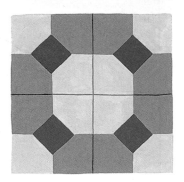

True Lover's Knot

Chimneys and Cornerstones

Bear's Paw

Carpenter's Wheel

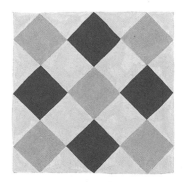

Grandmother's Pride

Sister's Choice

Peggy LeVasseur
11 Ingraham Dr.
Owls Head, ME 04854

The Master Quilter

AN ELM CREEK QUILTS NOVEL

Jennifer Chiaverini

SIMON & SCHUSTER
New York London Toronto Sydney

SIMON & SCHUSTER
Rockefeller Center
1230 Avenue of the Americas
New York, NY 10020

SIMON & SCHUSTER and colophon are registered trademarks
of Simon & Schuster, Inc.

For information regarding special discounts for bulk purchases,
please contact Simon & Schuster Special Sales
at 1-800-456-6798 or business@simonandschuster.com

Designed by Lauren Simonetti

Manufactured in the United States of America

1   3   5   7   9   10   8   6   4   2

Library of Congress Cataloging-in-Publication Data
Chiaverini, Jennifer.
The master quilter : an Elm Creek quilts novel / Jennifer Chiaverini.
p.   cm.
1. Compson, Sylvia (Fictitious character)—Fiction.   2. Women detectives—Fiction.
3. Quiltmaking—Fiction.   4. Quilters—Fiction.   5. Quilts—Fiction.   I. Title.
PS3553.H473M37 2004
813'.54—dc22
2003061711
ISBN 0-7432-3615-7

To Marty, Nicholas, and Michael, with all my love.

Acknowledgments

This book would not have been possible without the expertise and guidance of Denise Roy, Maria Massie, Rebecca Davis, and Christina Richardson. It is a privilege and a pleasure to work with such talented women.

I am grateful to the Wisconsin Historical Society for providing an outstanding collection of historical resources and for thoughtfully locating it in Madison. Thanks also to Lisa Cass and Christine Lee for playing with my boys while I worked.

Many thanks to the incomparable Anne Spurgeon for reading an early draft of this novel, for the research assistance, for the Monday lunches, and for her friendship.

Thank you to the friends and family who continue to support and encourage me, especially Geraldine Neidenbach, Heather Neidenbach, Nic Neidenbach, Virginia and Edward Riechman, Leonard and Marlene Chiaverini, Rachel and Chip Sauer, and the Tuesday morning moms: Mia McColgan, Leah Montequin, Jane LeMay, and Lori Connolly.

Most of all, I am grateful to my husband, Marty, and my sons, Nicholas and Michael, for everything.

CHAPTER ONE

Sarah

❧

January 7, 2002

Dear Friends of Elm Creek Quilts,

Wedding bells rang at Elm Creek Manor much earlier than any of the Elm Creek Quilters could have predicted! While Sylvia Compson's friends were helpfully—we thought—planning her wedding to Andrew Cooper, Sylvia and Andrew made plans of their own. Friends and family gathered at Elm Creek Manor to celebrate Christmas Eve and found ourselves unsuspecting guests at the union of two very dear friends.

The bride was beautiful, the groom charming, the ceremony moving, and the celebration joyful (although admittedly a few of us spent most of the reception recovering from shock). It was a perfect wedding save one glaring omission: Sylvia's bridal quilt. We had not yet sewed a single stitch!

Diane says Sylvia deserves to go without, but the rest of us know that that would be a cruel punishment for someone who has brought quilting into the lives of thousands of aspiring quilters. That's why we're asking all of Sylvia's friends, family, former students, and admirers to help us create a bridal quilt worthy of everyone's favorite Master Quilter.

If you would like to participate in this very special project, please make a 6-inch pieced or appliquéd quilt block using green, rose, blue, gold, and/or cream 100% cotton fabrics. Choose any pattern that represents how Sylvia has influenced you as an artist, teacher, or friend.

Please mail your blocks so they arrive at Elm Creek Manor no later than April 1. If you have any questions, contact Sarah McClure or Summer Sullivan at Elm Creek Manor. Thanks so much for your help, and remember, this is a surprise! Let's show Sylvia we can keep a secret as well as she can.

Yours in Quarter-Inch Seams,
The Elm Creek Quilters

"Did Diane really say that?" asked Summer as she read over the draft.

"No," admitted Sarah, "but it sounds like something she would say, and I thought it was good for a laugh. Should I delete it?"

"No, leave it in. Just don't send her a copy."

Sarah and Summer exchanged a grin, imagining Diane's reaction. Diane had been the last of the Elm Creek Quilters to admit that the Christmas Eve surprise wedding had been truly wonderful—and that was not until a week later, and only grudgingly. For all they knew, maybe Diane had indeed declared that Sylvia deserved to go without a bridal quilt for not sharing her secret with her closest friends.

"Don't you think Sylvia will get suspicious when dozens of blocks start piling up in the mailbox?" asked Summer.

"I'll ask Bonnie if we can have the blocks sent to Grandma's

Attic," said Sarah. Bonnie would probably be able to find room in her quilt shop to store the blocks, too, rather than leave them lying about Elm Creek Manor where Sylvia might discover them.

A phone call to Bonnie and a few revisions later, Sarah saved the final version of her letter and began printing out copies for every former camper, every quilt guild that had invited Sylvia to speak, and everyone in Sylvia's address book, hastily borrowed for the cause. She needed to refill the paper tray twice and replace the toner cartridge before the last letter emerged from the printer. Summer seemed to think they would receive dozens of blocks, but Sarah was less certain. Quilters were generous, helpful people, but they also tended to be quite busy. For all their good intentions, most might not be able to contribute a block by the deadline.

With all those hundreds of requests, surely they would receive the 140 blocks Bonnie had calculated they would need for a queen-size comforter. As Sarah affixed stamps to the envelopes, listening carefully for Sylvia's footsteps in the hall outside the library, she reflected that they might be fortunate to settle for a ninety-six-block lap quilt.

The bridal quilt was Sarah's idea, but the other Elm Creek Quilters were just as enthusiastic about the project—even Diane, who now only rarely complained about having to return the "perfect summer dress" she had purchased for the anticipated June wedding. Sylvia was the heart and soul of Elm Creek Quilt Camp, the business the eight friends had founded, jointly owned, and operated each year from spring to autumn, and not only because Elm Creek Manor was her ancestral home. Sylvia's passion for the artistic, historical, and social aspects of quilting so permeated the quilting retreat that the campers felt her influence in every class, every lecture, and every late-night chat with new friends that took place within the manor's gray stone walls. She had earned the respect, admiration, and affection of every quilter who had passed through the doors of Elm Creek Manor, yet she alone seemed unaware of this. Whenever Sarah tried to explain, as she did on each anniversary of the founding of Elm Creek Quilts, Sylvia cut her off and dismissed her praise as "preposterous." This bridal quilt would finally tell Sylvia what she would not allow Sarah to say.

To Sarah's delight, the first quilt block arrived only a week after the letters went out. The next day, Bonnie phoned with news that two more blocks had come in the morning mail, and after that, packages came so frequently that Bonnie stopped calling to report them. When she offered to bring them to their upcoming business meeting, Sarah couldn't resist. She and Bonnie told all the Elm Creek Quilters except Sylvia to meet in the kitchen thirty minutes early. Sarah figured that would give them plenty of time to examine the blocks, read the accompanying letters, and return the packages to Bonnie's car before Sylvia expected them in the formal parlor.

That Thursday evening, Bonnie arrived first, hustling through the back door and into the kitchen with a Grandma's Attic shopping bag in her arms. "Maybe this was a mistake," she said as Sarah eagerly took the bag and set it on the long wooden table in the center of the room. Bonnie shrugged off her coat and sat down on one of the benches. "All Sylvia has to do is look out the window at the parking lot and she'll know we're here."

"Sylvia's room faces the front of the manor," Sarah reminded her, emptying the bag onto the table. "It's twenty degrees outside, so the windows are shut and the furnace is running. She won't hear the cars pull up."

Bonnie raked her fingers through her close-cropped dark hair and glanced at the doorway. "Even so, we should keep our voices down."

"We're here," Diane sang, strolling into the kitchen, her blond curls bouncing. "Do we have to wait for everyone or can we see the blocks now?"

"Diane, hush, dear," warned white-haired Agnes, following close behind. Her blue eyes were exasperated behind pink-tinted glasses. "Stealth, remember?"

"She's about as stealthy as a thirsty elephant at the only water-hole on the savanna," remarked Gwen, peering in over Diane's shoulder. "You're also blocking the doorway."

"Well, excuse me, professor," Diane shot back, but she took a seat beside Sarah and reached for the envelope on top of the pile.

"Is Summer coming?" Sarah asked Gwen as she helped Agnes with her coat. "I sent her an email, but she didn't write back."

"Who knows what my daughter's up to anymore?" said Gwen. "I've had more meaningful conversations with her answering machine than with her lately."

"Summer has already seen most of the blocks at the quilt shop," said Bonnie. "But I'm sure she'll be here for the meeting."

"Summer never misses them," added Judy as she hurried into the kitchen, removing her gloves. "Unlike some of us. I honestly didn't think I'd make it tonight. When did juggling the schedules of two parents and an eight-year-old become so complicated?"

"When was it not?" asked Bonnie.

Sarah glanced at her watch and opened an envelope. "Let's keep an eye on the time, everyone."

"And keep one ear pointed toward the door," added Judy.

They agreed in whispers and soon were engrossed in passing the blocks around the table, praising them in hushed voices, silently reading the letters their makers had sent. Little Giant, Mother's Favorite, Three Cheers, Trip Around the World—the blocks were as imaginative and as varied as the women who had made them; while Sarah usually couldn't decipher the hidden meaning at first glance, the letters never failed to explain what the blocks represented. Sarah's favorite was a Spinning Hourglass block, which the maker wrote was inspired by a conversation she and Sylvia had participated in over dinner one evening at camp.

One of the women at the table had complained that she never had time to quilt at home and had to cram an entire year's worth of quilting into the one week each summer she spent at Elm Creek Manor. "We make time for the things that are important to us," Sylvia had remarked, and she listed several activities people typically participated in out of habit rather than necessity or enjoyment.

The writer said that Sylvia's words resonated with her and when she returned home, she scrutinized her routine to see where she could make better use of her days. After cutting out mindless television watching and delegating some household chores to her husband and teenage sons, she found several hours each week that she could devote to her own interests, including quilting. "Sylvia showed me that although we never have enough time for all the things we want to do," she concluded, "if we simplify our busy lives, we can keep them from spinning out of our control."

Sarah tucked the block and letter back into the envelope, ruefully running through her mental checklist of daily activities and wondering which she could sacrifice.

"Sarah?" called a distant voice. "Where is everyone?"

They scrambled up from the benches. "Quick," Gwen hissed, but the others were already returning the quilt blocks and letters to their envelopes and tossing them into the bag.

"Someone stall her," whispered Sarah frantically just as someone thrust the bag into her arms.

"Sarah?" Sylvia's voice came louder now, her footfalls swiftly approaching. "I don't have time for hide-and-seek."

Sarah flung open the pantry. She threw the bag inside and slammed the door just as Sylvia entered the kitchen.

"Sarah—" Sylvia stopped short in the doorway and eyed the gathering. "Well, for goodness' sakes. Why are you here so early?" She fixed her gaze on Sarah. "And why are you clinging to that door for dear life?"

"Because—" Sarah opened the door and retrieved the first item her hand touched. "They came early to help me make brownies. I was just getting the mix. Do you know if we have eggs? I was going to stop at the store, but—"

"You need six people to make brownies?"

"Sarah's never been much of a cook," offered Diane.

"Nonsense," said Sylvia, and gestured to the cellophane-wrapped plate on the counter. "She made lemon squares this morning."

"Should we get started?" asked Judy, reaching for an apron hanging on a peg beside the pantry door.

"Don't be ridiculous," said Sylvia, glancing at the clock. "We have a lot to cover tonight. We shouldn't waste time preparing extraneous desserts."

"Chocolate is never extraneous," said Gwen, but the others quickly agreed with Sylvia, eager to get her out of the kitchen.

They gathered in the formal parlor, where the original west wing of Elm Creek Manor intersected the south wing, added when Sylvia's father was a boy. The antique Victorian furnishings might have seemed stuffy if they were not so comfortably worn. Sylvia had once mentioned that her paternal grandmother had brought the overstuffed sofas, embroidered armchairs, beaded lamps, and ornate cabinets to Elm Creek Manor upon her marriage to David Bergstrom. No one else in the family had cared for the young bride's tastes, so they had arranged the furniture in a spare room and proclaimed it too fine for everyday use. Thus the newest member of the family had not felt slighted, and the Bergstroms were able to keep the west sitting room, their preferred place for quilting and visiting, exactly as it was. In more recent decades, the Bergstroms had grown more fond of the room, but even now the only nod to modernity was a large television in the corner, concealed by a Grandmother's Fan quilt whenever it was not in use.

Sarah began the meeting with an update on registration for the coming season. Enrollment was up fifteen percent, and there were so many requests for Gwen's Photo Transfer workshop that they had decided to add a second weekly session. "If you're up for it," added Sarah, glancing at Gwen.

Gwen shrugged. "Why not? Once the spring semester ends, I'll have plenty of time."

"Bonnie, I also thought we should add a few extra shuttles into town so campers can shop," Sarah continued. "Since they'll want to visit Grandma's Attic, we'll arrange them for when you can be fully staffed, okay? I wouldn't want one person to get swamped."

"Oh. Great." Bonnie hesitated. "Do you need to know the best times of the day now? Because I'm not really sure—"

"Just get back to me whenever you know." Sarah gave Bonnie an encouraging smile. She knew the quilt shop owner appreciated the extra business Elm Creek Quilt Camp sent her way, but she always seemed embarrassed by it, as if she thought she was taking advantage of their friendship. "You'll probably want your camp course schedule first."

Bonnie nodded, so Sarah glanced at her notes. "Oh. One more thing. This goes for everyone. Please remember to charge anything you use in your classes to supplies, not overhead. If we ever get audited—"

"I'm here," said Summer, rushing in red-cheeked from the cold and struggling out of her coat. "I'm sorry I'm late."

"Relax," said Diane. "This isn't the first time."

"Yes, but your tardiness has been increasing lately," mused Sylvia. "I can't imagine what has been keeping you so busy."

Summer draped her coat over the back of a chair and sat down. "What did I miss?"

"Sorry, Sylvia," said Judy with a laugh. "I don't think Summer wants to discuss her boyfriend."

Everyone except Summer laughed, but she managed a wry smile. "Fine. I was having supper with Jeremy. Satisfied?"

"You guys spend so much time together you might as well live together," said Diane.

"Don't suggest such a thing," protested Agnes. She patted Summer's hand. "She meant after you get married, dear."

Summer blanched, and Gwen said, "Married? Are you crazy? Don't go putting thoughts of marriage in my daughter's head. Or of living together. My daughter has more sense than that."

"As a newlywed myself, I object to the implications of that remark," retorted Sylvia. "Sometimes getting married makes perfect sense."

Agnes nodded, but Bonnie said, "Sometimes marriage makes no sense at all."

"Can we please get back to business?" begged Summer, throwing Sarah a pleading look.

Sarah promptly returned to her agenda despite grumbles from Diane, who apparently found teasing Summer far more interesting.

Midway through the meeting, Sylvia offered to return to the kitchen for refreshments, but Bonnie leapt to her feet and announced that it was her turn. She returned with the lemon squares, coffee, and a look of relief so plain that Sarah knew the quilt blocks were safely hidden away in her car.

That night, as Sarah and her husband prepared for bed, she told him about the afternoon's mishap. Matt laughed and said, "Why didn't you just go to Grandma's Attic and look at the blocks there?"

"Because every time I say I'm going downtown, Sylvia asks to come with me. I can't very well ask her to stay in the van while I go into the quilt shop."

"No, I guess not," Matt acknowledged. "And I guess delaying your trip downtown until you could go alone was out of the question?"

Sarah drew back the quilt and climbed into bed. "Absolutely."

Matt grinned and shook his head as he joined her. "Sorry to be the one to have to tell you this, but there's no way you're going to keep this quilt a secret very long."

"What do you mean?"

"You've never been good at keeping secrets."

"That's not true," Sarah protested, nudging him. "My friends trust me implicitly. I could tell you stories—but of course I *won't.*"

"Not other people's secrets. Your own. You have this over-whelming need to confess."

"I do not."

"I bet Sylvia will know about this bridal quilt before the first day of camp."

"And I know for a fact she won't." Sarah propped herself up on her elbows and regarded him. "Okay, if you're so sure, let's do it."

"Do what?"

"Make a bet. I say that Sylvia won't know about the quilt until we give her the pieced top. You can say whatever dumb thing you like, because you're going to lose."

"I'm not going to lose," said Matt firmly. "Okay. You have a bet. What am I going to win?"

"Nothing, but I'm going to win breakfast in bed for a week. Pre-pared by your own hands, so don't pass the work off on the cook."

"It won't be a problem, because I'm going to win five new apple trees for my orchard."

"Five? Then I get two weeks of breakfast, with the newspaper and a foot massage."

"Done." Matt held out his hand. "Shake on it?"

Sarah smiled, took his hand, and pulled him close. "I'd much rather kiss."

❧

For the next two weeks, Sarah resisted the temptation to invite Bon-nie to bring the most recently arrived blocks to Elm Creek Manor, resigning herself to hasty descriptions over the phone and Bonnie's assurances that if this pace continued, they would have all the blocks they needed well in advance of the deadline. Nearly three weeks passed before Sarah finally managed to sneak away to Grandma's Attic after dropping off Sylvia at her hairdresser.

Sarah drove the white Elm Creek Quilts minivan onto Main Street, which marked the border between downtown Waterford and the Waterford College campus. She tried to park in the alley behind Grandma's Attic, but an unfamiliar car already occupied the space reserved for Bonnie's employees. Because Bonnie's only remaining employees were Diane and Summer, she invited the Elm Creek Quilters to use the extra space, since downtown parking was scarce. But none of the Elm Creek Quilters owned the gleaming luxury sedan parked beside Bonnie's twenty-year-old compact. In fact, only a few of them could have afforded the payments.

Apparently a customer had discovered the secret parking space. Sarah hoped the driver liked to spend as much on fabric as she did on transportation. Bonnie never complained, but Sarah suspected the competition from the large chain fabric store on the outskirts of town had been siphoning off her revenues more than usual. Grandma's Attic had sometimes dipped dangerously into the red, but even then, Bonnie had managed to keep any hint of trouble far from her customers' view. Lately, however, Sarah noticed she had begun rearranging her shelves to conceal gaps in her inventory rather than restocking them.

Sarah found another spot not far away on Second Street and hurried down the hill to Main, turning up her collar and thrusting her hands in her pockets since she had forgotten her scarf and gloves. In the front shop window, beneath the familiar red sign with the words GRANDMA'S ATTIC printed in gold, hung several sample quilts Bonnie and Diane had made as demonstration projects for their classes at quilt camp. The front bell jingled when Sarah entered, but a glance at the cutting table in the center of the room and a quick survey of the aisles told her Bonnie was not in the main store area. "Bonnie?" Sarah called over the folk music playing in the background, just as she glimpsed her friend through the window of the back office. Bonnie was speaking earnestly—or heatedly—with a man in a well-tailored coat of rich black wool, who at that moment turned his back on her and strode briskly from the office. Something about his smug, self-satisfied grin plucked at Sarah's memory and, as he passed her and nodded on his way to the door, recognition struck her with the shock of cold water. She spun around and watched the door swing shut behind him, then turned back to Bonnie, who had followed him from the office.

"Wasn't that Gregory Krolich?" asked Sarah. Bonnie nodded and sat down on a stool behind the cutting table. "I knew it. The real estate business must be treating him well. He's driving an even more expensive car than the last time I saw him."

"You know him?"

"Barely. I haven't seen him in years, not since I first moved to Waterford. He wanted to buy Elm Creek Manor and raze it so he could build a few hundred student apartments on the property."

"Obviously he didn't," said Bonnie. "So he's just a lot of threats and bluster in a nice suit?"

Sarah shook her head. "On the contrary, I'm sure he would have gone through with it if Sylvia hadn't found out about his plan. She refused to sell to him once she learned the truth."

"Oh." Bonnie studied the cutting table for a moment. "So. Do you want to see the blocks?"

"Of course," said Sarah, removing her coat. "I have about twenty minutes before I need to pick up Sylvia."

Bonnie disappeared into the storage room and returned with a large cardboard box, which she said contained thirty-four blocks. She seemed so pleased that Sarah hid her dismay. A month into the project, and they had received only a small fraction of the blocks they needed. As Bonnie separated the newest packages from the ones Sarah had already seen, Sarah reminded herself that they were averaging one new block a day, and that contributors typically provided their blocks either right away or at the very last minute. Surely in the last week before the deadline, Grandma's Attic would be inundated with blocks. If not, Sarah would work overtime at her sewing machine to make up the difference.

"Look at this," Sarah marveled as she opened the first envelope and found an exquisite Bridal Wreath block. "I will never be able to appliqué this well."

"Only because you won't practice."

Sarah returned the block to its envelope and opened a second. "Queen Charlotte's Crown? It's lovely, but what does it have to do with Sylvia?"

Bonnie watched as Sarah put the block away and reached for another. "Why don't you read the letter and find out?"

"Can't. Sylvia expects me back at twenty past, and if I'm late, she's sure to ask questions." Sarah admired a Steps to the Altar block. "She'll know if I'm lying, too."

"Well, you can't leave without reading this one." Bonnie handed her a package somewhat thicker than the others. "You know the quilters who sent it."

Intrigued, Sarah took the thick padded envelope and withdrew two blocks, a Grandmother's Pride and a Mother's Delight. "I'm guessing these two are related," she said, unfolding the letter.

February 6, 2002

Dear Elm Creek Quilters,

Thank you so much for inviting us to participate in this gift for Sylvia. We know it will be a spectacular quilt and look forward to seeing it when we return to camp for our annual reunion of the Cross-Country Quilters.

Deciding to participate was easy, but choosing appropriate blocks proved far more difficult. Fortunately, we see each other frequently, so we have been able to share our thoughts. Sylvia has inspired us with her courageous attitude toward life, her insistence upon excellence, her steadfast dedication to her craft, and in so many other ways that we're sure it's evident why no single block could express what we feel for her.

So instead we decided to focus on how Sylvia most directly influenced our lives simply by creating Elm Creek Quilt Camp.

Vinnie, as you recall, was one of the first campers of Elm Creek Quilt Camp's inaugural season. Recently widowed, she wanted to attend camp during the week of her birthday rather than try to celebrate in the home she had so recently shared with her husband. At quilt camp she found friendship and fun, and discovered in Sylvia a fellow widow, but one with a far more tragic past. Sylvia's story of how she had lost her husband in World War II reminded Vinnie that she should not dwell upon what she had lost, but cherish and be thankful for the many decades she and her husband had spent together.

A few years later, Megan first attended quilt camp and, although she did not then realize it, meeting Vinnie would prove to be one of the most important moments of her life—and not only because Vinnie is as remarkable and inspirational as Sylvia herself. Vinnie was eager to find a sweetheart for her favorite grandson, Adam, and with a little meddling that Megan failed to appreciate at the time, she finally succeeded in arranging for the two to meet. The couple had the usual ups and downs (and a few that were not at all usual) on the path to love, but six months ago, Adam and Megan were married in St. James of the Valley Church in Cincinnati, with Megan's son, Rob, as best man. Adam, Megan, and Rob are all thrilled that in July a new baby will join their family. Rob says we should name the baby Sylvia if she is a girl and Elmer if he is a boy, because this child never would have come into the world if not for Elm Creek Quilt Camp.

How can one or even two quilt blocks adequately represent what Sylvia has done for our family? We admit no single pattern could, but we think Grandmother's Pride and Mother's Delight come close.

Please let us know if we can do anything more to help complete Sylvia's bridal quilt. If you need additional blocks, Vinnie has six all ready to put in the mail to you!

> Love to you all,
> Vinnie Burkholder and
> Megan (Donohue) Wagner

At the bottom of the typed page was a postscript added in spidery handwriting: "I'm sure you can tell Megan wrote this letter and kindly allowed me to add my name to it. It doesn't sound like me at all! I never would have bragged I was as remarkable and inspirational as Sylvia, not that anyone would have believed it anyway! I hope the baby is a girl, not just because I don't care for the name Elmer but because I've already made her a pink-and-white Ohio Star quilt. Hugs and Kisses from Vinnie."

"Megan and Vinnie's grandson got married!" exclaimed Sarah. "Sylvia will be thrilled."

"Don't tell her yet," said Bonnie, taking the blocks and the letter. "You'll have to explain how you know, and you're a terrible liar."

"I suppose you're going to tell me I can't keep secrets, either."

Bonnie winced. "No offense. I trust you with my secrets—most of them—but when it comes to your own—"

"You can stop there. I've heard it before, from Matt."

"Sorry."

"Frankly, it's not the worst thing in the world to be a terrible liar. At least everyone knows when I'm telling the truth."

"Even so, you'd better think of a convincing story pretty fast," advised Bonnie, nodding to the clock.

It was already a quarter past eleven. Sarah glanced about in dismay and put her hand on the nearest bolt of fabric. "Cut me a yard of this, would you?"

Bonnie rang up the charges quickly, and within two minutes Sarah was hurrying back to the minivan. As she rehearsed her cover story on the way to the salon, she realized Sylvia would never believe she had spent the entire time in the quilt shop only to emerge with a single yard of fabric. She took a sharp left at the town square and parked in front of the Daily Grind. Sylvia might more readily accept that Sarah had lost track of time in a coffee shop.

The early lunch crowd was just beginning to gather as Sarah joined the line. She bought herself a large latte and ordered a hot cocoa with whipped cream to appease Sylvia. As she stirred sugar and vanilla into her steaming cup, she glanced up and saw a familiar figure at a corner table. She didn't have time to chat, but just as she turned to go, Judy caught her eye and froze.

Sarah smiled and waved, but Judy appeared so discomfited that Sarah realized her friend must have noticed her attempt to avoid her and wondered at the cause. A cup in each hand, she made her way to the table Judy was sharing with a shaggy-haired man in a business suit.

"Judy, hi," she said, smiling at Judy and her companion in turn. "I thought I'd get my caffeine fix while Sylvia's getting her hair done."

"You must have had a late night," said Judy, noting the two cups.

"Oh, no, this one's a peace offering for Sylvia. I'm late."

"Sorry you can't join us," said the man with a smile.

With a start, Judy quickly introduced him as a colleague visiting from the University of Pennsylvania. Sarah set down her coffee long enough to shake his hand, then made a hasty exit. She would be even later now, but at least she had a truthful and, better yet, believable excuse.

To Sarah's surprise, when she arrived, Sylvia wasn't waiting by the front door in her coat and hat. Sarah found her in the back of the salon with her hands beneath a nail dryer. "Sarah, dear," Sylvia greeted her. "You were so late they talked me into a manicure."

Sarah apologized and offered her the hot cocoa, which Sylvia couldn't pick up at the moment anyway. Sarah rambled through an account of Grandma's Attic and the Daily Grind, which was mercifully cut short by the timer on the nail dryer. "Do you know I never get my nails done?" said Sylvia, admiring her hands. "Quilting is so hard on them that I usually don't bother, but the young lady was so persuasive. You showed up just in time or they would have convinced me to let them do my toes, too."

Sylvia paid the manicurist and gave her a healthy tip, then happily took her cocoa. She lifted the lid and inhaled the fragrance of the still-steaming chocolate. "If this is real whipped cream, don't you dare tell Andrew."

"It's the real thing and I wouldn't breathe a word."

Sylvia laughed and tucked her arm through Sarah's and, to Sarah's deep satisfaction, nothing in her manner suggested she doubted Sarah's ability to keep their little secret. It wasn't until they were halfway home that Sarah realized she had forgotten to ask Bonnie what Greg Krolich had been doing in Grandma's Attic. She resolved to phone Bonnie that evening and inquire, but at supper, Matt quickly made her forget all about the unexpected encounter.

"You look great, Sylvia," he began as he passed the bread basket to Andrew. "Did you do something different with your hair?"

Sylvia touched her hair, pleased. "Why, thank you for noticing, Matthew. My stylist talked me into some highlights."

"Take a look at those nails," said Andrew. Sylvia obliged by regally extending a hand. "My bride's gotten herself all dolled up, and I keep scratching my head wondering what special occasion I forgot."

Sylvia laughed. "The only special occasion is that Sarah was late picking me up."

Matt turned to Sarah, his eyes wide with false innocence.

"Sarah, late? Usually she's the one keeping us all on schedule. What kept you?"

"Nothing, sweetheart." Sarah gave him a look of warning. "I stopped for some coffee—"

"And fabric," added Sylvia. "You can't forget that, although why you left with such a small purchase I honestly don't know. Bonnie could use the business."

"That is strange," exclaimed Matt. "What were you doing at Grandma's Attic all that time if you weren't shopping?"

"You know how it is. I got started talking with Bonnie, and then, well, I looked up at the clock and I barely had enough time to get coffee before Sylvia expected me." Sarah set down her fork and glared at Matt. "If it bothers you so much, I'll go back tomorrow and spend all the money for your Valentine's Day present on fabric for myself."

Matt could barely hide his grin. "You don't have to go that far."

"Sarah, dear, relax," said Sylvia, astounded. "Goodness. Every-one's allowed to be late once in a while. He's only teasing you. There was no harm done."

"You're right." She smiled sweetly at Matt so that he would be sure to know the real harm was yet to come. "I'm sorry, honey."

Sylvia seemed satisfied, but Matt could only manage a weak grin.

She cornered him by the kitchen sink after Sylvia and Andrew retired to the parlor to watch the news. "All right," she said, snap-ping a dish towel at him. "We're adding a codicil to our wager. If Sylvia finds out about the quilt because of you, it doesn't count."

"I'm not going to tell her," he protested.

"That's not good enough. If you force the truth out of me in front of her, or trick any of our friends into revealing the secret, or acci-dentally on purpose leave one of the quilt blocks on her chair, I win the bet." She extended her hand. "Shake on it."

He took her hand gingerly. "No kiss?"

"Not this time."

"Does this mean you're not getting me a Valentine's present?"

"Oh, no. You'll get exactly the present you deserve."

Two days later, a still-contrite Matt brought Sarah breakfast in bed, and he gave her a thorough foot massage while she read the paper. Only afterward did he mention that he was trying to make up for all the breakfasts in bed she would not receive once he won the bet. Sarah didn't take offense. Instead she made him a Dutch apple pie to compensate for the apple trees she had no intention of buying him.

The first day of the new season of quilt camp was rapidly approaching, and Sarah's days were filled with the minutiae of the business: processing registration forms, scheduling classes, ordering supplies, mailing out welcome packets, assigning rooms and sometimes roommates. Amid the chaos, Sarah wondered how the campers could not fail to notice how she scrambled to make everything run smoothly. Summer assisted her by planning evening entertainment programs and inviting guest speakers, and together they wrestled with the problems of last-minute course adjustments. Already it seemed apparent that Gwen's Hand-Dyeing and Agnes's Baltimore Album courses would not be filled throughout March, while Diane's class for beginners and Judy's seminar in computer design were in heavy demand. It was no small feat to adjust the schedule in a way that would please everyone.

When Sarah and Summer decided they had done the best they could, Summer phoned the instructors involved to see if they would agree to the changes. In the meantime, Sarah went through invoices and contacted the distributors who—for reasons they could not explain—had still not delivered supplies Sarah had ordered months before. Summer hung up the phone in defeat long before Sarah had sorted out her own problems. "What is wrong with everyone this year?" asked Summer, dropping into a chair in front of the library fireplace, which still held a few logs in cynical mistrust of the calendar. "Agnes was home, of course; you can always count on Agnes. But Diane, Judy, and my mom are incommunicado. My mom won't even pick up her cell phone."

"She's probably in class."

"Not all day. She ought to be in her office by now." Summer let her head fall back against the cushions. "People could try to be a little more accessible at this time of year."

"Diane's so stressed out about Todd's college acceptances that she's probably too jittery to sit by the phone. Judy's either at work or with Emily, and you know better than anyone how busy your mom is."

Summer snorted in grudging acceptance.

"Besides, if anyone's inaccessible, it's you," remarked Sarah. "You rarely answer your email anymore and never answer your phone. All anyone can ever get is your machine. By the way, I think it might be broken. There's no outgoing message anymore, just a beep."

"Oh. Thanks. I'll look into it."

"You should. Last week I called three times in a row just to make sure I had the right number." Sarah leafed through a pile of registration forms and sighed. "How does Agnes feel about canceling her appliqué class?"

"She'd rather not. She doesn't care if there are only four students. If they want to learn to appliqué, she's willing to teach them."

"I guess we should keep it on the schedule, then." Better that than writing apologetic letters to the four campers and trying to squeeze them into their second-choice classes.

"Did you know Agnes started piecing the top for Sylvia's bridal quilt?"

Sarah set down the forms, instantly attentive. "No. Does that mean we have enough blocks?"

"Not quite. She's adding an elaborate pieced border to compensate."

Sarah smiled ruefully. "I had hoped to receive a better response."

"We still might. There's a whole month before the deadline. Agnes just wanted to work ahead since camp starts in almost three weeks." Summer studied the unlit fireplace. "Have you decided what block you're going to make?"

"I have no idea." Sarah had been so preoccupied with the other blocks that she had never given her own a thought. She had not even checked her fabric stash to see if she had the right colors. "What pattern did you choose?"

"I was hoping to steal some ideas from you." Summer rose and stretched. "Back to work. Maybe my mom's in her office by now."

Sarah nodded, lost in thought.

What block could possibly convey all that Sylvia meant to her?

Either Summer was unable to reach her mother or she forgot that she was supposed to contact Sarah with Gwen's response, because Sarah did not hear from either woman until their business meeting the following Thursday evening. In the past Gwen had protested any cuts in her teaching schedule, insisting that holding a class with only one student was far preferable to disappointing the one camper who had registered. Sarah and Gwen had gone through the same debate so often that this time Sarah came prepared with documented evidence proving that one-student classes, while good enough in theory, could be a financial disaster. But when she took Gwen aside before the meeting and recommended that they cancel her dyeing workshops for the first two weeks of camp, Gwen merely shrugged. She added something vague about possibly directing a seminar on the sociopolitical implications of quilt contests instead, but she drifted off to the parlor before waiting for Sarah's response.

Throughout the meeting, Sarah gradually realized that Gwen was not the only one who seemed inordinately distracted. Bonnie looked tired and pale, as if she had not slept in days. Agnes, too, must have noticed, for she watched Bonnie all evening with a look of carefully muted concern. Summer paid more attention to her watch than to Sarah's updates about enrollment, and twice Judy left the room to take calls on her cell phone. Their behavior was puzzling, but Diane's was downright irritating; she stormed in twenty minutes late muttering about admissions counselors and tuition payments, then spent the rest of the meeting tapping her pen against her notebook and scowling.

Finally Sarah had had enough. "While we're on the subject of guest lecturers, Jane Smith has agreed to speak to our campers in August. That's perfect timing because, as you know, Jane is the world-famous Naked Quilter, and she requires that all of her lectures be conducted entirely in the nude. Students included. I decided we should make all of Elm Creek Quilt Camp go naked for the whole week so her students don't feel self-conscious. Matt, Andrew, and the rest of the male staff should wear fig leaves so our more sensitive campers aren't offended."

Everyone but Sylvia nodded absently. "Are you out of your mind?" Sylvia gasped.

"What?" said Summer. "What did she say?"

"If any of you had been listening, you would know." Sarah took a deep breath and made herself count to ten. "Look. I realize you're all busy and that you have lives and jobs outside of camp. But it seems to me that you're beginning to take Elm Creek Quilts for granted. I realize we've been very successful very quickly, but contrary to appearances, this camp does not run itself. I can't do it without you, so please, while you're here, really be *here*, okay?"

Abashed, the Elm Creek Quilters nodded and murmured apologies.

"Jane Smith, the Naked Quilter, indeed," said Sylvia. "I suppose there is no such person. Pity. That certainly would have been an interesting week."

"Jane Smith the who?" said Diane.

"No one." Sylvia shrugged. "Serves you right for not listening."

As far as Sarah could tell, they hung on her every word for the rest of the meeting.

※※

Whenever Sarah could find a spare moment from the frenzy of camp preparations, she pored through Sylvia's library of quilt-pattern books trying to find the perfect block. With no time to idly admire the illustrations, she began with the index and read through the names, trying to find one that was suitable. A block called Homecoming evoked Sylvia's return to Elm Creek Manor after a fifty-year absence and also the launch of Elm Creek Quilts, but one glance at the pattern told Sarah it would be too difficult. Many blocks incorporated the word *Friendship* into their names, but while Sarah liked several of the designs, she suspected everyone else would be looking for some sort of "Friendship" block, too, and she wanted her choice to be more distinctive. With only one week before the first day of camp, Sarah finally settled on Sarah's Favorite, for Sylvia was certainly Sarah's favorite quilter and ran a very close second with Matt for her all-around favorite person. The approaching deadline nagged her, but as the organizer of the project, she figured she could extend the deadline if circumstances warranted. Readying Elm Creek Manor for its first guests of the season certainly qualified.

Sarah found a perfect rose-colored floral print in her stash and stopped by Grandma's Attic to pick up a few coordinating fat quarters in blue and leaf green. She cut the squares and triangles that same day and sewed the pieces together late at night, after Sylvia retired.

"Nice," Matt remarked a few evenings later, when she had nearly finished. He had come to the sitting room adjoining their bedroom, Sarah's de facto sewing room, to see when she planned to come to bed.

Sarah thanked him and sighed as he began rubbing her shoulders. She hoped her block would be good enough. It was well made—she'd had an exacting teacher—but most of the blocks sent to Grandma's Attic were far more elaborate.

"You know," she mused, "I think I might want shoulder rubs on alternate days rather than foot massages for the entire two weeks."

"I still have two more days to win this bet."

Sarah laughed. "I admire your confidence, misplaced though it is."

"You have to admit you skewed the odds in your favor with your codicil."

"And you have to admit that dropping hints to Sylvia would have been unfair."

"Explicitly telling her about the quilt would have been cheating," Matt acknowledged. "But hints would have been fair. Tricking you into revealing the secret would have been the best of all."

Sarah turned in her chair and regarded him. "Why are you so eager for Sylvia to find out about our surprise?"

"I'm not. I just want those apple trees." Matt paused. "Want to play double or nothing?"

"When I'm this close to winning? No, thanks."

"You'd turn down four weeks of breakfast in bed? You must be closer to spilling the truth than I thought."

"Hardly. What are your terms?"

"Double or nothing, Sylvia will find out about the quilt before it's finished."

"Finished as in all the blocks sewn together or as in quilted and bound?" They were planning to set up the pieced top in Sylvia's quilt frame on the ballroom dais so campers could contribute stitches throughout the spring and summer. Sarah had planned to present the pieced top to Sylvia before then, for they would be unable to conceal it and still allow the campers to work on it.

She hid her glee when Matt said, "I want to pick out my trees soon, so let's say until all the blocks are sewn into a top. But I want more leeway with this codicil."

"Sylvia can't learn about the quilt from you," Sarah warned.

"But anything else is fair game."

For four weeks of breakfast in bed, why not? Since Agnes had already begun to assemble the top, surely Sarah would only need to keep the quilt secret until mid-April, at the latest. "You have a deal." She extended her hand, but the words had barely left her lips before Matt bent down and kissed them.

⟋

A week of late nights and early mornings followed. Sarah finished her block on the last evening before quilt camp and spent most of that night lying awake, running over last-minute details in her mind. She fell asleep sometime after three and stumbled down to the kitchen the next morning, bleary-eyed and yawning, to find Sylvia, Andrew, and Matt already seated at the kitchen table. As Sarah took her seat beside Matt, the cook, recently returned from his annual monthlong vacation, placed steaming plates of blueberry pancakes before them.

"Sarah, dear, you look exhausted," said Sylvia.

"She should," said Matt. "She stayed up half the night quilting."

"I did not."

"Sarah," scolded Sylvia gently. "You should have gotten more rest. Today's a busy day."

"That's what I told her, but she kept at it," said Matt.

"What on earth was so important that you had to finish last night?" asked Sylvia. "It couldn't have been a class sample. You aren't teaching this week."

Sarah took a hasty bite of pancake. "These are delicious," she called to the cook.

"Sarah?"

"Oh, Sylvia, don't believe a word Matt says. I was done sewing by ten-thirty and in bed by eleven. You know how it is when you see a new quilt pattern and just have to try it out right away."

"Hmph." Sylvia looked dubious. "Well, do I get to see this amazing quilt block?"

Matt shot Sarah a look of triumph, but she did her best to sound unconcerned. "Sure. Later. If I remember." It was the first day of quilt camp. She would have abundant excuses to forget.

Satisfied, Sylvia let her off with a warning that she should make sure to go to bed early that night. Sarah laughed, knowing how impossible that would be, but assured Sylvia she would try. As the conversation turned to other matters, Sarah raised her eyebrows at Matt, smug. He lifted his coffee mug to her to acknowledge his defeat, but she suspected he considered it a temporary setback. Matt wanted those apple trees, and he intended to fight dirty.

At twelve o'clock, the first sixty quilters of the new camp season began to arrive. The Elm Creek Quilters had gathered well before then to arrange registration tables in the grand front foyer and to go through the guest rooms to be certain no detail had been over-looked. Agnes and Diane arranged fresh flowers from the cutting garden on each bedside table to assure every guest received a proper welcome, while Judy and Gwen checked with the cook to be sure all was ready for the Welcome Banquet. Bonnie and Summer gave the classrooms one last inspection, as Sylvia helped Sarah set out forms and organize room keys. Matt and Andrew stood ready to assist arriving guests with their luggage, while the rest of the staff bustled about, filled as they all were with the expectation and excitement that heralded each new season of Elm Creek Quilt Camp. As far as Sarah could discern, the distraction that had afflicted her friends earlier that month had completely disappeared.

A few minor problems surfaced during registration: Two friends who had wanted to room together had been paired with total strangers, and a woman who had registered for the following week had shown up early, totally unaware of her mistake. Sarah and Sylvia resolved these minor crises before anyone had time to become too anxious, and once again Sarah marveled at their illu-sion of flawless service. No wonder people assumed the camp ran itself!

The Welcome Banquet was the best one yet, and the Candlelight ceremony at sunset on the cornerstone patio was like a warm embrace, drawing campers and faculty alike into a close circle of friendship. After the last guests retired for the night—or, more likely, gathered in neighbors' rooms to renew old friendships and initiate new ones—Sarah returned to her library office to go over a few last-minute details for the classes that would begin the following morning. She could not keep the smile off her face as she listened to footfalls going from room to room and laughter muffled behind closed doors. Elm Creek Manor had become her home and she loved it in any season, but it truly came to life when it was filled with quilters.

Sarah did not get to bed as early as she had promised Sylvia, but Matt was even a few minutes later. As the manor's caretaker, his workload increased exponentially when the estate was full of visitors. He seemed so content, though, that Sarah knew he had come to enjoy his role in the company as much as she did hers.

Still, as they lay down beneath the sampler quilt she had made for him as an anniversary gift so many years before, she could not resist teasing him. "I sure hope camp runs as smoothly as Sylvia's bridal quilt project," she said, exaggerating a yawn. "Agnes finished her pieced border, and is just waiting for the last blocks to arrive so she can sew it all together."

Matt feigned sleep, punctuating Sarah's remark with a snore.

Sarah's alarm woke her at half past six, and by seven she was descending the carved oak staircase and hurrying to the kitchen. The cook and his two assistants had breakfast well in hand—and seemed surprised and even hurt that Sarah had felt it necessary to check—so she returned to the banquet hall to join Matt. Sylvia and Andrew, both early risers, had already finished eating and were nursing cups of coffee and chatting with a group of campers. Matt had joined them, so Sarah hurried through the buffet and took the seat he had saved for her. So many enthusiastic campers came by to greet her that Sarah had barely managed to take a few quick gulps of coffee before she was summoned to the phone.

She grabbed half a bagel and munched on it as she hurried to the nearest private phone, in the formal parlor. Judy was on the line, breathless. "Sarah, I'm so sorry to do this—"

"What's wrong?"

"I have to go out of town, so I can't teach my classes today or tomorrow. I might be able to make it back by Wednesday, but I won't know until later today. I'm sorry I can't at least teach my ten o'clock today, but I have to leave for Philadelphia by nine—"

"Is your mom all right?"

"Yes, yes, she's fine. It's for work. I have to meet with some professors at Penn."

"But it's spring break." They always scheduled the first week of camp to coincide with spring break, to lighten the burden on Judy and Gwen.

"It's Waterford College's spring break, not Penn's. I'm so sorry for the short notice. I just found out five minutes ago. Apparently they sent a letter, but I never received it."

"That's all right," said Sarah bleakly. "These things happen. We'll find someone to cover for you."

"Thank you, Sarah. Thank you. I swear I'll make it up to you. Look, I have sample quilts for display and handouts and lesson plans. I'll drop them off on my way."

"That would be great." It was as far from great as Sarah could imagine, but what else could she say?

Judy thanked her profusely and hung up. Sarah tossed her bagel in the trash and raced upstairs to the library. Ordinarily she could recite the teaching schedule from memory, but at the moment, she couldn't think of a single available instructor. She rifled through her files, found the weekly class schedule, and let out a moan. Judy's morning workshop was Bindings and Borders, and only Diane was free from ten o'clock until noon. Judy's class taught participants how to draft original pieced borders and how to finish the quilted tops in unusual fashions—scalloped edges, spiral bindings, contrasting piping, prairie points. While Diane might be able to handle the drafting-borders segment of the class, she had never attempted the unusual bindings. For that matter, neither had Sarah.

She sank into the high-backed leather chair and spread the papers out on the desk. Judy's afternoon class was a weeklong program in computer-aided design. Summer knew how to use that software—Sarah shuffled some pages—and she was free from four until five every day that week except Wednesday, when she worked a longer shift at Grandma's Attic. Agnes had that afternoon off, as did Bonnie and Gwen. Gwen. Perfect.

The door opened and Sylvia entered. "I thought I'd find you here." She crossed the room and set a steaming cup of coffee on a coaster on the desktop. "When you didn't come back to breakfast, I made some inquiries and discovered you had been spotted racing upstairs, a look of sheer panic on your face."

Sarah filled Sylvia in on Judy's abrupt cancellations and her attempts to adjust the schedule. "The afternoon class should be fine, as long as Summer and Gwen agree. As for this morning—" She folded her arms on the desk and buried her face in them. "I don't see how to resolve this."

"It's simple, really," said Sylvia, patting Sarah's shoulder. "I'll teach it. I've made all of those bindings and borders more times than I could count."

"You? But you have . . ." Sarah sat up and shifted around some papers. "You have your Hand-Quilting class from ten to eleven. Do you mean change the seminar from eleven until one? Because we can't. We need the classroom, and the students will need time for lunch."

"No, dear, that's not what I mean. I'll take over Judy's seminar. You'll teach my Hand-Quilting class."

"Me?"

"Why not? You're a fine hand-quilter."

"But I've never taught that class before." She had only taught Beginning Piecing and Quick Piecing, and she always planned the classroom time down to the minute and would rehearse for weeks in advance. "There must be someone else."

"I'm sure Andrew would do it if we asked, but since he's never quilted before, I'm confident the students would much prefer you."

Sarah tried to laugh, but it came out as a whimper. "Maybe we should cancel."

"Out of the question. There are twelve eager campers waiting to learn hand-quilting, and we can't disappoint them. You'll do just fine. Just go in there and teach them everything I taught you. What could be easier?"

Canceling the class, for one, but Sarah took one look at Sylvia's raised eyebrows and folded arms and decided against saying so. Sylvia would never admit that Sarah might not be up to the task, perhaps because she honestly believed Sarah capable of it. Worse than disappointing the twelve students would be disappointing Sylvia by not even trying.

"After I call Summer and Gwen, I'll run downstairs and bring back some breakfast," said Sarah, resigned. "I'll start preparing while I eat."

"You go ahead and get ready," said Sylvia. "I'll fix you a plate myself."

Sylvia did more than that; before leaving for her own nine o'clock lecture, she helped Sarah outline the topics she should cover the first morning and gather the appropriate supplies. Sarah went over her notes until the very moment class began, and although the students seemed disappointed by Sylvia's absence, the lesson went better than Sarah had expected.

She spent most of the rest of the day in the office catching up on all the work set aside that morning. She joined the faculty and guests for supper, and later that evening assisted Summer with the evening program, a slide show of antique quilts from the Waterford Historical Society's Quilt Documentation Project. She was too exhausted to join the rest of the Elm Creek Quilters for a celebratory cup of hot chocolate afterward, as was their tradition. She might have joined them if she could have her cocoa laced with rum, but as it was, sleep seemed the preferable option.

In comparison, the next day went remarkably well, with a broken slide projector and an overscheduled Machine Quilting workshop the worst crises she had to solve. She joined in the evening program, Games Night, with her old enthusiasm, and by Wednesday morning, the familiar excitement and anticipation of the first week of camp had returned. She went to the office cheerfully, the stress of Judy's last-minute cancellation faded, her confidence in her ability to manage Elm Creek Quilt Camp restored.

It was nearly eleven o'clock, and Sarah was considering returning to the kitchen for another cup of coffee when she heard someone running in the hallway. The library door opened suddenly and Matt rushed into the room. "Honey," he called. "There's a problem."

Sarah was already on her feet. "What happened?"

"Summer sent me to tell you Bonnie never showed for her ten o'clock workshop. Her students waited for twenty minutes before leaving. Those that weren't too angry just joined other classes, but the others . . ." He shrugged.

Sarah sank into her seat. She had been within arm's reach of the phone since breakfast and had checked the voicemail only fifteen minutes before. Bonnie had not called.

She glanced at the clock. There was still an hour left in the workshop. If Matt helped her gather the students, Sarah could teach the class. She could extend it past noon so they received the full two hours they had paid for, if the students didn't have scheduling conflicts, if the classroom space was available . . .

She scrambled for the schedule. Bonnie's workshop was on sewing tailored quilted jackets. Sarah could barely hem a pair of pants.

"We'll refund their money," said Sarah. She closed her eyes and rested her head against the soft leather chair.

Wherever Bonnie was, she had better have a very good excuse.

CHAPTER TWO

Summer

Summer would have stayed to help Sarah revise the letter for Sylvia's bridal quilt, but Jeremy had just returned from semester break the night before, and she had not yet had a chance to see him. After suggesting a few changes—most importantly, having participants send their blocks somewhere other than Elm Creek Manor—she hurried outside to her car and drove downtown to Jeremy's apartment.

She parked behind his apartment building, a three-story red brick walk-up on the opposite end of Main Street from Grandma's Attic. Jeremy's car was in the lot, but he walked to and from campus, and a glance at his darkened windows confirmed he was not yet home. She retrieved the groceries from the trunk and hurried upstairs to the third floor. After two weeks apart, Jeremy would be as eager to see her as she was to see him, and she wanted to get dinner started in case he came home early.

She let herself in with the key Jeremy had given her after his roommate moved out upon graduating at the end of fall semester. A pile of unopened mail sat on the table and a snow shovel was propped up beside the front door. Summer hung up her coat and went to the kitchen, where she found a bottle of wine chilling in the refrigerator. She smiled and put a pot of water on to boil.

Not half an hour later, she heard the door open. "Summer?"

She set down the spoon. "In here," she called, hurrying out of the kitchen. Jeremy met her in the doorway, where she flung her arms around him.

"I missed you," he said, hugging her. He had cut his curly dark hair and was wearing the organic aftershave she had given him for Hanukkah.

"You better have," she teased, kissing him.

"I don't want to spend this much time away from you ever again."

"Does this mean no more locking yourself away in the library for days?"

He picked her up, and she wrapped her legs around him as he carried her to the sofa. "I'd gladly flunk out first."

"That's what you say now." She ran a hand through his dark curls. "We'll see what happens when you're closer to defending your dissertation."

"Please don't remind me. My advisor doesn't expect it until September."

"I bet you spent your entire break writing."

"I should have spent it here with you."

Summer wished he had; most graduate students stayed close to campus during breaks. But Jeremy's parents had been surprised and disappointed when he suggested remaining in Waterford, so he'd loaded his car with books and research notes and driven home.

She gave him a long kiss. "You're here now."

He smiled and stroked her arm. "Yes."

The timer went off in the kitchen. "Hope you're hungry," Summer said, climbing off him. "I made gnocchi with rosemary and sun-dried tomatoes."

Jeremy followed her into the kitchen. "No sprouts and tofu?"

"Not tonight. It's a special occasion." She emptied the gnocchi into the colander in the sink and motioned for him to set the table. "It's still vegetarian."

"It smells great." He gave her a sidelong look. "I promise I won't do anything as tacky as to ask what's for dessert."

After supper, which to Summer's satisfaction was perfect, from the tender gnocchi to the crusty Italian bread, they sat on the sofa finishing the bottle of wine and catching up on the time they had spent apart. "I missed you," Jeremy said, setting their empty wineglasses on the assemblage of milk crates that passed for a coffee table.

"So you've said."

"I meant what I said about not wanting to be apart from you ever again."

She kissed him, then lay down on the sofa, resting her legs in his lap. "After two weeks without you, I feel the same way."

"Then move in with me."

She stared at him. "What?"

"Move in with me."

"I heard you. I'm just surprised."

"Surprised?" He looked hurt. "The only real surprise is why you haven't moved in already. Officially. You practically live here as it is."

She sat up. "Not quite."

"Come on. It makes perfect sense." He took her hand. "I have to get a new roommate to share the rent anyway, and your lease is up at the end of the month."

"I was planning to renew."

"But if you move in here instead, we'll see more of each other."

He was so earnest that she almost laughed despite her discomfort. "Yeah, maybe more than we want."

"This way we won't have to drive back and forth between apartments. We won't have to play phone tag just to arrange to have dinner together."

"If you think I'd cook like this for you every night, you're out of your mind."

"That's not what I expect at all." He put his arm around her shoulders and held her close. "You'd have your own room, your own space. Anytime you want to shut your door and be alone, I won't bother you."

Summer found that hard to believe, but instead of saying so, she said, "Let me think about it."

"Okay. Sure." He was clearly disappointed. "I guess you want to check with your mom first."

Sharply, she asked, "Why would I want to do that?"

He shrugged. "To see if she approves. Or more accurately, to see if she disapproves too much."

"There's a guy sharing my apartment now."

"Yes, but you're not dating him, and there are two other women." He grinned. "Anyway, I don't think she'll object, do you? From what you've told me, your mother was pretty wild when she was younger. I don't think she'd argue about propriety."

No, Gwen would object on entirely different grounds. "Whatever decision I make, my mother will have nothing to do with it."

Summer's copy of the bridal quilt letter arrived three days later, the same day she met Jeremy for coffee and told him she would move in at the end of the month. She could use a change, anyway; the neighborhood of fraternities and undergraduate apartments had seemed exciting when she was a student, but now that she was almost five years out of college and holding down two jobs, the party atmosphere was more of a nuisance than a pleasure. By moving, she would save almost seventy dollars a month on rent for a newer building with its own laundry and free parking. And the company was much better.

Jeremy wanted to start packing at once, but Summer laughed and reminded him that he had to study and she had to work.

"Elm Creek or Grandma's Attic?" asked Jeremy.

"Both. Grandma's Attic until two, then I'll be at home working on some lesson plans for camp."

"Did you tell Bonnie yet?"

"Not yet. But I will."

"The sooner you tell her, the more time she'll have to find someone else."

Summer knew that, but she also knew circumstances were more complicated than Jeremy thought. She had worked at Grandma's Attic since she was sixteen, and Bonnie had hinted that since none of her children were interested in running a quilt shop, she intended for Summer to take over upon her retirement. Once, Summer would have been happy to do exactly that, but her responsibilities at Elm Creek Manor had expanded more than she had anticipated. She could no longer divide her attention and remain sane, and since Elm Creek Quilts was without question the more promising opportunity, she had chosen it.

Grandma's Attic would be fine without her, Summer told herself. If, despite their diminishing sales, Bonnie thought she needed the extra help, she could hire one of her loyal customers or expand Diane's job to full-time. But telling Bonnie would be much easier if Summer didn't feel as if she were abandoning her friend when Bonnie needed her most.

Bonnie was in such good spirits when Summer arrived that she immediately decided not to spoil it. "Holiday sales were better than we thought," Bonnie told her. "We made a profit for the month of December."

"That's fantastic." Summer tucked her backpack away on the shelf beneath the cutting table. "How much of a profit?"

"Enough to pay off all the overdue ninety-day invoices and some of the sixty-day."

"Great," said Summer, with somewhat less enthusiasm.

"If this keeps up, we'll be able to get out of debt by March."

Summer nodded and began straightening bolts of fabric. It wouldn't keep up, and if Bonnie weren't so indefatigably optimistic, she would admit it. The year-end rush of quilters seeking materials for holiday projects and husbands seeking gifts for quilting wives had ended with Christmas. "We could get out of debt faster if you pressured some of our delinquent customers to pay their bills."

Bonnie shook her head and began cutting a remnant bolt into fat quarters. "We've been through this."

"If they want to buy on credit, they should use a credit card."

"And pay seventeen, eighteen percent interest if they can't pay off their cards in full?"

"If they can't pay off their cards, they shouldn't buy more stuff."

"Summer . . ." Suddenly Bonnie looked tired. "Customers expect that kind of service from a shop like mine. If I don't keep them happy, they'll shop at the Fabric Warehouse instead."

Yes, Summer thought, *where they would pay with cash, check, or credit card.* Granted, customers were fickle and sustaining their loyalty was important, but in Summer's opinion, Bonnie could well afford to lose a few of those so-called loyal shoppers. Summer could name at least twenty who owed Grandma's Attic much more than two hundred dollars each. If they were any more loyal, they would sink the shop so deeply into the red that Bonnie would never drag it out.

Summer would just have to figure out some other way to generate more revenue. Then she might be able to leave with a clear conscience.

At least her three roommates took her news without complaint. One even confided that their real worry had been that Summer would invite Jeremy to move in there. Aaron, the lone male in the household, said he had a friend who would be glad to take over the lease. Karen, who had been her friend since their undergraduate days, asked, "What will your mother say?"

"Probably something to the effect that I must be crazy to sacrifice my independence and autonomy for a guy."

"Really." Karen folded her arms and regarded her with interest. "My mother would be more concerned about all the implied sex."

Aaron, on his way from the kitchen with a bag of chips, added, "Your mom's going to let you move in with a guy?"

"Let me?" echoed Summer, incredulous. "I'm twenty-seven years old."

"Well, yeah, but you know. You and your mom . . ." Aaron shrugged.

"My mom and I what?"

"Ignore him," said Karen, glaring at Aaron in disgust. "Don't worry. Tell your mom when you're ready to tell her. We'll cover for you until then."

Summer thanked her and frowned at Aaron, who managed a sheepish grin before backing away. Things were worse than she expected if even her friends questioned her autonomy. She had learned to expect that from the Elm Creek Quilters, who had known her most of her life and who, despite their assurances to the contrary, still thought of her as little Summer in pigtails with her stuffed bear in the basket of her bike. If she had gone away to college or had found work in a far-off city after graduation, her mother and the other Elm Creek Quilters would have been forced to acknowledge her as an independent adult long ago. The tuition waiver Waterford College offered the children of faculty had been too persuasive, however, and once she had earned her degree she had not wanted to leave her mother or the fledgling Elm Creek Quilts, despite tempting offers from graduate schools. Often Summer wished she had experienced life in other places, experiences deeper and richer than the few glimpses that vacations and one semester of study abroad had afforded. Sometimes she even envied Jeremy, who within a year would be leaving Waterford College with his doctorate for an exciting job somewhere. She wondered what it would be like to have no idea where she would be living or what she would be doing this time next year.

⸙⸙

For the next three weeks, Summer concentrated on the details of moving, and on the last day of January, Jeremy borrowed a friend's pickup truck and hauled Summer's belongings to his apartment. Summer left behind her answering machine in case someone called for her during the few days the phone company insisted they needed to switch over Summer's number to her new home. Jeremy had agreed to leave the outgoing message on his answering machine blank. "We just have to remember the different rings so we only pick up for our own calls," Summer reminded him as they stacked her books on shelves in her new room.

"Or we could just tell your mother you moved in, and not worry about who answers the phone."

"She wants me to come for supper on Sunday. I'll tell her then."

She worried that Jeremy would ask to accompany her, but he simply wished her good luck, adding, "And the next time you see Bonnie, you can tell her you're leaving Grandma's Attic at the end of March."

Summer agreed. She might as well offend everyone in the same week.

By Sunday morning, Summer had finished unpacking and was growing pleasantly accustomed to having Jeremy around, although she still felt like a guest in his apartment rather than an occupant of her own space. While making room for her soy milk and herbal teas in the kitchen and rinsing the tiny black hairs from his morning shave down the bathroom sink, Summer told herself the feeling would pass in time.

As suppertime approached, Summer prepared her mother's favorite three-bean salad and kissed Jeremy for luck. A light snow fell as she drove to her mother's neighborhood, the streets shrouded in midwinter dark despite the early hour. She parked in the driveway and steeled herself as she approached the front door. Her mother admired her independence and trusted her ability to make her own decisions—or so she said. Now was her chance to prove it.

"Mom?" she called, opening the front door. There was no reply. Summer set down the bowl on the hall table and removed her coat and boots when something else struck her: She detected no aroma of her mother's lentil and brown rice soup.

Hurrying into the darkened kitchen, Summer called out again and was rewarded with a muffled reply. She found her mother in her office, eyes fixed on the computer screen, papers strewn across the desk, academic journals scattered all over the floor.

"Hi, kiddo," said Gwen, frowning at the computer. "What's up?" She gasped and spun around in her chair. "Oh, no. Supper."

Summer grinned and tapped her watch. "Sunday at five o'clock."

"I completely forgot." Gwen absently smoothed her long auburn hair, the same shade as Summer's but streaked with gray. "We could send out for pizza."

"I brought a salad. If you have sandwich makings, we'll be fine."

As Summer set the table, Gwen layered Gorgonzola and crushed walnuts on sourdough bread spread liberally with pesto. "That's the best I can do on the spur of the moment," she said as she set one on her daughter's plate.

Summer assured her it was delicious, then couldn't contain her curiosity any longer. "What are you working on in there? Something for the conference?"

Gwen shook her head and loaded her fork with three-bean salad. "I don't want to talk about it. It's too depressing. This is fabulous, by the way."

"It's your recipe. What's too depressing?"

"As it happens, I'm not going to be in charge of the conference after all."

"Why not? I thought the new department chair always ran things." Her mother winced, and Summer guessed the rest. "You weren't made department chair?"

"Nope."

"But you seemed so sure you would be."

"I was." Gwen took a bite of her sandwich, her expression hardening. "The outgoing chair informed me, on behalf of the committee, that they needed someone with solid academic credentials in, and this is a quote, 'substantial, hard research.'"

"What's wrong with your research? You publish at least three articles a year. The book you edited with Laurel Thatcher Ulrich is coming out this fall. Your last conference paper was quoted in *The Washington Post*. What could that committee possibly object to?"

"My topics."

Summer shook her head, uncomprehending.

"I write about quilts."

"Well, yeah. Quilts as cultural and historical artifacts. You've written about what certain quilts tell us about American society in particular eras. What else would they expect a professor of American Studies to do?"

"Write about a less frivolous art form, apparently."

"They said that? They used the word *frivolous*?"

"Merely implied, but the outgoing chair did encourage me to turn my attention to sculpture or painting or architecture if I'm that fixated on art."

"Let me get this straight," said Summer. "It is not okay to study quilts, which happen to be made primarily by women, but other arts are perfectly acceptable, especially those dominated by men?"

"You have an extraordinarily clear grasp of our conversation."

"That's outrageous!"

"You put it more eloquently than I did." Gwen tore the crusts off her sandwich, frowning. "I told him that for a card-carrying liberal and someone who claims to be devoted to the pursuit of knowledge, he had an obvious and detestable bias for 'manly' topics. I also asked him when he turned into a Republican."

"You didn't."

"Unfortunately, I did."

"Oh, Mom."

"I know."

Summer sat back in her chair. "How can they say your work isn't substantial? What about how your analysis of the dyeing processes used in those New England quilts indicated how the settlers inter-acted with the Native Americans? What about your paper on those Confederate quilts and how their fabrics reveal the disruption of trade routes?"

Gwen shrugged and continued eating.

Summer had lost her appetite. "I can't believe a college, of all places, would discourage an intellectual investigation because the subject is 'women's work.'"

"Believe it, kiddo. I'm afraid it's all too true."

Summer reached across the table and took her mother's hand. "I'm sorry, Mom. You deserved that chair. You were robbed."

"Everyone knows being the department chair is a thankless job, anyway."

Maybe so, but Summer also knew it would have given Gwen the prestige she deserved, professional clout she had earned, and a not insubstantial increase in salary for the duration of her term. "Can you protest their decision?"

"I could." Gwen's reluctance told Summer that she had consid-ered that idea and dismissed it. Summer didn't need to ask why. Through the years, she had learned enough about the politics of academia to know her mother had to choose those battles wisely.

"So what were you working on?" asked Summer. "A new paper on a new topic?"

"I'll let you read it when it's done."

Summer nodded, concealing her disappointment. She had hoped that Gwen would tell her she would study whatever topic she thought relevant, regardless of her colleagues' disapproval. Her secrecy obviously meant she would no longer study quilts.

"When your book comes out this fall," Summer said, "and when it becomes a best-seller, and when you and your coeditor are nominated for the Pulitzer, those idiots in your department will eat their words."

Gwen managed a laugh. "I'm counting on it, kiddo."

❦

Gwen's rejection astonished Jeremy, who said that the committee's reasoning would never pass scrutiny in the history department. To Summer's relief, he readily agreed when she suggested waiting until Gwen had adjusted to her disappointment before telling her about the move.

Unfortunately, that excuse would not work with Bonnie. Two days later, Summer arrived for her morning shift at Grandma's Attic with a lump in the pit of her stomach. Bonnie was sitting at the cutting table sorting the morning mail. She wore her purple-and-green Pineapple quilted vest, which she seemed to choose whenever she needed extra courage to get through the day.

"Four more packages arrived today," she said. "Sylvia's bridal quilt is going to be gorgeous."

"Can I see the new blocks?" asked Summer, slipping out of her coat. She resolved to phone Sarah and assure her the project was on schedule. Sarah seemed unnecessarily worried about the bridal quilt, certain they would not receive enough blocks. Summer thought it more likely they would receive too many and would have to wrestle with the more difficult problem of deciding which blocks to include and whose to reject.

Bonnie had already inspected the newest blocks, so she handed the padded envelopes to Summer and turned her attention to the rest of the mail. "Bills," she muttered as she edged her stool closer to the table.

Since there were no customers, Summer lingered over the accompanying letters explaining the quilters' inspiration for their pattern choices. A woman who had sent a Rocky Road to Dublin block explained that Sylvia's investigation into the lives of her ancestors had compelled her to learn more about her own fore-bears, a search that eventually led her to Ireland and some long-lost relations. A Blazing Star block was pinned to a three-page letter extolling Sylvia's accomplishments and praising her with phrases like, "the brightest star in the firmament of the quilting world," and "truly the most gifted and giving quilter of her generation."

Summer smiled as she returned the letter and block to their envelope. Sylvia wouldn't be able to read through half a page before setting it aside in embarrassment.

The next envelope contained a simple Variable Star and a note apologizing for its simplicity. "I hope this is good enough to be included," the maker wrote. "I'm just a beginner. I took my first les-son at Elm Creek Manor last summer. As you can see, Sylvia has inspired me not to give up! It might not look like it, but I've made a lot of progress since the Nine-Patch I made at camp."

Summer recognized the name of a frequent camper on the last envelope.

February 1, 2002

Dear Elm Creek Quilters,

I was thrilled to hear about Sylvia and Andrew's wedding. I wish I could have been there, but I suppose they couldn't have invited every former camper without giving away their secret. And not even Elm Creek Manor is large enough to host a reception that big! I guess I'll just have to congratulate them when I see them again in August.

Thanks for inviting me to participate in Sylvia's bridal quilt. I sat down and made my block right away rather than add this project to my growing list of UFOs. My reason for choosing the Quilter's Dream pattern is probably obvious: Sylvia herself is the friend and teacher every quilter dreams of, and she has turned her home into a wonderful haven where quilters' dreams can come true.

I don't think I ever told Sylvia this, but I started quilting because I saw a picture of one of her quilts in the newspaper when she came to Minnesota to speak at a quilt show twenty-three years ago. I was expecting my first child, and I knew right then and there that I had to make my baby a quilt. I took the article to the nearest fabric shop and begged them for lessons. Apparently, that happens a lot, because half the women in their beginner's class were pregnant!

Twenty years later, I attended Elm Creek Quilt Camp for the first time. I went for two reasons: to finally meet my long-time internet friend in person, and to avoid meeting my daughter's future in-laws. The friends I met at camp that week convinced me to trust my instincts that the marriage was a mistake. With their support, I was eventually able to convince my daughter to leave what I did not yet realize was an abusive relationship.

Sylvia is a wonderful role model for women of all ages. She is self-reliant and makes those of us who know her want to be that way, too. When we come to a situation where we will either sink or swim, we think of Sylvia and start paddling.

I'm pleased to say that my daughter has been doing wonderfully ever since I taught her what Sylvia taught me. She loves film school at USC and, thanks to another one of my quilt camp friends, has been able to work on several well-known feature films. My younger daughter is a freshman at the University of Wisconsin in Madison where she is studying pre-law. It's hard to have both of my girls so far away, but I'm so proud of both of them and I don't want to hold them back from following their dreams.

As for me, for the past year I have been volunteering at a local shelter for abused women. We were able to take in our daughter when she left her fiancé's apartment, but many women have nowhere to go, and often they bring children with them. The shelter provides women with a safe place to stay until they can make their own way, and it also directs them to whatever counseling or work placement assistance they need. I admit the work is stressful sometimes, but when I think of what might have happened to my daughter, I stick to it and do what needs to be done. I think that's what Sylvia would do.

This is probably more information than you wanted about why I chose that block! Thanks again for letting me be a part of this quilt. I can't wait to see it.

Sincerely Yours,
Donna Jorgenson

"How totally cool," said Summer as she put away the block and the letter. "I wonder what movies her daughter worked on. Maybe we've seen some of them."

Summer looked up when Bonnie did not reply. In one fist, she held a crumpled envelope, in the other hand, a crisp sheet of paper.

"What is it?" asked Summer. A list of their angriest creditors flashed through her mind.

"The building's been sold. All tenants have to sign new leases if we want to stay."

"Of course you'll stay," said Summer, aghast. "Where do they expect you to go? They won't raise the rent, will they?"

"The letter doesn't say."

"But you have a lease. They can't change anything until that lease is up, can they?"

"A new owner takes precedence over existing leases. That's city law." Bonnie had once belonged to the Waterford Zoning Commission; she would know. "I wonder what this means for the condo."

Bonnie and her husband lived in the flat directly above the shop. "You guys own that, right?"

"We do, but our landlord owned the building as a whole. It's complicated." Bonnie looked up from the letter. "Do you know anything about University Realty?"

"A little. They manage my old apartment building."

Bonnie's eyebrows rose. "Old apartment?"

"Yeah. I mean, you know, my apartment. It's old. Not that old. Just older than this."

"The new owner says he'll be around to meet all the current tenants and discuss the transition." Bonnie smoothed the crumpled envelope and returned the letter to it. "I'll just have to wait to hear what he says."

"I guess so," said Summer, and decided one transition was enough for Bonnie to worry about at the moment.

Bonnie took the letter into the back office. Through the window, Summer watched her file it and sit down in front of the computer. She did not emerge until the end of Summer's shift, and Summer could tell from her expression that she didn't want to discuss the sale.

After work, Summer stopped by her old apartment to collect her answering machine. Her former roommates apologized for forgetting to tell her about the eight messages on the tape, but they assured her they had not revealed anything to Gwen the time she stopped by on her way to work. Summer thanked them and wondered why her mother had not mentioned the visit.

Jeremy came home later than usual that evening bearing Thai takeout since it was his night to cook. Over Phat Thai, Summer told him about Bonnie's situation, the exasperation of her roommates' forgetfulness, and Gwen's visit to the old apartment.

"She probably thought you spent the night at my place," said Jeremy.

"I know. I didn't want her to."

"Why not? It's the truth, sort of."

Summer sighed and toyed with her chopsticks. "Jeremy, your parents must be incredibly accepting for you to be so clueless about why this bothers me."

"Are you kidding? My mother would faint if she ever finds out the truth." He quickly added, "I'm kidding. They already know."

"They don't mind?"

"That's the benefit of being the youngest of four. They've already been through everything with my sisters and brother."

"Great," said Summer dryly. It was far too late to hope for any siblings to help share her burden of maternal attention.

Throughout February, Summer managed to rationalize away several more opportunities to mention the move to her mother or give notice at Grandma's Attic. She had even begun to forget her anxieties enough to feel at home in Jeremy's apartment until one evening during supper when three hang-up calls on the answering machine convinced her that Gwen had figured out the truth. Summer waited a reasonable interval before calling her mother on some camp-related pretext only to find her engrossed in her new research project.

Relieved, she hung up and wondered aloud who had called, but Jeremy was annoyed that Summer had not gone ahead and unburdened her obviously troubled conscience. That led to their first fight as roommates. They made up that same night, but not before Jeremy told her that if she was so ashamed to live with him she ought to move out, and Summer retorted that she had considered it.

The next morning they lingered in bed and shared a leisurely breakfast, still apologetic and careful, wanting reassurances that everything was fine between them before they parted for the day. Despite her late start, Summer managed to get to work on time since Jeremy's apartment was only a five-minute walk from Grandma's Attic. She arrived to find the quilt shop dark, the sign in the front door still turned to CLOSED. Bonnie should have unlocked the door an hour earlier. Summer fumbled in her backpack for her key and let herself in.

"Bonnie?" she called, flipping the sign. She turned on the lights and the music system, taking advantage of the opportunity to slip in one of her favorite CDs instead of Bonnie's usual hammered dulcimer and flute. She restocked the empty shelves with what little was left in the storage room, but when another half hour passed with no sign of Bonnie, she phoned upstairs. The answering machine picked up; Bonnie's husband's voice announced that she had reached the home of Craig Markham and that he would return her call later. Summer hung up without leaving a message.

At that moment, the door burst open and Diane came in. "Oh, hi," she said, taking off her coat. "I thought no one else was working today."

"I work every Friday when camp isn't in session," said Summer, puzzled. Diane knew that. "Bonnie should be here, too, but she didn't show up this morning. I'm worried. No one answered the phone upstairs, either."

"She's not coming in today." Diane hung up her coat on a peg on the back wall and stored her purse under the cutting table. "Agnes called and asked me to open the store. I guess she didn't know you would be here."

"Agnes? Why would Agnes have called?"

Diane shrugged. "I have no idea. I imagine Bonnie asked her to."

"But Bonnie knew I was working and she would have called you directly."

"Well . . ." Diane paused. "I don't know. But I'm here, so I'm going to work. I need the hours. Todd is still holding out for Princeton. Do you have any idea how expensive that is? Thank goodness Michael decided to go to Waterford College so we could take advantage of the family tuition waiver."

Summer nodded. Michael had been something of a troublemaker since the fifth grade, but as his former and favorite babysitter, Summer tended to see harmless mischief where others saw an inmate-in-training. When Michael enrolled at Waterford College, Diane had been so relieved that she would have paid any amount of tuition without complaint. Now completing his sophomore year, Michael seemed to be thriving as a Computer Sciences major. When the time came, Summer hoped he would find a job outside of Waterford so that, unlike herself, he would be accepted as the adult he had become instead of perpetually seen as the child he had been.

The morning passed with no word from Bonnie. When a call to Agnes went unanswered, Summer considered phoning Bonnie's husband at work, but she had carried on only a handful of strained conversations with Craig in all the years she had known the Markhams. She didn't want to risk making trouble by bothering him at his office. If something was seriously wrong, he wouldn't be there, anyway. He would be with his wife.

A slow but steady flow of customers kept Summer and Diane too busy to have much time to chat, but it tapered off long enough for them to go to lunch. After Diane's turn, Summer went to the Daily Grind for coffee and a salad. Judy was there, an empty plate on the table beside her laptop. Summer did not want to interrupt her work, but when she stopped by to say hello, Judy invited Summer to join her. Summer agreed and, as she seated herself, she couldn't resist a glance at the computer screen. She glimpsed what looked to be lecture notes before Judy shut it down.

They chatted about quilt camp while Summer ate and Judy

nursed a cup of black coffee. "Have you started your block for Sylvia's quilt yet?" Summer asked.

"I confess I forgot all about it," said Judy. "I don't even have the fabric yet."

"If you run out of time you could always buy one of those bargain kits at the Fabric Warehouse," teased Summer, and had to laugh at her friend's stricken expression. "I'm just kidding. You have plenty of time. I haven't started my block, either."

"I don't know what's more insulting," said Judy, tossing her straight black hair over her shoulder and feigning moral outrage. "That you think I have such poor time management skills or that I'd take my business anywhere but Grandma's Attic."

Summer assured her she knew otherwise on both counts.

She would have stayed to talk longer, but she couldn't linger with a clear conscience knowing Diane was at the store alone. Judy encouraged her to stay, but she had her computer switched back on before Summer pushed in her chair. On her way out, Summer passed two young men joining the line at the counter, digging in their back pockets for folded bills. She recognized the tall blond on sight, although she hadn't baby-sat Diane's sons in years. The younger of the brothers, Todd was handsome, athletic, and therefore popular, and his companion seemed much the same. The boys laughed and talked loudly like the lords of the local high school class that they were, wanting and expecting to be noticed, oblivious to the utter lack of interest of the college students and professors who had no idea how important they were among their peers. Summer smiled and left the coffee shop. She shouldn't be so hard on Todd and his friend, who looked vaguely familiar. Troubled Michael had always been her favorite, and Todd couldn't help that his perfection made him so annoying.

Back at Grandma's Attic, the stream of customers slowed to a trickle by midafternoon, and despite Bonnie's absence, Summer considered leaving early. Quilt camp would begin in almost three weeks, and Summer should have been at Elm Creek Manor helping Sarah. Out of guilt for her intended resignation, she had not reduced her hours at the quilt shop as she usually did by that time of year. Sarah rightly could have complained, but she probably had everything so well under control that she barely noticed Summer's absence. Even so, come Monday, Summer would revert to her camp season hours. Maybe that would provide a natural transition into leaving permanently.

Eventually customer traffic slowed so much that Diane suggested that to pass the time they read the letters accompanying the blocks for Sylvia's bridal quilt. Summer agreed, but thoughts of her enormous workload nagged at her so much she could not enjoy herself.

Just as she was about to ask Diane if she would mind closing on her own, the front bell jingled. A customer entered wearing a red wool coat trimmed with black fur, and black pumps rather than the snow boots nearly everyone else in Waterford favored this time of year. She removed a black fur hat and smoothed her platinum blond pageboy with a leather-gloved hand, "Isn't Bonnie here today?"

"No," said Diane abruptly, sitting down at the cutting table with her back to the woman and unfolding another letter.

"Diane," whispered Summer, incredulous.

"Don't worry. She's not a customer."

Diane's voice dripped with disgust, but fortunately she had spoken too softly for the woman to overhear. Suddenly Summer recognized her. She had been a brunette the last time Summer had seen her, but she was unmistakably Mary Beth Callahan, the perennial president of the Waterford Quilting Guild and Diane's next-door neighbor.

Summer decided to avoid giving Diane another opportunity to address Mary Beth, since their mutual loathing was legendary. "Bonnie's not here, but may I help you?"

"I suppose so. You're Summer, right? Summer Sullivan?"

"That's right."

"Your name is in the letter, so I guess you'll do." Mary Beth withdrew an envelope from her purse and unfolded it. "I believe this was sent to me by mistake."

She held out the envelope until Summer took it. One glance told her it was the invitation to participate in Sylvia's bridal quilt.

"We definitely meant to send it to you," Summer assured her. "Actually, to the entire guild. You're listed as the guild contact, so we sent it to your home, hoping you would announce it at your next meeting."

She tried to return the letter, but Mary Beth waved it away. "Oh, no, I couldn't do that."

"Why not?" asked Diane.

"I couldn't impose on my fellow guild members like that. They'd probably feel obligated to participate, and that isn't fair. Sylvia is not a charity case. If I endorse your project, where does it stop?"

"We're not asking you to endorse it, just announce it," said Diane. "Just tell them about the quilt and let them decide whether they want to help."

Summer raised a hand to quiet her friend. "I understand your concerns, but many of your guild members have known Sylvia for years. Don't you think they would want to know about her bridal quilt?"

"Don't you think once they see the finished quilt they'll be ticked off that you kept them from participating?" Diane added.

Mary Beth regarded her sourly. "If those few members of my guild are such good friends of Sylvia's, I'm sure you have their addresses and can contact them individually. Our guild happens to be very busy, Diane, so regardless of their feelings for Sylvia, we would appreciate it if nonmembers didn't come around begging for blocks."

"How would you know if you never ask them?" said Diane. "If they don't want to participate, fine, but you won't even give them the chance to refuse for themselves!"

Mary Beth ignored her. "Make sure to take our address off your mailing list," she called to Summer over her shoulder as she departed.

"Gladly," retorted Diane as the door closed behind her. "Can you believe that woman? What is her problem?"

"I have no idea." Summer tossed the letter into the trash. "She seems easily threatened."

"Absolutely. Remember how she freaked out when I opposed her for guild president? I would have been elected if she hadn't reminded everyone that I had never won a ribbon in a quilt show."

"Winning lots of ribbons can't make someone a good president," said Summer. "You need an entirely different set of skills." She didn't point out that the Waterford Quilting Guild apparently believed Mary Beth possessed them or she wouldn't be elected every year. Diane would merely argue that she ran unopposed because everyone feared her wrath.

"She's deliberately trying to ruin Sylvia's quilt," said Diane, opening and closing her rotary cutter with an ominous glint in her eye.

"Why would she do that?" Summer gently guided Diane to the cutting table. "Remember, that's to cut fabric, not throats."

"Because she's jealous of Sylvia's success. And Bonnie's. And mine, too, probably."

Summer couldn't dispute that, but said, "She can't ruin Sylvia's quilt. It would have been nice to have some contributions from more local quilters, but we'll have enough blocks without them."

"Oh, really? The mail came while you were at lunch. The three blocks we got today brings us to a grand total of fifty-eight. We need one hundred forty." Diane frowned and tapped the rotary cutter on the table. "Think about it. Mary Beth has had our letter since the beginning of January. Why would she wait two months to tell us she can't announce it at the guild meeting?"

"I imagine you're about to tell me."

"To make sure we couldn't get around her, that's why. Even if we do send letters to someone else in the guild and ask her to make the announcement, and even if she manages to sneak it past Czarina Mary Beth, the guild members won't have enough time to make any blocks."

Summer had to admit that Diane's explanation of Mary Beth's motives sounded plausible, but she couldn't believe that one spiteful woman could ruin the entire quilt. They had plenty of time. She had not started her own block yet, but she would definitely complete it before the deadline.

Summer left shortly afterward, making Diane promise to call her if she received word from Bonnie. Over the weekend she worked on sample projects for a new course she hoped to teach later that season, and on Sunday afternoon, she phoned Bonnie to remind her she intended to cut back her hours in preparation for camp. She left messages at Bonnie's home as well as at Grandma's Attic, but Bonnie did not return them.

Before driving out to Elm Creek Manor Monday morning, Summer dropped by Grandma's Attic just in case Bonnie failed to show. To her relief, the quilt shop was open, and Bonnie was inside helping a customer. Summer stopped in just long enough to remind Bonnie about her changed schedule—and to notice the dark circles beneath her friend's eyes. Bonnie apologized for not returning her messages but offered no explanation for her silence, and with a customer listening in, Summer could not ask.

Summer spent the rest of the day in the library of Elm Creek Manor helping Sarah prepare for the start of the new camp season. After several hours arranging and rearranging the course schedule, they finally acknowledged that they would have to cancel a few classes. Summer volunteered to phone some of the Elm Creek Quilters to confirm schedule changes, wanting to spare her overworked friend that unpleasant task. Summer contacted Agnes, but could not track down her mother, Diane, or Judy.

Frustrated, Summer hung up and flung herself into a chair in front of the library fireplace, complaining about their friends' inaccessibility. Sarah laughed and as usual offered a logical explanation for their absence, then added that Summer was the least accessible of them all. "All anyone can ever get is your machine. By the way, I think it might be broken. There's no outgoing message anymore, just a beep."

"Oh," said Summer guardedly. "Thanks. I'll look into it."

"You should. Last week I called three times in a row just to make sure I had the right number."

Summer nodded. So Sarah was the mysterious caller.

That evening, Summer told Jeremy what she had learned, making light of the misunderstanding and the argument that had followed. Jeremy laughed with her about it, adding, "I don't want another fight over something so stupid. Record whatever message you want. My callers will just have to get used to it."

"No, you record it. If my mom calls, problem solved."

His eyebrows shot up. "Are you sure that's the best way for her to find out?"

"No, it's not. Now I'll have some incentive to tell her soon."

She resolved to do so before the Elm Creek Quilters' next business meeting.

On the following Thursday, she tried all day to reach Gwen and offer her a ride out to the manor. They could talk in the car. Summer would time it so she delivered the bad news just as they were crossing the bridge over Elm Creek. Gwen would have to settle down for the meeting, and by the time Summer drove her home, she might be better able to conduct a rational discussion. Unfortunately, Gwen did not cooperate with her daughter's plans. She did not respond to calls to home, office, or cell phone, so eventually Summer gave up and drove to the meeting alone. She still hoped for a few minutes alone with Gwen beforehand, but Gwen arrived just as Sarah opened the meeting.

"Mom, hi," whispered Summer, edging her chair closer. Sarah frowned slightly but continued speaking. "Listen, can we talk after the meeting?"

"Hmm? Oh, hi, kiddo. Sure, if things wrap up before eight-thirty. I have to get back to the library before it closes."

So that was where she had been hiding. Summer hoped Sarah would get through the meeting with uncharacteristic brevity. She willed Sarah to quicken her pace, instinctively checking her watch every time Sarah paused between topics, but as the minutes passed, her thoughts wandered from Gwen to Jeremy to Bonnie's still unexplained absence from Grandma's Attic. Summer would have asked for an explanation, but considering her own secrets, it seemed hypocritical—

"Are you out of your mind?" Sylvia cried out.

"What?" said Summer, looking from Sarah to Sylvia and back. "What did she say?"

"If any of you had been listening, you would know." Clearly distressed, Sarah begged her friends to pay attention. Summer, who already felt guilty over helping Sarah less that year than in the past, resolved to concentrate on Elm Creek Quilt Camp for the rest of the meeting. When Sylvia and Diane exchanged a few quips about some naked woman, Summer paid no attention and nodded at Sarah to encourage her to continue.

The meeting concluded at eight twenty-five. "What did you want to talk about, kiddo?" Gwen asked as she put on her coat.

"Nothing." Nothing they could discuss in five minutes. "I just wanted to catch up. Let's talk on Sunday, okay? Want to try supper again?"

Gwen agreed, gave her a quick hug and kiss, and hurried out the door. Summer was reaching for her own coat when she felt a hand on her arm. "Summer, dear," said Sylvia. "Do you have a moment?"

"Sure."

Sylvia beckoned her to take a seat and waited for the others to leave the room. "I hope you won't think me a nosy old biddy, but I wonder how you're doing these days. You seem somewhat troubled."

Summer forced a smile. "I'm fine."

"I see. Apparently I was mistaken, then, when I assumed all was not well with your, shall we say, domestic situation."

"What do you mean?"

"I phoned yesterday and was greeted by a pleasant young man's voice on the answering machine. A familiar voice—Jeremy's, I believe."

"Oh. Right." Summer tried to sound nonchalant. "Actually, I moved in with Jeremy in February."

"In February? Goodness, you can keep a secret. I assumed this was a much more recent development."

Feeling foolish, Summer said, "I have my own bedroom."

"Of course you do," said Sylvia, without missing a beat. "I assume you haven't told your mother?"

"I haven't told anyone except you." Summer hesitated. "I guess you're going to tell her?"

"Oh, my, no," said Sylvia with a little laugh. "I'm afraid that's in your hands. It's not my place to tattle on you, nor to judge. However, as your friend, and as someone who cares about your well-being, I'm compelled to ask why you would choose to do anything you're ashamed for your mother and your friends to know about."

"I'm not ashamed." Summer slumped against the backrest. "But I know how everyone will react and I'm not looking forward to it. They still think of me as a little kid."

"Some of our friends would object to your living with Jeremy whether you were twenty-seven or fifty-seven. It's not a question of age, but of marital status."

"They have a right to object," Summer countered, "but I have the right to make my own choices."

"So you do," said Sylvia, nodding. "Then you believe Jeremy is 'the one'?"

"I don't know. I suppose not."

"My understanding is that moving in together is often a precursor to marriage."

Summer shook her head. "Jeremy has to know that isn't possible. My life is here, right?"

"Are you asking me or telling me?"

"My career, my mom, my friends are all right here in Waterford," said Summer firmly. "I couldn't leave if I wanted to."

Sylvia's eyebrows rose. "Couldn't you?"

Summer let the question pass. "Jeremy will eventually get his Ph.D. and move on to some faculty position elsewhere. He knows I can't come with him."

"Are you certain he knows? Men have a way of ignoring what they don't want to see."

Summer couldn't argue with that. She toyed with a loose string on her shirtsleeve. They had never discussed marriage or made any long-term plans. Summer loved Jeremy, and she would be brokenhearted when he left, but she knew it would happen and accepted it. He occasionally mentioned different colleges he aspired to work for after receiving his degree, and Waterford College was not among them. Even if he did prefer a small, rural school, departments seldom hired their own Ph.D.s for tenure-track positions. It was just the way things were.

"I know our time together is limited," said Summer. "One of the reasons I moved in with Jeremy was to make the most of that time."

"I see."

"He has less than a year before he graduates." Summer forced a laugh. "Most couples break up sooner than that. Jeremy and I probably will, too, and so none of this will matter."

"If none of this matters, why haven't you told anyone? And if you honestly believe you're going to break up anyway, isn't it rather foolish to move in with him?"

Summer had no answer for her.

Sylvia reached over and patted Summer's hand. "I believe you two should have had this discussion before you gave up your old apartment, but you should still have it. Better late than much too late."

Summer nodded. Sylvia was right, but that meant one more discussion she loathed to have. Speaking to Gwen seemed easy in comparison.

⟡

On Sunday, Summer decided to get it over with.

She waited until after supper, then, in a calm, controlled voice, told Gwen she had moved in with Jeremy. She omitted a few details, such as when the move had taken place and her former roommates' assistance in deceiving Gwen. She waited for her mother to respond, but finally prompted, "Mom?"

"Why?" Gwen choked out.

With barely a tremor, Summer carefully went through the reasons again. Jeremy needed someone to share the rent. She was tired of her old place. The new apartment was better in every respect, including rent. She loved Jeremy and wanted to spend more time with him, something their busy schedules would not permit otherwise.

"But you've only been dating since last summer," said Gwen, with remarkably less hysteria than Summer had anticipated. "How could you give up your freedom, your independence?"

Summer couldn't help it; she rolled her eyes. "I knew you would say that. I'm not chained to the kitchen table. Jeremy doesn't shove a toilet brush into my hand when he leaves for campus in the morning."

Gwen shook her head. "I can't believe you didn't discuss this with me first."

"I'm not a teenager, Mom."

"But apparently still not mature enough to understand the consequences of your decisions."

Gwen rose and began to clear the table, refusing Summer's offer of help. Summer carried plates to the sink anyway and tried to change the subject by asking about Gwen's progress on her new research project. Gwen told her she did not want to stir up more negative energy that evening, and maybe they could talk about it another day, when Gwen felt less hopeless.

Summer did not know what else to do, so she went home, where Jeremy was waiting to hear how it had gone. She told him both better and worse than she had expected, and left it at that. He gave her a searching look, but left his books and papers to make her a cup of her favorite chamomile tea.

Summer drank it curled up on the futon with a book that could not hold her attention. Her mother's reaction was a disturbing echo of Sylvia's. Summer trusted her own instincts, she was comfortable making her own decisions, and she enjoyed living with Jeremy. Still, somehow she wished she had talked to someone before making the move.

"Jeremy," she finally said, "do you think moving in together has changed things?"

"You mean, between us?" A book closed. "Of course. For the better. Don't you?"

She chose her words carefully. "I'm happy with the way things are right now."

"So am I."

"But you know, they can't stay like this forever."

A pause. "No, I guess not, but I love you, Summer, and when the time comes to take the next step, we'll take it."

She could only nod in reply. She wondered what he thought that next step was when they both knew he would be leaving Waterford someday.

The remaining two weeks before the first day of camp passed in a flurry of activity. The Elm Creek Quilters were too busy to spare much time for gossip, so Summer's news spread more slowly than it would have at any other time of the year. Judy was the first to find out; she expressed surprise, but like Sylvia maintained a nonjudgmental front. When Summer admitted she had waited more than a month after moving to tell her mother, Judy seemed more impressed than shocked. "How did you keep it a secret for so long?" she asked admiringly. "The Elm Creek Quilters tell each other everything."

"Not everything," said Summer, thinking of Bonnie. One secret was enough to keep from Bonnie, Summer decided, so she mentioned her change of address casually during her next shift at Grandma's Attic. Bonnie stared at her for a long moment before saying, "Are you sure you know what you're doing?" When Summer assured her she did, Bonnie studied her for a moment before finding an excuse to work in the storage room. Later she emerged, forced a smile, and told Summer that she was probably right to test the relationship before making a more permanent commitment. Summer managed not to flinch as she nodded.

Summer knew Agnes had been told when the older woman began studying her mournfully when she thought Summer unaware. She became so flustered in Summer's presence whenever certain words came up—*apartment* and *boyfriend*, of course, but also unavoidable words such as *together*, *living*, *trouble*, and *wrong*—that they could no longer carry on a conversation. Summer tried to put her at ease, but Agnes's disappointment in her was so apparent than it became easier to avoid her. Dreading that Sarah, Diane, and the rest would share Agnes's feelings, Summer decided to let them find out on their own rather than telling them herself. One friend's dismay was difficult enough to bear.

Then the deadline for Sylvia's bridal quilt, once so distant, was only a week away. Summer thought of all the blocks she had ever made, but none of the names captured what she felt for Sylvia. Unlike the quilters who had mailed blocks to Grandma's Attic, she knew Sylvia too well to pick out one particular conversation or encounter that had transformed her life. She found the perfect fabrics in her stash—better organized than in years past, now that she had a room to herself—but the inspiration she waited for did not come.

On the morning of the first day of camp, Summer decided to ask for an extension. Surely the deadline was somewhat flexible for Elm Creek Quilters, and maybe the block choice guidelines were, too.

Summer made it to Elm Creek Manor by eleven, her worries momentarily forgotten in the excitement of the first day of camp. Sarah buzzed about the grand front foyer setting up tables and delegating tasks, her frenzy barely tempered by Sylvia's reassuring confidence. When Sarah asked Bonnie to inspect the classrooms, Summer quickly volunteered to assist, determined to talk to her alone.

As they checked the classrooms for equipment and furnishings, Summer asked Bonnie why she had not shown up for work on the first of March. When Bonnie hesitated, Summer prompted, "Did it have something to do with the building?"

Bonnie busied herself with testing a sewing machine. "Yes, I guess you could say that."

"Are they going to raise the rent?"

"Oh, sure, but only by seventy-five percent."

"Seventy-five?" Summer dropped into a chair. "They can't do that."

"They can, and they're going to."

"How do they expect you to pay that much?"

"They don't. They want me out."

"Why? It can't be that easy to find a new business to fill the vacancy."

"Oh, they have big plans for the building. They're going to turn it all into student apartments."

"Even the condos?"

Bonnie nodded.

"They can't," said Summer, although she was beginning to wonder about the limits of their power. "You own the condo. They can't force you to sell."

"They assume I'd prefer that to living surrounded by partying sophomores. And these days I'm not too attached to the condo, so moving wouldn't be the end of the world." She paused. "But it is my one bit of leverage over University Realty. They want me to sell the condo, but they know I'll dig in my heels if they force me out of my store. As long as we're still holding on financially, I'll never give up Grandma's Attic."

Summer clasped her hands together in her lap. "I know one way you can cut your expenses."

"I know." Bonnie nodded, resigned. "It's awful, but it's the most obvious solution. I have to fire Diane."

"What? No, not that! I'll resign."

"Oh, Summer. It's sweet of you to try to save Diane's job, but I couldn't manage without you. Your ideas are what have kept us afloat this long."

"I was planning to quit anyway. I can't keep holding down two jobs, and Elm Creek Quilts is my first choice."

Bonnie managed the first smile Summer had seen from her all day. "I appreciate what you're trying to do. I know Diane's concerned about paying for Todd's tuition—"

"That's not it." Summer placed her hands on Bonnie's shoulders and looked her directly in the eye. "Let me make this as clear as I know how: I quit."

Bonnie patted her hand and rose. "I'm glad people like you still exist in this world. Believe me, I'm in no hurry to fire my friend. I'll tell you what. I'll keep Diane on for another month. If we can turn things around by then, I won't let her go. If not . . ." She took Summer's hand and pulled her to her feet. "Come on. We still have three classrooms. Sarah probably thinks we ran off."

⮆⮄

"She wouldn't let you quit?" Jeremy asked as they prepared for bed that evening. He had waited up for her to hear how the banquet and Candlelight welcoming ceremony had fared.

"It's not that she wouldn't let me. She didn't believe that I wanted to." Summer vigorously brushed her long auburn hair. If she had quit weeks ago, she wouldn't be in this mess. Neither would Diane.

"Put it in writing," said Jeremy. He lifted her hair off her shoulders and kissed the nape of her neck. "Then stop showing up for work."

"I still have a month to save Diane's job," she reminded him, but resolved to write a letter of resignation first thing in the morning.

The next day, she had just kissed Jeremy good-bye and was settling down at her computer with a cup of tea when Sarah phoned. "Would you mind teaching Judy's four o'clock Computer Design class this week?" Sarah asked. "I know you're busy Wednesday afternoon, but I thought your mom could sub then."

"Sure," said Summer, puzzled. She had arranged that schedule herself and knew she had not overlooked a conflict. "What happened to Judy?"

"She had to go out of town unexpectedly on business." Sarah sounded even more frazzled than usual. "I think we have her other class covered, though."

"Are you sure?"

Sarah let out a bleak laugh. "Unfortunately, yes." She said something about needing to prepare for some hand-quilting, said a hasty good-bye, and hung up.

Summer shook her head, hung up the phone, and typed her letter of resignation. She rehearsed what she would say on the drive to Elm Creek Manor. Bonnie spent her mornings at Grandma's Attic, so Summer didn't bother to look for her until after the morning sessions. She found her at lunch engaged in an animated conversation about quilted clothing over burritos and margaritas. "I'm sure you understand how much I regret this," said Summer, jumping into a momentary pause in the discussion. She handed Bonnie the letter and smiled at the assembled campers, who looked on curiously. "This is to prove I'm serious."

Bonnie laughed and tucked the letter into her pocket without reading it. "Sure you are. Remember, you work the closing shift on Wednesday."

Summer frowned. And Sylvia said *men* ignored what they did not want to see. She left to grab a sandwich before her afternoon classes. Obviously Bonnie would not wish to discuss her resignation in front of the campers but, like it or not, she would have to accept it.

Summer's classes were full of fun and over too soon, reminding her again why, when forced to make a choice, she had chosen Elm Creek Quilts over Grandma's Attic. Her students' energy and enthusiasm rekindled her own passion for quilting and reminded her anew why she had first begged Gwen to teach her the art.

Except for Judy's absence, camp seemed to be off to a fine and unusually smooth start, from classes to evening entertainment programs to the mundane details such as laundry and parking. Summer thought so as late as Wednesday morning, as she began the third day of her weeklong workshop in color theory. At half past ten, she noticed two students lingering in the doorway, but they moved on when they realized she had seen them. Then, five minutes later, three other students slipped into the room and quietly took seats in the back. A murmur of voices came from the hallway, rising, falling, and yet another student entered the room. Apologizing to her students, Summer quickly went to see what was happening.

The source of the commotion was the room next door; Summer had to wait for two students to exit before she could enter. Six students remained within, talking irritably. They fell silent when they caught sight of Summer. "Are you our new instructor?" one woman asked.

"What happened to Bonnie?" demanded another.

"I don't know," said Summer. "Did she have to leave?"

"She never showed up," said another peevishly. "I've never seen anything so unprofessional in my life."

"Oh, hush up, Phoebe," said a third student. "Emergencies happen. She was so nice to us at lunch yesterday."

"Let me see what I can do," said Summer, and hurried from the room. She ran from the ballroom into the front foyer, where through the tall double doors she glimpsed Matt working outside. She called him over and asked him to run upstairs and inform Sarah what had happened. Then she hurried back to her own students and carried on with the class.

At noon, Summer found Sarah in the foyer on her way to the banquet hall with an armful of schedules and other papers. She had no idea what had become of Bonnie. "She never called," said Sarah. "I've tried Grandma's Attic and her home, but all I get are answering machines. Something strange, though. Craig seems to have recorded over Bonnie's family greeting on the home machine."

"It's probably nothing," said Summer, thinking of her own answering machine problems. "Their youngest moved out years ago. They were overdue for a change."

Sarah nodded dismissively. "You're right. I don't know why I even mentioned it. We have enough to worry about."

"I'm going to Grandma's Attic right now," said Summer. "I'll call you as soon as I find out what's wrong. Maybe she just had car trouble."

"Car trouble *and* phone trouble?" said Sarah. "Unlikely."

In response, Summer nodded and ran up to the office for her backpack. In a few minutes she was driving through the leafy wood surrounding the estate on her way downtown. She wished she had her mother's cell phone so she could try to reach Bonnie. Why had she failed to call—again?

Fifteen minutes later she pulled into the employee parking

space behind Grandma's Attic and ran around the block to the front entrance.

Parked in front of Grandma's Attic were two police cars.

Summer stopped short for a heartbeat, then caught her breath and hurried inside.

"Bonnie?" she cried, searching for her friend. The quilt shop was a shambles. Notions were scattered across the floor, bolts of fabric knocked from their shelves and unrolled in a snarl of color, books and patterns flung about as if by a great wind.

Bonnie looked up from a far corner of the room, her face ashen, but she did not break off her conversation with the two uniformed officers before her. She leaned against an empty bookcase as if she might faint without its support.

"I'm afraid you can't come in, miss," said a third officer Summer had not noticed. "This is a crime scene."

"What?"

"We had a break-in," said Bonnie, picking her way across the room. Her eyes were filled with unshed tears, but she held out her arms to comfort Summer.

Summer embraced her. "What did they take?"

"Everything in the cash register." Bonnie clung to her, trembling. "Last night's deposit. I didn't have time to take it to the bank after closing."

Why didn't you take it upstairs? Summer almost cried out, but she held back the instinctive criticism. It was pointless.

"Some rotary cutters and scissors, pens, a sewing machine." Bonnie's voice was distant, disbelieving. "And the quilt blocks."

"What?"

"All of the blocks for Sylvia's bridal quilt, except for those I had already given to Agnes." Bonnie shook with sobs. "They're gone."

CHAPTER THREE

Gwen

A s soon as the spring semester began, Gwen began checking her office mailbox twice daily for official notice that she had been named chair of the Department of American Studies. She waited, but in the first three weeks of January, the most interesting piece of mail she received was the invitation to participate in Sylvia's bridal quilt, and she had already known about that. Of course, she already knew what the committee's letter would say, too, but before she told all her friends and celebrated, she wanted official confirmation of the hints and veiled promises the outgoing chair had dropped during the past year and a half.

They would have to reveal their selection soon. Although the official transition would not take place until the end of May, the incoming chair traditionally assumed some of the duties by the end of January. Every summer the Society for the Study of American Culture held a four-day conference at Waterford College, which the department chair directed. A good portion of the work had already been completed, but the incoming chair would be expected to take over just in time for reviewing paper submissions, scheduling speaking times, and making sure Food Services remembered to order enough alcohol for the opening reception, which never failed to set the tone for the entire conference. Gwen had seen chairmen's careers falter over too little wine or the wrong brand of beer.

"Chairmen" was the accurate term to use, too, even for someone who generally eschewed gender-exclusive language. Only three women had directed the department in its entire history, and the last had retired fourteen years earlier. The department was long overdue to select another woman, but Gwen considered herself the strongest candidate regardless. She had seniority over the other professors who had not yet served, her record of publications was outstanding, her graduate students performed well and consistently found tenure-track positions in respected universities, and her undergraduate teaching evaluations were excellent. So why did the committee's reticence trouble her so much?

Because, she admitted to herself, she had been a tenured member of that faculty for too long not to have been chair already. Twice before she thought she deserved the job at least as much as the person who was eventually named. If she were passed over again, she would have to consider seriously whether she ought to spend the rest of her career at Waterford College.

The news finally came one Wednesday morning when a knock sounded on her office door. "Gwen?"

"Come on in, Jules," Gwen called. The door opened and one of her graduate students entered. "Ready for the candidacy exam?"

"Almost. Ask me again next month." Jules settled his lanky frame into the opposite chair. "How are you doing?"

"Me?" Gwen turned away from the computer to find him peering at her, his expression guarded. "I'm fine. Why wouldn't I be?"

"So you haven't heard? Or is it just a rumor?"

"Is what a rumor?"

"One of Professor Brannon's grad students says she's going to be chair."

For a moment Gwen just stared at him, absorbing this. "There hasn't been any official word yet. It's a bad idea to spread rumors. Or to listen to them."

"I know. I know. But this rumor's spreading fast, and no one's refuting it." He hesitated. "We wanted to see how you were taking it."

He meant the rest of her grad students had sent him in to gauge whether it was safe to approach or if they ought to avoid her for the next few days. "Thanks for keeping me in the loop." She saved her document and rose, adding with forced confidence, "I'll get this cleared up."

Bill's assistant buzzed her in to the department chair's office with little delay, with a look of sympathy that spoke volumes. She had probably known the committee's decision weeks before Bill did.

When Gwen entered, Bill rose and offered her a seat. His atypical politeness so unsettled her that she almost involuntarily dropped into the chair. "I think I know why you're here," he said, scratching a graying sideburn.

"I've heard some rumors."

"Annette Brannon has been appointed department chair."

"I see." She inhaled deeply but held his gaze. "Based upon our conversations of the past two years, it was my understanding that I was first in line."

"If it makes you feel any better, you were our next choice if Annette refused."

"No, it does not make me feel any better." No one who would consider refusing was ever offered the position. "Why? What happened?"

He spread his palms. "The same process that happens every three years. The committee scrutinized a number of relevant factors and determined that Annette was the best choice."

"I have been a member of this department for nearly sixteen years." Gwen studied the photos on his desk: Bill and his wife in tuxedo and gown, his wife alone, Bill and William, Jr. wearing identical Pittsburgh Steelers sweatshirts. When she was calm enough, she said, "Annette joined us five years ago. She has one book out, her dissertation. I have four and another slated for the fall. She has not yet led so much as one department committee to my six. Compare our journal publications and you'll find—"

"Gwen. Please. The decision's been made." Bill glanced at his watch discreetly, but not discreetly enough. "Maybe next time will be your turn."

This time was supposed to have been her turn, and she was not about to go through this same humiliation three years hence. "I'd appreciate hearing how the committee reached its decision since you didn't dispute my comparison of our qualifications."

"Maybe you should take it up with the committee."

"I've had a little too much bureaucracy for one day, so I'd prefer to take it up with you." Gwen reminded herself to be civil. "I'd appreciate it, especially since, inadvertently or not, you led me to believe I would be offered the job."

"Annette is the most appropriate choice for the department at this juncture," said Bill. "You're focusing on quantity of work and ignoring quality. The committee felt the department needed someone with solid academic credentials in substantial, hard research, and Annette is that person."

The implication stung, but Gwen let him continue unchallenged.

"Undergraduate majors have been declining over the past decade. We've lost students to history, government, and women's studies at alarming rates. Annette's research is cutting-edge and well regarded, and the political angles have caught students' attention. Her teaching evaluations are off the charts. She's brought in two six-figure grants. She'll invigorate this department at a time when we desperately need it." He rose to indicate the conversation was over, but added, "Does that clear up the situation?"

"Almost. One more question. Are you saying my work is not 'hard, substantial research'?"

"Gwen—"

"What is soft and insubstantial about my research?"

"Is that a rhetorical question? You study quilts. That's nice, but it's not politically or socially relevant."

"Haven't you read any of my papers? How can you say art is not politically or socially relevant within a culture?"

"Art? Come on, Gwen. Quilts aren't art. My mother-in-law makes quilts." He came out from behind his desk and rested his hand on the doorknob. "I know you're disappointed. Personally, I think you'd make a fine chair. Here's some advice if you want to improve your chances in three years. If you want to study the arts, study the arts that matter—architecture, maybe. Sculpture or painting."

He opened the door and gave her a sympathetic grimace.

Somehow his attempt to be helpful infuriated her even more. "For a card-carrying liberal and someone who claims to be devoted to the pursuit of knowledge, you and your committee have an obvious and detestable bias for 'manly' topics. Since when did you all turn Republican?"

He looked wounded, but she did not linger to apologize. She stormed from his office and back to her own, ignoring the curious glances from colleagues and students alike.

Jules had wisely not waited for her return. Fuming, Gwen shut down the computer and packed books and papers into the quilted satchel she used as a briefcase. "The arts that matter," she muttered, locking the door behind her. If Bill had read any of her research— for that matter, if he had any common sense—he would realize that home arts and folk arts revealed more about a culture than the isolated, esoteric pieces preserved in museums for the benefit of the elite. She was sick and tired of having her work dismissed as frivolous because it centered on a largely female occupation. If most quilts had been made by men, no one would question her interest in exploring the role of quiltmaking in American history.

She crossed the wooded campus carefully, her footsteps unsteady on the snow-covered sidewalks. A snow squall had struck while she was in class, too recently for the maintenance crews to have cleared the icy dusting from anything but the main roads. Two men, one probably a student, were shoveling snow from the steps of the Computer Sciences building when she arrived. The older man greeted her by name as she climbed to the front door. She did a double take before she recognized Bonnie's husband, Craig. She smiled and made some joke about his getting out of his office to enjoy the fine weather, but he didn't get it. "We're understaffed," he replied instead. "Everyone has to help out."

Gwen had never particularly liked Craig, so she merely smiled again, nodded, and went on her way rather than explain. Bonnie and Craig were a prime example of opposites attracting, although Gwen had never figured out what Bonnie found so appealing. Of course, she found little to admire in the institution of marriage, so she probably wasn't looking hard enough.

She found Judy in her lab studying a long printout of rows and columns of numbers and letters—incomprehensible to Gwen, but apparently holding Judy and two of her graduate students spellbound. When Gwen asked if she had a moment to talk, Judy handed the printout to one of her students and led Gwen into an adjacent office. The room, though small, had a window, two laptops, and a color laser printer Gwen had coveted ever since Judy unpacked it. The walls were lined with bookcases—the shelves so full they bowed in the middle—and on the back of the door hung a quilt designed from a fractal pattern.

"What's going on?" Judy asked, leaning against the edge of a desk and gesturing to a seat.

Gwen sank heavily into it. "I wasn't named department chair."

"I thought the committee had all but given you the keys to the office."

"Never again will I believe anything until I see it in writing."

Judy shook her head, her long black hair slipping over her shoulder. "So they chose another man after all."

"No, they cleverly rendered me unable to complain on those grounds. The woman they chose is bright, capable, and only five years out of graduate school. She doesn't even have tenure, but her work is hip, political, and socially relevant, which mine isn't."

"Since when?"

"Since I started concentrating on textiles, apparently." Gwen's head throbbed. She buried her face in her hands and massaged her forehead. "And naturally I had to make everything worse. I couldn't just take the news stoically and write up a well-reasoned, formal protest after I regained control of my temper. I had to storm into Bill's office and demand an explanation."

"How did that go?" When Gwen hesitated, Judy winced. "Never mind. I can guess." She reached out and squeezed Gwen's shoulder. "I wouldn't worry about it. He's probably more embarrassed than you are, no matter what you said. He must be ashamed of the committee's ridiculous excuses."

"I doubt it. He seemed sincere when he told me to switch to studying 'the arts that matter' if I hope to be considered three years from now."

"So what are you going to do?"

"I might write him a letter of apology."

"Sounds like overkill to me. I meant, what are you going to do about your research?"

"I don't know." She wanted to pursue research that fascinated her, but had her passion blinded her to the obvious? Was her work irrelevant? She never wanted to become one of those academics who churned out journal article after journal article that no one would ever read. For a time, a time she had enjoyed enormously, studying the lives of women in history had been celebrated as the archiving of the almost forgotten past of an enormous, disenfranchised population. When had the climate shifted?

"You have tenure, so they can't fire you simply because they don't like your research," Judy reminded her. "But they can prevent you from advancing within the college and otherwise make your life miserable. I suppose you have to ask yourself which is more important: impressing the committee or continuing your current research, which until an hour ago you couldn't have imagined abandoning."

"I could always return to it after my term as chair."

"That's true, but three years is a long time to study something that bores you."

Gwen doubted she could stand even one year bored out of her mind simply to make a point. Worse yet was the idea of herself humbled, acquiescent, willingly switching research topics to please the selection committee. She might be able to do so if she accepted their assessment of her work, but she did not. "Not all departments believe that women's stories are irrelevant," she said.

Judy shrugged. "It is possible to outgrow a college. You can be happy for many years, but one day, you realize you've gone as far as you can go. Sometimes the best and only way to pursue your research is to pursue it somewhere else."

Gwen would hate to leave Waterford College, Elm Creek Quilts, Summer. But she was a long way from retirement and refused to be shuffled off to her rocking chair where she could work on her girlie projects while younger women like Annette were celebrated for their important work.

She had to find a middle ground. If her ongoing research wouldn't impress the department, she would find something new, but she would not abandon quilts simply because some stuffy old men didn't understand their significance. It was her job as an educator to make them understand.

But it wouldn't hurt to find something that would also win her a grant.

※

Gwen managed to avoid Bill and Annette the next day, but she found little comfort in the sympathies of the two American Studies professors who stopped by her office once the official announcement was made. Her grad students, perhaps warned away by Jules, did not seek her out, so she left campus right after her last class. She would work at home until it was time to leave for the weekly business meeting at Elm Creek Manor. Bonnie wanted them to arrive early so she could show them the first blocks of Sylvia's bridal quilt.

Was it any wonder Gwen preferred the energy and camaraderie of the manor to the suspicious temper of the Liberal Arts building? Elm Creek Quilts was collaborative, cooperative, and—she dared to say—matriarchal, while academia was still a rigid hierarchy despite the varying political winds that drifted across it, altering its surface without changing the deeper layers. As an idealistic student, she had thought the university was a place where the love of learning and the sharing of ideas were celebrated; now she knew that argument and backbiting were the norm, the egalitarian exchange of knowledge an afterthought.

Or maybe she was just bitter. Judy never seemed to encounter politicking and backstabbing. All she ever complained about was inadequate funding and too many boring department meetings.

The gray stone manor was a welcome sight as Gwen crossed the bridge over Elm Creek. She parked near the middle of the lot, where a patch of snow-covered grass encircled two towering, bare-limbed elms. Summer's car was not there, but inside Gwen found Bonnie, Agnes, and Diane, and Judy soon joined them. Gwen wished Summer was there; she never failed to help Gwen put her disappointments in proper perspective. Still, Gwen joined in the usual banter and admired the blocks until Sylvia's sudden arrival sent them scrambling. Fortunately, Sarah managed to fling the blocks into the pantry before Sylvia saw them, but her feeble cover story made Gwen cringe. Miraculously, Sylvia believed it, or pretended to, and the Elm Creek Quilters went to the parlor to begin the meeting.

Sarah began with the good news that enrollment for the coming season was up fifteen percent. "Your Photo Transfer workshop is especially popular, Gwen," she added. "Summer and I thought it would be a good idea to offer a second session each week. If you're up for it."

Gwen shrugged. "Sure. Why not? Once the spring semester ends, I'll have plenty of time." Much more time than she had intended or hoped, but she needn't tell Sarah that. No one but Summer and Judy knew how much she had counted on that appointment.

Not long into the meeting, Summer burst in, slipping out of her coat and full of apologies. She wore her long auburn hair in a loose knot at the nape of her neck, and if Gwen wasn't mistaken, she had secured it with a number-two pencil. "Relax, kiddo. You're not that late," whispered Gwen, but Summer was too distracted by the others' teasing to hear. Naturally they assumed she was late because of her boyfriend, which Gwen thought ridiculous until Summer confessed they were correct.

"You guys spend so much time together you might as well live together," said Diane.

Agnes looked horrified. "Don't suggest such a thing. She meant after you get married, dear."

Summer blanched as Agnes patted her hand.

"Married? Are you crazy?" said Gwen. "Don't go putting thoughts of marriage in my daughter's head. Or of living together. My daughter has more sense than that."

She gave Summer a reassuring grin. The other Elm Creek Quilters still felt cheated out of planning Sylvia and Andrew's wedding, and they saw Summer as the most likely candidate for matrimony. They obviously hoped to nudge her closer to the altar so their investigation of local florists and bakeries wouldn't go to waste. What they could not possibly understand was that Summer was just like her mother in her need for personal freedom. Summer was too wise to commit to anyone when she had so much of her own life to live first. No one would ever accuse her of either settling or settling down.

The teasing subsided when Sarah resumed the meeting. Afterward, Gwen stopped Summer before she could put on her coat. "Kiddo, can we talk?"

"About what?" said Summer, wary.

"Nothing important." Gwen forced a smile. Clearly Summer was in no mood for a heart-to-heart. "It can wait. Can you come for supper on Sunday?"

"Can we make it the following week?" Summer tugged on her coat and wrapped her scarf around her neck. "I'm swamped until the end of January."

Puzzled, since January was far from their busiest season, Gwen agreed and promised to make the lentil and brown rice soup Summer loved. Summer thanked her with a quick kiss on the cheek and bounded out the door, and Gwen watched her go. It was hard to believe that Gwen herself had once been so slender and lovely, but she had the photographs to prove it. Summer would accomplish much more with her life than Gwen had, though, because she was brighter and braver than Gwen had ever been.

"You must be very proud," remarked Sylvia as she cleared away the cups and plates left over from their midmeeting snack.

"Proud beyond reason," said Gwen with a laugh.

She stayed behind to help Sylvia tidy the room, and as they carried the dishes to the kitchen, she found herself telling the older woman about her disappointment at work. Sylvia put on a fresh pot of tea and they sat at the kitchen table while Gwen confessed the whole sorry tale.

"I spent most of my teaching career trying to convince people quilting was art," said Sylvia when Gwen had finished. "Now you're trying to persuade them it's a relevant art. I suppose that's progress of a sort."

"At that rate, in another forty years, no one will have these arguments anymore." Gwen stared glumly into her teacup, wishing she could read the leaves. "Just in time for my great-grandchildren."

"The woman they chose instead—what is her field of study?"

"Media and the political process, mostly. How campaigns have changed over time, the role of debates in elections." She forced herself to add, "I have to admit it's interesting work."

"I'm sure it is, but that doesn't make your work dull or irrelevant." Sylvia drummed her fingers on the tabletop. "I wish I could think of a quilt that figured heavily in politics, but I'm afraid nothing comes to mind. The closest I can come is the time Mrs. Roosevelt was presented with the prizewinning quilt from a contest held at the 1933 World's Fair in Chicago."

Gwen set down her teacup. "Eleanor Roosevelt?"

"That's right. This was the biggest quilt competition ever held, before or since. Nearly twenty-five thousand quilters submitted quilts, and my sister and I were two of them." Sylvia chuckled. "We bent the rules a little by making our quilt together. When we signed the form saying that the quilt was entirely of our own making, Claudia wrote, 'Claudia Sylvia Bergstrom.' That was her idea. I thought no one would believe a mother would name her child Claudia Sylvia, but they must not have noticed, because we made it to the semifinals."

Gwen laughed. "Sylvia, I'm shocked. You cheated in a quilt competition?"

"Only in a sense," she protested. "Keep in mind, I was only thirteen and my sister fifteen. If we combined our ages we were still younger than most of the other participants, so we decided we weren't really cheating."

Sylvia explained that they weren't the only participants to interpret the rules liberally. The woman who claimed the grand prize had not put a single stitch into the quilt submitted in her name. Instead she sent the fabric and pattern to one woman who pieced the top, while another added beautiful stuffed work, and still others contributed the exquisite, sixteen-stitches-to-the-inch quilting. The winner paid her team of helpers a modest fee for their labor, but refused to share any of the prize money with them after she won.

"They were poor women, too, and it was the Depression," said Sylvia disapprovingly. "The grand prize of one thousand dollars was an enormous sum in those days, more than a year's salary for most people. I never understood why she wasn't more generous."

"How does Eleanor Roosevelt figure in this story?"

"After the World's Fair, the grand prize quilt was presented to her and kept at the White House. It has since disappeared. Now, that would be a project worth researching. I'd give a lot to know what happened to that quilt." Sylvia sipped her tea, thoughtful. "But whatever happened to it, and however one regards the woman who won, that's not what I think of when I recall that quilt show. The theme of the fair was 'A Century of Progress,' and the interpretations those quilters produced were simply remarkable. There were quilts that celebrated advances in technology, transportation, industry, women's fight for equal rights—and remember, this was at a time when the nation was truly struggling. To see all those expressions of optimism and hope when we had so recently seen the worst of times in the Great War and were now mired in the Depression—well, it certainly impressed me, even at my age."

"You saw the quilts? In person?"

"Yes, indeed. My father took my sister, my brother, and me to the World's Fair that year. It was a long journey to Chicago with three children in tow. I can't imagine what he was thinking, but I'm glad he did it." Sylvia rose and inclined her head to the doorway. "I saved a box full of souvenirs, if you would like to see them."

Gwen wouldn't have dreamed of doing otherwise, so she followed Sylvia up the oak staircase to the third floor, where Sylvia gestured to the narrow set of stairs leading to the attic. She declined to accompany Gwen farther, but she described the old walnut bureau so well that Gwen found it easily, halfway down the west wing. Gwen retrieved an engraved tin box from the bottom drawer and dusted it with her sleeve as she carried it down the creaking staircase.

They went to the library, where the embers of an earlier blaze still glowed in the fireplace. Sylvia seated herself nearby, but Gwen sat on the floor at her feet, the better to spread out the box's treasures. Inside she found brochures, ticket stubs, programs, photographs, and other items that must have been added later— newspaper articles from around the country featuring local quilt- makers whose entries had made it to the finals, advertisements from Sears Roebuck announcing their sponsorship of the contest, commercial patterns taken from prizewinning quilts, a tattered rib- bon with writing in faded ink naming Claudia Sylvia Bergstrom as the first-place winner from the Harrisburg Sears.

Before long Gwen became so engrossed in examining the arti- facts that she hardly remembered to thank Sylvia when the older woman rose to go to bed, telling her to stay as long as she liked. Alone, Gwen lost track of the hours as she pored over the yellowed newspaper articles and studied the show catalogue. The picture that emerged from the fragile scraps of history was not the little- known anecdote from the life of Eleanor Roosevelt that Gwen had hoped to find, but something far more intriguing. The quilts entered in the 1933 World's Fair contest had captured the national mood during a time of extreme trial. Granted, the theme "A Cen- tury of Progress" would have encouraged more optimistic interpre- tations in those days than in Gwen's ironic era, but even if the quiltmakers had been steered toward a rosier perspective, their quilts still could be considered an accurate record of how those women defined progress.

This was it, Gwen realized. This was her new book.

She surveyed the orderly groupings of souvenirs on the floor all around her. Sylvia's treasure trove of information was surely just the beginning. If nearly twenty-five thousand quilts had been sub- mitted, surely there were more newspaper articles about the women who had made them, more scandals like the one surround- ing the dubious honor of the grand prize winner, more mysteries such as the disappearance of the winning quilt—and, of course, the quilts themselves. A few hundred or even a few thousand of them might still exist, and if their makers were still around or had left diaries behind or had told their children stories—

"Sylvia's quilt," Gwen suddenly exclaimed. Sylvia had shown her the souvenirs, but not the quilt she and Claudia had made. She scrambled to her feet, left the library, and hurried down the hall to Sylvia's room. She rapped softly at the door and drew back when Andrew opened it, squinting.

"What's wrong?" he asked in a hoarse whisper.

"I'm sorry. Did I wake you?"

His brow furrowed. "Of course. It's ten after one."

"What?" She should have checked her watch. "Never mind. It can wait until tomorrow."

"Is this a quilt thing?"

"What else would you expect at this hour? I'm sorry, Andrew. Go back to sleep."

He shrugged as Gwen pulled the door shut softly. It was probably good she had woken him instead of Sylvia. Gwen doubted she herself could have managed so much tolerant humor in Andrew's place. He was a rarity among his sex, the sort of man she could understand a woman wanting to marry.

She returned the souvenirs to the box and placed it carefully on a bookcase away from the fireplace and windows. As she drove home, her mind raced with possibilities. Tracking down her primary source materials would be a challenge, most likely involving travel—which meant finding grants to pay for it.

The next morning, she arrived at her office so jubilant that when Jules came to see her—once more either the bravest of her graduate students or the one who had drawn the short straw—he looked at her as if unsure whether she had indulged in some mind-altering substances more potent than caffeine. She immediately sent him off to the library to search the online newspaper archives for articles on the 1933 Chicago World's Fair. "What about my other assignments?" he asked, halfway out the door.

"Forget about those for now. This is our new project."

He didn't ask why. Gwen supposed the previous day's announcement provided reason enough.

Jules must have spread the word to her two other graduate students that it was safe to approach, because they stopped by before noon for their new assignments. As for herself, she alternated between searching the internet for leads on funding sources and scanning her reference books of Depression-era quilts for possible Sears National Quilt Contest entries, even if they were not expressly identified as such. In a ten-year-old auction catalogue she found a floral appliquéd medallion quilt with "A Century of Progress" embroidered in a scroll across the top, but nothing in the item's description alluded to the World's Fair contest. It had to be connected, and a bit of research would uncover the particulars. Exultant, she concluded that this lucky find was a positive omen and thanked whatever divine spirit had inspired Sylvia to tell her about the contest.

The rapidly approaching camp season, the deadline for Sylvia's bridal quilt, and even the committee's misguided decision slipped to the back of her thoughts as her new research consumed her time and her imagination. Even her graduate students caught her enthusiasm after she explained the scope of the project and made them swear on the fate of their doctoral dissertations that they would discuss it with no one. Before their weekly business meeting on the last day of January, she and Sylvia arranged to meet at the manor in the afternoon to search for the Bergstrom sisters' entry.

"I know where it ought to be," said Sylvia, huffing slightly as she led Gwen up the narrow staircase to the attic. "My concern is that it was moved during a search for something else."

Gwen switched on the light and sneezed, waving away dust motes. "Is it possible Claudia sold it?" She had sold many other family heirlooms during Sylvia's fifty-year absence from Elm Creek Manor, including their mother's own bridal quilt.

"It's possible, but I doubt it. Claudia rarely won ribbons for her handiwork. I doubt she would have parted with any quilt of hers that earned such recognition. Of course, she never would have made it to the semifinals working on her own."

"Of course not," said Gwen, hiding a smile.

Sylvia directed Gwen to a section of the attic not far from the walnut bureau and gestured to a collection of trunks and boxes. "If it's here, this is where we'll find it."

There they found papers, books, china, clothing, and assorted items Gwen would have tossed out with the trash if they were in her house, but no quilts. When Gwen decided to broaden their search area, she discovered a bundle of Storm at Sea blocks pieced from the pastel cottons common to the late 1920s and early 1930s. Sylvia examined them and announced that Claudia had made them, judging from the poorly matched seams that she never would have permitted in her own work. "You're on the right track, dear," said Sylvia approvingly, and took up the search nearby.

Before long they found the quilt, nestled into a paper box all its own. Gwen held it up so Sylvia could examine it. The quilt was in fine condition for its age, a testament, Sylvia noted, to the excellent care it had received, except during shipping and at the judging venues. Even so, few stains marred the green, lavender, rose, and ivory quilt, which was accented with appliquéd features in bold red, blue, and black.

The design itself was a compromise, Sylvia explained. Sylvia had wanted to create an original pictorial quilt inspired by the "Century of Progress" theme, but Claudia thought they would stand a better chance of pleasing the judges if they used a traditional pattern and devoted their time to flawless, intricate needlework rather than novelty. After an argument spanning several weeks—which would have been better spent sewing—they agreed that Sylvia could design a central appliqué medallion depicting various scenes from colonial times until the present day, to which Claudia would add a border of pieced blocks. "Odd Fellow's Chain," said Sylvia, fingering the border. "Obviously, she chose it for its appearance, not its name."

"Unless she meant to make a statement about contemporary notions of progress."

"Hmph." Sylvia showed a hint of a smile. "Claudia was not that clever. The block did give us the quilt's title, however. We called it Chain of Progress."

Gwen draped the quilt over an upholstered armchair to better examine it. She could see in this early example of Sylvia's work how her tastes and skills had developed through the decades. The uneven quality of the needlework she attributed to the widely differing abilities of the two sisters, but even the worst pieced Odd Fellow's Chain block proved that Claudia could not have been as poor a quilter as Sylvia suggested. The green Ribbon of Merit still attached to the quilt attested to that.

Gwen was imagining how Chain of Progress would look on the cover of her book when Sylvia began folding it. "It's almost time for the meeting. Shall we take this downstairs and surprise our friends?"

"No," Gwen exclaimed. "I don't want anyone to know."

"Why on earth not? If you want to track down other contest entries, the more people who know about your project, the better. You never know who might provide a useful lead."

"I will tell them eventually. Soon," she amended, when Sylvia raised her eyebrows. "First I want to be sure there is a book in this. Then I'll be grateful for help."

"You'll be lucky if you get any, keeping secrets from your friends as if you're afraid they'll steal your ideas," admonished Sylvia. "Whenever the Elm Creek Quilters keep secrets from one another, it always means trouble."

"Not always," said Gwen, remembering Sylvia's bridal quilt and the block she had yet to begin.

The next day, Gwen received a response to an email she had sent to the Chicago Historical Society. They agreed her idea was worth pursuing and would consider funding a portion of her research if she submitted a full proposal by their annual deadline, February 5.

That left Gwen with only a few days to pull together all the information they needed, but fortunately, she had no plans for the weekend. On Friday afternoon after her last class, she hurried home, turned off the ringer on the phone, and hid her cell phone in a kitchen drawer. She resolved not only to complete her proposal in time, but to write the best, most persuasive proposal the Chicago Historical Society had ever seen. One late night blurred into an early morning, and another, as she feverishly raced to meet her deadline. If she succeeded, it wouldn't be one of Annette's six-figure triumphs, but it would be a start.

"Mom?"

Gwen jumped at the sound of Summer's voice from elsewhere in the house. "In here," she called, typing frantically even when she heard her daughter enter the room. "Hi, kiddo. What's up?" Then she remembered, and she spun her chair around, dismayed. "Oh, no. Supper."

"Sunday at five o'clock," Summer said, grinning and tapping her watch.

"I completely forgot." How could she forget inviting her only child for a meal? "We could send out for pizza."

Summer assured her she would be satisfied with a sandwich to accompany the salad she had brought, and Gwen suddenly realized she had taken nothing but coffee since breakfast. Her refrigerator was shamefully empty, as she had skipped her customary Saturday morning trip to the grocery store, but Summer, as always, was a good sport. She was also always very curious, and she soon asked her mother what she was working on.

Gwen couldn't tell her. She knew her idea would make a fascinating, informative book—but maybe she was not the person to write it. She could not bear to tell Summer later that she had abandoned a brilliant research project because, ultimately, Bill and his committee were correct: She was good enough for what she did, but she need not aspire to anything greater.

Gwen tried to put Summer off, but Summer persisted, so Gwen told her about the committee's decision not to appoint her department chair. Summer's indignation warmed her and reminded her that she had made some important discoveries in her tenure at Waterford College. Too bad Bill lacked Summer's insight—or bias.

Then Summer asked, "So what were you working on? A new paper on a new topic?"

"I'll let you read it when it's done."

Summer nodded, but Gwen knew she was disappointed, despite her lighthearted reassurances about Gwen's forthcoming book. She thought her mother was giving up the study of quilt history to appease the committee.

Gwen wanted to assure her she wasn't, she wouldn't. She wanted to see pride shining in her daughter's eyes again. But she could not commit that hope to words until she knew she would not have to relinquish her new project to a more able scholar.

She tried to change the subject by asking how Jeremy was doing. Summer said he was fine and she saw him often, but offered no more than that. They talked about the upcoming camp season and Sylvia's bridal quilt, but Gwen was too conscious of disappointing Summer to enjoy the rest of the meal.

The next morning, she decided to stop by Summer's place on her way to work. It wasn't really on the way, but Gwen was eager to apologize for her forgetfulness and her evasive behavior the previous night. Karen opened to her knock and told her Summer had left not long before, but Aaron hovered in the background, his expression so alarmed and wary that Gwen knew at once Summer had not spent the night there.

So. Summer must have slept at Jeremy's. Gwen thanked the roommates, who were visibly relieved not to be interrogated further, and departed without leaving a message. She could hardly criticize Summer for doing something many other young women her age did, something she herself had done. She just hoped Summer wouldn't make a habit of it, and build up Jeremy's expectations when she surely had no intentions of leaving with him upon his graduation.

Surely Summer had no such intentions?

With a knot in the pit of her stomach, Gwen continued on to campus, pausing only to drop her grant proposal in the overnight express pickup box.

February passed in a frenzy of classes, research, writing, and the submission of grant proposals, with worries about Summer and Jeremy lingering in the back of Gwen's mind. She would have forgotten Sylvia's bridal quilt entirely if not for the invitation letter pinned to the bulletin board behind her computer, and she had so neglected her preparations for the upcoming quilt camp season that at the first business meeting of March, when Sarah told her they needed to cancel some of her classes, Gwen felt too guilty to argue. That feeling was compounded when Summer, who had asked to speak to her afterward, changed her mind, obviously sensing Gwen's eagerness to get back to work. They made plans to have supper the following Sunday, and this time, Gwen vowed not to forget.

When the evening arrived, she set aside her notes, which were accumulating with reassuring speed, to make a batch of almond cookies to follow Summer's favorite vegetable stir-fry. Summer showed up right on time with pot stickers and spring rolls from their favorite carry-out, and they spent an enjoyable hour eating and talking about Elm Creek Quilt Camp. Summer had some great ideas about new seminars she wanted to try, but she confessed to having no idea which block to make for Sylvia's quilt. "I hope Elm Creek Quilters get an automatic extension," she added. "I'm planning to run my block over to Agnes's house at midnight on the very last day."

Gwen laughed and admitted to her own difficulties. "On the surface it seems like an easy project," she said. "Make one six-inch block. What could be simpler?"

"Adding the condition that it represents all that Sylvia means to us, that's what," said Summer. "The blocks accumulating at Grandma's Attic typically express that in their names. But what if you can't find a block with an appropriate name? What if you'd rather express yourself visually?"

"Exactly," said Gwen. She and Summer never failed to find the same bandwidth. "I've decided the only way to resolve the problem is to design an original block. I know it's taking the easy way out—"

"I doubt it, Mom," said Summer, laughing. "It won't be easy to invent a completely original pattern."

"At least I can name it whatever I like."

Summer agreed that Gwen's method had its merits, but she planned to keep looking. Then, suddenly, she hesitated. "Mom, remember last Thursday, when I said I needed to talk to you?"

Gwen recalled that Summer had said she *wanted* to talk, not that she *needed* to talk, a significant difference in mother-daughter parlance. Suddenly she thought of Jeremy, then Jeremy in his doctoral hood clutching a diploma under his arm as he helped Summer load a moving van.

"Sure, kiddo." She steeled herself. "What's up?"

"You know that Jeremy and I are very close." She paused so long that Gwen realized she was supposed to nod, so she did. "Well, his roommate moved out at the end of fall semester, and he needed to find someone to share the rent. Remember how great his place is?"

It was nice enough, for a student apartment. "He's having trouble finding someone?"

"No, actually. He found someone. Me." Summer took a quick breath and plunged ahead. "It's so much more convenient than my old place, and much less expensive, too. I don't even have to pay for parking anymore, and I *so* don't miss all the partying every weekend."

She continued, but what registered in Gwen's mind was, first, that Summer was not planning to leave Waterford with Jeremy in the immediate future, and second, that she was speaking in the present tense. She had already moved. Without seeking Gwen's advice, without giving Gwen a chance to talk some sense into her.

"Mom?" Summer prompted, worriedly.

All Gwen could say was, "Why?"

Summer repeated the list of reasons almost verbatim, as if she had rehearsed many times. Gwen forced herself to remain calm, then pointed out—quite reasonably, given the circumstances—that Summer and Jeremy had not been together very long, surely not long enough to know whether he was worth the sacrifice of her independence. Summer rolled her eyes, a gesture Gwen loathed; it signified that she was an old-fashioned, closed-minded throwback to the olden days rather than the hip mom of the twenty-first century she liked to imagine herself.

Summer was twenty-seven, old enough to make her own decisions. Gwen knew that. She wasn't sure, however, if Summer understood the entirety of the decision she had made.

Give her your blessing, Gwen told herself. But she held back. Summer had made decisions Gwen had disagreed with before, and her announcements had always come with a hint of concern that Gwen would not approve. This time Gwen sensed something more, that Summer sought her approval in order to convince herself she had not made a mistake.

What bothered Gwen most of all was that despite her obvious uncertainty, Summer had not talked it over with her before making her choice.

A few days later, Gwen took a break from her research to shop for fabric. Grandma's Attic was cheaper than therapy.

Although she had chosen one of Summer's afternoons off, Gwen still glanced around from the doorway before entering the quilt shop to make sure her daughter was not there. Bonnie was in the back office, looking morose as she paged through a folder. She happened to glance up as Gwen entered the shop, then mouthed something inaudible through the glass as she put away the file and rose to meet her.

"Keep working if you want," said Gwen as Bonnie exited the office, wondering what in that file had the power to make her optimistic friend look so glum. "I'll just browse for a while."

Bonnie sighed and seated herself on a stool by the cutting table. "No, I could use a break."

"If you don't mind my saying so, you're looking rather grim today."

"Thanks. I can always count on my friends to cheer me up with praise." But Bonnie managed a wan smile and indicated the office with a nod. "This should be a profitable business. Even with high rents and a competitor undercutting me at every turn, I should be in the black every month. What am I doing wrong?"

"You're too nice," said Gwen, recalling many conversations with Summer on that subject. "People take advantage."

"Customers, friends, husbands, children—I know, but what can I do?" She peered at Gwen. "You know, you're looking rather grim yourself."

"Funny you should mention children," said Gwen dryly. "I just found out Summer moved in with Jeremy."

Bonnie said nothing.

Gwen stared at her. "You knew?"

"Only since yesterday."

"Oh." At least Gwen wasn't the last to know; that was something. "At first I thought she was crazy. Then I decided it was a delayed form of rebellion. My current theory is ignorance."

"Ignorance?"

"Ignorance of what she's getting herself into."

Bonnie looked dubious. "Maybe that's what she wants to explore, I mean, before she gets in any deeper."

"Don't tell me you approve."

"Actually, I'm surprised you don't. Isn't this better than rushing into marriage?" She rubbed her chin absently. "If I had lived with Craig before marrying him, I might have decided against it."

"Then it's a good thing you didn't, right? Anyway, that doesn't always work. I lived with Summer's father before we got married, and we split up soon after."

"You lived in a van with a bunch of other flower children," Bonnie reminded her. "And you were probably high most of the time."

"I was not," Gwen retorted. "That's slander. Pot gave me migraines."

"So you say." Bonnie sighed. "Listen. If I had found out before you, would you have wanted me to tell you?"

"Absolutely. I would have counted on it." Gwen studied her, then, with some effort, hopped up to sit on the cutting table. "Why? What else do you know?"

"This isn't about Summer."

"But clearly it's about someone we know, so spill it."

Bonnie hesitated. "I was in the liquor store the other night—"

"Rough day?"

"You have no idea. Anyway, you'll never guess who I saw buying beer."

"Who?"

"Michael."

"Michael? Diane's son Michael?"

Bonnie nodded. "He showed the clerk an ID, but it must have been fake. Michael saw me, too, and froze right there at the counter. I gave him a look, you know, like he'd better watch out, but I didn't say anything. Should I have? He just bought the beer and left as fast as he could. Should I have stopped him, told the clerk, something? What would you have done?"

"I don't know." Gwen pondered the question. "I think I would have been too startled to react. I probably would have done the same as you."

"You mean, done nothing." Still, Bonnie looked somewhat relieved. "So what should I do now? Should I tell Diane?"

"How old is Michael, anyway? Nineteen?"

"Twenty."

Gwen shook her head. "I don't know. He can drive, he can join the military, he can vote—who are we to say he can't drink?"

"We aren't saying it. Pennsylvania state law says it." Bonnie let her hands fall into her lap, helpless. "He could get into a lot of trouble, if not with the drinking, then with using a fake ID. Aren't friends supposed to keep an eye out for each other's kids?"

"Maybe just thinking you'll tell Diane will keep him honest."

Bonnie shrugged, unconvinced. "I don't want to turn a blind eye. If he should get hurt, I'd never forgive myself. Diane would never forgive me, and I wouldn't blame her."

"Then why haven't you told Diane already?"

"Well, like you said, he is twenty years old."

"You don't have to tattle to Diane," said Gwen. "You could talk to Michael himself."

"What would I say?"

"You're a mom. You know what to do. Tell him what you're worried about. Remind him he's breaking the law." Gwen grinned. "And then threaten to tell Diane if he doesn't clean up his act."

Bonnie said she would think about it.

With Bonnie's help, Gwen searched the shelves until she found several bold geometric prints in the appropriate hues for Sylvia's bridal quilt. She bought twice as much fabric as she needed with the excuse she might attempt several different designs in her search for an original pattern. Bonnie gave her a sidelong look, but she said nothing to indicate she knew Gwen was trying to alleviate her financial worries one yard of fabric at a time.

Gwen decided she would set aside fifteen minutes each day to work on the block, but her resolve quickly eroded under the mounting pressures of her new research project and the upcoming camp season. With only a week to go, she scrambled to revise her lesson plans, assemble samples, and gather materials, glad for the activity to consume time she otherwise would have spent worrying over Summer.

It took an all-nighter, but somehow she managed to finish by the first day of camp, which only involved registration and welcoming ceremonies, not the more challenging and enjoyable work of teaching. The second day of camp had a less promising start, with an early-morning phone call from Sarah asking her to take over an afternoon class for Judy later that week. Gwen agreed, wondering what was going on and why Judy had not told her about the trip to Philadelphia. Guiltily, she reflected that she had not stopped by to chat with her friend since the day she had found out about the department chair. They usually got together for coffee or lunch at least once a week. The last few times they had spoken at business meetings, Gwen had not even remembered to ask how Judy's mother was recovering from a serious bout of pneumonia that had afflicted her throughout January. She would have to apologize when Judy returned.

Gwen's quilt camp seminars went well, as she expected, and she didn't regret the one that had been canceled. Mindful of how she had neglected friendships and camp responsibilities of late, she gave herself a few days' vacation from her research. It was spring break, after all, and her grad students needed the time off even if she didn't. Besides, the first week of camp usually brought with it a few unexpected surprises. She needed to be flexible in case of another curveball like Judy's absence.

The wild pitch came out of nowhere on Wednesday. At

lunchtime, she found Sylvia, Sarah, Diane, and Agnes sequestered at a table at the back of the banquet hall rather than scattered among the campers as usual. She joined them, only to find her friends huddled over the daily schedule.

Sarah looked up at her approach, harried. "Could you emcee the quilted clothing fashion show for the evening program tonight?"

"Sure," Gwen said with a shrug. "I thought Bonnie was doing it."

"Maybe she will, but she didn't show up for her workshop this morning, so I thought I should have a backup plan."

"Didn't show up?" Gwen sat down. "Why not?"

"No one knows," said Agnes, fingering her beaded necklace worriedly. "She didn't call in, and no one's answering the phone at the store."

"You tried her at home, right?"

"Well, yes, but—well, she's not there, either," said Agnes.

"Summer drove to Grandma's Attic a few minutes ago," said Sylvia. "She'll call us when she learns anything."

Gwen nodded. Summer worked an afternoon shift at the quilt shop on Wednesdays. If Bonnie had not shown up for work there, either, Summer would be unable to look for her elsewhere and too busy to call.

As soon as her afternoon workshop concluded, Gwen found Agnes in the hallway and told her she was on her way to Grandma's Attic. She parked behind the store next to Summer's car, then hurried around to the front entrance. The door was locked, the sign in the window turned to CLOSED several hours ahead of time. She cupped her hands around her eyes and peered inside.

Summer and Bonnie worked amid overturned shelves and piles of scattered cloth and notions, deliberately, wearily, battling the mess.

Gwen gasped and pounded on the door. Bonnie started, but quickly recognized Gwen and carefully made her way across the room. "What happened?" Gwen exclaimed after Bonnie let her in.

"We had a break-in." Without pausing to elaborate, Bonnie returned to work.

Gwen stood rooted in place, stunned, until Summer came over and hugged her. "Come on, Mom," she murmured. "We could use the help."

Gwen nodded and joined her. Quietly, Summer explained the little she knew as they tried to restore unwound yards of fabric to their bolts. Surprisingly little had been taken. Money and tools. A sewing machine. Several packs of Pigma pens. Blocks for Sylvia's bridal quilt. The police had spent all morning and most of the afternoon combing the store for clues, dusting for fingerprints, questioning Bonnie and Summer, taking photographs. They had found no evidence of a forced entry, so they suspected an inside job.

"What?" said Gwen, astounded. An inside job meant someone with a key: Bonnie, Summer, Diane, possibly Craig. "That makes no sense."

None of it made any sense. Why take Sylvia's blocks instead of an extra sewing machine? Why trash the place instead of fleeing with the most expensive merchandise? The bizarre scene suggested vengeance—or a horrible prank.

"Someone must have left the door unlocked," she told Bonnie later as together they struggled to right an overturned bookcase. "Some college students must have passed by on their way home from the bars and found it open. Drunken kids have a sick idea of fun."

"I locked the door myself." Bonnie's mouth set in a hard, worried line. "No college students did this. There are three keys. I didn't do it, and I know Diane and Summer didn't, so it must have been someone with access to one of our keys. At first I thought—"

"Thought what? Who?"

"Nothing. Someone who as it turns out wasn't anywhere near a key." Bonnie glanced at Summer on the other side of the room and lowered her voice. "Then I remembered."

"What?" Gwen glanced worriedly at Summer. Surely Bonnie didn't suspect Jeremy—or herself.

"Last Friday I ran into Michael. I warned him about the dangers of alcohol abuse, of breaking the law—you know, the standard mom lecture."

Gwen nodded, heart sinking.

"I also told him to give me his fake ID or I'd tell his parents what I had seen him do with it." Bonnie took a deep, shaky breath. "He gave it to me, but he was furious. He stalked off without another word, but he gave me a look over his shoulder I'll never forget. Gwen, now that ID is gone."

"How can you be sure, with this mess?"

"I'm sure."

"We've known Michael since he was a baby," said Gwen in a whisper, glancing at her daughter. Summer used to baby-sit Michael and his brother. She defended him against all criticism, especially when he most deserved it. "He's made mistakes, but he would never do anything like this."

"Wouldn't he? Remember when he was in the ninth grade, and he vandalized the school?"

Gwen could not reply. Until that moment, she had forgotten the incident.

Bonnie scrubbed a hand through her short hair and glanced about as if desperately seeking another answer amid the debris.

Quietly, Gwen asked, "Did you tell the police?"

"No," said Bonnie, shaking her head. "Not yet."

CHAPTER FOUR
Bonnie

C raig was gone when Bonnie woke, but she knew he had come home because the bed in the guest room had been slept in. Still in her flannel nightgown, Bonnie made the bed and plumped up the pillow. When Craig had first stopped sharing the master bedroom, Bonnie had been troubled, even hurt, but she had grown accustomed to his absence. It was easier than lying beside him wondering what she could do to inspire some affection in him, wondering if it was worth the bother.

There was a time when Craig would have called to let her know he was working late. There was a time, Bonnie thought ruefully as she showered and drew on her bathrobe, when he would have turned down overtime in his eagerness to come home to his family. That time was so long ago it preceded the children, Grandma's Attic, her first gray hairs.

At least with Craig gone she could eat breakfast in her bathrobe without snide comments about her appearance. At least she could read the newspaper without worrying about irritating him by getting the sections out of order. In many ways his absence was preferable to his silent presence. Even that was far better than their one-sided arguments, in which Craig complained and criticized and Bonnie simply let his words wash over her. He didn't really mean it, she would tell herself, until a particularly harsh jab provoked her into reminding him that someone who had been forgiven for a cyber affair had little room for error. He would explode then and accuse her of not really forgiving him, of enjoying her grudge, of finding a perverse pleasure in taunting him forever for his one mistake.

But it was not his one mistake; it was simply his biggest mistake. As far as she knew. And wasn't that part of the problem, that she would never know and always wonder?

He probably had worked late. The Office of the Physical Plant was understaffed, and winter meant sidewalks to clear of snow and frozen pipes to thaw. But Craig could very well have decided that anyplace was preferable to home. Bonnie often felt that way.

Grandma's Attic was her haven. She could not imagine how she would have endured the past few years without it. The quilt shop was one sign that she had not wasted her life, that she was not a failure. Her children were the other. But they were so far away and visited so rarely that they probably had no idea that an equally vast distance separated their parents.

Bonnie put on a warm pair of slacks and her oldest but most favorite quilted vest, made from miniature purple-and-green Pineapple blocks. She'd had to rip out many a seam during the months it had taken her to complete it, and she wore it whenever she needed a reminder that even the most difficult times would eventually pass.

She opened the shop and worked in the office until customers arrived. She dreaded looking at the accounts. Holiday sales had boosted their gross income, allowing her to pay off their worst debts, but January sales were down from the previous year, and February seemed to be matching that disappointing pace. She was not surprised. She could hardly open the *Waterford Register* without seeing an advertisement for the huge chain fabric store on the outskirts of town. If not for Summer's help, Bonnie would have been forced to close the shop years before. Whenever Grandma's Attic teetered on the brink of bankruptcy, Summer would somehow come up with an inspired idea for bringing quilters into the shop. Sales would surge for a time, then dwindle as the novelty of their innovation faded. The one exception was their virtual quilt shop on the internet, which had garnered consistently strong sales since its inception. One day, Bonnie surmised, email orders might account for the majority of their profits.

A few customers came in, some merely to browse, drawn inside by the colorful display in the front window. Then morning mail arrived, and with it, more bills. Bonnie set those aside and opened the larger packages, which contained more contributions for Sylvia's bridal quilt. They were lovely, but Bonnie would have been grateful for them even if they were only half as well made. At their current pace, they would have only enough blocks for a modest lap quilt, although she wouldn't admit that to Sarah until absolutely necessary.

Summer arrived moments later and, as always, her confidence and good cheer made Bonnie glad she would be leaving the quilt shop in such good hands after her retirement. Summer greeted her as she slipped off her coat, her eyes lighting up at the sight of the packages on the cutting table. "Can I see the new blocks?" she asked. Bonnie handed them over and forced herself to sort through the rest of the mail. Good news rarely came to Grandma's Attic in a business-size envelope.

The phone bill was lower than usual; Bonnie congratulated herself for keeping to her resolution to use email whenever it would save her a long-distance call. The power bill was higher, as expected, due to the recent cold snap. She sighed and opened the last envelope, something from University Realty, most likely an advertisement. Anything but another bill.

February 1, 2002

Dear Ms. Bonnie Markham:

I am pleased to announce that Waterford Commercial Properties has sold your building to University Realty, Inc. Welcome to the University Realty family. A fixture in the Waterford community since 1957, University Realty is the area's finest resource for commercial and residential properties.

Within the next week, a representative from University Realty will visit your business in order to discuss the terms of our rental agreement for any tenants who wish to remain in their current location. The visit for Grandma's Attic is scheduled for Tuesday, February 12, at 10:45 A.M. If this is not convenient, please contact our office. However, please note that new leases must be signed within ninety days of the sale to University Realty, after which expired tenants risk eviction.

Again, thank you for joining the community of properties owned and operated by University Realty. We look forward to a long and rewarding relationship with you.

Sincerely,
Gregory H. Krolich
Vice-President

Bonnie read the letter a second time, disbelieving. How could something like this happen without any word to the tenants? What would this mean for the condo upstairs? She could not recall all the clauses of their purchase agreement. Surely University Realty could not touch their home, and even if they raised the rent on the shop, they couldn't afford more than a modest increase. Far too many storefronts in downtown Waterford stood empty already. The new owners had to offer competitive rents or risk losing all their tenants.

"What is it?" asked Summer, watching her with concern.

"The building's been sold. All tenants have to sign new leases if we want to stay."

"Of course you'll stay," said Summer. "Where do they expect you to go? They won't raise the rent, will they?"

"The letter doesn't say." But Bonnie was sure the rent would go up. Why else would Gregory Krolich have included that vague, threatening line about the dangers of missing her scheduled meeting and becoming an "expired tenant"?

She tried to answer Summer's questions about the stipulations of her lease, but she was too upset, her thoughts a swirl of confusion. The last thing she needed, what with Craig so distant and the shop already in financial trouble, was to have to worry about the expense and hassle of moving.

She spent the rest of Summer's shift in the office, going over books, paying the utility bills, and ordering products from the few suppliers who had not yet suspended her credit. At the end of the day she closed the shop, walked to the corner grocery for milk and coffee, and went home. On her way upstairs she checked the mail, only to find a second envelope from University Realty. She set it on top of the pile of bills and advertisements on the counter and started supper, taking a chance on making enough for two. So far Craig had never stayed away for more than a day without calling.

When the chicken was in the oven, Bonnie steeled herself and opened the envelope. Inside she found a letter announcing the sale in slightly more cordial tones than before. This time Gregory Krolich expressed his hopes that the Markhams would consider selling the condo to his company so that they might make it available for "other residential purposes." He promised to phone within the next few days to arrange a meeting.

"You have a different attitude when you want to buy, don't you?"

muttered Bonnie as she tossed the letter on the counter. Did this Gregory Krolich even notice he had written to her twice? Perhaps not; the condo was in Craig's name, too, while the shop was in Bonnie's alone. Still, if Krolich wanted them to sell their home, he ought to be more civil regarding her shop—and more flexible about the new lease.

With the first stirring of hope she had felt since morning, Bonnie finished preparing supper. She did have some leverage after all. Though the thought of lying to Krolich made her uncomfortable, she could not allow him to believe she might sell the condo until they had settled on the terms of their new rental agreement for the shop. She would do anything to save Grandma's Attic. If she could consider firing one of her closest friends, she could mislead Krolich for a few weeks. Businesspeople did that sort of thing all the time. Just because she was new at it—

The outside door opened and shut. Craig did not call out, but she knew it was her husband from the familiar sounds of snow boots thumping on the linoleum and the closet door squeaking as he put away his coat. "Supper will be ready soon," she said without turning around when she heard him enter the kitchen.

"What are we having?"

"Baked chicken, the kind with parmesan cheese in the crust. Mashed potatoes and peas."

He grunted his acceptance and took a beer from the refrigerator. She waited, but he said nothing about his absence. She vowed not to ask, but she did a slow burn as she set the table and served the meal.

They ate in silence, Craig's face hidden behind the newspaper.

"We received some interesting mail today," she said eventually. "Our building has been sold. The new owners want to buy our condo."

"What?" said Craig. She repeated herself, and he set down the paper. "What was their offer?"

"They weren't that specific." Bonnie wished she wasn't so pleased that she finally had his attention. "I'll also have to sign a new lease for the shop."

"They'll probably raise your rent."

"Yes, I rather expect them to."

He shrugged and picked up the paper again. "Maybe now's a good time to get out, then."

Bonnie stared at him, hard. "Why would I want to get out?"

He glanced at her, his expression full of disbelief and exasperation, as if he could not believe he had to argue the same points again when he had made himself perfectly clear many times before. "When's the last time you made a profit? It's a hobby, not a business. Everything you earn from Elm Creek Quilts goes into keeping that store afloat. We have better uses for the money." He wiped his mouth and dropped his napkin onto his plate. "If you'd let go of that place, we could finally move into a real house."

"You want to leave our home?"

He glanced around, taking in with impatient distaste the rooms she had decorated so lovingly. "Did you ever think we'd stay here this long? Maybe you don't care, but I've always wanted my own house with my own yard. Do you realize I never got to play ball with my own sons on my own lawn? If I'd wanted this kind of lifestyle I would have moved to the city, but that store of yours has always come first."

"How dare you," said Bonnie, incredulous, furious. "I never put the store before my children."

"Well, you put it ahead of other things. Other people."

She almost laughed. "You blame Grandma's Attic for our problems?"

"Maybe. Yes. I don't know." He pushed back his chair and rose. "I don't know. Give me the letter and I'll find out what they're willing to offer us for the condo."

"I don't want to move."

"Where's the letter?" He rifled through the stack of mail on the counter. "Never mind. I'll find it and call them tomorrow."

"I don't want to move," Bonnie said again, but Craig found and pocketed the envelope. He indicated the conversation was over by leaving the room. A moment later, she heard the door to the guest room close.

❧

In the week that passed between the arrival of the letter and her appointment with Gregory Krolich, Bonnie saw little of Craig and spoke to him even less. He offered scant explanation for his erratic comings and goings. "By the time I know I won't be coming home," he said, "it's too late to call."

"You won't wake me," she said. "I'm usually awake wondering where you are. Where do you go, anyway? You must be sleeping somewhere."

"I catch a few hours on the sofa in my office."

Bonnie found that hard to believe. She had seen the furniture he picked out when he redecorated after his last promotion, and it looked as uncomfortable as it was worn. She assumed he had bought used rather than new to save money, but she never understood why he did not at least have it reupholstered and refinished. He said he would get around to it when he had time, but Bonnie doubted it since the furniture resembled some antique pieces they had seen in the President's House on the Penn State campus. Craig was a fervently loyal alumnus, and Bonnie had expected him to be pleased when she had remarked upon the similarities, but instead he had grumbled something about never wasting hard-earned money on designer stuff and ushered her from his office. Still, even if he had intended the resemblance, Bonnie was not convinced he could actually sleep comfortably there.

"Where do you shower and shave?" she asked him.

"I don't," he said, as if it were obvious. "The guys don't care."

On the day of the meeting, Bonnie went to Grandma's Attic carefully attired in her one suit rather than a quilted jacket, determined to make a strong, businesslike impression. The shop was remarkably busy that morning, so that when a man in a black wool coat arrived promptly at ten forty-five, a group of cheerful, well-satisfied customers passed him on the way out. "You must be Mr. Krolich," Bonnie greeted him, pleased that his first impression of Grandma's Attic was that of a lively, thriving business.

"Please call me Greg," he said, removing a leather glove and shaking her hand. "Are you Ms. Markham?"

"Bonnie. Yes."

He glanced around the room, but Bonnie suspected his quick glance took in much more than it appeared. "Is there somewhere we could talk undisturbed?"

The shop was now empty, but Bonnie led him into the back office and offered him the best chair. He removed his coat and sat down, smiling all the while. "Based upon my conversations with other tenants, my guess is this sale came as something of a surprise."

"Shock is the word I would use," said Bonnie, managing a laugh. She seated herself, her hands clasped tightly in her lap.

"I trust you began considering your options when you received our letter."

"Well—" What options? "I think I'll be more able to make an informed decision once I see the rental agreement."

"Of course." He opened his briefcase and withdrew a sheaf of paper in a clear plastic binder. "We have several attractive properties in the downtown area, some within walking distance of your current location. However, I've taken the liberty of highlighting one I think you'll find ideal." He opened the binder and placed it on the desk before her.

At the top of the page was a color photocopied picture of a store in a strip mall. BUTTONS AND BOWS was painted in blue and pink on a window that displayed frilly lace frocks and blue sailor suits. Beneath the picture was a detailed description of the property—square footage, available utilities, address—which Bonnie skimmed before realizing what Greg had assumed.

"Thank you, but I don't intend to move," said Bonnie, smiling apologetically and closing the binder. "I want to see your rental agreement for this location."

"Oh." Greg's expression turned puzzled and alarmed. "You want to stay."

"What's wrong?"

"Basically, you're the first of our tenants who wasn't grateful for the opportunity to find a more suitable location." He turned a winsome smile on her and opened the binder again to the correct page without glancing at it. "I understand change can be difficult, but if you drive out and inspect this property, all you'll want to know is how soon you can move in. That's immediately, by the way. The current tenant is retiring."

"I don't need to drive out and see it. I don't want to move Grandma's Attic away from downtown, especially not there. That's right next door to our biggest competitor."

"Exactly. Traffic into the Fabric Warehouse would naturally drift over to you, and if you don't mind my saying so, you look like you could use more business."

More likely Bonnie would lose even more customers to the chain store, but she kept her voice even and asked, "May I please see the new lease for this shop?"

Greg frowned and dug in his briefcase. "Here," he said, slapping it down on the table.

Bonnie skimmed the first page before she stopped, aghast. "This increase in the rent—it must be close to seventy percent!"

"Seventy-five, to be exact." He smiled, and for the first time, Bonnie detected a smug satisfaction in his manner. "Please also note that our leases are for six months and the rent may increase semiannually. It's safe to assume that it will."

Bonnie returned to the document, afraid to ask if seventy-five percent was the standard increment. Some clauses sounded similar to those in her current lease; others seemed to tack on fees for everything from late payment of rent to improper use of the trash receptacles to new distribution of parking in the back alley. She tried to absorb it all, but her mind was fixed on the rent, that outrageous, impossible rent.

"I can't afford this," she finally said, returning the lease. "I suspect none of my neighbors can, either, and that's why they're leaving. I used to serve on the Waterford Zoning Commission and I can tell you these rates are unreasonable for this area in this economic climate. You're going to end up with an empty building and a lot of angry business owners, who might have something to say at the next public review of your business license."

He blinked, clearly unprepared for a challenge from a nice little middle-aged quilt lady. He recovered quickly, but all pretense of helpfulness vanished. "An empty building would be ideal," he said. "We already have plenty of commercial properties. What we need are more student rentals."

Bonnie stared at him. Other buildings on her street had been transformed from offices into apartments, but her building would require extensive remodeling for such a drastic change in purpose. Except for the condos. Suddenly Bonnie pictured her home surrounded by wild undergraduates, the shop, her haven, thrust into the middle of a twenty-four-hour fraternity party.

"You'd be amazed at what students are willing to pay for housing directly across the street from campus," remarked Greg. "Or, rather, what their parents are willing to pay."

"I have no intention of moving," Bonnie said, but less firmly than before. "From the shop or from my home."

His perplexed frown deepened into a scowl as he made the connection. "You've already admitted you can't afford the rent," he said, rising. "Your husband might not find living among college kids as appealing as you do."

"My husband and I stand together on this."

"We'll see." He put on his coat and nodded toward the binder. "Keep that. Like it or not, you're going to need a new location. If you don't like the one I picked, choose for yourself, but choose fast. All of the other tenants have the same binder."

"I already said I'm not moving." She thrust the binder at him. "And if I were to move, I would never rent from you."

"We would have offered you a good price for the condo and an excellent rent in another building." He returned the binder to his briefcase, shaking his head. "Now you'll have to take what you can get."

He picked up his briefcase and strode from the office. "I'll do just fine, thank you," she said, but he ignored her. Beyond him she saw Sarah standing in the middle of the store.

Sarah turned to watch Greg leave, then spun back around to face Bonnie, eyes wide. "Wasn't that Gregory Krolich?"

Bonnie nodded, drained, and sank onto a stool behind the cutting table. What was she going to do? What could she do? She could not have afforded that outrageous rent even in the shop's best days.

"I knew it," declared Sarah. "The real estate business must be treating him well. He's driving an even more expensive car than the last time I saw him."

Suddenly it registered that Sarah had identified him by name. "You know him?"

"Barely. I haven't seen him in years, not since I first moved to Waterford. He wanted to buy Elm Creek Manor and raze it so he could build a few hundred student apartments on the property."

"Obviously he didn't. So he's just a lot of threats and bluster in a nice suit?"

"On the contrary, I'm sure he would have gone through with it if Sylvia hadn't found out about his plan. She refused to sell to him once she learned the truth."

"Oh." Bonnie dropped her gaze and tried to compose herself, her momentary hopes swiftly fading. She would have to come up with a plan, and Craig would have to help her. Even if he did want to move, even if he was no longer in love with her, surely pride would compel him to intercede when someone tried to intimidate his wife and drive them from their home.

But that evening Craig did not come home, nor did he call. The next morning Bonnie phoned his office from Grandma's Attic, but his assistant said his morning was booked solid with staff meetings and maintenance on campus to supervise, and that he would proba- bly not return until lunch. "Should I have him call you before he leaves for his appointment?" she asked.

"What appointment?"

"I don't know. He just told me he has to leave for an appointment at four." His assistant chuckled. "Maybe he's planning a big sur- prise for Valentine's Day."

If he was, it was not for Bonnie. She hung up and eyed the store's displays of pink, red, and white fabric and ribbon with dis- taste. They should have reminded her, but she had forgotten today was the fourteenth. She had probably blocked it out. Craig seemed to every year.

She searched the storage room for their St. Patrick's Day deco- rations and selected green and white fabrics from the shelves so that she could expunge all signs of the romantic holiday from her shop first thing the next day. As she worked, pausing to assist the occasional customer, the idea that Craig might be planning a Valen- tine's surprise for someone else gnawed at her. He was obviously up to something. A man didn't stay away from his wife that long without cause. While she longed to believe he had been staying up nights planning that second honeymoon in Paris they once talked about, she knew they had moved well beyond any chance of that. It was a bitter truth to accept, but she forced herself to be realistic.

He had planned to cheat on her once. He might have cheated on her since.

She had to know what this appointment was about.

When Diane came in at two, Bonnie made an excuse about needing to leave early. Diane assured her she would be happy to close the shop alone, so at three-forty, Bonnie bid her good-bye and hurried across campus on foot. She wished she had departed earlier. If his appointment was far away, he might have left already. Then another realization stopped her in her tracks: He might have already returned home for his car. He never drove to work; the employee parking lot was farther from his building than their home. She had not checked for his car before leaving.

She would just have to wait outside the Physical Plant building and hope for the best, she told herself, and resumed walking at a brisker pace. She rounded a copse of snow-shrouded evergreens and nearly crashed into a couple engrossed in an intense discussion.

"Excuse me," she mumbled, hurrying on.

"Bonnie?"

Bonnie stopped short and whirled around. She recognized Judy before her friend lowered her scarf. "Oh, hi. Hi, Steve."

"Hi," said Judy's husband, smiling. "Where are you going in such a hurry?"

"Oh, well—" Bonnie fumbled for an excuse before realizing she didn't need one. "I'm going to see if I can catch Craig before he leaves work. You didn't happen to see him pass this way?"

They shook their heads. "If we do, should we tell him to meet you somewhere?" asked Steve.

"No, that's all right." Bonnie forced a smile and backed away. "I'd better hurry."

"See you tonight at the business meeting," said Judy. As Bonnie turned to go, she heard her ask Steve, "Do you think she overheard?"

Bonnie understood at once that she had interrupted an argument and wished with all her heart she had not. If the happiest married couple she knew argued, what chance did she and Craig have if he made her resort to spying?

She reached Craig's building with ten minutes to spare and brushed snow off a bench partially concealed from the front entrance behind the bare limbs of a lilac bush. She sat down and waited, mittened hands clutching the tote bag on her lap. Students passed on their way to and from classes, but just then she glimpsed a familiar burly figure in a blue Penn State coat and blaze-orange knit hat exiting by a side door. Bonnie tracked him with her eyes as he hurried across the quad toward downtown, but not in the direction of home.

She waited as long as she thought she could afford before pursuing him. She almost lost him trying to cross Main Street, but his blaze-orange hat stood out among the crowd on the other side. Once across, she had to run to close the distance between them. When she was within two blocks, Craig turned down an alley lined with bookstores and coffeeshops, then headed south. He was on his way to the residential area, Bonnie guessed, but he turned again and climbed the stairs of a three-story Victorian, one of the many former private homes on that street converted to offices. Outside, a steel blue-and-gray sign read UNIVERSITY REALTY.

Out of breath from the chase, Bonnie gasped and ducked behind a street sign. Her heart pounded; her face burned. What was Craig doing here? He must be meeting with Krolich, and not to demand an apology for the way Krolich had treated Bonnie.

Bonnie pulled up her hood and hurried away before either man chanced to step outside. Craig could have come to find out what University Realty was prepared to offer for the condo, but a phone call would have sufficed for that information. Bonnie paused, glanced back at the office, then crossed the street and entered a coffee shop. She ordered a mocha latte and found a seat by the front window with a decent view of University Realty. Her cup was empty by the time Craig emerged. He descended the steps with a jaunty gait. He appeared to be whistling.

Sick at heart, Bonnie gathered her coat and purse and left.

She took the long way home, longing for the comfort of Grandma's Attic but too stricken to face Diane, too distracted to think of an explanation for her unexpected return. Exhaustion weighted her footsteps as she climbed the stairs to the condo. Craig was not there.

She wanted to crawl into bed and sleep until spring, but she went to the kitchen and cut up vegetables and leftover turkey for soup. The latest *Contemporary Quilting* magazine had come in the mail. She curled up on the sofa beneath a flannel Lady of the Lake quilt and read while the soup simmered.

At six she decided Craig wasn't coming home, so she warmed a few slices of sourdough bread in the oven and ladled soup into a single bowl. The door opened just as she began to eat. "That smells great," Craig called from the hallway as he hung up his coat.

It was the kindest thing he had said to her in weeks. Tears sprang into her eyes, but the automatic thank-you died on her lips. He bustled in, cheeks red, rubbing his palms together for warmth. Bonnie sipped her soup and pretended not to notice how he hesitated at the sight of her eating alone.

"Bread smells good, too," he said on his way to the kitchen. She heard him fishing a spoon from the drawer, taking a bowl down from the cupboard, opening a beer. A few minutes later he joined her at the table.

She ate without looking at him, waiting for him to speak. Oblivious to her silence, he ate with his eyes glued to the paper. Bonnie returned to the kitchen for seconds, then sat at the table swirling the barley and thick slices of carrot without tasting a mouthful, realizing only then that she was no longer hungry. She had refilled her bowl only to prolong the meal.

Finally she said, "Don't you have something you want to tell me?"

He set down the paper and studied her for a moment. "Oh. Right. Happy Valentine's Day."

"That's not what I'm talking about."

"What were you expecting, chocolates and a dozen roses?"

It was all Bonnie could do not to fling her bowl at him. "I have a meeting," she said, rising, clearing away her dishes. "Please put the leftovers in the fridge when you're done. I'm taking the car. Don't wait up."

"Don't worry."

Fighting off tears of rage, she grabbed her tote bag and left. She endured the meeting, finding no comfort in her friends' presence or their anticipation of the upcoming camp season. Then it was time to go home, but Bonnie dreaded the discussion—the argument—that would inevitably follow her return. She had to confront Craig; if he intended to tell her why he had met with Gregory Krolich, he would have done so over supper. Whatever secrets he kept could not be good for their home or Grandma's Attic. Or their marriage.

When she pulled into the parking space behind their building, all the second-floor windows overlooking the back alley were dark. Inside, she found the pot of lukewarm soup sitting uncovered on the stove. Craig was gone, and so was the large duffel bag that once carried his workout clothes, but had sat on the floor of his closet, unused, for most of the past year.

He stayed away for three days. In the meantime, Bonnie called University Realty and left a message on Krolich's voicemail declaring that the Markham home was not for sale. She wrote lessons for camp. She pored over the shop's finances and concluded that she would have to cut her employees' hours in half or let one of them go. Summer was out of the question, so it would have to be Diane. Reluctantly, she spent Sunday morning with the classifieds circling ads for commercial properties. There weren't many choices, since three-quarters of the listings belonged to University Realty.

On Sunday afternoon Craig finally returned home. He ignored her as he went down the hall, tossed the duffel bag into the guest room, and continued on to the bathroom.

She went to the kitchen to fix a cup of tea. Eventually Craig came to the kitchen for a beer. "We need to talk," she said, but he pretended not to hear as he rooted in the refrigerator. He left the kitchen and in a moment she heard a basketball game on the television.

She followed him into the living room and sat down. "I know you met with Gregory Krolich."

He raised the can to his lips, eyes fixed on the television screen.

She clasped her hands around her mug of tea. "I want to know why."

"So he could make an offer on this place."

"I already told you I don't want to sell."

"It's a good offer. Better than we could get if we tried to sell on our own."

"I don't want to sell."

"It's not up to you."

"Yes, it is." Her hands shook so badly she had to set the mug on the table. "It's up to both of us."

"You're a spoiled brat." He looked at her with such venom that she shrank back into her chair. "You won't admit this is the best opportunity we're likely to see. Ever. You won't admit you can't afford the new rent for the shop. You can't admit you should close that place before it sinks us any deeper."

"Grandma's Attic means the world to me," said Bonnie. "I still have many loyal customers who would hate to see it go. For them, and for me, I won't close it short of total bankruptcy."

"Then we won't have long to wait."

After that, Bonnie no longer noted when Craig slept in the guest room or how many days he stayed away. A week after their confrontation, she was vacuuming the carpet when words came into her mind, so suddenly that it shocked her, so clearly that she knew she had been considering them for weeks.

I want a divorce, she thought, then said aloud, "I want a divorce."

She shouldn't. He didn't beat her. He had not, as far as she knew, been unfaithful. He had been a reliable if critical father to their children. Maybe he was right and she was a spoiled brat. But she could not endure the current situation. Spending the rest of her life in a state of perpetual animosity was unthinkable. She didn't think she loved him anymore; she barely even liked him most days. She was tired of the tension, tired of feeling at her worst when he was around, tired of feeling inconsequential when he did not even bother to tell her he wasn't coming home.

Whatever happened with the store, with their home, they had to try marriage counseling again. It had helped them reconcile five years before when she had discovered and thwarted his planned rendezvous with a woman he had met on an internet mailing list. They simply could not throw away a shared history of thirty years. Things had never been worse between them, but she had to believe they still had a chance.

She wrote him a short but heartfelt note asking him to please come home for supper so they could discuss resuming counseling. She left it on the pillow of the guest room. It was gone by the time she returned home from work the next day, but Craig left no reply behind, and he did not show up for supper.

The last day of February was cold and overcast, with gusty winds that sent newspapers and trash scuttling down the alley behind their building. Bonnie rose early to pay the household bills before going to Grandma's Attic, where she would have to complete the same chore. Craig's paychecks were direct-deposited into their joint checking account at the end of each month; usually he brought home a pay stub telling her the amount, but this week he had not left the familiar envelope by the computer. Bonnie wasn't sure how many of his late nights had actually been overtime, so she estimated conservatively when she entered the deposit into the account. She would inquire at the bank for the actual amount when she withdrew funds on her lunch break.

The ATM was down when Bonnie arrived, but she had beaten the midday rush and used her brief time in line to fill out a withdrawal slip. "Could you check on a deposit for me?" she asked the teller while he counted out her bills. "It was made by direct deposit either this morning or yesterday afternoon."

The teller entered a few keystrokes, frowned at the monitor, and shook his head. "Sorry. The last deposit was on the twelfth for twenty-two seventy-eight."

"That can't be right. My husband's paycheck comes by direct deposit from the college at the end of each month."

"Yeah, I know. They all come the same day." The teller, freckled and far younger than her children, pressed another key. "The last direct deposit was on January thirty-first."

"Maybe the college delayed their transfer for some reason. A computer glitch or something."

"I doubt it, ma'am. People with Waterford College IDs have been coming in all day."

"Well—" Bonnie didn't know what to think. "What is my balance without that deposit?"

"Oh. Sorry." He handed her the receipt he had forgotten to give her with her cash.

Bonnie stared at the receipt in shock—$215.74. In a moment of confusion she thought the checks she had written that morning had somehow already cleared, then she realized the envelopes were still in her bag. "There's been some mistake," she said. "There should be at least a thousand dollars in this account."

"Um." The teller glanced over his shoulder. "Well, there was a big withdrawal yesterday. I could print out a statement for you, or you can see it online. Do you know about our online banking?"

Bonnie went cold. "What about the savings account?"

"You want me to check the balance?"

"Yes, yes, please."

Her distress motivated him to hurry. "Twenty dollars and fifteen cents," he said, not wasting time on a printed statement. "Just enough to keep the account open."

"I don't understand." But she did understand. Craig. "Can you tell me if the money was transferred to another account? Or was it in cash?"

He studied the screen. "It was a cash withdrawal."

"Did my husband—" She took a deep breath. "Did he open a new account and deposit the money in it?"

"I'm sorry. I can't give you any information about accounts not in your name."

"Please," she said, fighting off tears. "Please make an exception just this once."

His fingers clattered on the keyboard. He glanced over his shoulder again, then said, "I'm sorry. I'm not allowed to tell you that your husband did not open a new account at this bank."

"Thank you." Bonnie forced a shaky smile, which faded when she remembered the bills in her purse. "While I'm here, I need to transfer money from my business account into the checking account."

"Are you sure you want to do that?"

Bonnie stopped short, her hand on the stack of transfer slips. "What do you mean?"

"They're still joint accounts."

Bonnie withdrew her hand, slowly. "No." She ducked her head as she returned her checkbook to her bag. "No. I suppose I don't. Thank you."

He nodded, with more sympathy and understanding than she expected from a boy his age.

Bonnie hurried back to Grandma's Attic, rushed past Diane with barely a greeting, and shut herself in the office. She tore up the checks she had written that morning and wrote new ones drawn on the Grandma's Attic account. Craig could not have touched those funds, she reminded herself after a quake of fear made her hands tremble as she signed the new checks. The Grandma's Attic accounts were in her name alone. Craig did not even know the account numbers. Ordinarily she was scrupulous about keeping her personal and business accounts separate, but this was an emergency. As long as Craig had not taken a plane to the Cayman Islands, she would be able to return the money soon.

Diane readily agreed to close for her that evening. "I'll open tomorrow, too, if you want to sleep in," she offered with a grin.

Bonnie forced a smile and thanked her, but declined. How could she offer Diane more hours one week and fire her the next?

Later, upstairs in the condo, she waited in the living room, hugging her knees to her chest on the sofa, the flannel quilt draped over her, until the winter light faded. She knew she should start supper, but she could not even rouse herself to turn on a light. Finally hunger overcame her immobility, and she went to the kitchen for tea and toast with honey. The clock on the microwave told her it was half past eight.

She waited on the sofa long past her usual bedtime. At eleven she brushed her teeth and put on the evening news. When that ended, she switched between Leno and Letterman, but their jokes seemed inane and the celebrity guests fatuous. She put on the History Channel and tried to concentrate on an account of the Battle of Stalingrad, but the narrator's voice sounded so much like Gregory Krolich's that she finally turned off the television.

Not long after midnight the door quietly opened. She sat in the dark watching Craig remove his boots and hang up his coat. He switched on the dining room light, then turned and nearly leapt into the air at the sight of her. "What're you doing up?"

"I went to the bank today."

He disappeared into the kitchen. "So?"

"So, what did you do with our money?"

There was a long pause in which Bonnie heard the refrigerator door open and the microwave heating something. Soon Craig returned with a beer and a slice of pizza on a paper plate. "*Our* money? I earned it. Everything you earn goes straight into that money pit you call a store."

"That is not true." Bonnie had the ledgers to prove it. "You can't drain our accounts so much without at least telling me. I paid bills this morning, and all those checks would have bounced if I had not happened to go into the bank today."

He shrugged and sat down in his recliner, his mouth full of pizza. He reached for the remote and put on a sports network.

"I think we should try marriage counseling again."

Craig barked out a laugh. "Right, since it was so successful the first time."

"If you won't come with me, I'll go alone."

"Suit yourself, but you're paying for it."

"Craig—" She fought back tears. "I want to sort this out, but if we can't, I think we should separate."

"You mean divorce."

"I didn't say—"

"No one gets a separation unless they really want a divorce. Why don't you just say what you want for a change?"

She stared at him in bewilderment. "Will you please just go?" she said after what seemed an interminable silence. "Pack an overnight bag. Tomorrow—tomorrow, when I'm at work, come back for whatever you want."

He watched her balefully as he chewed his pizza. "Go where?"

She lifted her hands and let them fall into her lap. "Wherever it is you go when you don't come home."

"Why should I be the one to leave? You're the one who wants a divorce."

Didn't *he*? "You hate it here."

"It's not so bad, now that it's for sale. Why don't *you* leave? Go move into that Elm Creek Manor with the rest of the crones. You practically live there anyway."

Her home was not for sale, she thought, but she said, "Please,

Craig. Let's not make this any worse. For the kids' sake if not for ours. Please, just go."

He jabbed the remote at the television and shook his head. "If the Penguins keep playing like this, they'll never make the playoffs."

She watched him, but he acted as if she had already left. So she put on her shoes and coat, shouldered her tote bag, and went.

She was so accustomed to walking everywhere except to Elm Creek Manor that she never thought to take the car. It was nearly one o'clock when she rang Agnes's doorbell. After a while she rang again, but no one answered. She was debating whether she ought to walk to Diane's and endure the third degree in warmth or risk freezing to death by spending the night on Agnes's front porch swing when a light went on in a second-story window. A few moments later, Agnes opened the door, squinting without her glasses and holding her fuzzy pink robe closed at the neck.

"Bonnie, honey," she said. "What's wrong?"

"May I spend the night?"

Agnes immediately opened the door wide. "Of course."

The older woman bustled about, showing her to the guest room, setting out fresh towels in the adjoining bath, offering her a cup of tea or glass of milk, but Bonnie refused, clutching a borrowed flannel nightgown to her chest and wanting desperately not to cry. She wanted to kiss Agnes for not asking any questions.

Once alone, she put on the nightgown. It was warm but too snug and it only came down to her knees, so she crawled into bed with her socks on. She fell asleep as soon as her eyes closed and did not dream.

She woke to bright sunlight and felt a moment of contentment before realizing that she was not at home, and then, that she had left her husband. Sick dread filled her as she rose and saw from the clock on the bedside table that it was after eleven.

She showered quickly and dressed in the clothes she had worn the day before. She found Agnes in the kitchen. "I overslept," she said, wondering where she had left her shoes. "I have to get to work."

Agnes smiled and shook her head, gently guiding her to a chair. "Not without breakfast. Do you want scrambled eggs or waffles?"

"But the shop—"

"Don't you worry. I called Diane. She said she'd head over as soon as she could. She probably didn't get there on time, but she got there."

Agnes closed Bonnie's hands around a cup of coffee. Bonnie sank back into the chair as Agnes brought her cream and sugar. "Thank you," said Bonnie.

"I had waffles myself," remarked Agnes, patting her shoulder and returning to the refrigerator. "I like to add cinnamon and vanilla. Have you ever tried them that way?"

"I haven't, but I'd love to."

Agnes nodded and left her to drink her coffee in silence. A few minutes later she set a plate in front of Bonnie and refilled her coffee, then brought a second cup for herself. She sat down as if friends showed up unexpectedly on her doorstep every night.

"I left Craig," said Bonnie.

"For good?"

"I think so."

Agnes nodded, apparently not surprised. Bonnie told her what had happened the night before, and in the weeks leading up to it, and all the months of loneliness and arguing and pretending that everything would be all right eventually if she just weathered the current storm. When Bonnie said she still intended to speak to a counselor, Agnes said, "As long as you speak to a lawyer, too."

Bonnie nodded. She supposed Craig already had.

They washed the dishes together. "You can stay here as long as you need to," Agnes said as she wiped off the table.

"Thanks, but I intend to stay at home tonight." She dreaded the thought of seeing Craig again, but she would not give up her home to him. "He doesn't usually sleep there anyway." She managed a small laugh. "I have to go home, if only to change clothes."

"I'll come with you, if you like."

Grateful, relieved, Bonnie nodded.

They linked arms as they walked, with Bonnie unsure who was supporting whom. The Markhams' parking space was empty, but Diane's car filled the one beside it. Bonnie knew she ought to stop by and thank Diane for coming in on a moment's notice, but not before she changed clothes.

The outside door stuck on a crust of ice. Bonnie shoved it open and led Agnes upstairs to the second floor. She hesitated before slipping her key in the lock, wondering if she ought to ask Agnes to watch for Craig. The key did not turn. Bonnie withdrew it and checked that she had the right key, since it resembled the one for Grandma's Attic. Neither key worked. She tried again, jostling the knob and shoving the door with her shoulder, but it would not budge.

"He changed the locks," she said, not believing it.

She tried the Grandma's Attic key again, but Agnes gently pulled her away. "Come on. We'll go shopping. Buy yourself something nice and send the bill to Craig."

Bonnie pressed her lips together and nodded, holding her breath to fight off sobs. "Please don't tell anyone about this," she managed to say as they emerged in the alley below.

Agnes glanced at her to see if she meant it. "I won't breathe a word."

They walked downtown, past the fancy boutique where five years before Bonnie had tried on expensive, flattering dresses in an attempt to find one that would lure Craig out of his cyber-girl infatuation, to Bonnie's favorite department store. Woodenly she selected slacks, sweaters, blouses, sweats; she would have forgotten undergarments if not for Agnes's delicate reminder. She did not know how much to buy. Ordinarily she never would have purchased so many items for herself, but she did not know when she would be able to go home.

Standing in line, Agnes did her best to amuse Bonnie with a story about how Sarah's husband, Matt, had spied pieces for Agnes's block for Sylvia's bridal quilt in her sewing box. He had been so interested in seeing her current project that she had had no choice but to show him. "Right in front of Sylvia," she said, chuckling, as the clerk rang up Bonnie's purchases and took her credit card. "I know Sarah told him Sylvia's quilt is a secret, but of course he didn't know that particular block was my contribution or he wouldn't have insisted upon seeing it. Fortunately Sylvia wasn't paying attention or the surprise would have been ruined."

"That was lucky," Bonnie agreed, remembering her own half-finished block on the table in her sewing room. It had once been her daughter's bedroom. The kids. What would they think when they learned what had happened? How would Bonnie tell them?

"Ma'am?" said the clerk. "I'm sorry, but your card didn't go through."

"Oh." That bill, still in her purse from yesterday. It was late, but not that late. "Here's my bank debit card. No, wait." She remembered just in time and snatched the card away before the clerk could pick it up. She extended a second card. "Here, use this. May I have the other one back?"

"I'm afraid I can't do that. I have to cut it up. It's been reported stolen."

"What?" said Agnes.

The clerk looked uneasy. "I'm sorry. Your credit card company insists."

"That's outrageous," Agnes began, but Bonnie placed a hand on her arm to silence her. She should have anticipated this. She returned the second card to her wallet and handed the clerk her Grandma's Attic corporate card without a word. The clerk scrutinized it, dubious, but the card cleared. As soon as the humiliating transaction ended, Bonnie snatched up her bags and fled.

Agnes hurried to catch up with her. "Come home with me," she said. "You can change clothes and call your lawyer."

"I don't have a lawyer."

"I do. He's a wonderful young man. His father looked after our affairs for years, and he took over the firm after his father passed."

"Does he handle divorces?"

"If not, he'll know someone who does."

Bonnie took the lawyer's number but did not call. She reminded herself that less than two weeks before she had been cleaning the condo and contemplating divorce. For five years, since Craig's first betrayal, she had struggled to hold their marriage together, but in her heart she knew it was over. It was time to salvage what she could and move on.

And yet she could not bring herself to make the call. She did not know why and did not want to think about it.

She spent the weekend with Agnes, helping her cut fabric for the pieced border of Sylvia's bridal quilt. Agnes arranged for Diane to cover for her at Grandma's Attic on Saturday before Bonnie remembered to ask. On Monday she returned to work as if she had not been away. Summer stopped by in the morning, her concern and curiosity apparent, but fortunately Bonnie was helping a customer so she avoided uncomfortable questions.

"You have nothing to be ashamed of," said Agnes that evening, when Bonnie returned to her house in defeat. She had tried to outwait Craig at the alley door since he would not return her calls, but her resolve faltered as the night grew colder. "Our friends would be a great comfort to you if they knew you needed their support."

"I'm not ashamed," Bonnie said, but she was. Ashamed that she had failed at her marriage, ashamed that she had not heeded the obvious warning signs and left Craig five years before.

On Wednesday, at Agnes's urging, she camped in Craig's office until he showed up for work. She pleaded with him to let her come home, but he said, "You're the one who decided to abandon the property. Now you've got to live with it."

She didn't like his gleeful tone or the odd emphasis he gave the words *abandon* and *property*, but she was too emotionally exhausted to argue within earshot of his coworkers, whom she had known for years and had entertained in their home. She considered it a triumph when he agreed to let her come home that evening to pack her clothes and other necessities. Agnes accompanied her and stood glaring at Craig as Bonnie quickly filled two suitcases and sorted the mail. She left the bills for him to pay, since she had drawn on Grandma's Attic as much as she could afford, but took her magazines and an unopened letter from their daughter.

"I forgot to ask him if the children called," she told Agnes in dismay as they struggled to her house with the suitcases in hand.

"The light on the answering machine was blinking," said Agnes, breathing hard from exertion. "I doubt if he even saw it, buried under all that mail."

Bonnie waited until late the next morning, then called and checked the messages using the remote code. There were three messages, none very important, but Bonnie did learn that Craig had changed the outgoing announcement.

The days passed. Bonnie often felt as if she were watching a dream of someone else's life. She went to work, returned to Agnes's for supper, and spent her evenings helping Agnes with the bridal quilt or working on lesson plans for camp. Some mornings before unlocking the door to the shop, she would stare up at the windows of her home from across the street and wonder what Craig hoped to accomplish by throwing her out and cutting her off from their joint resources. She had no idea what her next step should be, no foresight into what Craig intended. Did he want her to suffer longer before he allowed her to return? Was he keeping her out just long enough to sell their home without interference?

A week and a day after she left the condo, she understood. He had no intention of allowing her to return. He had already divorced her in his heart. The legalities of their relationship he would leave for the lawyers.

New resolve filled her the day she accepted the inevitable. She still dreaded the confrontations to come, the astonishment of the children, the frightening questions of how she would manage financially, but she would no longer pretend these problems would disappear if she ignored them.

Somehow she felt like celebrating—she also felt like weeping, but she was determined not to. She had cried every night since leaving the condo and she felt too wrung out for more tears. After work, she stopped off at the market for a crown roast and all the fixings for a special dinner to thank Agnes for all she had done, suppressing a wave of guilt as she handed over the Grandma's Attic corporate card. Afterward she passed a liquor store, something of a dive but popular with the students, and decided to stop for a bottle of wine.

She knew next to nothing about wine, but Agnes never criticized anyone except for bad manners, so she could hardly go wrong. She chose a red she had enjoyed at Gwen's last Winter Solstice feast and got in line behind a young man hefting two cases of beer onto the checkout counter. When he dug in his back pocket for his wallet, Bonnie glimpsed his face in profile—and nearly dropped the wine. His hair was shorter than he had worn it in years, but he was unmistakably Diane's eldest son, Michael.

The clerk asked for Michael's ID, and Bonnie held her breath—waiting for Michael to run, for the clerk to call his supervisor, the police—but Michael said, "Sure," and handed him something that looked like a Pennsylvania driver's license. It couldn't have been; at least, it wasn't Michael's. But the clerk looked from the photo on the card to Michael's face and back, then returned the license and rang up the beer. Bonnie watched, dumbfounded, as Michael paid him and pocketed his wallet. He turned to go and stopped short at the sight of her, his expression giving way to shock and dismay. He left quickly, without a word.

He was nowhere in sight by the time Bonnie exited the store. She had no idea what she would have said to him anyway, had he lingered to shower her in excuses. She must tell Diane, of course. Shouldn't she? She could imagine how that conversation would unfold: "Diane, I saw your underage son buying beer last night. Since I'm managing my own domestic situation so perfectly I thought I should tell you how to raise your son. Oh, by the way, Grandma's Attic is in even more trouble than my marriage, so I'm afraid you're fired."

She didn't tell Agnes about the encounter—Agnes had baby-sat Diane as a child and they had remained close, so she was almost a surrogate grandmother to her boys and could hardly be objective—but she did tell Gwen when she stopped by the shop a few days later. Gwen seemed more concerned with her daughter's perfectly legal decision to move in with her boyfriend than by Michael's breaking the law, but that was not surprising. Gwen did offer one offhand suggestion and, after mulling it over, Bonnie decided it was actually quite good: She could talk to Michael herself. She was no prude, and she knew college students started drinking as soon as they hit campus regardless of age, but that fake ID could get him in serious trouble. Diane and Tim were so proud of how their rebellious son had turned his life around. Bonnie could not sit back and wait for him to disappoint them, or worse.

But first Bonnie had to pay back Grandma's Attic. The following Thursday evening she took a cab out to Elm Creek Manor and found Sylvia in the formal parlor, tidying up for their business meeting. After procrastinating with small talk, Bonnie awkwardly asked her for an advance on her first quilt camp paycheck. "I wouldn't make this request lightly—"

"I know you wouldn't," interrupted Sylvia. "If you say you need the money now, you must have good reason."

"I think I owe you an explanation."

"Well, you don't. Now, let's go upstairs so I can write you a check before everyone else gets here and wants their first paycheck early, too."

Bonnie managed a smile as she followed Sylvia from the room, but as they climbed the stairs, she said, "I left Craig."

Sylvia nodded. "I thought it was something like that. Have you contacted a lawyer?"

"I meet with him tomorrow." Bonnie gave Sylvia a sidelong glance. "You're not surprised?"

"Frankly, no. I've been expecting something like this for the past five years."

Bonnie stopped short on the landing. "Really."

"Of course, dear. Once the trust between a husband and wife is broken, it's very difficult to repair, even with the best of intentions."

Sylvia continued down the hall toward the library, but Bonnie caught her arm. "You're not going to tell me I should try harder?"

Sylvia looked shocked. "I wouldn't presume to. You stuck it out for more than thirty years, by my reckoning. You would know far better than I whether you've done all you could."

"But what about all your talk about forgiveness, about reconciling before it's too late?"

"Oh. That." Sylvia sighed and shook her head. "In an ideal world, your forgiveness would have inspired Craig to mend his ways and be an exemplary husband. You gave him five years to prove himself, which is about four and a half more than I would have managed in your place. If you're still miserable, if you still can't trust him, you're far too young to live that way for the rest of your life."

"I didn't leave because of that woman from the internet," said Bonnie, and while Sylvia wrote out a check, Bonnie filled her in on the events of the past few months. Sylvia's expression grew more grave as the story tumbled out, and at the end, she gave Bonnie one long, wordless hug. They returned downstairs together, ten minutes late for the meeting.

❧

The next day was unseasonably mild, with sunny skies and warm breezes that promised of the coming spring. Students basked in the sun on the main quad across the street from Grandma's Attic, while others clad in shorts and T-shirts packed their cars for spring break. Business picked up a little that week, as residents of outlying small towns took advantage of the students' absence to venture into Waterford. Bonnie tried to take some hope from this and the fine weather as she locked the door to the quilt shop and walked to her lawyer's office.

She had collected some of the papers he had requested, but the most important documents were unattainable in the condo. Not for long, however, if her new lawyer could be believed. Darren had told her it was unfortunate that she had abandoned the property, but he could argue that Craig gave her no other choice. The echo of Craig's words made her uneasy, but she decided to believe Darren when he said he would have her back in her home soon. She didn't ask where he expected Craig to go.

Scanning front doors for the address, she glanced through the window of a coffee shop and spotted Michael pouring sugar and cream into a to-go cup. She hesitated, then checked her watch and went inside.

Michael eyed her warily as she approached. "Hello, Michael."

"Hi, Mrs. Markham," he mumbled.

She smiled pleasantly. "Do you have any plans for spring break?"

"Stayin' here."

When he did not elaborate, she decided to get to the point. "Michael, I've been concerned ever since I saw you at the liquor store."

"It wasn't all for me," he broke in. "I wasn't going to drive after."

"I'm relieved to hear it, but that doesn't change the fact that you used a fake ID."

"I'll be twenty-one in six months."

"Do you think the police would care? Do you have any idea what would happen to you if you got caught?" He shrugged, and since Bonnie didn't know either, she let the ominous threat hang in the air. "I could tell you all the reasons why you shouldn't drink, but I'm sure you've heard them before. What you might not have considered is that breaking the law so you can drink makes a bad situation worse." His scowl deepened, so she finished in a rush. "I want you to give me that ID."

"What?"

"It's for your own good." She could have cringed; she shouldn't have put it that way. "I haven't told your parents what I know, and I won't, as long as I know you can't do it anymore."

"What if I just promise?"

"If you promise, and if you intend to keep your promise, you won't need the ID." She held out her palm. "Please, Michael. Either give it to me now or to your parents later."

He looked as if he might protest, but then he whipped out his wallet and shoved the card into her hand. He stalked off as she tucked it into her purse, but at the door, he turned and gave her a look of such unmitigated rage that her breath caught in her throat. Then he was gone.

She composed herself and continued on to her lawyer's office, to prepare for another confrontation she did not want but could not avoid.

❧❧

Two days later, Bonnie and the other Elm Creek Quilters welcomed the first group of campers for the season. It was a scene so customary that it should have comforted her, but instead its sameness in the context of sudden and unwelcome change unsettled her. First there was the excuse she invented for being at Agnes's house when Diane stopped by to pick her up—although she would have been uncomfortable around Diane regardless. Then, when she finally confided to Summer that she would have to let Diane go, Summer actually tried to resign in order to save her friend's job. Bonnie was deeply touched that Summer would offer to make such a sacrifice without even pausing to consider the consequences, and if Summer were not so crucial to the survival of Grandma's Attic, Bonnie might have taken her at her word.

Still, as the Candlelight welcoming ceremony concluded, Bonnie began to fall under the spell of the campers' joy. Even Judy's unexpected absence seemed reassuring as the sort of ordinary emergency the Elm Creek Quilters had learned to expect and absorb. By the end of the first day of classes, Bonnie almost managed to forget her grief over the loss of her marriage, the indignity of having to rely on Agnes for a place to live, her fear that one day soon she might have to lock the door of her beloved quilt shop forever. The familiar rhythms of quilt camp reminded her that she had a life beyond Craig, beyond Grandma's Attic.

True to her predictions, business did pick up slightly as spring break began, so that as she walked to the quilt shop Wednesday morning, she considered that they might just be able to save the store without losing Diane.

But then she reached the front door, and before unlocking it, she knew that she had already lost.

She was too shocked to cry. She stepped carefully over the rubble of her dream, turning around, taking it all in. She could not believe it, but it had to be real. It hurt too much to be a nightmare.

Craig. He had always hated the shop. He had smirked when he said she was close to losing it. She never suspected he would be vicious enough to push her over the edge. Until that moment, she had not understood the depth of his contempt for her.

The cash register was empty, as she had suspected it would be. Then, a shiver of alarm ran through her. In her haste to meet her lawyer, she had stashed the previous day's deposit in a filing cabinet rather than taking it to the bank. She ran to the office, tripping over fabric and spools of thread, but that room, too, had been ransacked, the filing cabinet overturned. The money bag was gone.

With a sob, Bonnie sank down onto a chair. She stared at the disarray, seeing Craig hurling fabric bolts across the room, knocking over shelves, tearing sample quilts from the walls and grinding them beneath his feet, until she remembered she ought to call the police. She fumbled for the phone and made her report numbly. When the squad car pulled up in front of the store, lights flashing, she was picking her way through the mess in a daze, trying to determine exactly what had been stolen.

One officer questioned her and took notes while the other looked around, studying the front and back doors and the windows carefully. They asked what was missing. When Bonnie told them, the second officer's eyebrows rose. "That's all?" she asked.

"As far as I know," said Bonnie, indicating the mess with a wide, despairing sweep of her arm. "It's difficult to say."

They urged her to look around, carefully. Bonnie complied, gradually understanding the reason for their surprise. Common thieves would not have wasted so much time destroying the shop, and they would not have left so many expensive items behind. Whoever had done this had wanted to hurt her. Bonnie wanted to dismiss the thought—it would be easier to believe thieves had struck rather than the man with whom she had shared most of her life—but it became an irrefutable conclusion when she discovered the thief had also taken the carton of blocks for Sylvia's bridal quilt.

Bonnie could no longer stand. She managed to reach a stool and brace herself against the cutting table, but not before the officers noticed. When she told them what else was gone and explained the significance of the project, they exchanged a knowing look she doubted she was meant to see.

The first officer finally asked the question she had been dreading: Did she have any idea who the culprit was? She could not bring herself to speak, so she shook her head. The officer frowned and tapped his pad with a pen. "Do you have any enemies?" he asked. "Anyone who would like to see you driven out of business? Any competitors who play hardball?"

"No," Bonnie said, since the Fabric Warehouse was succeeding in that without destroying her shop. Then she thought of Krolich and gasped.

"What is it?" the second officer asked.

"There is someone . . . I don't want to accuse anyone lightly, but the new owner of the building doesn't want me to stay. He wouldn't need to resort to this, though. The rent he wants to charge is enough to drive me away."

"We should probably talk to him anyway," said the first officer. "Can you tell us how to reach him?"

Bonnie nodded and made her way to the front counter, where the contents of her card file had been scattered on the floor beneath the register. She picked through the pile but she could not find Krolich's business card, and then suddenly she froze, realizing what else was missing.

Michael's fake ID. She had put it in the card file for safekeeping, not quite willing to discard it in case she had to go to his parents after all. A momentary relief flooded her when she realized Craig was not to blame, but the feeling vanished when she thought of what this would mean for Michael, and for Diane.

Then she spotted Krolich's business card and quickly scooped it up and rose before the officers noticed her distress. "Here's his card," she said, handing it to the first officer.

He glanced at it before tucking it into a pocket. "I assume that as the owner Mr. Krolich has a key to the building?"

"I suppose he must," said Bonnie. "Why?"

"There's no sign of forced entry," said the second officer. "It must have been an inside job, if you're sure you locked the door."

"I'm sure, but I really don't think Gregory Krolich did this."

The officers nodded noncommittally and resumed their work.

Krolich would likely have access to a key. So would Michael, but not Craig. Michael could have taken Diane's key from her purse, while Craig had not been within blocks of Bonnie's key for weeks.

Another officer arrived shortly afterward and began dusting for fingerprints and photographing different areas of the store. The officers' questions shifted from points of entry and the motives of her enemies to Bonnie herself, and how she felt about her shop. Bonnie supposed they were trying to put her at ease, but explaining that she and her husband were estranged and admitting that Grandma's Attic was not in the best fiscal health only made her more uncomfortable. Just when she was considering asking them to allow her to sit down for a moment, alone, Summer burst in. The third officer tried to prevent her from entering, but Bonnie was so glad to see her she almost could not tell her what had happened. She clung to her young friend and, finally, let her tears fall when she admitted that Sylvia's blocks were missing. Why would Michael have done that, when most kids would assume losing the expensive sewing machines would hurt her most deeply? How would Michael have known to do that?

It was midafternoon before the officers said she could straighten up the areas they had already searched and photographed. As soon as they departed, Bonnie and Summer got to work. They had made little progress by the time Gwen arrived several hours later. Since Summer had a tender spot in her heart for Michael, Bonnie waited until she was out of hearing to confide her suspicions to Gwen. At first Gwen denied the possibility that the Michael they had known since childhood could have done such a terrible thing, but soon doubt appeared in her eyes.

Bonnie had no doubts.

CHAPTER FIVE

Agnes

Agnes's New Year's resolution was to update her will and get her affairs in order, so after the traditional New Year's Day feast of honey-glazed ham with all the trimmings, she took her two daughters aside and told them if they especially wanted any of her belongings, they should let her know so she could set them aside.

She was not surprised when both of her girls recoiled. "Mom, that's morbid," said Stacy, her eldest. "That's not something you need to worry about yet."

Laura, as always, suspected she had not been told the entire story. "Are you ill?"

Agnes laughed. "Of course not. I'm perfectly healthy, or so my doctor tells me. But I'll be seventy-four in two months, and no one lives forever. I'd like to know things are settled so there won't be any arguments after I'm gone."

"You aren't going anywhere," Stacy assured her, patting her on the arm and guiding her to a seat on the sofa. "Is something else bothering you?"

Agnes sighed. She should have anticipated this, although she wished her daughters would show more respect for her intelligence. She was well aware she would not be the first immortal woman in the history of the species, but the gentle, soothing tones in her daughters' voices suggested they thought they could convince her otherwise. "If there's a certain quilt you would like, for example, or a piece of furniture, let me know so I can put it in writing. Soon," she added, and hid a smile when they exchanged a look of dismay at the implied urgency. They deserved to be needled a bit for patronizing her.

"Just divide up everything fifty-fifty," said Laura. "We won't argue over anything."

"Of course not," Stacy chimed in. "For goodness' sake, Mom, how could we care about *things* when we've lost you?"

Laura nodded, so Agnes merely smiled, patted their hands, and suggested they return to the family room where her sons-in-law and grandchildren were watching football on television. Even as youngsters Stacy and Laura had indeed gotten along much better than the average pair of sisters, but Agnes had witnessed the sad legacy of friends whose children's amicable relationships had fractured into bitter animosity over the ownership of an antique armoire or a set of books worth only sentimental value. She did not want to think of that happening to her girls, nor did she want to stipulate that they sell everything and divide the cash. After seeing what Sylvia had gone through to find her mother's heirloom quilts Claudia had sold off, Agnes was determined to spare her daughters that ordeal.

The girls said nothing of her proposal for the rest of their visit, so two days after they departed, when their absence and the enduring winter made the house seem especially lonely and quiet, Agnes sorted through her collection of quilts with a pad of paper, a pen, and a box of new safety pins by her side. She admired the handiwork of decades, reminiscing about the creation of each quilt and mulling over who might appreciate it best. Each daughter would receive one of her two queen-size Baltimore Album quilts—Stacy the one in pastels and Laura the one in brighter hues. Sarah, who loved samplers, would adore the floral appliqué wall hanging, and the Pinwheel lap quilt simply had to go to Summer, who had encouraged Agnes to piece it from Summer's own favorite vivid Amish solids. Come to think of it, she ought to put Summer's name on the leftover fabric, too, which had sat untouched in her fabric stash since she had completed the quilt five years before.

As for Sylvia—Agnes chuckled as she wrote Sylvia's name on a piece of paper and carefully pinned it to a cheerful scrap Double Wedding Ring quilt. Surely Sylvia would remember Agnes's first quilting lessons, when Agnes, who knew nothing of sewing except needlepoint, decided to learn to quilt in order to pass the time while their men were in the service. Sylvia suggested Agnes choose a simple pattern or a sampler as her first project. Then Claudia drew her aside and told her she would master the skills more quickly and thoroughly if she chose a more challenging pattern. Agnes unwisely took her advice, for the bias edges and curved seams of the Double Wedding Ring proved too difficult for her inexpert stitches, and the resulting half-ring buckled in the middle and gapped in the seams. She never finished that quilt—the news of the men's deaths and Sylvia's subsequent departure brought the quilting lessons to an abrupt end—but twenty years later she had attempted the pattern again. Practice and a more knowing eye for color and contrast enabled her to create a lovely, comforting reminder of how far she had come since leaving Elm Creek Manor to remarry. If Sylvia inherited that quilt, she would be clever enough to understand the symbolism and generous enough to forgive Agnes one parting joke.

For each quilt and each friend or relation, Agnes affixed an identifying tag and added the information to her list. She intended to type up the list, sign it and date it, and keep it with her will in the fireproof box beneath the bed in Stacy's old room. After going through the quilts, she would consider the furniture and other belongings. She had already decided what to do with the contents of her sewing room. Since neither of her daughters quilted, she would bequeath her fabric stash, pattern books, and all her tools to Elm Creek Quilt Camp. They would surely find a good use for them.

Agnes was nearly finished when the phone rang. She climbed to her feet, shook the stiffness from her legs, and picked up in her bedroom. "Hello?" she said, gingerly lowering herself onto the edge of the bed. She should have known better than to sit on the floor for so long.

"Grandma?"

"Why, hello, Zachary," she said. "This is Zach, right, not Norman?" His voice sounded so much like his father's that it was difficult to tell.

Zach laughed. "Yeah, it's me."

"What a lovely surprise. How are you? Are you back at school already?"

"I moved back into the dorm this morning. Classes don't start until Monday," her grandson said. "Grandma, the reason I'm calling is that—well, my mom and dad were talking in the car on our way home from your house last week."

Agnes could guess the topic of discussion, but she said, "Talking about what, honey?"

"About your will. Mom said you asked her and Aunt Stacy what they wanted to inherit, you know, if there was something in particular they wanted."

"I imagine your mother didn't discuss this calmly."

"You know Mom. She was kind of upset, but Dad said it was thoughtful of you to spare them a tough job at what would obviously be a stressful time."

Good old Norman. "What do you and your sister think?"

"Rebecca's like Mom. She thinks if you pretend something can't happen to you, it won't. She made Mom and Dad stop talking about it."

"And you?"

"I didn't like talking about it, either. I don't want to think about you dying, Grandma. I don't want you to ever die."

"I appreciate that, honey."

"But since you asked—" He paused. "I know you just asked Mom and Aunt Stacy, not the kids, but—"

Gently, Agnes asked, "Is there something special you would like?"

"You know that quilt with the different colored triangles and all the black?"

"Of course," said Agnes, surprised. She was not aware he had ever given the quilt a second glance. "Would you like it?"

"Yes, please. And—your journals."

"My what?"

"Your journals. You know, the ones you started keeping during World War II."

Agnes had to think a moment before she understood. Her notebooks. She had begun the first when Richard went off to war to note news from home to include in her letters. After he was killed, she continued out of habit for nearly ten years, filling fifteen notebooks with reminders to herself, appointments, to-do lists, and the like. She wondered when Zach had learned of them, then vaguely remembered an occasion several years before when Laura was filling out a medical form and needed to know if she had ever had a particular illness. Agnes had consulted her notebooks and determined that Laura had been vaccinated at age eight.

"Why would you want those old things?" asked Agnes. "They're not very interesting, just a lot of lists, mostly. They don't read like a story, even a dull one."

"I don't care. They're an important record of our family history."

Agnes had to laugh. Her old grocery lists and hairdresser's appointments, family history? "There aren't any fascinating family stories in those old notebooks, Zach. I should have thrown them away a long time ago."

"That's exactly what you shouldn't do, and that's why I want you to set them aside for me. Someone might throw them away not knowing what they are. You're wrong to think they're trivial or worthless. They're irreplaceable and important, and that's the truth, even if you don't think so."

"Why, if they're that important to you, they're yours, of course," said Agnes, surprised.

He thanked her, and they talked of other, more pleasant matters. After they hung up, Agnes rummaged in the kitchen cabinet until she found a large padded envelope. She located her old notebooks under her sweaters in the bottom drawer of her bureau, frowned ruefully at their battered state, and slipped them into the padded envelope with a shrug. She still couldn't see why Zach wanted them so badly. Likely he would read the first few pages and wonder the same thing. Agnes ought to save him the trouble of discarding them by taking care of the job herself, but she couldn't now, not after promising to save them.

She wrote his name on the outside of the envelope and added her notebooks to the list on the pad. Then she took Summer's name from the Pinwheel quilt and pinned Zach's in its place, marking the change on the list. She would have to find something else for Summer to supplement the leftover Amish solids from her fabric stash. Summer would understand. Friends were dear, but grandchildren came first.

The invitation to participate in Sylvia's bridal quilt had arrived in the meantime, but Agnes already knew the requirements and had not bothered to read the letter thoroughly. When she had finished sorting out the future ownership of her quilts and a few other special belongings, she filed the list and decided to turn her attention to her quilt block. This time she read the letter over carefully, and tsked when she read that Diane had said Sylvia deserved to go without a wedding quilt since the surprise wedding on Christmas Eve had thwarted her friends' plans for an elaborate June affair. Agnes could imagine Diane thinking that, briefly, but not blurting it out where someone might overhear. Despite her sometimes abrasive manner, Diane cared for her friends too much to wish them any disappointment. If she had gone a bit overboard in planning the couple's wedding, it was only from the desire to please them and spare them the trouble.

It was too late to ask Sarah to change the letter, so Agnes could only hope she and Summer had been wise enough not to send Diane a copy, and not only because she might be hurt. They could not afford to discourage anyone from participating, especially one of their own. While Sylvia had many friends and admirers around the world, 140 blocks were a great many to collect in such a short period. Even if Sylvia and Andrew had not surprised them with an early wedding and had married in June, as the Elm Creek Quilters had anticipated, they still should have begun the quilt much earlier, ideally as soon as the couple announced their engagement. Agnes blamed the demise of their weekly quilting bees for the delay. Their business meetings were so full of details for Elm Creek Quilt Camp that the friends rarely had the opportunity to chat just about quilting. Finding such a time when everyone but Sylvia was present was even more difficult, since Sylvia never missed a meeting unless she and Andrew were traveling. Agnes considered the quilt camp a great adventure and was thrilled to be a part of it, but she missed some aspects of the old days.

"So many blocks," said Agnes with a sigh as she sorted through her fabric stash for hues suiting those described in the guidelines. The other Elm Creek Quilters had gladly accepted her offer when she had volunteered to assemble the blocks into a quilt top, since they knew the task meant much more than simply stitching all 140 blocks together. To avoid a cluttered or chaotic quilt, she might need to separate the blocks with strips of fabric called sashing. If not enough blocks arrived, she would need to employ more elabo-rate tricks, such as setting the blocks on point or alternating them with squares of solid fabric. Either way, she ought to make a few extra blocks just in case. If, as Summer had predicted, they received enough blocks or more than they needed, she would sim-ply save her extras for another project.

Since she could not think of one single block that represented all that Sylvia meant to her, she decided instead to make blocks reminiscent of their shared history. She began with a Bachelor's Puzzle block. How shocked Sylvia would be to learn that Agnes had known about the nickname almost from the time the Bergstrom sis-ters had bestowed it upon her! Long ago, Agnes and Richard had been unable to send word when Agnes decided on the spur of the moment to accompany him home from school in Philadelphia for the Christmas holidays, and her presence—and Richard's obvious affection for her—had confounded the sisters. Sylvia, especially, was jealous that someone had stolen away her beloved baby brother's attention, and decided to find nothing redeemable in her rival. She saw Agnes as a flighty, spoiled, pampered princess, and nothing Agnes said or did could persuade her otherwise. It was a puzzle, Sylvia said, what Richard saw in her.

Agnes chuckled to herself as she worked on the block, imagin-ing how flustered Sylvia would be to discover her little meanness had not been a secret for decades. So as to not spoil the joke, Agnes would allow Sylvia to believe Agnes had overheard the sisters using the nickname. She would not reveal that while their menfolk were overseas, Claudia had confided the secret in a spiteful attempt to win Agnes to her side after an especially heated argument with her sister.

Next Agnes pieced a Sister's Choice block for Sylvia's rash and oft regretted decision to leave Elm Creek Manor upon learning that Claudia's future husband, Harold, could have saved the lives of Richard and Sylvia's husband, James, but, out of cowardice, had done nothing. Sylvia's decision to abandon her ancestral home transformed her life, her sister's, and the manor itself. Perhaps nothing more than Agnes's own choice to marry into the Bergstrom family had influenced the course of her fate more than Sylvia's departure from the manor. If Sylvia had remained to run the family horse-breeding business, Claudia and Harold would not have driven it into bankruptcy. If the couple had not depleted the family fortune and begun selling off parcels of land and precious family heirlooms, Agnes would not have met the history professor who advised her on antique markets and later became her husband. If she had not married Joe, she would have lived out her days in the manor that had become as full of grief and despair as it had once been blessed with love and prosperity. She would not have become a mother and a grandmother. She would not have known the greatest joys of her life.

Upon completing that block, Agnes somberly began a Castle Wall. Sylvia would know at once why Agnes had chosen the pattern. More than a year after Sylvia's departure, in a rare moment of regret, Claudia had agreed to help Agnes complete a memorial quilt for Sylvia, whom they still believed would soon return. Together Agnes and Claudia had sorted through James's closet, selecting shirts and trousers and ties they knew Sylvia would recognize. From the cloth they cut diamonds and triangles and squares and sewed them into the pattern whose name conveyed all that the founders of Elm Creek Manor had wanted their descendants to find within its walls: safety, sanctuary, family, home. For a year the forsaken sisters pieced the tribute to the husband Sylvia mourned, but Claudia's own marriage had begun to crumble under the strain of grief and guilty secrets, and as she withdrew into her solitary bitterness, Agnes layered the top in the frame and quilted it alone. It had yet been incomplete when she had left Elm Creek Manor to marry Joe. After Sylvia's return to the manor, Sylvia and Agnes had finished the quilt together, and it now hung in the library, where

Sylvia and James had spent so many happy hours discussing the family business, planning for a future that would not come to pass.

Rather than evoke only sorrowful memories, Agnes next pieced a Christmas Star in celebration of Sylvia and Andrew's Christmas Eve wedding. That pattern called to mind Sylvia's favorite block, the eight-pointed LeMoyne Star, and all the variations that found their way so often into Sylvia's quilts: Virginia Star, Snow Crystals, Blazing Star, Carpenter's Wheel, St. Louis Star, Dutch Rose, Star of Bethlehem. Once Agnes completed these, she made her own favorites, the appliquéd Whig Rose, American Beauty Rose, and Bridal Wreath.

By the end of February, Bonnie had collected thirty blocks at Grandma's Attic, which she delivered to Agnes so that she might begin planning their final arrangement. To these Agnes added her own twenty-four blocks and arranged them on the design wall Joe had put up for her when she had converted Laura's old bedroom into a sewing room. The pieced and appliquéd blocks clung to the flannel surface where she placed them, and as she admired their beauty and variety, she decided that a border of split LeMoyne Stars would be just the thing to set them off best. She would start on it right away. She could always stitch a few more blocks later, if they were needed.

Agnes dreamed of a balmy summer day, Joe in his shirtsleeves cooking steaks and hot dogs on the charcoal grill, her daughters shrieking with delight in pink and yellow bathing suits as they ran through the sprinkler. She threw the red-and-white checked tablecloth over the picnic table and returned inside for plates and napkins, where she found Zach sitting at the kitchen table reading one of her notebooks. He looked up and smiled. "This is an important family record," he said, grinning. "But what the heck is oleo?"

She opened her mouth to reply but was distracted by a distant ringing. She turned to find Laura, suddenly a grown woman, ringing the doorbell on the screen door. Her expression was solemn and she did not speak. Confused, since the back door had no bell, Agnes watched as Laura rang again.

"You should probably get that," advised Zach. The summer day vanished, and Agnes woke to the dark winter night of her bedroom. She jumped and clutched her quilt, heart pounding, as the doorbell rang downstairs. She glanced at the clock on her nightstand. Good news never came to the door at nearly one o'clock in the morning. She put on her robe and slippers and hurried downstairs, remembering to check through the window before opening the door. What she saw made her fling it open.

"Bonnie, honey," she said, gasping at the sudden cold. "What's wrong?"

Hollowly, Bonnie said, "May I spend the night?"

"Of course," said Agnes, opening the door still wider and ushering in her friend. Her mind raced with questions, but Bonnie seemed dazed, shocked, lost in an uneasy dream. "You must be exhausted at this hour," Agnes said instead, leading Bonnie upstairs to Stacy's old room. "I won't need but a moment to set everything up for you. Would you like a cup of tea while you wait? A nice glass of warm milk? I like to put just a touch of vanilla in it."

Bonnie shook her head, eyes downcast. She seemed to be fighting back tears.

At a loss, Agnes made nervous small talk as she showed Bonnie the adjoining bath and set out fresh towels for her. Bonnie would need a nightgown, she thought, noting for the first time that Bonnie had brought nothing with her. She hurried to her own room and retrieved the largest and warmest nightgown she owned, and hoped it would do. Bonnie took it and shook her head again when Agnes asked her if she wanted to try it on first, if Agnes should look for something better.

It was apparent Bonnie wanted nothing more than to surrender

to a dreamless sleep. "I'll say good night, then," said Agnes, lingering with her hand on the doorknob. "Just call me if you need anything."

"Thank you," said Bonnie, stroking the flannel nightgown
absently.

Agnes shut the door and went to her own room, where she lay
awake in bed listening to floorboards creak, water flowing in the
pipes, the settling of bedsprings. When all was silent once again,
she drifted off to sleep.

Agnes woke at six, her first thoughts of Bonnie. What on earth had
brought her friend to her door, on foot, on a cold winter's night? It
could not have been a disaster with the children; Bonnie would
have remained at home with her husband and called her friends to
her side. Knowing Bonnie, she would have waited until morning to
trouble them no matter how she longed for the comfort of their
presence. No, the most logical explanation was a fight with Craig.
Trouble with a husband was what most often sent a woman from
her home in the middle of the night.

Agnes bathed and dressed, then tiptoed downstairs, pausing by
Bonnie's door. When she heard nothing, she continued on to the
kitchen, where she put on a larger pot of coffee than usual and fixed
some waffles. She read the newspaper while she ate, and a large ad
for Fabric Warehouse reminded her with a jolt that Bonnie worked
on Fridays. She would surely be in no fit state to work today, especially considering that her husband would be right upstairs. Agnes
waited until half past seven before phoning Diane and asking her to
fill in. Diane agreed, but not before asking too many questions that
Agnes evaded with difficulty. Agnes hung up, hoping she had not
given Diane any reason for suspicion besides the obvious, calling
on Bonnie's behalf when Bonnie typically took care of such matters
herself. With any luck, Diane's harried morning rendered her too

distracted to notice, which was why Agnes had phoned her instead of the more perceptive Summer.

Still listening for noises above, Agnes washed her breakfast dishes, then crept softly upstairs to her sewing room and gathered the fabrics for the pieced border, her rotary cutter and ruler, and a cutting mat. She set up her tools on the dining room table and cut fabric pieces in silence, working off her worries in the familiar, repetitive motions of measuring and cutting. Shortly after eleven o'clock, she heard Bonnie walking about upstairs, followed by the sound of the shower. Agnes set her work aside and met her friend in the kitchen. Bonnie appeared fairly well rested given the circumstances, but was clad in the clothing she had worn the previous night. Agnes had not thought of that or she would have searched around for an alternative.

"I overslept," Bonnie said. She looked around the room as if she had lost something. "I have to get to work."

"Not without breakfast," said Agnes, leading her to the table, then turning to pour her a cup of coffee. "Do you want scrambled eggs or waffles?"

"But the shop—"

"Don't you worry. I called Diane. She said she'd head over as soon as she could. She probably didn't get there on time, but she got there."

As she returned to the counter for cream and sugar, Agnes watched from the corner of her eye as Bonnie relaxed and sank back into the chair.

"Thank you," said Bonnie softly.

As far as Agnes was concerned, it was the least she could do. She convinced Bonnie to have some breakfast, and while Bonnie ate her waffles, Agnes poured herself another cup of coffee and joined her at the table. Every ounce of willpower she possessed went into appearing nonchalant as she sipped the hot, fragrant coffee and waited for Bonnie to speak.

"I left Craig," said Bonnie suddenly.

Agnes was not surprised, but she wondered if it was rude not to appear so. "For good?"

"I think so."

Bonnie continued with an account of the argument that had sent her to Agnes's for the night, and then the more heartbreaking story of the lonely, angry months that had preceded it. As Bonnie spoke, Agnes could only listen, speechless and sympathetic, her heart aching with one relentless question: Why? Why had Bonnie not shared her anguish with her friends? Each would have rallied to her side, lent her their strength. Worse yet, why had they not noticed how much she was hurting?

When Bonnie's voice trailed off at the end of her story, she stirred her coffee idly and added, "I still have the number of our marriage counselor. I'm going to ask if he can see us—or even just me—as a sort of emergency rescue case."

Agnes hid her astonishment. Nothing Bonnie had just told her suggested the marriage was salvageable. "That's fine," she said carefully, "as long as you speak to a lawyer, too."

To her relief, Bonnie nodded.

As they cleaned up the kitchen and finished washing the dishes, Agnes told Bonnie she was welcome to stay as long as she liked, but Bonnie shook her head and staunchly assured her—or herself—that she fully intended to sleep in her own bed that night. In the meantime, she had to return home for a change of clothes. Agnes offered to accompany her, and prepared to insist upon it, but Bonnie nodded almost before Agnes finished speaking.

But Bonnie's intentions would not be fulfilled. They arrived at the condo to find that Craig had changed the locks; when Bonnie tried to buy new clothes, they discovered he had canceled her credit cards. Agnes would have put the purchase on her own account, but Bonnie handed over the Grandma's Attic corporate card impassively, as if she had expected such vindictiveness from her husband. Agnes was so shocked she hardly knew what to do, but on the walk home, she certainly knew what to say.

"Come home with me," she said. "You can change clothes and call your lawyer."

"I don't have a lawyer."

"I do. He's a wonderful young man. His father looked after our affairs for years, and he took over the firm after his father passed."

"Does he handle divorces?"

"If not, he'll know someone who does."

She gave Bonnie his card as soon as they returned home. Bonnie nodded and took it upstairs with her shopping bags, but when she returned in her new knit pants and sweatshirt, she shrugged when Agnes asked her when her first appointment with the lawyer would be.

"You didn't call him?" asked Agnes.

"I don't feel up to it." Indeed, Bonnie looked as if she needed a good soak in a warm tub, preferably with a huge plate of chocolate chip cookies within reach. Or, failing that, a strong right cross capable of knocking Craig on his rear.

"Bonnie, honey, I don't think you should delay."

"I'm not even sure if I want a divorce. I don't know if I could go through with it."

"Maybe not, but a lawyer could at least tell you what your options are. And your rights."

Bonnie nodded and wandered into the dining room. Agnes followed and found her fingering the strips of fabric cut for the bridal quilt's border. Agnes did not want to add to the pressure already weighing down her friend, but Craig had proven to be more spiteful and cruel than Agnes could have imagined, and she was certain he wouldn't demur when it came to getting a lawyer on his side. "He nearly cleaned out your bank accounts," said Agnes. "He canceled your credit card. He locked you out of your home and gave you nothing to live on. That can't possibly be legal."

"At least the kids are grown." Bonnie picked up a stack of fabric diamonds and set them back down. "If they were still living at home, this would be a hundred times worse."

Agnes figured things would rapidly become a thousand times worse if Bonnie didn't take care. Agnes took her by the shoulders. "I know this is an enormous shock. I know divorce would be a drastic change and you don't want to think about it. But right now you have to do what's in your own best interest. You can be sure Craig is."

Bonnie blinked, then frowned, hard. "I wouldn't doubt it. That's what he's always done."

Finally, Agnes thought with relief. A bit of well-deserved anger. Bonnie would need that if she were to shake off this wounded bewilderment and steel herself for what was likely to be an unpleasant fight. Agnes could see it coming, even if Bonnie refused to look.

❦

Agnes knew that until Bonnie found her bearings, what she needed most was companionship and activity, so she enlisted Bonnie's help in assembling the split LeMoyne Star border. Over the weekend they cut fabric and assembled the four-pointed half stars, taking turns at Agnes's sewing machine. They worked uninterrupted except for meals and sleep, and, without consulting Bonnie, Agnes arranged for Diane to cover at Grandma's Attic. They spent the hours working in tandem, at first conversing little except to discuss the progress of Sylvia's bridal quilt. But as the weekend passed, Bonnie broke the silences more frequently with other dismaying revelations about the Markham marriage—and surprising confessions about the financial status of the quilt shop. Revenues were down, debts were high, and the rent was going up. The building's new owner seemed as unscrupulous as Craig, and Agnes concurred with Bonnie's suspicion that they intended to arrange the condo's sale with or without her consent. Agnes was not sure how that could happen since Bonnie's name was on the deed, but that was all the more reason Bonnie ought to consult a lawyer without delay.

To Agnes's consternation, Bonnie seemed as unwilling to confront this Gregory Krolich fellow as she was Craig. Her friend seemed deflated, skittish; on Sunday evening she sounded reluctant when she told Agnes she planned to return to work in the morning. Agnes quickly assured her she thought that was an excellent idea. Grandma's Attic had been Bonnie's favorite place from the day of its grand opening, and Bonnie's former confidence and optimism were more likely to be restored in familiar, beloved surroundings.

Indeed, early Monday evening Bonnie returned to Agnes's house in better spirits and was more resolute than she had been in weeks. Agnes even managed to persuade her to go to Craig's office and refuse to leave until he allowed her back into the condo. "You need it more than he does," Agnes pointed out, "since he enjoys staying away so much." Bonnie agreed, and on Wednesday morning, after arranging for Diane to open the shop, Bonnie headed for the Waterford College campus. Agnes was so proud of her that she resolved not to let her fight alone.

First she phoned her lawyer herself and told him about Bonnie's situation. He recommended a divorce attorney named Darren Taylor, describing him as smart, honest, and relentless. "Call him soon," her lawyer advised. "He's the best in the county, and you don't want your friend's husband to retain him first."

Uneasy, Agnes decided not to wait for Bonnie to return home from work. She phoned Darren Taylor herself, left a message with his assistant, and worked on Sylvia's bridal quilt impatiently while she waited for him to return the call. At noon the phone rang, and Agnes told the attorney as much of Bonnie's story as she could remember.

"Your friend's husband sounds like a real louse," said Darren.

"It's too bad Bonnie had to leave the property, but it's obvious he left her no choice. We'll have a strong case against him if she can document his actions."

"So you're willing to take the case?"

"I'd prefer to speak to your friend first, but I see no reason why not."

"Considering how her husband has frozen her assets, I'd be happy to send you a check myself if it's a matter of your retainer."

"Thanks, but what I really want to know is if your friend truly wants to go through with a divorce."

"She does," said Agnes firmly, thinking, *She will*.

"Then have her call me and we'll set up a meeting. In the meantime, tell her to secure any assets her husband might not have thought of yet—investment accounts, properties, autos—and to go over their bank records very carefully to see if there were any other unexplained withdrawals before the one that all but closed the accounts. He could have been siphoning off money from their joint accounts for years and concealing it somewhere. He acted so quickly I bet he's been planning this for some time."

Agnes quickly took notes as he spoke. "I'll tell her."

"I'm afraid this next business is rather ugly. You said he's spent a lot of nights away from home. Ask your friend if she knows where he's been staying, and with whom. If we can sue on the grounds of infidelity, any claim that she abandoned the property will lose its impact."

"I'll ask," said Agnes, but she doubted Bonnie knew or she would have mentioned it.

"This business with University Realty might prove a difficult knot to untie. Some of my colleagues have dealt with them before, and while they're unscrupulous, they always manage to keep everything nice and legal. If your friend can get me copies of her lease for the store and purchase agreement for the condo, I'll pass them along to our property law specialist."

Heartened by Darren Taylor's confidence—and the fact that they finally had some steps to take—Agnes assured him that everything would be taken care of, and that Bonnie would call him soon.

"The sooner the better," Taylor emphasized.

When Bonnie returned from work, she glowed with accomplishment: She had refused to budge from Craig's office for three hours until he had finally appeared. "And that's not idle boasting," she said with a laugh. "That old furniture in his waiting room is uncomfortable. Craig bought it because it looks like some antiques he saw at Penn State once, not because he cares about the poor visitors who have to use it."

Agnes sniffed. "How typical." Craig's reputation as a cheapskate was well earned.

"I think he would have stayed away even longer except he had to get some papers from his desk for a meeting."

Agnes smiled, proud of her. "Did he agree to move out and let you return home?"

Bonnie's face fell. "No, he didn't. But he did say I could come home to pack a suitcase."

"Well, he's become quite the altruist, hasn't he," said Agnes, and insisted that she accompany Bonnie. She was neither strong nor intimidating enough to defend Bonnie if Craig tried to harm her physically, but experience had taught Agnes that often the presence of an older woman encouraged younger men to be on their best behavior. Furthermore, her conversation with Darren Taylor had put her in a litigious frame of mind, and she thought it prudent to witness Bonnie's visit home. Heaven only knew how Craig would describe it later.

As they walked to the condo, Agnes summarized her phone conversation with Darren Taylor and urged Bonnie to contact him first thing the next morning. Bonnie hesitated and said, "I'll think about it."

What more was there to think about? Agnes wanted to ask, but determined to be a supportive friend, she linked her arm through Bonnie's and nodded.

Having some of her belongings back and wearing her own favorite clothes brought about a marked change in Bonnie's attitude, even greater than her triumph of facing down Craig at his office. Three days after her return to the condo, Bonnie came home from work bearing two grocery bags and a bottle of wine, and announced that she intended to prepare Agnes the best meal she had ever eaten. Agnes was too pleased by her friend's good cheer to ask how she could afford such a feast and instead tied on an apron and offered to help. They had a delightful evening preparing and indulging in a crown roast, sweet potatoes, salad, and a luscious chocolate soufflé for dessert. Agnes even finished off a glass of wine, but what made the occasion truly worth celebrating was that Bonnie announced her intention to contact Darren Taylor and begin divorce proceedings. "I can't be afraid of being alone," she said. "The wrong man is much worse than no man at all."

"Oh, Bonnie." Agnes reached out and touched her hand. "You have so many friends, you'll never be alone."

Tears filled Bonnie's eyes. "Now I just have to explain things to the kids."

"Do they have any inkling of what has been going on between you and Craig?"

"Who knows? I doubt it. To them we're just old mom and dad, fixtures, a unit." Bonnie sighed and swirled the last drops of wine in her glass. "They're old enough to understand the reasons why couples divorce, but I can't imagine they ever thought their own parents would. I wish for their sake Craig and I could keep things amicable, but I think once you've crossed over into hostility, you can't go back."

"You don't have to be nasty, regardless of what Craig does," Agnes assured her, and was rewarded with a grateful smile.

Agnes would take care of the nastiness herself.

❧❧

On Monday morning after Bonnie left for Grandma's Attic, Agnes waited a suitable interval before setting off on the same route. Rather than enter the quilt shop, she circled around behind the building and ducked into a shallow alcove at the rear entrance of a drugstore just across the alley. The hiding place provided a good view of the back door to Bonnie's building, but no one leaving the building would see her unless they knew to look.

She had arrived just in time; within ten minutes the door banged open and out came Craig, clad in his blue Penn State coat and blaze-orange knit hat, whistling, his hands in his pockets. Agnes sighed with relief as he walked past the car without a glance—she would not have been able to follow him driving—and continued east down the alley. She waited a few moments to see if an overnight guest would emerge a discreet few moments later, but when the door remained closed, Agnes hurried after Craig.

From the mouth of the alley Agnes spotted Craig jaywalking north across Campus Drive and turning east again down Main. She pursued him for several blocks, dodging students and professors hurrying to class, until he pushed his way through the revolving door of The Bistro, a favorite breakfast and lunch spot for locals and faculty, a popular student hangout after six.

Agnes pretended to study the menu posted in the window. She glimpsed Craig inside as he removed his hat and finger-combed his hair. She frowned and sniffed. Primping for his lady friend, no doubt, for all the good it would do him. No amount of grooming would conceal the flaws in Craig's character for long.

As Agnes watched, a man clad in a black wool coat and carrying a leather briefcase joined Craig in line and clapped him on the back. Craig seemed glad to see him, but not surprised; they shook hands like fond colleagues and waited together to be seated. "My," breathed Agnes as she watched, but unless she had completely misread Craig all these years, this particular breakfast companion was not the reason for Craig's nights away from home.

The hostess appeared, menus in hand, and led the two men through a doorway and out of sight. Agnes hastened to a window farther down the sidewalk, but although she rose up on her tiptoes, she could not see where they had been seated. She cupped her hands around her eyes and peered through the glass—and then became aware of the curious and pointed stares of the couple eating pancakes at the table on the other side of the window. Agnes felt her cheeks grow warm. "Sorry," she mouthed, backing away. Then she retraced her steps and entered the restaurant.

She sidestepped the hostess's stand and headed into the main dining area, pretending to be in search of the ladies' room. Suddenly she spied Craig and the man, who had removed his coat to reveal a suit of equally fine quality, chatting up the pretty young waitress as she poured their coffee. The man had opened his briefcase and set a thin sheaf of papers on the table, promptly distracting Craig's attention from the waitress. Agnes strolled by, heading for the REST ROOMS sign on the far wall, but stealing quick glances at the papers as she passed. They were clearly legal documents of some sort; she knew this not because she could read the small print, but because the man uncapped a silver pen and passed both pen and papers across the table to Craig as they spoke. She caught snatches of conversation from the man—"property under contention," "sole resident," and "closing"—and confident assurances from Craig consisting mostly of "No problem."

Agnes reached the hallway to the rest rooms and ducked around the corner. No problem indeed! She would bet her last spool of silk thread that the man in the well-tailored wardrobe was that despicable Gregory Krolich, and the property under contention must surely be the condo. She peered around the corner and watched as Craig capped Krolich's pen and returned it to him. They shook hands, and Krolich gathered up the papers and filed them in his briefcase.

Agnes did not linger to observe what coldhearted snakes ate for breakfast. She marched home, indignant. If she recalled correctly, Sylvia had met with that Gregory Krolich years before, when she still intended to sell her estate. She might be able to confirm his description.

To her disappointment, when Sarah answered the phone at Elm Creek Manor, she reported that Sylvia and Andrew were out running errands. "Oh, dear," said Agnes. "I have a rather urgent question for her. Could you have her call me back as soon as she returns?"

"Of course," said Sarah. "Is there anything I can do in the meantime?"

"Thank you, honey, but I don't think so. I have some questions about a local real estate company and recalled Sylvia had some dealings with them."

"Are you planning to move?"

"No," said Agnes, determined to stay on the fair side of truth. "A friend of mine may be, and she could use some advice."

"Well, the only company Sylvia's dealt with since I've known her is University Realty."

"I thought so. That's the one."

"I can tell you what Sylvia would say: Your friend should run, not walk, to another agency as soon as possible. Did you know one of their people wanted to raze Elm Creek Manor and build student apartments in its place?"

"That was Gregory Krolich, right?"

"That's right."

"Is he tall, dark hair with gray at the temples, would be distinguished if not for the obsequious smile?"

"Expensive clothes, flashy car—that's the guy."

"Thank you, Sarah," said Agnes. "You've been very helpful. Please tell Sylvia she doesn't need to return my call."

How far could Craig proceed with the sale of the condo without

Bonnie's consent? The little Agnes had overheard suggested that Craig had implied he had her consent, or at least that she could raise no objections. Krolich had seemed perfectly willing to believe him.

Agnes's sleuthing had uncovered more questions than answers, and nothing she had learned explained who or what had kept Craig away from home all those nights.

She pondered this all day as she worked on Sylvia's bridal quilt and made some last-minute revisions to her lesson plans for her Baltimore Album Appliqué class. Perhaps there was no lady friend. It was possible Craig had spent each night sleeping in his office, alone, but that seemed a great many nights to toss and turn on what Bonnie had called old, uncomfortable furniture, regardless of its resemblance to something finer at his beloved alma mater. Bonnie could not afford to hire a private detective to follow Craig, as a suspicious wife on television would do, nor could Agnes herself stake out the condo every evening.

In Agnes's experience, if a man was having an affair, his best friends knew about it. The betrayed wife usually found out from their wives, if they were close, or from clues the husband carelessly left behind. Bonnie either had found no such clues or had ignored them, and she and Craig did not seem to socialize with other couples much, other than gatherings of the Elm Creek Quilters and their families. Agnes could not imagine Craig confessing an affair to one of the Elm Creek husbands.

The only people who knew Craig as well as his friends were his coworkers, and they probably saw more of him than his family. If Craig was involved with another woman, he had probably conducted the affair from the office rather than home, especially since five years earlier Bonnie had caught him in that awful liaison with that woman from the internet.

When Bonnie called at five to say she planned to eat takeout at Grandma's Attic for supper while she caught up on some paperwork, Agnes decided to pay Craig an office visit.

First, she stopped by the Grandma's Attic building to see if his car was there and if any lights were on in the condo above. The car was parked in its usual place and the condo windows were dark, so Agnes continued on foot along the most direct route to Craig's building. As she left the back alley, she remembered what Darren Taylor had said about securing other joint assets. She would suggest to Bonnie that she drive the old compact home from work one day and store it in Agnes's garage. Let Craig walk or bum rides from his good buddy Krolich. It would serve him right.

Craig did not pass her on the way across campus. She reached his building at a few minutes to six and checked the directory posted in the lobby for the room number of the director's office. Since students rarely came to the Office of the Physical Plant, the halls were deserted except for an occasional custodian with a cleaning cart. Light spilled through one open doorway at the end of the corridor; as Agnes approached, she saw the sign announcing OFFICE OF THE DIRECTOR posted on the wall beside it. She peered inside and saw three desks bearing computers, papers, and the assorted photos and personal knickknacks that attempted to make the workspaces more homey. Not far from the desks was a waiting area, and Agnes understood at once why Bonnie had commented about it. The pieces were enough alike in design—a sort of hybrid of Shaker and Arts and Crafts—to be considered a set, but the chairs and sofa were upholstered in different fabrics and their wooden armrests and legs had been finished in stains of slightly different hues, as were several tables scattered among them. Their only other unifying features were the dings and scratches of what appeared to be generations of hard use. Unless Craig had more comfortable accommodations in his private office, he surely wasn't spending the night here.

Agnes glanced at the two doors on the far wall; one was closed, light visible through the long, narrow window beside the door. The other was open and, at that moment, Agnes heard the unmistakable sound of a file drawer slamming shut. Before she could duck out of sight, a slim woman, who had short blond hair with a touch of gray, emerged from the room, a stack of files in her arms. "Oh, hi," she said, smiling briefly at Agnes before seating herself at the largest desk with the most impressive-looking computer. "Can I help you with something?"

Agnes forced herself to smile. "No, I just wanted to see who else was working late. Is Craig still in?"

"Of course. We can barely pry him out of this place lately."

Agnes nodded knowingly. "I've heard he has . . . company most nights."

The woman's eyebrows shot up. "Who? Craig? Not unless his computer counts as company. He's too cheap to run up his own internet bill at home."

"I should have known they were only rumors." Agnes chuckled and gestured at the waiting area. "I guess they would have to be, if the furniture in his private office is as awful as this stuff. No one could sleep—or anything else—on this."

"What do you expect when he insisted on redecorating at his own expense? Between you and me, though, he's roughed it more than once. His wife was here the other day and—" Suddenly her eyes narrowed. "But that doesn't mean I believe those rumors floating around your office. Where do you work, again?"

Agnes made a dismissive gesture. "Oh, I'll bet you can guess. The office everyone hates and everyone fears they'll be transferred to. Thankfully, I'm just a temp, which is probably why you don't recognize me. At least, you don't seem to. Maybe you do. That would be nice."

The woman nodded, her brow furrowed, but Agnes didn't wait for her to puzzle it out. She bid her good-bye and hurried away.

She walked home, too absorbed in what she had learned that day to notice the chill that had descended with darkness. So. Craig stayed up late "surfing the net" as her computer-savvy younger friends liked to say. For a man with his history, that counted as having illicit company, although his assistant seemed certain he was not seeing anyone in the physical sense. Craig did not seem overly fussy, as his choice in new furniture confirmed, and Agnes could picture him being too lazy to do anything more than slouch over to the nearest sofa, lumps and scratches and all, rather than return home after a late night of computer-assisted romance.

That furniture. Something about it . . . Agnes paused and frowned. That unusual hybrid of Shaker traditions and Arts and Crafts. She had read about that style somewhere, or had seen something like it before.

"Likely at a yard sale," she said aloud, and continued homeward. Craig's assistant was right: Craig was cheap and always had been. He would leave Bonnie with nothing to show for their thirty-some years of marriage except for their children and memories unless Agnes found something more substantial than assumptions and intuition to use against him. He'd shake down Bonnie for her pocket change, if he could.

As the last two weeks before the start of the new camp season passed, Agnes learned little more about Craig or the hypothetical computer girlfriend, despite frequent attempts to follow Craig as he left the condo in the morning or work in the afternoon. She did discover that Craig took two-hour lunches at a sports bar near campus at least twice a week, where he sat alone in the clubhouse, had a beer with his sandwich, and watched three separate cable sports networks on the three giant televisions that rivaled movie screens. Her investigation of Gregory Krolich, however, turned up a few important details. Posing as a prospective tenant, she phoned University Realty and inquired about Bonnie's condo, which she had heard was for sale. The pleasant young woman who answered told her that while it was true the current tenants were moving out, all of the condos were going to be converted to student apartments, so unless that interested her . . .

"No, no," said Agnes, laughing to disguise her outrage. "How disappointing, though! It would have been so convenient to live just upstairs from that charming little quilt shop. I've always wanted to learn, you see."

But the quilt shop was moving, too, Agnes learned. They had decided not to renew their lease, and while University Realty was sorry to lose them, they welcomed the opportunity to take over the space themselves. They had outgrown their current building, which like the other businesses on that block had been converted from a single-family home, and they had long desired a storefront closer to campus, to better serve the student market.

University Realty was proceeding as if Bonnie had already signed away both condo and shop, but although Agnes made a risky visit to University Realty to obtain a brochure or flyer or something, the receptionist at the front desk told her they had no rental literature yet available, no matter how urgent her grandson's need for a student apartment was, and that despite what she might have heard, they had not yet "finalized" their plans for the building. She also asked, politely but with an edge to her voice, where Agnes had heard otherwise, but Agnes quickly left before turning in the helpful assistant, who had really been a dear and whose name she didn't recall, anyway.

Without any evidence to back up her suspicions, Agnes reluctantly decided to say nothing of her investigation to Bonnie. Passing on rumors would accomplish nothing, only fuel Bonnie's anxieties.

The first day of camp brought a welcome respite from worry. Agnes was glad to see Bonnie preoccupied with the last-minute preparations for the campers' arrival rather than Craig or Grandma's Attic. Indeed, all of her friends seemed cheerful in their work, except for Diane, who spent much of the time she and Agnes were arranging fresh flowers in the guest rooms grumbling about Bonnie's failure to appreciate her work at Grandma's Attic. Agnes hid her exasperation and pointed out that Bonnie might have other concerns on her mind, problems more significant than who worked more hours than whom. Diane snorted dismissively, but she kept her complaints to herself for the rest of the day until she drove Agnes home after the Candlelight welcoming ceremony. Bonnie had insisted on departing the manor later, by cab, rather than reveal that she was staying with Agnes. When Bonnie finally arrived, Agnes encouraged her to reclaim the Markham family car, but Bonnie only laughed and considered her suggestion a joke even when Agnes told her she was in earnest.

Bonnie insisted on returning to Elm Creek Manor separately the next morning to preserve her secret, even though that meant a bus ride that ended at the main road and a rather long walk through the woods surrounding the estate. Agnes urged Bonnie to tell her friends the truth, or at least to confide in Diane so she could ride with her and Agnes, but Bonnie said that telling Diane was like telling the entire town, and she wasn't ready for all of Waterford to know.

For the first few days of camp, Bonnie's arrangements seemed to work adequately well. She got to work almost on time, and returned home only a little later than usual. Then at lunchtime on Wednesday, Sarah came to the table where Agnes sat eating with her four Baltimore Album students and asked Agnes to join her. Sarah's voice was so urgent that Agnes immediately agreed and excused herself, following Sarah to a separate table at the back of the banquet hall where Sylvia and Diane already waited.

"Has anyone seen Gwen?" asked Sarah as she sat down. Sylvia and Diane shook their heads.

Their solemnity sent a shiver of alarm through Agnes.

"Bonnie didn't show up this morning," said Diane. "We've called the shop and the condo, but no one answers."

"Didn't show up?" Agnes looked around the circle of friends, confused. "Of course not. She had to open Grandma's Attic this morning. She isn't due in until her workshop."

"Her workshop began at eleven," said Sylvia.

"Or at least it was supposed to." Beneath Sarah's concern lingered a trace of irritation. "We had to juggle the schedule to cover for Judy, remember? It was Bonnie's idea to close Grandma's Attic for a long lunch."

Agnes did not recall; probably Sarah had been too harried to tell everyone. "Maybe she forgot." But why did she not answer the phone? Likely she had missed the bus and had been forced to take a later one, and even now was en route to the manor. Agnes should have insisted she take her car. What if Bonnie had tried to, and Craig had stopped her?

Agnes tried to disguise her fear. "Someone—one of us ought to go down there and make sure she's all right."

Sylvia patted her hand. "Summer's already on her way."

"Well—I think we should call again anyway. Sarah, may I borrow your cell phone?"

Sarah agreed and showed her how to use it. Cupping the phone in her palm to conceal the display, Agnes quickly dialed Grandma's Attic and then her own home. Only answering machines responded.

She returned the phone to Sarah, who meanwhile had been going over the schedule with the others. "No answer," she said, and pretended to listen as her friends debated how to cover for another absent instructor. They should call the police. Something was dreadfully wrong, and Agnes knew it.

Just then Gwen arrived, and cheerfully admonished them for huddling together rather than mingling among their guests. In response, Sarah asked her to emcee the evening program.

Gwen shrugged. "Sure. I thought Bonnie was doing it."

"Maybe she will, but she didn't show up for her workshop this morning, so I thought I should have a backup plan."

"Didn't show up?" Gwen pulled out a chair and sat down. "Why not?"

"No one knows," said Agnes. But Bonnie had meant to come; they had spoken about her workshop at breakfast. "She didn't call in, and no one's answering the phone at the store."

"You tried her at home, right?"

"Well, yes," stammered Agnes, "but—well, she's not there, either." It was not exactly a lie; she had not wasted a call to the condo, but someone else had tried.

Sarah and the others explained the situation to Gwen, but Agnes sat silently with her own churning thoughts. She should tell their friends what she knew. Craig was a strong and unpleasant man, and he was furious with his wife. Bonnie could be in danger, and Agnes's silence might prolong it.

As soon as Sarah finished with the schedule, Agnes hurried to the parlor, where she took a few deep breaths to calm herself as she flipped through the phone book for the Waterford College listings. She called Craig's office. "Is Mr. Markham in?" she demanded.

"Yes, he is. May I ask who's calling?"

Agnes recognized the voice of the blond woman she had met in the outer office and lowered her voice half an octave. "This is Jane in accounting. He was supposed to return my call. What time did he get in this morning? Did he just arrive?"

"He was here at eight-thirty when I arrived. I'm sorry he didn't return your call right away. He probably didn't realize it was so urgent. Please hold and I'll transfer you."

"Never mind," growled Agnes and slammed down the phone, heart pounding. At least she knew Craig was not driving to Mexico with Bonnie tied up in the trunk of his car, but that did not mean he had not harmed her. Summer was on her way to Grandma's Attic. If there was any sign of foul play, she would call.

Ordinarily Agnes had Wednesday afternoons off, but today she lingered at the manor, assisting Sarah to make up for the absent Judy,

Bonnie, and now Summer, who did not call with news. Three times Agnes slipped away to call Grandma's Attic and home, and once she even tried the condo, but Bonnie did not answer. At midafternoon, Gwen passed her in the hallway on her way out the back door. "I'm going to Grandma's Attic if anyone needs me," she said.

"Promise you'll call," said Agnes.

"I will," promised Gwen, with a reassuring grin, "unless the phones have been knocked out."

When Gwen did not call by supper, Agnes figured that was precisely what had happened.

She had no appetite, but Sarah had asked her to stay to disguise the dwindling numbers of Elm Creek Quilters. Diane had already left to feed her family before the evening program, so after the meal, Agnes asked Matt to drive her home in the Elm Creek Quilts minivan. It was almost seven by the time she unlocked her own front door and hurried inside. There was no sign of Bonnie, not downstairs or in the guest room. She returned downstairs to the dining room and, as her glance fell upon the split LeMoyne Star borders she and Bonnie had assembled together, she berated herself for putting Bonnie's desire for secrecy ahead of her safety.

She hurried to the phone and dialed Craig's office again. When only voicemail responded, she called the condo.

He answered on the fourth ring. "Hello?"

"Craig? This is Agnes Emberly."

"Oh. Hi." There was wariness in his tone, but no hostility, no guilt.

"Bonnie didn't come to work today, and we're all a bit worried. I wondered if you might know where she is."

"My guess is she's still downstairs cleaning up the mess."

"Cleaning?" Then she was all right. "What mess?"

"I don't know exactly. Maybe a robbery. There were cop cars parked out front this morning."

"My goodness," exclaimed Agnes. "Are you sure Bonnie's not hurt?"

"Yeah, yeah, she's fine. She and a couple of other Elm Creekers keep coming out back to throw junk in the Dumpster. Looks like a lot of damage was done."

Agnes bristled at the satisfaction in his tone. "It's a pity you can't find it in your heart to sympathize with your wife. You know how much that shop means to her."

"Listen, you don't know anything about me or my wife or how that store has dragged us down. If this is what it takes for her to give up on it, that's fine by me."

"Bonnie deserves far, far better than you," Agnes declared, but he had hung up the phone with a crash.

It was nearly midnight before Bonnie came home. She sank into a chair, wordless, exhausted, as Agnes ran to fetch her a warm quilt and fix a cup of tea. She refused Agnes's offer of food, but Agnes made her a sandwich anyway, and when she brought it to her, Bonnie wolfed it down as if she had not eaten all day.

"I heard there was a robbery," said Agnes, and Bonnie told her the whole story. Agnes listened with tears in her eyes as Bonnie described the destruction.

"The police think it was an inside job," Bonnie concluded dully.

Agnes was not surprised, but she asked, "Why do they think so?"

"Because there were no signs of a forced entry, and because more was ruined than taken."

Agnes took her hand. "Bonnie," she said gently, "do you think Craig is responsible?"

"No." Bonnie shifted in her chair and pulled her hand away. "I know he isn't."

Agnes remembered the satisfaction in his voice as he recounted the crime to her, and Darren Taylor's suspicions that he had been planning the divorce for a long time. "He could have used the spare key in the condo. He's entirely capable of something like this, especially given the circumstances."

"He's capable, all right, but he didn't do it. I gave the spare key to Diane a long time ago so she could open the shop occasionally. He obviously didn't use my key, since he hasn't been near it in weeks."

But before then he had had ample opportunity to duplicate it secretly. "Did you tell the police about the divorce?"

"The divorce, the debts, everything. They had so many questions. I heard Gwen tell them she thinks I forgot to lock the door last night, and they wrote that down, but I don't think they believed it. I know I locked the door, but I wish I wasn't so certain."

"Why not?"

"If the police say it's an inside job, the insurance company might refuse to pay."

Agnes felt a chill. Suddenly she thought of the personal expenses Bonnie had charged to Grandma's Attic in the past few weeks, the "debts and everything" she had confided to the police.

"Everything will be all right," she said, embracing her friend, and wishing she believed it.

CHAPTER SIX

Judy

I f Judy's mother had not come down with pneumonia soon after Christmas, Judy might never have considered leaving Waterford, even though her mother lived alone and the long drive to suburban Philadelphia made frequent visits difficult. Instead Judy had often reflected that one day she might be forced to put her mother in a retirement community or bring her to Waterford to live with them, taking her away from her Philadelphia home and the close, nearly lifelong friendships she had developed within the Vietnamese immigrant community there. But that January—for the fourth weekend in a row—Judy felt as if she spent more time in the car than caring for her mother, and it occurred to her that life would be so much simpler if she, Steve, and Emily were to relocate.

She allowed herself to imagine, for a moment, rainy Saturday afternoons chatting over tea with her mother in the big house where Judy had grown up, Emily and her grandmother on the sofa reading a book together, Steve helping his mother-in-law tend her garden. Then she reluctantly dismissed the notion. She was on track for a promotion to full professor in the Computer Sciences department, Steve enjoyed reporting the local news for the *Water-*

ford Register, and Emily was firmly attached to her second-grade teacher and circle of friends. Bringing her mother to Waterford was the far more logical solution, but Judy knew leaving her home would break her mother's heart.

The first day of the spring semester, Judy proposed the move to Steve over breakfast, presenting it as a joke. To her surprise, he told her he had entertained similar thoughts, adding that he had long wished for an opportunity to work for a larger paper. Moreover, Emily would benefit from a closer relationship with her grandmother, and Philadelphia was nearer to his family, but still far enough away that they could not visit without advance warning. "I'm all for it if you are," Steve assured her, but he regarded her curiously. "I can't believe you'd be able to leave Elm Creek Quilts, though."

"You're right," said Judy. "I couldn't."

Steve shrugged and finished his cereal so nonchalantly that she doubted he was genuinely disappointed. Still, she wondered why he had never mentioned his desire to work for a larger paper.

Besides, Steve was right. She could never leave Elm Creek Quilts. Her friends would never understand.

Her mother fully recovered and soon insisted that Judy stop dragging her family across the state every weekend just to check on her. Relieved, and guilty because of her relief, Judy agreed, and soon she was too caught up in the busy routine of the new semester to think about moving. She might have forgotten about it altogether if not for an unexpected email from a former graduate-school classmate, now a full professor at Penn. He had read her most recent paper in the *Journal of Theoretical Computer Science* and could not believe she had not applied for the opening in his department, where they were just embarking on a more advanced stage of related research in a new, state-of-the-art facility. Had she missed the advertisement in the *Chronicle of Higher Education*, or was Waterford College really treating her that well?

Judy never bothered skimming the want ads, and Waterford College treated her fine, but she clicked on the link Rick had provided to an online article from the *Philadelphia Inquirer.* Reading the description of Penn's facility made her alternately admiring and envious. Waterford College's computer systems were adequate to her needs, but Penn's read like the catalogue of her wildest dreams. She could shave years of number-crunching from her current projects, which would allow her to develop her theories in ways she never could have otherwise contemplated.

"Rick, you are more fortunate than you know," murmured Judy, recalling the brilliant but unfocused student who had never made it into the lab before noon and who had twice written half a dissertation before scrapping it for a new subject. On impulse, she went to the home page for the *Chronicle* and searched the archives for the ad. Rick was right to contact her; her experience and interests dovetailed with their criteria perfectly. She would be ideal for the job— as would hundreds of other professors at far more prestigious universities, professors who had not spent their entire careers at small, private, rural colleges much better known for their achievements in the liberal arts than anything in the sciences.

It was nice of Rick to think of her, but she was far too busy to apply for a job she had no chance of getting.

She tried to put Penn and its wonderful new research facility out of her thoughts. She didn't even tell Steve about the job, knowing he would insist she apply anyway. Then, two days later, Gwen came to her office, angry and miserable. Once again the search committee had passed her over for department chair, this time with the asinine excuse that her research was irrelevant. As a scientist, Judy was hard-pressed to find any relevance in most of the papers churned out on that side of the campus, but Gwen's research had always seemed to provide valuable, fascinating historical information. Judy wondered if other factors had influenced the decision, but Gwen was so depressed Judy decided not to pester her with questions.

She thought it over after Gwen left and decided her friend might have struck the infamous glass ceiling head-on without realizing it, deceived because the committee had, in fact, chosen a woman. They clearly thought Gwen had gone as far as she could, despite her past accomplishments. The same could one day be said about Judy, once scholars at other schools made advances in her field that her limited resources simply would not allow.

She told Steve about the position that evening, and he agreed that she would be foolish not to apply. Unfortunately, he also insisted she was guaranteed to get the job, which displayed a charming faith in her abilities and an overwhelming ignorance of the competition. "Don't clear out your desk at the *Register* yet," she begged. "And don't tell the Elm Creek Quilters. They'll take it personally. They'll wonder what they did to make me want to leave, when to them, leaving is incomprehensible."

It would also save her embarrassment later when she had to tell them she didn't get the job.

She started assembling her application package that weekend, wishing she had updated her curriculum vitae long ago, wishing she had begun more than six days before the deadline. Unfortunately, she could not work at the office without attracting the attention of her graduate students, who would be dismayed to hear she would consider leaving them. Instead she took her laptop to coffee shops between classes and student conferences, and stayed up long after putting Emily to bed. Caffeine, Steve's encouragement, and images of that gleaming new research facility sustained her until she ran headlong into her deadline. A former professor of hers had a saying: "Better finished than perfect," and Judy repeated his words glumly as she dropped off her application package at the overnight delivery service the day before it was due. She sent Rick a confirming email, and then there was nothing to do but wait.

Wait, and catch up on all the work she had neglected in the meantime. A stack of papers awaiting grades collected dust on her desk, a graduate student needed to discuss his upcoming candidacy exam, and the first day of quilt camp was barely two months away. Judy had taught computer quilt design many times before and would need only to update her materials, but the Bindings and Borders workshop would be entirely new, and she had yet to finish a single sample. The block for Sylvia's bridal quilt was due a week after the start of quilt camp, which Judy considered rather poor planning. They were all swamped at that time of year despite spring break at the college and, given that they had already missed the wedding, it would have been more reasonable to give themselves an extra week.

She knew the perfect pattern to use for Sylvia's quilt, but since the sample quilts were needed sooner, she decided to complete the border examples first, snatching spare moments from her obligations to her family and the college wherever she could find them. On impulse she decided to sew her sample borders into a quilt top of ten horizontal rows and to finish each of the four sides in a different style. Days later, as she draped the completed quilt top on the living room floor for inspection, she couldn't help laughing. It was without a doubt the most eccentric quilt she had ever made.

"What's so funny?" Emily entered the room and took her hand, inspecting the quilt top. "Wow, Mom. That's great."

Judy put her head to one side and studied the quilt top critically. "Do you really think so?"

"Yeah, I like the colors and how every row is different."

"You don't think it's a little too bizarre?"

"Uh-uh. Can I use it in my room when it's done?"

Judy smiled, thinking of how the exotic batiks would clash with the pastel floral decor Emily had selected three years before. "It doesn't really go with your room."

"I could paint the walls. Please? I'll do it myself."

Judy laughed. She should not have been surprised that Emily, who over the past year had developed a keen affinity for German opera with no encouragement from her tone-deaf parents and who had more recently begun wearing her straight black hair in two asymmetrical braids bound by anything from yarn to bread bag twist-ties, would appreciate her quilt enough to redecorate her bedroom to suit it. "No way I'd let you paint your room by yourself," Judy said, "but your dad and I will talk about it." When Emily cheered, Judy added, "Remember, this quilt isn't finished yet, and I'll still need it all summer at quilt camp."

Disappointed, Emily said, "Maybe I can use it before quilt camp. When are you going to finish it?"

"As soon as I can." She glanced at her watch; on Saturdays, Grandma's Attic stayed open until five o'clock. While Emily went off to her room to dress for soccer practice, Judy found Steve working in the computer room and asked if he would mind taking Emily so Judy could shop for backing fabric and batting in the meantime.

Steve agreed, adding, "Are you finally going to use that gift certificate?"

"Absolutely not. You know I can't set foot in the Fabric Warehouse. It's incredibly disloyal to Bonnie. What if someone I know sees me?"

"That's not likely, since none of your friends will shop there, either." Steve grimaced in sympathy. "I know how you feel, but my mother has been bugging me ever since Christmas."

"I wish she had never bought it for me."

"I'm sure to her it seemed like the perfect gift for a quilter. Look at it this way. If you spend the certificate on batting and backing, you'll satisfy my mother without acquiring any fabric you'll use in a quilt top later. The Elm Creek Quilters will never know."

It still seemed traitorous, but Steve's mother had already paid for the gift certificate, so at least Judy wouldn't be giving them any of her own money. As for her guilt and the money she otherwise would have spent at Grandma's Attic, she would just have to make up for them with an extravagant shopping spree that would leave Bonnie gaping in astonishment.

The Fabric Warehouse took up most of a strip mall on the northwest fringes of town. When Emily was a toddler, Judy used to shop at the children's clothing boutique next door, whose windows were now empty except for a sign announcing the space was available for rent. Judy's last trip to the mall had occurred years before, when she and Summer had accompanied Bonnie on a scouting mission during Fabric Warehouse's holiday sale. Bonnie had ordered them to disguise themselves in head scarves and dark glasses, which only drew attention, made Judy feel ridiculous, and probably fooled no one.

Once inside, Judy steered her shopping cart directly to the batting section and chose two large rolls. Determined not to browse, she went straight to the shelves of fabric bolts along the far wall and selected a cream tone-on-tone print similar to one she had seen in Grandma's Attic. Beneath the fluorescent lights, it looked good enough for the back of a quilt, and if her friends happened to see it, they would assume she had purchased it from Bonnie.

She joined the line at the cutting table where two unsmiling employees in long green aprons unrolled bolts of fabric and snipped away at them with shears. The wait troubled Judy less than the realization that she had not seen such a long line at Bonnie's shop since her last fall clearance.

"Don't I know you?"

The voice behind Judy was unfamiliar, so she ignored it and waited for one of the ten people in front of her in line to turn around. Then she felt a tap on her shoulder. Stifling a groan, she turned her head enough to take in a woman in a red wool coat and a platinum blond pageboy. "Hi, Mary Beth," said Judy weakly. "How are you?"

Mary Beth eyed her with suspicion. "Surprised to see you here, that's for sure."

Judy gestured to her shopping cart. "My mother-in-law got me a gift certificate for Christmas."

"I would kill for a mother-in-law like that. Mine's always buying me these horrible tacky sweaters." Mary Beth shrugged, then brightened. "Does this mean you're no longer in with Bonnie Markham and that gang? If that's the case, you're always welcome to rejoin my guild. Those Elm Creekers are so high-and-mighty, don't you think? Expecting everyone to drop everything and make their precious Sylvia a quilt block. What is she thinking, getting married at her age? What is she, eighty-five or something?"

"Not quite," said Judy shortly, turning back around. "And I'm still in with that gang."

"Oh, pardon *me,*" said Mary Beth, in a falsely sugary voice. "No offense. Speaking of offense, I wonder what Miss Bonnie will think when she finds out you were shopping here."

Judy said nothing. She should have invented an excuse for her mother-in-law, anything rather than shop the competition. But it was too late now. Let Mary Beth tattle if she felt so compelled. "Bonnie's heard about my mother-in-law. She'll understand why I had to use the gift certificate. She'll understand, and she won't hold it against me. That's what friends do." She couldn't resist adding, "I don't suppose you'd know that."

She sensed Mary Beth seething behind her and heard her storm away. Judy glanced over her shoulder to find Mary Beth halfway to the thread display and the rest of the line moving forward to fill her place.

❧

Two days later, Judy received an email from Rick. He would be passing through on his way home from Pittsburgh tomorrow and hoped she wouldn't mind treating him to lunch. Judy wrote back that she didn't mind and sent directions to her office.

He arrived shortly after ten. His longish red-blond hair had gone gray at the temples and he had put on a good forty pounds, but otherwise he could have been the same perpetual student she had known back in grad school. He had been working on his doctorate for five years before Judy joined the lab at Princeton, and he had remained for at least three years after she had graduated. Rumor had it their advisor called in favors so that Rick would not be dismissed for failing to complete his degree within the required time span, but whenever any of his friends tried to confirm this, Rick grinned and made up even wilder tales.

Judy showed him around her lab, painfully aware of how it must compare to his, but Rick nodded agreeably and demonstrated unusual restraint in his jokes about the age of her computers. Her graduate students were awed to meet the man who had authored so many of the papers Judy distributed as required reading and, to Judy's delight, Rick seemed impressed with their work and how well they discussed it. Suddenly it occurred to Judy that at that moment she could be in the middle of a job interview.

Before he could mention the position in front of her students, Judy got their coats and suggested they go to lunch. They walked a few blocks south of campus to a popular coffee shop with surprisingly good food, where Judy teased, "This is what you get when you invite yourself to lunch at the last minute."

"Next time I'll offer to treat," said Rick, as he eyed the café with mock distaste. Judy happened to know he had virtually camped out in his favorite coffee shop back in grad school, and she doubted he had changed much. Inside, he ordered the largest sandwich on the menu plus a luscious pastry Judy had often been tempted to try but had managed to resist. She settled on the tabbouleh and hummus platter and black coffee.

They grabbed a table in the corner and caught up on the news of their families while they ate. Rick pretended not to remember Steve's name and referred to him as the guy every heterosexual male in the department had hated from the moment he and Judy went on their first date. Judy teased him by pretending to have lost count of his divorces, then was astounded to hear he actually had one more than she recalled, and that he was planning to marry again in October. "Maybe you should quit while you're ahead," she told him, to which he replied that he couldn't stop now, so close to the record.

After he returned to the counter for a second cup of coffee, he took a sip and remarked, "They love you."

"Who?"

"The search committee."

"How much do they love me?"

"You're in the top five."

Her heart thumped, but she forced a nonchalant grin and said, "That's it? Not even the top three?"

He shrugged. "Sorry. I did what I could."

"I don't doubt it." She sat back, taking this in. "What exactly do I owe you?"

"Not a cent. Just accept the job if they offer it, come to Penn, and do brilliant work for the rest of your career."

She folded her arms and regarded him. "Do you help all your old grad school friends like this?"

"No, just those friends who are underserving themselves and the academic community by spending their careers in a backwater when they ought to be at the forefront of their fields."

Judy had to laugh. "You sounded exactly like Dr. Saari when you said that."

"Did I?" For a moment Rick looked guilty. "Would you be offended if I confessed this was his idea? You always were his favorite student. Don't get me wrong. I wholeheartedly agreed with his recommendation; I just can't take credit for it."

"So you're promoting my application as a favor to Dr. Saari."

"I'm promoting your application because you're the best candidate. However, he did remind me that he could have let the graduate school kick me out on a technicality a year before I would have graduated."

"I'll have to thank him, then, not you." She sipped her coffee and found that it had cooled. "Waterford College is not a backwater."

"Not if you're in the liberal arts. Judy, your doctorate is in Computer Engineering. Your undergrad degree is in Electrical Engineering. You can't tell me you're satisfied teaching computer programming. It's not your fault you got knocked up and had to take the first job that came along, but you don't have to suffer for the rest of your life."

"That's not exactly what happened."

"Close enough. If your hubby had had a real job you would have been able to afford another year of grad school while waiting for the job offers to roll in."

"I might have been waiting a very long time. The economy wasn't especially kind to new Ph.D.s that year."

"Which is why you should have waited it out, and would have, if not for Emily, and if not for the instability of Steve's freelance writing income."

Judy reluctantly had to agree, but she refused to admit that to Rick. She looked away, pretending to check the line at the front counter. She was wondering aloud how long she would have to wait for a refill when she spotted Sarah stirring cream and sugar into a carry-out cup. Judy was so startled she could not return Sarah's wave, and she sat riveted in place as Sarah crossed the room to join them.

"Judy, hi," said Sarah, smiling and indicating the two cups in her hands. "I thought I'd get my caffeine fix while Sylvia's getting her hair done."

"You must have had a late night," Judy said, and silently scolded herself for being so nervous. Sarah could not possibly know what she and Rick were discussing.

"Oh, no, this one's a peace offering for Sylvia. I'm late."

"Sorry you can't join us," said Rick, grinning at Sarah.

"Oh. Rick, this is my friend Sarah McClure. Sarah, this is Rick Balrud, an old friend from grad school. He's visiting from the University of Pennsylvania."

Sarah set down one of the cups and shook his hand "Hi. Welcome to Waterford. I'm impressed you were able to find it without a Sherpa or a global positioning system."

"Who says I didn't have both?" Rick's grin deepened and he held her hand longer than necessary.

Sarah glanced at her watch and picked up her cup again. "I'm late. Got to go. Nice to meet you."

"You, too." Rick watched as Sarah hurried away, then turned back to Judy. "She's cute. Married?"

"Yes, happily," said Judy sharply. "This is why you go through so many wives. You always think your true soul mate is right around the next corner."

His eyebrows rose. "Who said anything about my soul mate? I'm not that deep. I'm content with a nice pair of—"

"Don't say it." Judy waved him to silence. "Not about my friend."

Rick feigned innocence. "Eyes. I was going to say eyes."

"You're awful. You always have been."

"I know." He sipped his coffee. "Fortunately, I'm also a genius."

On the walk back to Judy's office, Rick told her she would soon receive a letter asking her to be available to travel during the week of March 24. If she were one of the top three candidates, she would be invited for an interview with the selection committee, comprised of the department chair, several professors, two graduate students, and one undergrad. They would provide the usual campus tour, job placement conference for the spouse, and meals with selected members of the department, which, Judy knew, was where most of the committee members would make up their minds rather than at the formal interview. She would also need to present a graduate-level seminar and guest lecture in an undergraduate class, the topics of which she should send by return mail so that they could match her with suitable courses.

Judy thanked him for the advance warning. She was familiar with the standard interview hoops candidates were obligated to jump through, having served on several search committees herself, but the last job she had applied for was the one she currently held.

Steve was thrilled by the news, although Judy tried to temper his enthusiasm by reminding him she had not made it to the top three yet. "You'll make it," said Steve, kissing her. "Why is it that everyone else is so much more aware of your abilities than you are?"

"You're blinded by love."

"On the contrary, love has opened my eyes."

Judy rolled her own eyes at that, but she was moved and decided to give him an early Valentine's Day treat that night after Emily went to sleep.

Two days later, on the real Valentine's Day, Steve surprised her by showing up at the lab in the middle of the afternoon and inviting her on a walk. Snow had fallen that morning and the wind still blew cold, but Steve looked so earnest that Judy quickly bundled up in her coat and scarf and followed him outside.

They walked arm in arm until the cold compelled them to stuff their hands into their pockets. "I want you to know that I fully support you and your career," Steve began. "Whatever you've wanted to do, I've always backed you up. I've always adjusted."

"I know you have." He didn't need to remind her of that. He had moved to Waterford without knowing if freelancing for the local paper would ever develop into something more permanent. When Emily was younger, he had stayed home to care for her, putting off his writing for weekends and evenings when Judy was home. It made sense, he said whenever Judy told him how much she appreciated him. Judy's work paid more and provided benefits. If their roles were reversed, no one would remark about what a devoted parent Judy was if she stayed home. Judy couldn't dispute that, but she was still convinced that only three men in a hundred would have sacrificed their own careers for their wives' so willingly.

She took a deep breath through her scarf. "Are you telling me you don't want to adjust anymore? I'm overdue to sacrifice for you. I'll turn down the Penn job if you want."

"No. No. That's the last thing I want." He paused. "I sent a letter and a packet of clips to a guy I know on the *Inquirer* editorial board. The editor of the news division wants me to come in for an interview."

"That's great!"

"Thanks. It wouldn't be for some cub reporter position, either. They liked my investigative pieces on the college embezzlement scandal so much that they're considering me for a senior position, not just comparable to what I have now but a significant step up."

"Oh, Steve." She was so proud she flung her arms around him. "I always said you were too good for the local rag."

"They haven't offered me the new job yet, and if they do, it won't mean anything if you don't get the job at Penn. As much as I want to make the jump, I can't justify doing so if it means a commuter marriage."

"It wouldn't necessarily—"

"Judy, you can't quit your job for me." He said this with such resolve that she knew he had seriously considered it. "The cost of living is higher out there, and my increase in salary won't compensate for the loss of your income."

Not to mention Judy's work would screech to a halt if she lacked a research facility. She could hardly build one in the basement. "So where does that leave us?"

"I've thought about it, and—"

At that moment, a plump woman carrying a tote bag appeared from behind a cluster of snowy pines and veered away just in time to avoid crashing into them. As she murmured an apology and hurried on, Judy recognized her fellow Elm Creek Quilter. "Bonnie?" she called out, fumbling with gloved hands to lower her scarf.

Bonnie spun around. "Oh, hi. Hi, Steve."

"Hi," said Steve. "Where are you going in such a hurry?"

"Oh, well—" Bonnie glanced over her shoulder as if searching for an escape. "I'm going to see if I can catch Craig before he leaves work. You didn't happen to see him pass this way?"

They hadn't, but Steve asked if Bonnie wanted them to pass along a message in case they saw him before she did. Bonnie demurred through a shaky smile and told them she had to hurry off.

"See you tonight at the business meeting," Judy called after her, wondering at her haste. "Do you think she overheard?"

"Not a chance."

"But she looked so startled, like she had caught us plotting a political coup."

Steve laughed and put his arm around her as they walked on. "She's probably on her way to a romantic Valentine's Day rendezvous with Craig, and she's embarrassed that we caught her."

Judy knew enough about Craig to doubt it, but she wanted to believe Steve was right. "So," she said, remembering the question he had not yet answered. "What have you been trying to tell me?"

He stopped and took her gloved hands in his. "I want you to try very hard to get that job at Penn. And when they offer it to you, I very much want you to accept."

❧❧

Early the next week, a letter from the Department of Computer Sciences arrived and warmly informed her that she was one of five candidates for the position of associate professor. Thanks to Rick's warning, Judy was able to assemble the information they requested well in advance of their deadline. As she sent it off via certified mail, she hoped they awarded points for promptness.

A week passed. Judy knew the supplemental information had arrived, but all Rick would say in his email was that the top three candidates would receive information about their campus visits by mid-March. He told her to be optimistic and reminded her to keep the week of March 24 open. The date sounded familiar, and one glance at the calendar confirmed it: The twenty-fourth was the first Monday of spring break, which would have been ideal for any professor not involved with Elm Creek Quilts. Torn, Judy eventually decided against asking Sarah to cancel her classes for the opening session of quilt camp. Her computer design classes had been filled for weeks, and she couldn't ask any of her friends to take over her Bindings and Borders workshop when she had not yet had the chance to work the bugs out of her new lesson plans. Besides, she couldn't cancel without offering an explanation.

Just in case, she revised her lesson plans carefully, making them so detailed that almost any of her friends could pick them up and run the class from scratch. After that, and in between her usual obligations, she worked on her guest lecture and grad student seminar, just in case. She grew accustomed to lifting a fork to her mouth with one hand and typing furiously on her laptop with her other, since her lunch break was the only time she could work unobserved. She felt a twinge of guilt thinking of how long ago she had last arranged to meet Gwen for lunch, but she promised herself she would make up for it after she returned from Penn. If they invited her.

On the first Friday of March, Judy spent an extended lunch break at the Daily Grind revising the last section of her lecture notes for the undergraduate course and wondering how much longer she would be able to endure the twin burdens of waiting for news from Penn and keeping her application a secret from her friends, especially when Steve was bursting to tell his colleagues about his triumphant interview earlier that week. Judy was thrilled for him and glowed when she recalled how the editors had praised his work, but she cautioned him to keep it to himself. If one did not count the transient population of college students, Waterford was like any small town, with at most three degrees of separation between any two residents. It was not easy to keep secrets when everyone knew someone who knew everyone else.

A shadow fell across the keyboard. "Hey, Judy."

Judy jerked her head up, startled by Summer's sudden greeting. "Oh, hi. How are you?"

"Don't worry, I'm not here to interrupt. I just wanted to say hi."

"Don't be silly. It's too hard to find a free table this time of day. Sit down." Judy quickly saved her document and shut down the computer before moving it out of the way. "Are you working at Grandma's Attic today?"

"Yes, I'm working." A slight frown touched Summer's lips, but it quickly vanished. "Diane came in, too. You should come by some-time and see all the new blocks for Sylvia's quilt."

"I'd love to. I need to buy fabric for my block, too." Judy did not mention that she had stopped by the quilt shop on her way to work on that very errand and found the lights off and the door locked. Bonnie would not be happy to learn that her employees had not opened the store on time, but she wouldn't hear about it from Judy.

As Summer ate, they talked about the upcoming camp season and about their progress on Sylvia's bridal quilt, which Judy was embarrassed to admit had completely slipped her mind until the previous evening, when she had come across the invitation letter while cleaning her sewing table.

"If you run out of time you could always buy one of those bar-gain kits at the Fabric Warehouse," said Summer with a teasing smile.

Judy's heart thumped. They knew. That awful Mary Beth had told on her, just as she had insinuated.

Summer laughed. "I'm just kidding. You have plenty of time. I haven't started my block, either."

Relieved, Judy fought to compose herself and managed a feeble joke about Summer's poor opinion of her. Summer left soon after that, so Judy got back to work before her guilty conscience gave away something more important than anxiety over a quilt block deadline.

As she glanced up to be sure Summer had gone, Judy's gaze fell on two young men waiting in line. When the taller, golden-haired one turned her way, she recognized Diane's youngest son, Todd, but she did not know his friend. They were laughing and joking and jostling each other, heady with the freedom of their off-campus senior lunch privileges. Todd paid for a cup of coffee and two frosted crullers, which he left on the counter while his friend placed his order. Just then, Todd bent over to tie his shoe, and in the moment while the server's back was turned, Todd's friend removed the lid from Todd's cup, poured half the contents into the tip jar, and replaced the lid. By the time Todd rose and the counter clerk placed the friend's drink on the counter, the friend was scanning the bakery case, hands in his coat pockets.

Surprised, Judy watched while the friend paid the cashier and Todd picked up his plate and coffee, tested the weight of the cup, frowned, and removed the lid. Judy could not hear his exchange with the clerk, but it was evident Todd complained and asked for his cup to be filled to the top. The server checked it, frowned in puzzlement, and was about to oblige when the woman next in line spoke up and gestured to the tip jar. The server looked from the tip jar to Todd, his expression stormy, and his voice rose enough for Judy to make out a demand that the two boys clean up the mess. Todd's friend burst out laughing, grabbed his lunch, and made a quick dash for the door. Todd, obviously baffled, hurried after him.

"Don't come back!" the server shouted.

Judy sighed and shook her head as the server took the tip jar to the sink, carefully poured out most of the coffee, and fished coins and soggy bills from the bottom in disgust. Judy wondered what Diane thought of her youngest son's choice of friends. She was probably just relieved Todd got decent grades and kept his record clean, unlike his elder brother. To be fair, though, as far as Judy knew, Michael had given his parents no undue cause for worry ever since he had started college. Judy was thankful Emily was still young enough that she and Steve could exercise control over her social life, though she knew those days wouldn't last.

She frowned, wondering if she should tell Diane about the prank. She would have, except she was so anxious about the campus invitation that had not yet come that she forgot about the young men by the time she left the coffee shop.

Technically the seventh day of March could not be considered the middle of the month even by the most generous estimate, but Judy still fretted over the lack of any word from Penn. She called home every afternoon to ask Steve if the campus invitation had arrived in the mail, even though she knew he would have called if it had. She could have managed more patience if Rick had sent her regular updates, but it would never occur to him to do so.

By the first business meeting of the month, Judy was a mess of distraction and worry. She drove to Elm Creek Manor mulling over her options and decided that the only reasonable choice was to wait until the fifteenth—indisputably mid-March—and contact Rick. In the meantime, she had other work to occupy her thoughts, plenty to do to keep herself from going crazy.

Even so, she had to force herself to concentrate on the business meeting, for every other topic reminded Judy of her job search. Enrollment reminded Judy of the possibility that Emily might enroll in a new school next autumn. Classroom assignments called to mind the wonderful new facility at Penn. The schedule for the first week of camp made Judy wince when she thought that if all went well, she would need Sarah to make additional changes to the plan she had worked so hard to arrange.

Then, suddenly, her cell phone rang. Quickly retrieving it from her bag, aware of Sarah's subtle frown, Judy checked the display. She made a hasty apology and hurried into the hallway. "Steve?" she said breathlessly into the phone.

"Judy? I have great news."

"What is it?"

"They just called. I got the job."

A momentary rush of joy quickly dispersed. "*You* got the job?"

"Isn't that fantastic? They want me to start as soon as I can—do you believe it? If everything goes well, I might even get my own political commentary column within a year." He paused. "Honey?"

"Wow, Steve." She forced more enthusiasm into her voice. "I knew you'd get it. How could they not recognize your talent?"

"There's more, but we can talk about it when you get home. I just had to let you know."

"I'm glad you did." She took a deep breath and closed her eyes, then told him she had to get back to the meeting, but she'd come home immediately afterward.

They hung up, and Judy returned to the parlor with an apologetic smile for Sarah. She assumed a look of interest as Sarah continued on uninterrupted. Of course Steve got the job; he was talented and experienced. He deserved it. How soon would he have to respond? What could he say until Judy heard something from Penn? She had not even been asked to interview on campus yet. She might not be asked. How could she expect Steve to pass up this job when an opportunity like it might never come again?

The phone rang on her lap. She jumped, checked the display, and raced into the hall, treading on Bonnie's tote bag on her way. "Steve?"

"Honey, I'm sorry I got carried away. I shouldn't have interrupted your meeting."

She forced a laugh. "If you know that, why are you doing it again?"

"Because—look, I don't want you to think I have my heart set on this job."

"Of course not," she said, thinking, *Of course you do.*

"If you don't get the Penn job, I'll just tell them no."

"Well . . ." She glanced back at the doorway to the parlor. "Would they let you work from Waterford? Telecommute?"

He hesitated. "I didn't think to ask, but that's an option. I don't think that would be their first choice, but it wouldn't hurt to check."

"Don't ask yet. I might still get the job."

"Yeah." He sounded deflated.

"We'll talk when I get home, okay?"

He agreed. They ended the call and Judy returned to the meeting, pretending not to notice Sarah's glare. She tried to listen carefully for the rest of the meeting, but her thoughts were in turmoil, and within minutes Sarah issued a plea for attention. She addressed the entire group, but Judy knew she was the only one there who had earned the reprimand.

The days passed. Judy prepared for midterm exams and the first week of quilt camp and waited, but the only news she received was Gwen's mournful email telling her that Summer had moved in with her boyfriend. Judy wasn't surprised; although she sympathized with Gwen's tangible dismay, Summer was a grown woman and many grown women made similar choices these days. She tried not to think too much about what Emily would be doing at that age.

She decided a shopping trip to Grandma's Attic would lift her spirits and distract her for a while. She still needed fabric for Sylvia's block, and she also wanted to take Summer's suggestion and examine the other contributors' blocks. If several other people had used the same pattern she had selected, she would prefer to choose something else.

She took a chance on stopping by the quilt shop before work, glad to discover the late opening earlier that month must have been an anomaly. Perhaps that was because Bonnie herself was inside, rearranging a display of spring floral fabrics. She looked somewhat drained, as if it were the end of a busy workday rather than the beginning, but she was neatly attired in a pair of slacks and twin set Judy did not recognize.

"Good morning," Judy said with a smile, hoping to cheer up her friend. "I love that outfit. Is it new?"

Bonnie glanced down at her clothing absentmindedly. "Oh. Yes, it is. Thanks. Agnes helped me pick it out."

"Did she? Maybe I'll ask her to go with Steve next time he shops for my birthday present. Remember that cardigan he bought me two years ago, the one Diane called the lightning bolt sweater?"

Bonnie rewarded her joke with a smile. "Did he ever find out you always changed into something else when you got to the lab?"

"Are you kidding? He thinks it's still in the back of my closet, awaiting the right occasion."

Judy knew it was more likely he had completely forgotten the sweater, which was just an afterthought to the tickets to Vail they had bought for each other that Christmas, but Bonnie laughed, so Judy didn't mind a little exaggeration at her husband's expense. Bonnie herself often joked about Craig's annoying habits until she had the Elm Creek Quilters doubled over in laughter, but come to think about it, Bonnie had not shared any amusing stories about him in a long time. Maybe Craig just wasn't funny anymore.

When Judy asked for Bonnie's help finding fabric for her block for Sylvia's bridal quilt, Bonnie nodded and took her to a collection of fat quarters so perfectly suited to the project and complementary to one another that Judy surmised she must have set them aside for that very purpose. "I suppose many local quilters have asked for these same fabric suggestions," she said.

"Not as many as you might think." Bonnie shook her head. "I hope it's because they already have suitable fabric in their stashes and not because they aren't going to participate. Judging by the lack of local response, we're having a little trouble getting the word out."

"But all the quilters around here know Sylvia, at least by reputation. Should we send a letter to the Waterford Quilting Guild?"

"We tried that. President Mary Beth refuses to read the announcement."

Recalling their unpleasant conversation at the Fabric Ware-house, Judy wasn't surprised. "What does she have against Sylvia?"

Bonnie shrugged. "What does she have against any of us? Except Diane, of course. They've been unfriendly as long as they've been next-door neighbors. It's amazing that their sons are such good friends."

Judy suddenly remembered Todd and his companion from the Daily Grind. "Does Mary Beth's son have dark, curly hair? Shorter than Todd, but good-looking, with a big cocky grin?"

"That sounds like Brent. Why?"

"I think I've seen them around."

"Well, you usually can't miss them." Bonnie held out the basket of fat quarters to Judy. "They're big men on the high school cam-pus, and they want to be noticed wherever they go."

After Judy selected her fabrics, Bonnie brought out a large car-ton from beneath the cutting table. Inside were sixty-six blocks from all across the country, including two from the United King-dom and one from Australia. "Sixty-six?" asked Judy, taking a few packages from the top. "Isn't that a bit short?"

Bonnie admitted that she would feel better if they were closer to 140 than that, but they still had time. Judy smiled. Bonnie, the eter-nal optimist, would not admit defeat long after the other team went home with the trophy.

Although the return addresses on the packages did indeed indi-cate the conspicuous absence of Waterford's quilters, the blocks that had arrived were as beautiful and as varied as Judy could have hoped. She recognized some of the patterns as techniques taught in camp workshops, and many of their makers as favorite longtime students. One simple but striking block, an apparent variation on the Sawtooth Star, came from a camper who attended every year and could not help being the most recognized quilter there, with the exception of Sylvia herself.

February 20, 2002

Dear Elm Creek Quilters,

A bridal quilt for Sylvia—what an inspired idea! I'm honored and delighted to contribute a block, which you will find enclosed.

If you had told me on my first day of quilt camp that one day I would be asked to participate in such an important project, I never would have believed you. Actually, I probably would have called my agent and had him fax you a request for your terms, and I would have tried to exploit my benevolent donation for as much good PR as I could squeeze out of it, but thanks to friends I made at Elm Creek Quilt Camp, I have undergone a significant attitude adjustment since then.

Sylvia was the first to show me that the aloof, prima donna routine that served me so well in Hollywood would not go over well at Elm Creek Manor. My agent insisted that I take my meals in my room and that Sylvia forbid anyone to speak to me unless I addressed them first. But Sylvia would have none of that, and she told my agent so in her own inimitable style. She was right, and I knew it, but what impressed me most was that she managed to muzzle that arrogant loudmouth without breaking a sweat. This woman, I told myself, is someone to reckon with.

I came to learn later that she is also someone to trust, to respect, and to emulate. Her high standards for herself and her compassion for others inspire those of us inclined to selfishness and narcissism to do better. I can't say knowing Sylvia has entirely cured me of my faults and weaknesses, but she has been an example I have tried to follow ever since I came to know her. Years ago I thought the most I could learn from Sylvia would be enough quilting to pass myself off as an accomplished quilter for a movie role. Now I know she has far more important lessons to offer for those of us not too self-absorbed to learn.

So, we return to the enclosed block. I could not find a block that, as your instructions requested, captured what Sylvia has meant to me. Any blocks that had ideal names were too difficult for me to make, and those I could handle had names that wouldn't do. So I decided to take a simple block and change it just enough to make a unique block. (At least I hope it is. There are so many blocks out there I might have simply taken someone else's design.) I call it Prima Donna, and I mean that in the absolute best sense of the phrase, for Sylvia is truly the First Lady of the quilting world.

Best regards to you all, and I wish you great success in the completion of this grand project.

Affectionately yours,
Julia Merchaud

PS: I hope you have all had the chance to watch my PBS series, "A Patchwork Life," based upon my PBS movie of the same title. I adore the character of Sadie Henderson and hope you do, too, since I have drawn many of her characteristics and behavioral quirks from Sylvia. Our third season begins in September. Also, if you get the chance, I hope you'll head to the theater to watch me in *Lethal Weapon Eight*. I play Mel Gibson's grandmother (although I think I could pass for his mother) and my nursing home is beset by villains throughout almost the entire film. Wondering what happened to my resolution to appear in only highbrow, arty films? I assure you, making this movie was a momentary sacrifice more than compensated for by the many times I got to kiss Mel during rehearsals, even if it was only on the cheek.

Judy laughed. "Did you read Julia Merchaud's letter?" she asked Bonnie.

Bonnie nodded and, a little mournfully, said, "I would have paid good money to be her stand-in for that role. Of course, we all know I don't have the money, and with my luck, I would have ended up kissing Mel's understudy."

"I bet even his understudy is cute." Then Judy detected an undercurrent of fear in Bonnie's joke. "Are things really as bad around here as that?"

"Think of the worst they've ever been," said Bonnie. "They're worse this time."

She looked away, and no matter how much Judy asked her to explain, Bonnie the eternal optimist would say nothing more than that she would keep the shop open as long as she could.

On March fifteenth, a Friday, Judy emailed Rick to ask if the campus interview invitations had been sent. She did not expect to hear from him over the weekend, but when an entire week passed with no reply, she assumed the worst. After encouraging her so enthusiastically to apply, he would be too embarrassed to tell her she had failed. An assistant would send her a rejection letter soon enough.

"Wait until the end of the month, then call," Steve advised, unwilling to give up, reluctant to turn down his own job offer. Judy agreed, though she knew by that time the top three candidates would have concluded their campus visits, the selection perhaps already made.

The first day of camp came and went in a cheerful flurry of registration and welcoming ceremonies. Judy tried to find satisfaction in knowing she had not let down her friends by missing camp, but whenever she thought of Penn's new computer facility—and when she observed Steve leafing discouragedly through the *Waterford Register* at breakfast—she wished things had turned out differently.

On Monday morning, the first day of classes, the phone rang a half hour before her alarm was set to go off. Steve rolled over with a groan and answered. "Hello?" He paused. "Yes, it is." Another pause. "Yes, still married, and very happily. Do you want to talk to Judy?" He passed her the phone and put his pillow over his head. "It's Wild Man Rick."

Judy sat up and pressed the receiver to her ear. "Hello, Rick?"

"Hey, Jude."

"What are you doing up so many hours before noon?" And why in the world was he calling? To commiserate? To tease her? Most likely the latter. For that, the least he could have done was let her sleep in.

"What are *you* doing still in bed, or still at home, for that matter? I thought you would have spent the night in Philly."

"What are you talking about?"

"You must be as hung over as I am. Your interview, you dunce. Preceded by a lunch at the University Club and a campus tour, and followed by a multitude of other tedious activities. That's not a commentary on your lecture or seminar, by the way."

"You mean I'm one of the three finalists?"

Steve tore the pillow from his head and stared at her.

"Of course. It was all in the letter."

Judy scrambled out of bed and threw on her robe. "I never received a letter."

"I told you you'd hear by mid-March. Why didn't you call?"

"I sent you an email asking if the letters were sent. You never answered."

"Of course not," Rick shot back, but he did sound somewhat abashed, if one knew what to listen for. "And when you never wrote me again to follow up on your unanswered email, I assumed the letter had arrived."

"Rick, I swear—"

"Before you decide to kill me, may I remind you you're wasting time? You can still make it if you leave now."

"I can't leave now! I have to shower and pack, and look after Emily, and make arrangements for my classes—"

"I thought you were on spring break."

"—get directions—"

"Don't worry about those. I'll email them right away." In the background she heard the clattering of keys on a keyboard and a woman's voice, muffled. "Oh. Angie says she can watch Emily if you need to bring her."

"Tell her she's very generous and she deserves much better than you, but Emily's in school and Steve doesn't need the spouse job placement conference, so he's staying here."

Rick sighed. "You're coming alone, and here I am, engaged to someone else. Ow! Sweetheart, that hurt."

"Tell Angie to hit you again for me."

"I'll do that. Send me an email if the directions don't come through."

"Will you bother to answer it?"

"Maybe. You're wasting time, you know."

"I know." She promised—or threatened—to see him later, and hung up. A glance at the clock told her she had just enough time to race through a shower and throw some things into a suitcase. And call Sarah. Her elation dimmed for a moment. She had to call Sarah. But first she bounded back into bed to tell Steve the good news he had already guessed.

CHAPTER SEVEN

Diane

On the first day of March, Diane's phone rang while she was scrambling to get her husband and youngest son out of the house and on their way to work and school. Her assumption that the morning chaos would lessen by one-third when her eldest son started college had thus far proven to be laughably naïve.

She snatched the receiver a moment before the answering machine would have picked up. "Hello?"

"Hello, Diane? It's Agnes. Sorry to call so early, but I'm afraid there's an emergency."

"What's wrong?"

"It's not really an emergency. Let's call it—a situation."

"Call it whatever you like. Just tell me what's up." Diane covered the mouthpiece with her hand as Todd passed, selecting items from the kitchen counter and pantry at random and tossing them into a brown paper lunch sack. "Todd, leave one of those bananas for your father."

"He said he didn't want it."

"Then leave it for me. You ate both of my oranges for breakfast and there isn't any more fruit in the house."

Todd rolled his eyes, but he returned the banana to the otherwise empty fruit bowl. Diane uncovered the phone. "Sorry, Agnes. Where were we?"

"Todd's a growing boy. He needs fruit."

Diane sighed. "Todd," she called. When he turned, she tossed him the banana. "Okay, Agnes. Whatever crisis you called about, it will be over by the time you tell me."

"Bonnie can't make it into work this morning. Are you free to open Grandma's Attic today?"

"Why can't she come in? Is she sick?" Diane paused to kiss her husband, Tim, on his way to the door. "Why didn't she just call me herself?"

"It's a rather long story, and it doesn't sound as if you have time for a lengthy chat."

That was certainly true. Todd waved at her and, with a hopeful expression, held out a pen and a blue piece of paper. Diane scanned it. Oh. Right. That permission slip for the senior trip. She held the phone to her ear with her shoulder and scrawled her signature on the line.

"Thanks, Mom," whispered Todd as he carefully folded the form and tucked it into his backpack. "Come on. We'll be late."

"Just a minute." She glanced at the clock. "I'd be glad to work today, Agnes, but I can't get there right at nine. I have a dentist appointment and some errands I can't postpone."

"That's all right. As soon as you can get there will be good enough. I'm sure Bonnie would be grateful."

Diane wanted to believe that, but sometimes she wondered if any of her work at Grandma's Attic was appreciated or even noticed. "I'll call Bonnie at home when I get in."

"Mom, we have to go."

"Don't bother," said Agnes quickly. "She needs her rest."

"Okay, I won't." Diane nodded apologetically to her son, bid Agnes good-bye, and hung up. "Can you get another ride home?" she asked

Todd as she snatched up her purse and followed him out the side door into the garage. "I might have to work late at Grandma's Attic."

"No problem. Brent will drive me."

"Great." Diane managed not to clench her teeth. Since Todd was a little boy, she had tried to steer him toward other children in the neighborhood, but Brent had been his best friend since the second grade. In her own defense, she didn't object because Brent was the son of her worst enemy; she disliked him on his own terms. If Todd were a more rebellious, sullen sort—in other words, more like his elder brother—Diane would have suspected him of befriending Brent merely to annoy her, but Todd genuinely liked Brent and often mentioned his many admirable qualities in what he thought was a subtle attempt to win her over. Tim occasionally pointed out that if Brent were anyone else's son, Diane would be pleased Todd had chosen for his best friend a well-behaved, pleasant, athletic young man who earned good grades. While Diane couldn't deny the tiny grain of truth in her husband's mild censure, she had overheard Brent mock her eldest son, then turn around and speak to her with the utmost respect through an innocent grin far too many times. What bothered her most, though, was that Todd never defied Brent to defend his elder brother. She didn't like to think of Todd as a conformist follower, especially if Mary Beth's son was the designated leader.

If it were warmer, she would make Todd walk home from school. If Mary Beth had not bought Brent a new car for his sixteenth birthday, Todd would have had no choice. But since Diane could not fairly accuse Brent of poor driving, she could not withhold her permission without seeming unreasonable.

She dropped off Todd at school with time to spare and headed for the dentist. One routine examination later, she was back in the car en route to the post office and the bank. She hurried through her errands as quickly as she could, wondering about Bonnie's absence. It was odd that Agnes had called instead of Bonnie, but not surprising that Agnes had called her instead of Summer. Whenever Bonnie needed extra help around the store, she invariably contacted Diane. Although Diane had originally accepted the part-time job because she did not want to work any more than she had to, with all the extra shifts, she had regularly worked a two-thirds schedule for more than a year. She spent more time in a Grandma's Attic apron than Summer did, but Diane suspected neither Bonnie nor Summer realized that. Diane's name appeared on the official work schedule posted in the back office less frequently than theirs, and the fact that she worked more often escaped their notice.

Not that Diane minded the extra shifts; she welcomed them. It was not only to help Bonnie, although Diane was glad to do anything to take some pressure off her friend who, despite her outward optimism, had seemed shadowed by a cloud of gloom and worry for months. It was also not only because she appreciated the extra money, although she did, especially with Todd impatiently awaiting an acceptance letter from Princeton. She simply liked the job. The work was never boring or stressful, since Bonnie handled all the financial matters herself, and the customers were generally pleasant and not too demanding. Diane felt useful there, which was a good feeling considering that her sons seemed to need her less and less each day, and she enjoyed having shoppers ask her opinion about fabric selections or new patterns. When Todd went off to college, Diane hoped to work full-time officially. The next time she caught Bonnie in a good mood, she would suggest it.

Diane parked in the employee space behind the building and hurried around to the front door. To her surprise it was unlocked, and through the front window she spotted Summer on the phone. Disgruntled, she wondered if Bonnie or Agnes—or both—had called Summer in, doubting Diane's ability to handle the store by herself. If they had that little faith in her, she would be glad to point to the calendar and show them how many times in the past month she had opened and closed the store on her own.

Diane pushed open the door just as Summer hung up the phone. "Oh, hi," she said brightly, shrugging off her coat. "I thought no one else was working today."

Summer looked surprised to see her. "I work every Friday when camp isn't in session. Bonnie should be here, too, but she didn't show up this morning. I'm worried. No one answered the phone upstairs, either."

"She's not coming in today." Diane hung up her coat and put her purse in its usual place, on a shelf beneath the cutting table. "Agnes called and asked me to open the store. I guess she didn't know you would be here."

"Agnes? Why would Agnes have called?"

Diane shrugged. "I have no idea. I imagine Bonnie asked her to."

"But Bonnie knew I was working and she would have called you directly."

"Well . . ." Diane mulled it over, but all she could conclude was that the whole situation was a little odd. "I don't know. But I'm here, so I'm going to work. I need the hours. Todd is still holding out for Princeton. Do you have any idea how expensive that is? Thank goodness Michael decided to go to Waterford College so we could take advantage of the family tuition waiver."

She figured Summer would understand that, because she had attended Waterford College for the same reason. Or so Gwen had claimed at the time. In Diane's opinion, which no one had requested, Summer would have thrived at a larger university with more opportunities. She was certainly bright enough to succeed anywhere, and Gwen could have afforded even private school tuition. Diane had suspected Summer was afraid to leave Waterford and her mother, and that was why she had stayed. Her opinion was confirmed four years later when Summer turned down a generous fellowship to attend graduate school, in favor of Waterford, Grandma's Attic, and Elm Creek Quilts. At least Summer had those to fall back on; other young people who were too intimidated to leave their small town ended up underemployed in dead-end jobs unless they were fortunate enough to inherit a thriving family business. Diane was relieved her two sons had their sights set outside Waterford but, to be fair, she might not feel that way if she had not already made plans for their bedrooms.

Once Diane knew Summer had not come in to supervise her, she was able to enjoy the day. Business was brisk in the morning, more like the old days before the Fabric Warehouse opened. She and Summer even found an interval between customers to look through the carton of blocks for Sylvia's bridal quilt. The only unpleasantness—Mary Beth Callahan—arrived in the afternoon. The Neighbor from Hell apparently had nothing better to do than to complain about the letter Sarah had sent the Waterford Quilting Guild inviting members to participate in Sylvia's bridal quilt. Diane happened to know that quilters enjoyed making blocks for projects like this and were far more likely to be hurt if they were not asked to help than to be annoyed by "block begging" or whatever Mary Beth had called it.

Everything from Mary Beth's gleeful tone to the fact that she had waited two months to respond to the invitation told Diane she was determined to ruin Sylvia's quilt. And Diane knew why. Mary Beth wanted to be Waterford's best known and most respected quilter and, until Sylvia's return to Waterford, only Bonnie and perhaps Gwen had given her any competition. It was not Mary Beth's quilting that set her apart, of course; although she could count on collecting a ribbon at her guild's own quilt show each summer, she had either never aspired to enter the more competitive national shows, or they had rejected her entries. Her role as perpetual guild president, however, had lent her a certain local notoriety for years. Now all the Elm Creek Quilters were better known in the quilting world than Mary Beth—even Diane herself, the least able quilter among them.

Mary Beth couldn't stand it.

Diane usually enjoyed watching her neighbor stew in her jealousy, but she knew that concealed behind Mary Beth's impeccable makeup and designer clothes and perpetual, if insincere, perky smile lay a heart capable of plotting the most malicious vengeance. Diane would never forgive Mary Beth for complaining to the Zoning Commission and forcing the Sonnenbergs to demolish the skateboard ramp they had built in their backyard for Michael, just as she would never forgive her if she ruined Sylvia's quilt. Diane would not *allow* Mary Beth to ruin it.

After Summer left for the day, Diane fished Mary Beth's discarded invitation out of the trash. She had not received one herself, so once she figured out how to infiltrate the Waterford Quilting Guild, she would read from Mary Beth's. She rather liked the irony.

She unfolded the letter and was about to rehearse reading it aloud when her own name jumped out at her. "'Diane says Sylvia deserves to go without'?" she read, aghast. She had never said that! She had thought it, but not said it, and that didn't count, certainly not enough to be included in a letter sent out to hundreds of people!

She was going to have a little chat with Sarah as soon as she finished with Mary Beth.

When Diane returned home at six, Todd and Brent were watching music videos in the living room, open books and papers strewn on the coffee table before them. "No television during homework," she called out as she set her purse on the kitchen counter.

Todd, who knew the rule and usually obeyed it, turned off the television without complaint, but Brent grinned at her over his shoulder and said, "We're second-semester seniors. Homework doesn't really count anymore."

She returned his grin with a tight smile. "Homework always counts in this house. And yes, I realize colleges won't see your second-semester grades until after they've accepted you."

Brent shrugged and began closing books and collecting papers.

"You should just be glad we're doing it at all. Most kids in our class just blow it off."

"If that's true, which I doubt, I'm thrilled you two have a better work ethic." Diane would have added something about wondering what his mother thought of his smart mouth, but just then the phone rang and she snatched it up. "Hello?"

"Hi," a young woman responded. "Is, um, is Todd Sonnenberg there?"

"Yes." She glanced at the clock. Right on schedule. Ever since word got out that Todd and his girlfriend had broken up soon after she received an acceptance letter to a West Coast university to which Todd had not applied, the Sonnenberg phone had rung almost continuously from the end of the school day until ten o'clock at night, when Tim switched off the ringer on each extension. An unusual day of silence meant they had forgotten to turn the ringers back on in the morning. "May I tell him who's calling?"

"Um, it's Shelley from Calculus class."

"Shelley from Calculus," said Diane, holding out the phone to Todd. Brent shook his head and smirked as Todd ran a hand through his hair and straightened his shirt on his way to the phone.

"Hullo," said Todd into the receiver. "Uh-huh . . . Uh-huh . . . Yeah . . . I'm already going. Sorry . . . Okay. Bye." He hung up.

"I hope that conversation was more articulate on her end," remarked Diane as she searched the pantry for the extra box of pasta she was certain she had hidden in the back.

"It would have been more interesting here, too, if you weren't listening." But Todd smiled and patted her on the shoulder as he passed.

"Another invitation to the prom?" asked Brent.

"Yeah."

Surprised, Diane looked up from her search. "I didn't know you already had a date."

"He doesn't," said Brent before Todd could answer. "But he doesn't want to go with Shelley."

Diane kept her gaze fixed on her son. "I distinctly heard you tell that young lady you were already going."

Todd opened his mouth to speak, but once again Brent beat him to it. "You must not know Shelley or you'd get it."

This time Diane was too annoyed to ignore him. "If she's in Calculus, she must be fairly bright."

Brent began to laugh. "Yeah, but she's a dog."

Todd had the decency to look embarrassed, but Diane was nonetheless displeased with him. "Shelley's not so bad, but I want to ask this girl from Physics," he quickly explained, sensing her mood. "She's just as smart as Shelley, and she's on the soccer team. If she says no—"

"She won't," Brent interjected.

"—I'm going to ask Lisa."

Diane's eyebrows rose. "I thought you two broke up."

Todd shrugged. "We did, but we're still friends."

"If Lisa turns you down, can I ask her?" Brent inquired. Todd grinned and shoved him.

Brent finished packing up his things, none too soon as far as Diane was concerned, and before the door closed behind him, the phone rang again. The caller was a young woman from Physics class but not, judging from Todd's expression, the prospective prom date. She claimed to need the homework assignment, a transparent ruse Diane recognized from her own high school days. Only back then the boys did the calling; a girl never phoned a boy unless they were going steady.

Diane flipped through the mail while Todd carried out another brief, monosyllabic conversation. "You got a letter from Waterford College," she exclaimed, withdrawing the thick envelope from the stack as he hung up the phone. "Why didn't you open it?"

"You can, if you want."

She quickly did so. "Todd, this is great news! You got into Waterford College!"

He looked wounded. "You don't have to sound so surprised."

"I'm not surprised you got in." Not with his 4.0 GPA and 1520 SATs. "Just that you don't seem to care."

"You know it's just my safety school. I already got into Penn State, and I'd go there before I'd go to Waterford College."

"Before you stick your nose too far into the air, allow me to remind you that your father teaches at Waterford College."

"Yeah, but that's not where he got his degrees. It's probably a great place to work, but it's not where I want to go to school. Mom, no offense, but I really have to get out of Waterford."

"It's good enough for your brother." That was both feeble and defensive, and they both knew it. Michael would have gone elsewhere if he'd had the grades.

"It's fine for him since they have a good Computer Science department. But if I want to get into a top law school, I have to, you know, aim high. Like you and Dad are always telling me to do."

The argument was stupid and one-sided, so Diane dropped it. "Please don't complain about the college in front of your father or brother. They have their pride, you know."

"I know," he said, and he kissed her on the cheek.

That evening after supper, Agnes called to ask if Diane could work all day Saturday, because Bonnie most likely wouldn't be able to come in. Diane readily agreed and couldn't resist inquiring why Bonnie had not phoned herself, but Agnes promptly found an excuse to end the call. Ignoring Agnes's earlier admonitions not to bother Bonnie at home, Diane dialed her number, but hung up without leaving a message when the answering machine picked up. She didn't care for their new outgoing recording, which, thanks to Craig's brusque delivery, sounded like a suspicious demand for information and would lead a stranger to believe he lived alone.

The next day she enjoyed having Grandma's Attic all to herself. She moved the coffeepot from Bonnie's office to a table near the front of the store so customers could help themselves. She rearranged the shelves to disguise how bare they were, now that

Bonnie could not reorder stock as readily as before, and she managed to persuade two of their most negligent customers to make payments on their long-overdue accounts. By the time she flipped the sign in the front window to CLOSED and locked the door behind her, she felt satisfied that she had put in a good day's work. She wished Bonnie had been there to see it, but that would have defeated the purpose of proving how well she could handle the store on her own.

On Sunday, Michael came home to do his laundry, as he did almost every week. When he first proposed that arrangement after moving from the student dorms to a dilapidated rental house he shared with three other students, Diane had balked, certain that what he really meant was that he would dump his dirty clothes in the basement and expect to pick them up later that afternoon, washed and pressed. To her pleasant surprise, a year in a dorm with its own laundry facilities had taught Michael he could handle the work himself, and he actually did a fine job of it, though he still refused to iron. Most of the time Michael sat at the kitchen table studying—actually studying!—between changing loads, but occasionally he had time to sit and talk with her over a cup of coffee, especially if she had baked cookies earlier that day.

On that Sunday, however, he was sweating over a computer programming project and an English paper, both due before spring break, plus he had midterms coming up, so she knew better than to interrupt him once he sat down to work. When he took a break to stretch and put his whites in the dryer, she asked him what his plans were for spring break. She was curious, because by this time last year he had already hit her up twice for a trip to Cancún, requests she had flatly turned down. Still, she was surprised he had not tried again.

"I'm staying here," Michael told her. "I have a major design project due two weeks after spring break, and I've barely even started it since I have all this other stuff to do."

"That seems like poor planning on your professor's part. Does he expect everyone to work through spring break?"

Michael shrugged. "That's better than having it due during midterms along with everything else. College isn't like high school, Mom. You actually have to work."

"Yes, I seem to remember something about that from my own college years, back in the olden days," said Diane, but she was secretly thrilled, so much so that she didn't add a rebuke about how he actually should have worked in high school, too.

Michael turned down her invitation to stay for supper, citing too much work and plans to get pizza with his housemates. It was not until the next morning that Diane discovered he had left two pairs of jeans on the folding table in the laundry room. She knew he would wear the same pair he had worn Sunday every day for a week rather than make an extra trip home for his clean clothes, so she decided to drop them off at his house before her afternoon shift at Grandma's Attic.

She called ahead to warn him, since she and Tim had promised never to visit unannounced. As she drove through Fraternity Row to a street of student rentals as dilapidated as Michael's, she hoped the message she had left with a housemate counted as fair warning.

Michael, who had returned from class in the meantime, answered her knock and welcomed her in out of the cold. She handed him the jeans and looked around with misgivings, wondering how he would react if she raced to the store and returned with a carload of cleaning supplies. "Do you even have a vacuum?" she asked, eyeing the crumbs on the floor.

"No, we leave that to the mice. I'm kidding," he added hastily.

"Sure," she said, not sure at all, and she nodded to the interesting sculpture of empty beer cans on the floor beside a stereo system with enormous speakers. "One of your friends is an art major, I presume?"

Michael grinned. "Not exactly."

Diane snorted and decided to leave before she saw anything else. As she kissed him good-bye at the door, a young man shouted from another room, "Yes! I got it!"

"Great," Michael called back, and shook his head.

"What?" asked Diane.

"There's this girl he likes in his Econ class. She's not listed in the student directory, so he's been looking for her cell phone number."

"You can do that? Find cell phone numbers on the internet?"

"Sure." Raising his voice for the benefit of the unseen roommate, he added, "And it wouldn't take me two weeks to do it, either."

Suddenly inspired, Diane asked, "Could you get me Mary Beth Callahan's cell phone number?"

"Why?"

"It might come in handy someday."

"You mean like if Todd's out with her and Brent, and you need to contact him? Why don't you just ask her for it?"

"Michael . . ." She sighed. "Sometimes it's best not to ask too many questions. Can you get me the number or not?"

"Yeah, yeah, I can get it." He hesitated. "Can I use that line sometime, about not asking too many questions?"

"Not with me and your father you can't."

He grumbled but agreed, and told her he would have the number by his next laundry day. Diane thanked him and went home, the first fine threads of a plan gathering in her thoughts.

Three customers were waiting in line at the cutting table when Diane arrived at Grandma's Attic, so she quickly stashed her things, put on her apron, and took her place beside Bonnie. "Are you feeling better?" Diane asked as she unrolled a fabric bolt and measured out two yards.

"Hmm?" said Bonnie. "Oh. I suppose. Thanks."

"Was it the flu?"

Bonnie handed the first customer her pile of cut fabric and offered to help the next person in line. "Didn't Agnes tell you?"

"No."

"Oh." Bonnie fell silent as she sliced through a purple-and-green paisley cotton with her rotary cutter. "Well, I guess it was just one of those weekend things. You know."

That sounded rather vague to Diane, but she nodded. "You know," she said casually, "we had quite a few customers on Saturday. We—I should have said I, because I was here alone."

"I hope it wasn't too much for you."

"No, of course not." Diane handed the cut fabric to the customer. "Everything went quite smoothly. It was no trouble at all to open and close by myself, so if you ever need me to do it again, just let me know."

"Thanks." Bonnie finished assisting the last customer and headed to the cash register to ring up the three women's purchases. Diane rolled up the fabric bolts and returned them to their shelves. By the time she finished, the store was empty except for herself and Bonnie, who had taken a seat on a stool beside the front counter, visibly drained. No doubt she still felt the effects of her illness. "I apologize for imposing on you last weekend," Bonnie said.

"Not at all." Diane leaned back against the cutting table and smiled. She had thought that Bonnie's first day back would be the best time to approach her about going full-time, with her emergency substitution fresh in Bonnie's mind, but the conversation wasn't going as well as she had hoped. "You know how much I enjoy working here. It sure beats volunteering for another committee at the high school."

Bonnie's gaze had shifted past Diane to the shelves of sewing machines on the far wall. "Schools need involved parents."

"Well, of course, but once Todd graduates, I won't be a class parent anymore. Did I tell you Todd has pretty much rejected Waterford College? If he chooses Penn State, the tuition won't be that bad, but if he gets into Princeton—" Diane laughed. "Let's just say I'd rather work overtime than take out a second mortgage."

Bonnie said, distantly, "I'm afraid I can't afford to pay overtime."

"I know that," said Diane, bemused. "I was kidding."

"Oh. Okay, then." Bonnie rose and walked toward the back of the store.

"Not about working more," Diane called after her as Bonnie entered her office and sat down at the computer. "I wasn't kidding about that part."

If Bonnie heard, she gave no sign.

That evening, Diane drove to Elm Creek Manor to submit her proposed course schedule, already more than a week overdue and probably unnecessary since Sarah and Summer were well into arranging the master schedule. Her conversation with Bonnie ran through her thoughts, making her more displeased with each repetition. She should have been more forthright. When had delicacy and tact ever served her well? Bonnie had probably left the discussion thinking Diane resented working the extra hours, which meant Diane was now worse off than before.

She found Sarah in the second-floor library, which Sarah often referred to casually as her office, as if she were the only person who worked there. She was seated behind the large oak desk that had once belonged to Sylvia's father, looking every bit the overworked manager despite her jeans and faded purple turtleneck. Although she did not complain, she could not hide her exasperation when Diane handed her the overdue paperwork. "This would have been useful two weeks ago," she said as she leafed through the pages.

Diane knew she was only ten days late, not fourteen, but she said, "I'm sorry it's late. It's pretty much the same as last year, but if it creates any problems with your master schedule, don't change anything for my sake."

"Thanks," said Sarah dryly. "We won't." She set the papers aside and rubbed her eyes. "Diane, I'm sure you're very busy, but I'd really appreciate it if you could pay more attention to our deadlines."

"Sure," said Diane, giving her a tight smile. "You know, if it was that urgent, you could have called."

"It *was* urgent, which is why we gave it a mandatory deadline."

"Right. Got it." Irritated, Diane left the library before Sarah's reprimand could turn into an argument. "We," she muttered under her breath as she descended the grand oak staircase to the front foyer. Just what she needed, another employer who didn't respect her. Employer! What an unpleasant thought. A few years ago, she never would have thought of Sarah as her employer.

Fuming, she turned down the west wing hallway toward the back door. As she passed the kitchen, she heard Sylvia call out, "Diane, is that you?"

"Yes," Diane called back, reluctantly. She was not in the mood for another lecture.

"Would you mind joining me?"

Diane sighed and passed through the kitchen into the west sitting room. Sylvia's private sewing room was upstairs, but she often brought her work downstairs when she hoped for company. From her favorite armchair near the window, she had a fine view of the rear parking lot and, unless the cook and his assistants were raising a clatter in the kitchen, she could hear anyone passing in the hall.

Diane paused in the doorway as Sylvia looked up from the quilt hoop resting on her lap. "I'm afraid I can't stay long. I have to put supper on."

"I won't keep you but a moment." Sylvia smiled and indicated the opposite chair with a nod. "I hoped you might be able to clear up a mystery. You're very perceptive."

Flattered, Diane promptly seated herself. "I'll try."

"That's all I ask." Sylvia removed her thimble and set her unfinished quilt aside. "Tell me, is it my imagination or have people been acting rather strangely around here lately?"

"It's not your imagination," said Diane, thinking of Bonnie's unexplained absences from Grandma's Attic and Sarah's increasingly bossy tendencies.

"Ah! I knew it." Sylvia removed her glasses and let them dangle from the fine silver chain around her neck. "Now, if we can only figure out why. I admit I might not have noticed myself except for Matthew. He's the one who alerted me to everyone's odd behavior, although, come to think of it, he's behaved rather oddly himself. Would you believe I overheard him and Sarah arguing about foot massages and apple trees, of all things? I couldn't make any sense of it."

"Did you ask them what they were talking about?"

"Heavens, no. I would have been forced to confess my eavesdropping." Sylvia frowned. "But that's not all. Ever since that strange meeting where everyone showed up early and congregated in the kitchen, Sarah has been making the most ridiculous excuses why I can't accompany her on her trips downtown. And have you noticed no one talks about their current quilting projects anymore? We haven't had a show-and-tell after our business meetings in weeks. A few days ago, Matt asked Agnes to show him the quilt block in her sewing basket and you would have thought he had asked to see her unmentionables! This, from a group of quilters who usually can't wait to brag." She shook her head, then fixed a piercing gaze on Diane. "Have you noticed it, too?"

"Actually, no," said Diane weakly. "That's not the odd behavior I was talking about."

"Well, now that I've pointed it out, I'm sure you know what I mean. Do you have any idea what's wrong? I wouldn't be so concerned except the first day of camp is only three weeks away. If we have a serious problem, we must root it out before then."

Diane hesitated. It seemed unfair to allow Sylvia to worry when there was a simple explanation. Maybe she could reveal something—not the entire secret, but just enough to assuage Sylvia's fears.

While Diane struggled to decide what and how much she could say, Sylvia leaned forward slightly, her expression suddenly sharp and expectant. All at once, Diane understood. Sylvia had not invited

her to chat because she was unusually perceptive, but because she was—undeservedly—considered a bit of a gossip.

Indignant, Diane almost accused Sylvia of deceiving her, but remembered just in time that this would only confirm Sylvia's suspicions. "I'm afraid I can't explain," she said. That was the truth; she couldn't explain or the other Elm Creek Quilters would have her head. "But maybe you can help me with another mystery."

"What's that, dear?"

"Do you have any idea why someone might consider me an incompetent employee?"

"Incompetent? That seems rather harsh. I do recall Sarah grumbling about some missing paperwork recently, but she never called you incompetent."

"I wasn't talking about that." Silently Diane berated herself for ignoring the deadline. From now on she would submit everything early if it killed her. "I mean Bonnie. I've been working at Grandma's Attic for years and I don't think she appreciates a thing I do."

Sylvia smiled. "I suspect all employees feel that way from time to time. It must be especially difficult since Bonnie is also your friend."

"It's more than that," said Diane, and confided her entire list of hurts and grievances: her full-time schedule that invariably went ignored; her willingness to work extra hours on a moment's notice that no one appreciated; her good ideas for store displays and promotions for which she received little praise and no thanks; her exclusion from "management meetings" about the shop's future. "Maybe management meetings made sense when Bonnie had five employees," Diane said, "but not when Bonnie and Summer are management and I'm the only managee!"

"That does seem particularly unfair," said Sylvia. "I can't believe Bonnie is deliberately excluding you or ignoring your contributions. Have you told her how you feel?"

"Of course." Diane paused. "Well, actually, no. Not directly."

Sylvia laughed. "I'm not unsympathetic, dear, but how do you expect her to understand your concerns if you don't tell her?"

"I've dropped a lot of hints."

"I'm afraid that's not good enough." Sylvia reached over and patted her hand. "You've been working yourself into a fine state of hurt and resentment when what you needed to do was sit down with Bonnie and tell her what's troubling you, exactly as you've told me. On second thought, not exactly. You might consider shouting a little less."

"How am I supposed to get Bonnie to sit down and listen? Schedule an appointment?"

"That's a fine idea. Bonnie is a very busy woman, and it's clear she's had a great deal on her mind lately. Summer mentioned that the shop's rent is going up, and I can't open the newspaper without seeing an ad for another sale at Fabric Warehouse. I daresay Bonnie might have other worries, too, which have nothing to do with Grandma's Attic." Sylvia mused in silence for a moment, then smiled ruefully. "I suppose I've solved my own mystery. I must have forgotten that my friends have concerns apart from me, from Elm Creek Quilts. What I have perceived as odd behavior is probably nothing more than the actions of people dealing with problems of their own."

"That's possible," agreed Diane, reluctantly. She wanted Sylvia to find another explanation for her friends' recent secretiveness, but not if it excused Bonnie's behavior at work.

"Possible? I think highly probable." Sylvia put on her glasses, frowning. "It remains a mystery, however, why none of our friends have shared those concerns with the rest of us. Once it seemed we knew the most intimate details of one another's lives."

"That's because we used to have weekly quilting bees," Diane reminded her. "Then those turned into quilting bees tacked on to the end of our business meetings. Now the entire block of time is a business meeting. Each season we have more business to discuss and less time to talk about ourselves. Only Agnes bothers to bring handwork anymore."

"Yes, that's true." Sylvia smiled, regretful. "I suppose that's the price of success."

"It won't always be this way," said Diane. "This time of year is especially busy. Things will settle down once camp is under way."

Sylvia shrugged as she took up her quilt hoop and slipped her thimble on the first finger of her right hand. "You may be right. But nothing endures forever, Diane, perhaps not even the closest of friendships."

◈◈

A week later, Michael came home with a laundry bag full of dirty clothes and a phone number scrawled on a piece of notebook paper. "That's it," he said as he handed it to her.

"Are you sure?"

"Yep." Michael hoisted the bag on his shoulder and descended the basement stairs. "I tested it."

"From a pay phone, I hope," said Diane, pocketing the number with delight. "She might have Caller ID."

"I used my roommate's cell," he called from below. "Jeez, Mom, you watch too much *Law & Order.*"

Maybe so, but Diane was not willing to overlook any precaution where Mary Beth was concerned.

When Michael returned upstairs and began unloading his back-pack on the kitchen table, Diane set a plate of fudge brownies within reach. "A little token of my thanks," she said. "Would you like a glass of milk?"

"Sure," he said, helping himself to a brownie. "I hope giving you that number doesn't make me an accessory to a crime. I feel like I've corrupted my own mother."

"Don't be ridiculous. If you found it on the internet, it must be public information, right?"

"Well . . ." Michael hesitated. "Remember what you said about not asking too many questions?"

"Right. Understood." Diane handed him a glass of milk and hoped she had not tempted him into ruining his record for good behavior. She decided not to dwell on it. It was just a phone number; what harm could it do? "I won't ask how you got it, but if you did anything illegal, don't do it again. And thank you."

"I didn't, and you're welcome." He took a bite of brownie, opened a textbook, and uncapped his highlighter. "Um, if you really want to thank me, there's something I wanted to talk to you about."

Here it comes, Diane thought, noting his casual voice, the way he avoided her gaze. The annual Cancún petition. "You mean your mother's gratitude and fudge brownies aren't thanks enough?"

"They're great, but the thing is, I could really use some cash."

She folded her arms. "Michael, we've had this discussion before. Your father and I do not want you to go flying off to some postadolescent paradise for a week of free-flowing alcohol and drunken coeds in wet T-shirts. Cancún is out."

"Cancún?" he asked, bewildered. "Who said anything about Cancún? I need a new computer."

"Oh." She absorbed this. "No you don't. We bought you a computer for your graduation present. What happened? Did you break it?"

"No, but it's two years old. It's obsolete."

"For what we paid, it's not allowed to be." Diane tore a paper towel from the roll and swept brownie crumbs into the sink. "When you picked out the model, you assured us it would last you through college."

"Back then, I thought it would. I didn't know the kind of software my professors would make us use. Some of it is so new it barely runs on my computer."

"If it's a problem with memory—"

"It's not a problem with the amount of RAM; it's a problem with processor speed, peripheral compatibility—" He broke off and let out an exasperated, beseeching sigh. "Mom, I'm a Computer Science major. I need access to a better computer."

"Then use the college's computer labs."

"Do you know how long you have to wait in line for one of those?"

"No, but I imagine if you add up those hours and compare them to how many your father would have to work to pay for a new computer, waiting in line would still seem like a bargain."

He took a deep breath, and when he spoke again, he was clearly trying his best to sound reasonable. "In my major I need frequent access to a top-of-the-line computer, preferably a laptop. Ask Dr. DiNardo. I'm taking her class next fall. She'll tell you she always recommends students bring their own laptops to class."

Diane didn't doubt it. Judy was so fond of computer gadgets she would wait at the end of the assembly line to catch some new gizmo if the manufacturer would permit it. "If Dr. DiNardo requires a laptop, your father and I will discuss it. However, we spent a lot on the computer you have, and since it's practically new, you'll have to pay for a laptop yourself."

"Where am I going to get that kind of money?"

"Save your allowance. Get a job. Get two. If you start looking now, you'll definitely have something lined up for summer."

"'Definitely'? Have you ever tried to find a job in Waterford? What am I supposed to do, work at the quilt camp?"

"That's a fine idea. Matt might want an assistant caretaker for the summer, and I'm sure the cook will need help in the kitchen. In fact, you probably wouldn't need to wait until summer, since camp starts in March."

"Great," said Michael, disparagingly. "Just what I want. Mowing lawns and feeding quilters." He hunched over his book as if that would slam a wall in place between them.

Diane held on to her temper. "Michael, you know the value of money by now, and you know we can't throw it around just because your perfectly adequate computer doesn't have all the latest bells and whistles."

"Adequate. That's all it is," he muttered, not looking up from his book. "I guess if you don't care about my grades—"

"This has nothing to do with your grades, and you know it." Diane heard her voice rising and forced herself to maintain the appearance of calm. "I'll talk to Judy DiNardo. If she says you must have a laptop, you can buy one. You can earn the money to pay for it yourself. If you haven't saved enough by fall, your father and I will loan you the rest."

Michael said nothing. Diane watched him pretend to study, her irritation rising, until she wanted to snap at him that twenty going on twenty-one was too old to be acting like a spoiled brat. Instead she forced herself to leave the room. He was a bright boy, but he was too angry to see that her offer was entirely reasonable. She would talk to him when time, reflection, and frustration with his two-year old obsolete computer brought him to his senses.

Michael was still angry a week later when a full laundry sack compelled him to return home but, to his credit, he made an effort to be civil. Typically his grudges lasted a good two weeks, so Diane left him alone while he washed clothes and studied. Neither mentioned their disagreement, but Diane took it as an encouraging sign when Michael asked for a plastic bag so he could share some of her fresh-baked chocolate chip cookies with his roommates.

All she could do was wait until his anger blew over. She couldn't dwell on a ridiculous argument when she had other more immediate concerns: The following day was the third Monday of the month, the regularly scheduled meeting time for the Waterford Quilting Guild.

As Diane drove downtown to the public library, her cell phone,

Sarah's letter, and Mary Beth's number in her purse, she reflected that she ought to be nervous. She had no idea whether she could pull off this stunt or how the guild members would react if she did. But she could not afford second thoughts. Mary Beth never expected to see Diane or any of the Elm Creek Quilters at another guild meeting after they left in protest years before, when Mary Beth's dirty campaign tactics cost Diane the presidency. Tonight, Mary Beth's insufferably smug complacency would work to Diane's advantage.

In order to avoid detection, Diane parked on a side street and entered the library through the children's department. Her anticipation rose as she crossed the main lobby, adjusted her watch to the large clock over the circulation desk, and slipped into a stall in the women's rest room closest to Meeting Room C. She had to time her entrance perfectly. If she went in too early, she would risk recognition as later arrivals scanned the room for their friends, too late and the interruption would ruin the element of surprise. Mary Beth, anal beyond redemption, would begin the meeting at precisely seven o'clock and deliberately ignore the scurrying few who seated themselves at a few seconds past.

At seven o'clock and ten seconds, Diane left the rest room and hurried into the meeting room on the heels of five latecomers. Fortunately they, too, kept their heads down and eyes averted rather than draw Mary Beth's withering glare, so Diane's bowed head and slumped shoulders did not attract attention. She chose a seat on the aisle near the back behind two taller women and sat low in her chair. She surveyed the room quickly, enough to spot a few people who would know her on sight and to estimate the attendance at approximately seventy-five, down from the hundred or more who used to attend back when the Elm Creek Quilters were members. The room was arranged as for a formal business conference rather than a cozy quilting bee, with straight rows of padded folding chairs placed on either side of a broad aisle. At the front of the room, chairs for the guild officers and a second door leading to the hallway flanked a podium, where Mary Beth stood speaking into a tinny microphone. Folding tables lined the wall between the two doors and were stacked with books from the guild library, advertisements for local quilt shows, and back issues of the guild newsletter. Too late, Diane realized that she should have duplicated the letter—after making a certain editorial deletion—and distributed the copies. Reading it aloud would have to suffice.

The format for the meetings had not changed from the old days. Mary Beth introduced herself and the subordinate officers seated behind her, then asked for new members and guests to raise their hands. Those unwise enough to reply were promptly subjected to unexpected public speaking when Mary Beth urged them to rise and say a few words about themselves. The five unfortunates gave their names, mentioned their favorite quilting techniques, and sat down again as quickly as Mary Beth allowed. When no one nudged Diane to her feet or glanced at her as if to ask why she had not introduced herself, she congratulated herself on blending in.

Mary Beth moved on to guild business. The vice president took the podium and read over some proposed changes to the bylaws; the guild members voted and the measure passed. The treasurer came forward and read over the previous month's record of income and expenses. The social chair reminded everyone about the end-of-the-year picnic and urged them to pay their deposits soon or they wouldn't be able to rent a picnic shelter at the Waterford College Arboretum and would have to sit on blankets, which, as everyone probably remembered from last year, resulted in aches and pains for their older members and far too many insects in the potluck buffet.

Diane opened her purse and withdrew her phone, the invitation, and the slip of paper Michael had given her.

The program coordinator took the microphone next and listed the guild events remaining until the summer break and mentioned a few speakers who had already agreed to appear next year. Diane couldn't help rolling her eyes at the excited murmurs and scattered applause that greeted each name. More prestigious quilters than those gladly waited in line for the opportunity to appear at Elm Creek Quilt Camp. Some were so delighted they would offer to trade their speaker's fees for a few extra days at the manor. As a courtesy to the local quilting community, Sylvia always invited members of the Waterford Quilting Guild to attend such special events free of charge. Since few local quilters except those already on the Elm Creek Quilt Camp mailing list ever came, Diane figured Mary Beth had dispensed with those announcements, too.

She allowed the barest of sighs and keyed Mary Beth's cell phone number into her own, resting her thumb lightly on the Send button.

Mary Beth thanked the program coordinator and took her place at the podium. "Before we introduce tonight's speaker," she said, "does anyone else have any announcements?"

Before she completed the sentence, Diane pressed the button.

In the moment between when the call went through and when the faint, synthesized tones of Pachelbel's Canon sounded at the front of the room, it occurred to her that Mary Beth might have turned off her phone out of respect for the gravity of the occasion. But apparently she had not, and from the startled look she shot her musical purse, she had warned her family never to interrupt, and anyone else who might call her was present. Mary Beth raised her voice and carried on, growing flustered as the phone continued to ring, louder and louder with each stanza.

Finally the ringing stopped; simultaneously, a voice sounded over Diane's phone. She quickly covered the speaker with one hand and hung up.

Mary Beth smiled, relieved. "Voicemail," she said, and the guild members laughed in sympathy.

Smiling and nodding with the rest, Diane waited long enough

for Mary Beth to repeat her request for other announcements, then dialed again.

This time, at the ringing of the phone, Mary Beth went bright red. "I'm sorry," she said, hurrying back to her chair and snatching up her purse. "It must be an emergency. Sandra, will you take over?"

With that, she raced from the room and the vice president rose.

Diane didn't wait to be called upon; she met Sandra at the podium and seized the microphone. "I have an announcement," she said, smiling brightly. Sandra eyed her curiously but stepped back and gestured for her to continue.

"It's no secret that quilters love to contribute blocks to group quilts," Diane began, unfolding the letter. A few in the audience nodded; a few others, friends of Mary Beth, gaped in recognition. "There's a wonderful project going on right now, right here in Waterford, for a very special quilter who put our town on the map of the quilting world. On behalf of the Elm Creek Quilters, I'd like to invite each and every one of you to participate."

She launched into the letter. By the second paragraph, the vice president shook her head and murmured a complaint, but Diane ignored her. She read with conviction and feeling, omitting only that slanderous phrase about her thinking Sylvia deserved to go quiltless. Mary Beth returned as Diane read the block requirements; she steeled herself and clutched the podium as if she might be forcibly removed from it, but Mary Beth stood fixed in the doorway, mouth open in horror, until Diane finished the letter.

Prepared for a quick exit, Diane nevertheless relished the moment by smiling out at the audience. "Are there any questions?"

A few hands went up, but Mary Beth stormed to the front of the room, hands balled into fists, red-faced and spluttering. "This—this is an outrage!"

"Yes, it is," called out a woman seated in the front. "Why didn't you contact us sooner?"

"You aren't giving us much time," said another, dismayed. "I already have two baby quilts to finish by the end of the month."

A chorus of agreement rose, but Mary Beth wrestled the microphone from Diane and raised one hand for quiet. "May I remind you that this woman is not a member of our guild? She isn't authorized to make announcements."

Someone snickered; Diane looked in the direction of Mary Beth's glare and spotted Lee Kessenich, a frequent customer of Grandma's Attic. She had recently moved to Waterford from Wisconsin, too recently to have fallen under Mary Beth's influence. As Mary Beth shoved Diane toward the door, Diane leaned to the microphone and said, "I'm terribly sorry if I've broken any rules."

"Wait, don't go," another woman cried. "What colors should we use again?"

As others chimed in with questions, Mary Beth shouted, "Ladies, ladies, please! Obviously Diane's only reason for coming here tonight was to create a disturbance. Please just ignore her. If she really wanted you to participate in this quilt, she would have told you about it sooner."

"We tried," said Diane, incredulous. She held the envelope high. "We sent an invitation to the guild, care of Mary Beth. She returned it to us and said you couldn't be bothered. I have the envelope right here if anyone wants to check the postmark and the address."

A murmur of surprise and indignation rose, but Diane looked around uneasily at the guild members and realized that at least some of them were more upset with her than with their president. "Thanks for your time," she called out as she dashed back to her chair for her coat and purse. "If you have any questions, please call me or Bonnie at Grandma's Attic. Thanks!"

She hurried from the room as the chorus of voices swelled behind her.

❧

Diane went home and waited for her neighbor to storm over in a fury. Mary Beth's car pulled into the Callahans' garage twenty minutes later, but there was no furious pounding on the door, no shrill phone call. Diane regretted leaving the meeting so hastily, although it had seemed prudent at the time. She wished she knew what had happened after she left.

Whatever Mary Beth might have done to discourage her fellow guild members from contributing to Sylvia's bridal quilt, it soon became evident that she had failed. All that week, quilters phoned Grandma's Attic to inquire about the guidelines for block size and pattern choices. Every day several shoppers came in specifically to purchase fabrics for "Sylvia's quilt," and a few remarkably industrious quilters dropped off finished blocks. By Saturday they had added twenty new blocks to the collection and had received promises for many more. Bonnie and Summer were mystified by the sudden outpouring of interest. "I suppose Mary Beth had a change of heart," said Bonnie, dubious. "She must have announced the project after all."

"I know for a fact she didn't," said Diane sharply, and was about to explain when Summer pointed out that Mary Beth couldn't have, since she had left her invitation at Grandma's Attic. As if neither had heard Diane speak, Bonnie and Summer agreed that one of the other guild members must have spread the word. Diane was so irritated with them that she went off to alphabetize pattern books without confiding her role in the sudden windfall.

As the last week before the start of quilt camp passed, Diane waited for Mary Beth to exact her revenge, but she saw nothing of her neighbor except what she glimpsed through the windshield of Mary Beth's car as she pulled in and out of her garage. Even Brent, who came over nearly every afternoon to study for midterms with Todd, gave no sign that he knew anything was amiss.

Maybe Diane had so humiliated Mary Beth that she had not told her family. Maybe the guild had turned on her in fury when it sank in that their president had dismissed the Elm Creek Quilters' invitation without consulting a single member of the board. Maybe they would demand a recall election, and finally, finally Mary Beth would be deposed. New leadership might breathe life into that moribund institution, healing the rift between the guild and the Elm Creek Quilters.

For her next trick, Diane decided, she would drive Fabric Warehouse out of business. In the meantime, she had her own block to make for Sylvia's quilt.

Sylvia was one of the few people Diane knew whose sharp tongue could match her own, and she respected that. Somehow, though, Sylvia managed to speak her mind without annoying her listeners, a skill Diane had yet to master. Sylvia knew when to soften criticism with a compliment or humor, but when she was deadly serious, everyone knew it and listened with respect. Diane could sew for the rest of her life without becoming the accomplished Master Quilter Sylvia was, but she could, and did, emulate her way with words. Without Sylvia's example in mind when she crashed the guild meeting, she probably would have insulted everyone present and fled from the library meeting room with an angry mob on her heels. As it was, she had offended only Mary Beth and her inner circle, and that alone deserved commemoration in a quilt block.

Her block was nearly finished by the first day of quilt camp, but then the whirlwind of activity forced her to set it aside. Apparently she was not the only Elm Creek Quilter who had failed to plan well; on the first day of classes, Sarah had to juggle the schedule to accommodate Judy's sudden trip to Philadelphia and wound up teaching a hand-quilting class herself. Gwen ran out of fusible webbing in the middle of her workshop and had to send one of the cook's helpers to Grandma's Attic for more, and Bonnie and Summer had forgotten that running the evening program together left no one to close the quilt shop. Bonnie asked Diane to cover, and

Diane agreed, resolving on the drive over to schedule that appointment with Bonnie as soon as the busy first week of camp settled into an easier routine.

Closing the shop meant that she returned home later than usual. Not until she walked through the door and saw Todd and Brent foraging for food in the kitchen did she remember she had agreed Brent could spend the night, and that she was supposed to stop on the way home for pizza and videos. They had heard her enter, so she couldn't sneak back out to her car. Instead she called in the pizza order and drove the boys to the video store to pick out movies for themselves, which meant twice as many DVDs with twice as much carnage as Diane usually allowed. Tim and the pizza delivery man arrived soon after they returned home, so the evening was salvaged despite Diane's mistake.

Diane and Tim went upstairs to bed when the first movie ended, after urging Todd and Brent to remember to get at least a few hours' sleep. Diane heard them moving the sofa to make more room for the air mattresses, so she knew they had at least unrolled their sleeping bags, but the television was still playing when she drifted off to sleep.

She and Tim woke to the alarm clock early the next morning. While Tim took his turn in the shower, Diane went to rouse Todd for school. She had padded halfway down the hall before remembering spring break and the sleepover. With a groan, she returned to bed for a few more minutes' rest, but she could not allow herself to fall back asleep because she had to be at Elm Creek Manor by eight.

After her shower, she went downstairs, pausing by the family room to check on Todd and Brent. They had drawn the curtains and turned off the television the night before, and one of the boys was snoring. Diane crept away to the kitchen, where Tim was reading the paper and finishing his breakfast. She had planned to make pancakes, but the boys were unlikely to wake before she left for work, so she set out a plate of muffins and a few boxes of cereal for them and took a yogurt from the refrigerator for herself.

She kissed Tim good-bye when he had to leave, then hurried back upstairs to finish getting ready. She stopped by the family room again on her way back—still no sign of life from the two sleeping-bag-shrouded lumps on the floor—and went to the kitchen for her purse. Propped up beside it was a course catalogue for Waterford College, folded open to a page where a paragraph had been circled with a yellow highlighter. Diane picked it up and read a description for COMP 326—Advanced Programming, taught by Dr. Judy DiNardo. A sentence underlined in red ink read, "Students are strongly encouraged to obtain a laptop computer for use in class."

Diane sighed and stuck the catalogue between the phone and the answering machine. Trust Michael to arrange it so he would have the last word. She wondered what time he had come home the previous night. She was not aware that she slept that soundly. Perhaps the television had masked the sound of the front door.

Shaking her head, she picked up her purse and dug around for her keys on the way to the garage. They were not in their usual corner of the front pocket, but she always left the car door unlocked, so she got in and searched the main pouch and the change purse, to no avail. Sighing in exasperation, she emptied the entire contents of her purse onto the front passenger seat—still nothing. "This is ridiculous," she muttered, checking to make sure all the zippers and clasps were unfastened before turning the purse upside down and shaking it vigorously. Only a nickel and a crumpled tissue fell out.

Diane glanced at her watch and hastily shoveled her belongings back into her purse. She always returned her keys to her purse—always—and her sons had learned the hard way to follow suit whenever they borrowed the car. She raced back inside and dug around in the kitchen junk drawer for the spare set, blindly groping through birthday candles, address labels, and miscellaneous batteries until her fingers brushed against the Waterford College

Wildcats key ring. She pulled it free and shoved the drawer closed as best she could in her haste. The spare set included only the keys for the house and the car, but they would have to do until she could find her own set. Todd might remember where she had put them after they returned from the video store, but she had no time now to wake him and ask.

Fortunately, she was not teaching that morning, merely assisting Agnes and Gwen with their workshops, so she still arrived at Elm Creek Manor in plenty of time. With misgivings, she skipped what was certain to be an excellent lunch in the banquet hall in order to make sure she arrived for her afternoon shift at Grandma's Attic well before Bonnie departed for Elm Creek Manor and locked the door behind her. In passing, Bonnie told Diane she would be coming back later to go over the books, so Diane wouldn't need to close that evening. Diane used this as an excuse not to mention the missing key; she would surely find it before she was asked to open or close the shop again.

Todd was watching television in the family room, alone, when Diane came home to fix supper before returning to Elm Creek Manor for the evening program. "Where's Brent?" she asked.

Todd shrugged and switched off the television. "Hanging out with some ASB guys, I guess."

"I see."

Todd sounded dejected, and more than a little irritated. The Associated Student Body was not the same as student government, which was comprised of the traditional elected positions and actually did represent student interests fairly well. Anyone could join ASB—although no one outside the popular cliques ever did—if they had third period available and were interested in planning pep rallies, fund-raisers, and Homecoming events. Michael, who had mistrusted anything that reeked of school spirit, had avoided all things ASB with a passion, and even Todd, who would have been welcomed gladly, was unwilling to sacrifice an academic period for what he called a social hour with an occasional bit of work thrown in. Kids joined ASB for a break from real work and for something to add to their college applications to impress people who didn't know any better, Todd claimed, and he couldn't stand it when Brent invited his friends from ASB along when they got together. Diane, who had expected Todd to embrace ASB when he first enrolled with Brent as a freshman, had been astonished when he had declined to sign up for the second semester.

Diane asked, "Are the ASB guys going to monopolize Brent for the rest of spring break?"

Todd said he didn't know and that it didn't matter, because he had other plans with some of the guys from the basketball team anyway. Diane nodded, trying to hide her satisfaction. She wouldn't mind being rid of Brent for a while.

To cheer up Todd—and to assuage her guilt—Diane prepared his favorite supper, spaghetti and meatballs. Afterward, Todd and Tim helped her search for the keys, without success. Diane even phoned the video store and the pizza place, although she knew that was illogical, since she had driven home from the video store and the pizza had been delivered. "Did anyone see me toss my keys into the delivery guy's truck?" she asked wearily, when they had given up and sat in the living room, watching the last of Todd's rented DVDs.

"I saw you put them in your purse," Todd assured her for what must have been the tenth time.

"They'll turn up," said Tim. "Eventually."

Diane agreed, but she didn't have until "eventually." Bonnie could ask her to open the store any day, and Diane had too many doubts arrayed against her already without admitting she had lost her key to the store.

She decided to avoid Bonnie as much as she could for as long as she could, which would not be easy considering how frequently their paths crossed at quilt camp. She gave herself until the end of the week to find her keys. After that, she would confess the truth and ask Bonnie for another.

She did not see Bonnie at all the next morning at the manor, but at lunchtime learned that she had congratulated herself for her stealth undeservedly. Bonnie had never shown up that morning, nor had she called.

Diane agreed with her friends that this was troubling and uncharacteristic, but she wondered if any besides Summer knew that Bonnie had not shown up at Grandma's Attic two days in a row earlier that month. Since no one answered the phone at the shop or at Bonnie's home, Summer had driven downtown to investigate. She had promised to call as soon as she had news, but the afternoon classes ended without any word. Afterward, Diane wanted to stop by Grandma's Attic herself, but she did not have enough time between driving home to prepare supper for her family and racing back to the manor to help Gwen with the evening entertainment program. She was only supposed to assist Gwen, who had agreed to fill in for the absent Bonnie, but Gwen must have forgotten because she was nowhere to be found by the time the quilted clothing fashion show was to begin.

"She went to Grandma's Attic to find out why Summer didn't report back," said Sarah as Diane prepared for her unexpected starring role as fashion show emcee. "Something must be terribly wrong. No one's answering the phones and no one's checked in."

"Well, let's not send anyone else or they'll get sucked into the same black hole," said Diane cheerfully, donning the outlandish quilted and sequined jacket Bonnie had intended to wear. It hung on Diane's slender frame, but she figured that enhanced the humorous effect. "Bonnie's probably just sick or something and forgot to call. When Summer and Gwen found out it was nothing serious, they decided to wait until tomorrow to tell us. If it was something really terrible, someone definitely would have let us know."

Sarah looked dubious but said she hoped Diane was right.

The next morning, they all learned she could not have been more wrong.

Gwen and Summer had worked late into the night helping Bonnie restore some order to the ransacked shop, but so much remained to be done that Bonnie wanted to continue working throughout the day, if the Elm Creek Quilters could spare her. They quickly assented, and listened, shocked, as Gwen and Summer told them what they had seen, what the police had determined.

"They think it's an inside job," said Gwen, shaking her head in disbelief. "I think it's more likely Bonnie forgot to lock the door, but she insists she remembered."

Summer nodded in agreement and said, "What bothers me is that if the police are focused on this theory, they'll ignore other alternatives."

"Wait," said Diane, heart sinking. "Why do they think it's an inside job?"

"Because there were no signs of forced entry," said Summer. "So they assume the culprit or culprits must have used a key."

"Or the door was left unlocked," said Gwen. "They left no fingerprints, either, so they must have worn gloves."

"So the police think they were professionals?" asked Judy, who had missed the anxious waiting of the previous day and seemed even more shocked than her friends by the news that greeted her on her first morning back from Philadelphia.

"Anyone who has ever seen a detective drama on television knows to wear gloves during a robbery," said Sylvia.

"It was cold that night," said Diane, her voice tight. "Anyone going outside would have worn gloves. So does this mean everyone in Waterford is a suspect?"

They all looked at her, then returned their attention to Summer as she described the inscrutable lists of what had been taken and what had been left behind. Not surprisingly, all the money in the store was gone, as well as one of the most expensive Berninas, but only one. A handful of rotary cutters and shears. Some fine-point permanent pens. With a meaningful look to Sylvia, Summer added, "They also took blocks Bonnie had been saving for a special quilt."

The bridal quilt? Diane saw her own confusion mirrored in her friends' eyes.

Gwen's brow furrowed as it always did when she grappled with an especially difficult academic puzzle. "It makes no sense. They take some expensive things and leave others. They take quilt blocks and leave the computer."

"No, that makes perfect sense," said Summer. "Bonnie's Mac is eight years old, an antique by computer standards. I can't imagine the thieves would have been able to sell it for much, and if they want a computer, the money they stole is more than enough to buy one of the best."

Numb, Diane nodded along with the others when Agnes proposed they make a schedule so that anyone not immediately responsible for a class or workshop could be relieved of other quilt camp duties so they could help Bonnie set the store to rights.

She wanted to weep.

CHAPTER EIGHT

Mary Beth

❧

M ary Beth read the letter a second time, fuming. How dare those Elm Creek Quilters expect the members of her guild to help them with some silly gift for that overrated old Sylvia Compson? How dare they address her guild at all after Diane's vindictive attempt to assume the presidency? Diane had never won a ribbon in a quilt show, and yet she had thought herself fit to manage the Waterford Summer Quilt Festival. She couldn't meet a deadline to save her life, and yet she believed herself capable of organizing a dozen different guild subcommittees. The guild had neither needed nor wanted a "change of pace" or "fresh air to chase away stale ideas," as Diane had promised in her campaign speech, the first in the history of the guild. For ninety-three years members had been content to modestly mention their interest in the office to friends and allow word to spread, then feign surprise when they were nominated. Until Diane, no one had needed to bribe members with promises to invite better speakers or direct new workshops or spend the dues more frugally. Whoever had the most friends won, and wasn't that the democratic way? Mary Beth would never forgive Diane for forcing her to stand at that podium explaining

Diane's inadequacies for the job as if she were begging to be reelected. And she would never forget the added humiliation of Diane's walking out of the meeting the evening the results were announced and taking some of the guild's most talented and dedicated members with her. Bonnie Markham owned the only quilt shop in town, Gwen Sullivan actually published academic research on quilt history, and Agnes Emberly could always be counted on to contribute the work of four quilters to the annual service project. Their resignations stung, but the guild got along just fine without them—better, in fact, without Diane to create constant discord—but the shadow they had cast on Mary Beth's presidency that year had rankled her ever since.

"It's just like that Diane to complain about a present for her own friend, too," Mary Beth told her husband and son over dinner. "It's just another sign of her malignant sense of ingratitude. That woman never appreciates anything anyone does for her."

Brent and Roger merely nodded, so Mary Beth took that as encouragement to continue. "Those Elm Creek Quilters think their time is more valuable than ours, do they?" she said, helping herself to more broccoli, cheese, and rice casserole. "They think we have nothing better to do than sew blocks for some stupid bridal quilt, do they? Don't they know we make a quilt a year for a real charity? They ought to try giving back to the community for a change, but with them it's just take, take, take."

"They make quilts for hospitals," said Brent.

She frowned at him. "What?"

"I heard Mrs. Sonnenberg talking once. They all make quilts for the kids' cancer ward at Hershey Medical Center and for the, what's it called, for babies that are born too early—"

"Premature?" volunteered his father. "Neonatal?"

"Yeah, thanks. The neonatal unit at the Elm Creek Valley Hospital."

Mary Beth bristled at the disloyalty, but she hated to criticize her son. "Then they ought to understand how much work projects like that take."

"It's just one quilt square," said Roger tiredly. "It doesn't sound like that much effort."

"It's not the effort. It's the principle." Mary Beth's sour frown shifted into a smile as she turned to her son. "Honey, I'm sure you know better than to mention this conversation to Mrs. Sonnenberg."

His mouth full, Brent shrugged and nodded. Of course he would never tell tales on her to that conniving shrew next door, even though she was the mother of his best friend. Mary Beth had tried to root out that friendship before it spread like stinkweed, but Brent had taken to Todd Sonnenberg despite her best efforts. Mary Beth's only comfort was that Todd seemed a model son, and Brent shared her antipathy for his delinquent elder brother, Michael. Mary Beth saw Diane's attitude reflected in Michael whenever she had the bad fortune to run into him, but Todd's temperament was as unlike Diane's as Brent's or Mary Beth's. Mary Beth would have guessed Todd was adopted except he did resemble Diane physically. Todd's good characteristics must have come from his father. Tim wasn't that bad, despite his obviously poor taste in wives.

Mary Beth wished the Sonnenbergs would move away, far away, and leave the neighborhood in peace, but she had prayed for that for years with nothing to show for it. Mary Beth was stuck with Diane the way other people were stuck with miserable allergies or chronic lower back pain. There was no getting rid of Diane permanently, so Mary Beth could only struggle to hold the symptoms in check.

There was only one way to handle this most recent outbreak of Diane nastiness: file the invitation in her quilt room and hope no one else in the guild received one. There were factions in the guild—small and powerless, but still a presence—that might actually like to participate in the bridal quilt. Some members had even attended Elm Creek Quilt Camp! When the camp was in its third year, Mary Beth and her vice president considered adding a guild-wide boycott to the bylaws, but others on the board pointed out the rule would be difficult to enforce and might raise the ire of their members.

Mary Beth had been forced to settle for passive resistance, ignoring the patronizing invitations to activities at Elm Creek Manor and taking her business to the Fabric Warehouse and mail-order companies rather than Grandma's Attic. Fortunately, since all guild correspondence was sent to the Callahan home, she could filter out the junk before the other members discovered it.

Mary Beth put the letter out of sight but not out of mind, fuming over it whenever she saw Diane—which was far too often but inescapable since she lived next door—or any of the other Elm Creek Quilters. Once when she spotted Sylvia leaving the hair salon she was tempted to run up and blurt out the secret, but that tough-looking Sarah McClure was with her and she didn't dare. An anonymous note would ruin the surprise just as well, but in a much less satisfying manner. Eventually, since trying to forget the letter didn't work, she decided to return it and let those annoying Elm Creek people know once and for all that her guild was off-limits.

She waited until the first day of March, exactly one month before the quilt blocks were due—too little time for the Elm Creek Quilters to find an alternate way to reach her guild members but just enough to make them feel as if they ought to try. Let them scurry around like ants in a flooded anthill for the entire month. They deserved it.

Bonnie Markham was a soft touch and still on good terms with most of the guild and, best of all, Mary Beth could reach her in a public place. Grandma's Attic was a tolerable walk from her front door in fair weather, but not when the temperatures hovered at barely above freezing, so Mary Beth drove downtown. It might have been more convenient to leave the letter at Diane's house, but she could only imagine what that psycho would be capable of when provoked on her own property.

Mary Beth strode into the quilt shop and hid her consternation at the sight of Diane and a vaguely familiar auburn-haired girl looking at some quilt blocks spread out on the cutting table. She took off her hat, smoothed back her hair, and, addressing neither of them in particular, asked, "Isn't Bonnie here today?"

"No," Diane shot back rudely. She sat down on a stool with her back to Mary Beth and removed a padded envelope from a large carton on the cutting table. The auburn-haired girl murmured something as Diane took from the envelope another quilt block and what looked to be a letter. Diane muttered a response that Mary Beth could not make out, so she drew closer, suspicious.

The auburn-haired girl, who so strongly resembled a younger and much thinner version of Gwen Sullivan that she had to be her daughter, smiled and said, "Bonnie's not here, but may I help you?"

"I suppose so," Mary Beth said, reluctant. She would much rather deal with Bonnie. "You're Summer, right? Summer Sullivan?"

"That's right."

"Your name is in the letter, so I guess you'll do." Mary Beth produced the invitation and held it out. "I believe this was sent to me by mistake."

Summer took the page, skimmed it, and nodded. "We definitely meant to send it to you. Actually, to the entire guild. You're listed as the guild contact, so we sent it to your home, hoping you would announce it at your next meeting."

Summer tried to return the letter, but Mary Beth would have none of that. She explained as firmly and clearly as she could that the Elm Creek Quilters were out of line to impose on her guild when their members had so many legitimate charities to support already, but Diane kept interrupting with obnoxious objections, which only encouraged Summer to whine and beg for Mary Beth to reconsider. There was no reasoning with them, and since she was outnumbered, Mary Beth decided she had made her point as clearly as they would allow and left after insisting they remove the Waterford Quilting Guild from their mailing list immediately. The consternation and outrage on Diane's face were priceless, and as Mary Beth sailed out the door, she was glad Bonnie had not been there after all. She paused by the front window and peeked inside for one last glimpse and was rewarded with the sight of Summer throwing the invitation into the trash where it belonged.

At supper that evening, she couldn't resist boasting about how she had put Diane in her place. "And those blocks they had scattered all over the cutting table," she said, "I just know those were the blocks for the bridal quilt."

Roger and Brent nodded and continued eating.

"The ones I saw weren't anything special," she mused aloud. "I guess those Elm Creek people aren't the wonderful teachers they consider themselves to be. Or the people who sent the blocks didn't send their best work, which doesn't say much for how they regard Sylvia."

"Or they were beginners," said Roger, reaching for another piece of chicken, "and that *was* their best work."

"That couldn't possibly be the case," said Mary Beth. "Beginners know better than to ruin a group quilt with their sloppy blocks."

"It's a gift to congratulate a bride and groom, not a masterpiece to display in a show. If beginners want to express their good wishes, they shouldn't be criticized for the number of stitches per inch they use."

"Stitches per inch refers to quilting, not piecing," snapped Mary Beth. "Which just shows you don't know anything about it."

Roger shrugged and continued eating without another word.

"Mom, you've been going on about this stupid quilt for months," said Brent. "You should really just forget about it. It's not that big of a deal."

"It is a big deal. Diane and those Elm Creek Quilters think they're the best thing that happened to quilting in Waterford since my guild was founded, and it's not fair. They ignore everything my guild has done for this town as if it never happened."

When she said "my guild," she meant herself, but she didn't want to brag.

Brent shook his head. "I still say you should just forget about it. You're driving yourself crazy."

When he said "yourself," his expression suggested he meant "us," as did the affirming grunt from his father.

Tears sprang into Mary Beth's eyes. "This is what I get for living in a house full of men," she said, voice shaking. She rose and gathered up her dishes. "You couldn't possibly understand."

She saw them exchange a look of distress as she carried her dishes into the kitchen and dumped them in the sink. She worked so hard, for her family, for the guild, and all anyone ever did was criticize.

When she returned downstairs later that evening, she found that the dishes had been loaded into the dishwasher, the leftovers stored in the refrigerator, the table wiped clean. She smiled, seeing their apology in the completed chores.

As the week went by, she tried to take her son's advice and forget the quilt, but she could not shake the uneasy sense that Diane was plotting revenge. Brent said nothing to suggest he had overheard anything unusual at the Sonnenberg home, but Mary Beth wasn't sure if he would recognize the signs of a covert plan if he happened to stumble across them. She could never tell how much Brent absorbed and what he ignored. She might mention an upcoming appointment every night for a week only to return from it and find him genuinely surprised that she had not been home to greet him after school. Other times she might compliment only once, in passing, a book or blouse she had seen in a store, and receive it as her next birthday or Christmas present. Unfortunately, unless she came right out and asked him to spy on Diane, he wasn't likely to uncover anything. She was tempted, but not quite willing to resort to that.

As another week passed uneventfully, Mary Beth's sense of impending confrontation began to ebb. Maybe this time Diane realized that she was beaten, that retaliation was futile. By the third Monday of March, Mary Beth felt secure enough to savor her triumph, and as she dressed for the monthly meeting of the Waterford Quilting Guild, she decided to share her secret victory with Sandra, her closest friend and loyal vice president. Sandra didn't care for those Elm Creek Quilters either, although her spite was reserved for Bonnie, who had refused many requests to hire Sandra to work in her quilt shop, as if it were so grand a place only experienced salespeople could be permitted to don one of those ridiculous aprons.

Not since Diane sought the presidency had Mary Beth felt so at home behind the podium in Meeting Room C of the public library. At two minutes to seven, she tested the microphone and noted the filling seats with satisfaction, then returned to the officers' chairs long enough to bend close to Sandra's ear and whisper that she had big news to share later. She started the meeting at precisely seven o'clock, welcoming the members who were already seated and pointedly ignoring those who scurried in late.

Five prospective new members were in attendance, a number Mary Beth noted with satisfaction. One of her goals for the term was to increase the membership, which for no discernible reason had been declining over the past few years. She hoped the newcomers noticed how efficiently the officers went about presenting the business of their respective offices. When Diane and her crones had been in the guild, the announcements had been periodically interrupted by wisecracks and laughter, which wasted valuable time and almost always added an extra half hour to the meeting. Without their interference, the guild business was attended to in reasonable time, and before long Mary Beth reassumed her position at the podium and asked if any of the other guild members wished to make an announcement.

At that moment, on the chair several paces behind her, her cell phone began to ring. She pretended not to hear it, then pretended it belonged to someone else, but the distinctive tones Brent had downloaded from the internet were her signature ring and everyone in the room knew it. Come to think of it, all of her friends were in that room, it was too late for a call from Waterford High School, and her boys had been warned never to phone during guild meetings. "Anyone? Any other announcements?" she asked, raising her voice to drown out the phone.

At that moment, the ringing finally ceased. "Voicemail," she said, relieved, and the guild members laughed and nodded in sympathy. She cleared her throat. "Well, if no one has any announcements, our program chairwoman would like to introduce—"

The phone started up again. Mary Beth flushed and hurried back to her chair. "I'm sorry," she said, snatching up her purse. "It must be an emergency. Sandra, will you take over?"

She raced from the room without waiting for a reply. In the hallway she dug through her purse, seized the phone, and pressed it to her ear, all while hurrying away from the meeting room so that her conversation would not distract the guild while Sandra introduced the guest speaker. "Hello?" she barked. When there was no reply, she moved closer to the outside door to pick up a better signal. "Hello?"

Silence. She grimaced and read the display: "You have 1 new number!"

That made no sense; Roger's cell and their home phone were already programmed. She pressed the keys to bring up her Caller ID, but she did not recognize the number that appeared. Probably a wrong number, or worse yet, a telemarketer. She jabbed the key to clear the display, switched off the phone, and tossed it back in her purse.

Mary Beth stormed back to the meeting room, vowing to call that number back and let them have it as soon as the meeting ended. As she drew closer, she heard a lone voice speaking over the portable sound system, but none of the usual oohs and ahhs and applause that accompanied a guest speaker's trunk show. Curious, she tried to return unobtrusively, but she froze just inside the doorway, reeling from the sight of Diane at her podium reading the invitation to participate in the bridal quilt.

At first she was too shocked to do anything, but when Diane smirked, put away the letter, and asked for questions, she flew into action. "This—this is an outrage!" she exclaimed, hurrying forward.

"Yes, it is," someone called out. "Why didn't you contact us sooner?"

Another chimed in, "You aren't giving us much time. I already have two baby quilts to finish by the end of the month."

Other voices swelled, but Mary Beth, horrified, managed to pry the microphone from Diane's grimy fist and tried to regain order. "May I remind you that this woman is not a member of our guild?" she said, ready to remind them under what circumstances Diane had left. "She isn't authorized to make announcements."

Some traitor laughed derisively; Mary Beth ignored decorum and shoved Diane toward the nearest door. "I'm terribly sorry if I've broken any rules," Diane called out with false innocence, leaning close to the microphone.

"Wait, don't go," another woman cried. "What colors should we use again?"

"Ladies, ladies, please," Mary Beth shouted over the clamor. "Obviously Diane's only reason for coming here tonight was to create a disturbance. Please just ignore her. If she really wanted you to participate in this quilt, she would have told you about it sooner."

"We tried," retorted Diane, holding up an envelope. "We sent an invitation to the guild, care of Mary Beth. She returned it to us and said you couldn't be bothered. I have the envelope right here if anyone wants to check the postmark and the address."

Horror-struck, Mary Beth tried to snatch it away, but Diane suddenly blurted a hasty good-bye and sprinted for the door. Suddenly Sandra was at Mary Beth's side, gently taking the microphone from her hand. "Calm down, everyone," Sandra said, returning to the podium, her deep, gravelly voice making little impact on the rising din. "Don't pay any attention to that troublemaker."

"Is it true?" a voice rang out. "Did you deliberately keep that invitation from us?"

Mary Beth held up a hand as if it would keep back the accusing voices. She took a deep breath and willed herself to calm as she joined Sandra at the podium, her station of order. "I did, and I'll tell you why. I know how busy you are already, especially since so many of you have already been so generous with your time and talents for our service project, and I didn't want you to feel obligated to participate in something so, well, frivolous."

She cringed at the incredulous echo of her last word.

"That's for us to decide!" someone shouted.

"I'm the elected president. I had to use my best judgment. If I made a mistake, I apologize." Mary Beth forced a shaky smile. "From now on, I'll be sure to bring you every solicitation the guild receives, but don't be surprised when you're overwhelmed by all the requests."

"I don't care about next time," wailed a woman in the second row. "Sylvia's wonderful. I want to participate in *this* quilt."

Mary Beth tried to look apologetic. "I'm sorry, but as someone has already pointed out, it really is too late."

"There's plenty of time to make one block," said a woman in the back row. She had joined a year ago after moving to Waterford from Wisconsin; Mary Beth couldn't recall her name. Lee something.

"I've been on the Elm Creek Quilts mailing list ever since I attended quilt camp last summer. I received an invitation, too, and I'd be happy to make copies for everyone who wants them. Give me your names before you leave and I'll make a list."

A crowd of clamoring quilters quickly surrounded her. "Maybe this can wait until after the meeting," Mary Beth shouted into the microphone. "Let's not forget we have a very special guest tonight, a talented quilter from Boalsburg and a member of the Centre Pieces Quilt Guild . . ."

She trailed off when she realized no one was listening. The crowd around the traitor in the back row thickened. Mary Beth glanced at the guest speaker, who had taken a flyer from the table along the wall and was writing something on the back. Her address, Mary Beth realized, as she rose and carried the paper to the back of the room.

"Sandra." She plucked at the sleeve of her closest friend and ally, who was gaping at the scene. "Take over, will you? I think I'm— I think I should—"

Sandra gave no sign she heard. Mary Beth left the sentence unfinished and stepped away from the podium.

∞

She drove home in a daze. Inside, she clung to Roger and sobbed out the story. Brent had come downstairs to see what was wrong and now sat by her side, listening, wide-eyed and incredulous, as the story of her humiliation spilled from her.

Roger patted her back and sighed. "I guess maybe now you'll finally drop this silly feud with the Sonnenbergs."

"Dad," said Brent. "She's upset."

"That's your response?" Mary Beth pulled away from her husband and groped on the end table for a box of tissues. "Your wife is dishonored in front of all her friends, and that's how you respond?"

"Well, what do you want me to do? Run next door and challenge Tim to a duel?"

"Don't be ridiculous," she snapped, dabbing at her eyes. "This is between me and that—that evil witch. How can you call it a silly feud? It's much more than that, and that woman's behavior tonight proves it."

"All it proves," Roger muttered, "is that you two are equally committed to a to-the-death struggle over very small stakes."

Mary Beth ignored him and blew her nose. "Brent, I don't want you playing with that Sonnenberg boy anymore."

"That's not fair," he protested. "It's not Todd's fault his mom's a nutcase."

Roger gazed at the ceiling. "Why do I suspect an identical conversation is taking place next door?"

"If you can't be supportive, then be quiet," snapped Mary Beth. "I'm sorry, Brent, but that woman is a bad influence. I don't want you anywhere near her."

"I barely even see her when I'm over there."

"That's not good enough."

"But we have midterms coming up. Todd and I always study together. We're partners for the Physics project. Not to mention he's been my best friend since the second grade."

Mary Beth sniffled into her tissue. She hated to see him so distraught. "Well—"

"Please, Mom. This way, I might overhear her if she plans anything else."

"By all means," said Roger. "Let's take the high road. Let's spy on the neighbors."

"If she tries anything else, I'm pressing charges." Still, Brent had a point. "All right. You can still be friends with Todd under one condition: If that woman says a single word against me, you'll defend me." Unlike her husband. She glared at him, but he had let his head fall against the sofa cushions and was shaking his head at the ceiling.

"I promise," said Brent solemnly.

She reached out and drew him into an embrace. "That's my good boy."

Sometimes she thought Brent was the only person who understood her.

Sometimes Brent thought the main reason he and Todd were best friends was that they both had mothers who were certifiable. Still, while his mother was often embarrassing, at least she didn't have a mean streak like Todd's mom. When Brent went to the Sonnenberg house to study the next day, he was so furious he could barely look in her direction, much less speak to her. He ignored her so intently that it was some time before he realized Mrs. Sonnenberg was ignoring him, too. Then, in a flash of insight, he realized that she wasn't acting much different than usual.

She always tried to pretend he wasn't there. It wasn't just because of what happened at the library.

He wanted to talk to Todd about that night at the library, but he didn't know how to bring it up without starting an argument. He would have just let it go except he just couldn't understand what Mrs. Sonnenberg had against his mother. He wrestled with that question, but the answer was irritatingly elusive.

Finally he couldn't stand it anymore. "What's with your mom?" he asked on the Thursday after the quilt guild meeting, as he and Todd studied for their Calculus midterm.

Todd didn't even bother to look up from his differential equations. "What do you mean?"

"You know. Why'd she go off like that at the quilt thing?"

Todd looked genuinely perplexed. "What?"

"You know," repeated Brent, irritably. "The way she barged into my mom's quilt guild meeting and started ordering them around, telling them they had to make a stupid quilt."

"My mom says a lot of stuff about a lot of quilts, but the only quilt guild she talks about are her friends up at the manor."

Brent stared at his friend, head bent over his book, his pencil scratching on paper. Todd really didn't know. Mrs. Sonnenberg had made a fool of his mother in front of all her friends in the one place where she got any respect, and yet Mrs. Sonnenberg had thought so little of it she had not even bothered to tell her kid.

"Never mind," said Brent tightly, picking up his pencil and writing down equations with a vengeance. Sometimes he was seized by the urge to punch Todd in the face until he begged for mercy, but if he ignored it, the feeling always faded.

Although he wouldn't get his grades back until after spring break, Brent knew he had aced his midterms. His mom was so pleased that she hugged him, gave him fifty dollars, and agreed that he could spend the night at Todd's. She had smiled so rarely since that night in the library that out of guilt he put off accepting Todd's invitation until Monday. Unaccustomed to a weekday with no classes and no homework, they hung out for most of the day, watching TV, shooting hoops in the driveway, playing computer games, until they grew bored with the abundance of time. Todd halfheartedly suggested they work on their Physics project, but Brent said he would rather stare at a blank wall than spend one minute of his vacation working on an assignment that wasn't due for another month.

Mrs. Sonnenberg was supposed to bring pizza for supper and videos for later, but by five-thirty Brent and Todd were starved, so they raided the fridge and cupboards for pretzels and sodas and a few attempts at sandwiches. Brent suggested they order their own pizza and have it delivered, but Todd didn't have any cash and Brent wasn't about to blow his fifty bucks on food Mrs. Sonnenberg should have paid for, so he said he was broke, too.

It was after seven when Mrs. Sonnenberg finally showed up, with no pizza and no DVDs. Brent shook his head, disgusted, but she was too busy giving them some lame excuse about having to close the quilt shop to notice. She called for a pizza and herded them out to her car to drive them to the video store. When she wandered off to read the display case for some stupid Julia Roberts romantic comedy, Brent picked out three action movies and said to Todd, "You pick some and I'll pick some."

Todd eyed the stack in Brent's hands. "She said we could get two."

"Yeah, but she also said she'd bring them home for us. She's feeling guilty, so take advantage."

Todd shook his head, but grinned as he turned back to the shelves.

Brent nudged him. "Come on. Don't be such a craven poltroon."

Todd guffawed; one of their favorite inside jokes was to work vocabulary words from their SAT prep class into everyday conversation just to prove how awkward they were. But he selected two more DVDs, and when they took them to Mrs. Sonnenberg, she didn't complain.

Todd's parents finally went to bed after the first movie. "It's about time," muttered Brent, shoving the sofa aside to make room for the air mattresses.

Todd came over to help him. "Why? You tired already?"

"Not tired." Brent grinned and headed for the kitchen. "Just thirsty."

During their search for food, he had found where the Sonnenbergs had unimaginatively stashed their liquor, in a cupboard above the refrigerator. Todd realized where he was heading when he picked up a kitchen chair. "Brent, no. That's not a good idea."

"Why not?" Brent set the chair in front of the refrigerator and climbed up. "You don't complain at my house."

"My mom's a human Breathalyzer. She'll know."

"Not if we don't see them until morning." He selected a bottle of vodka three-quarters full, then took out a bottle of rum. "Hey. Rum and Cokes."

"Keep it down," said Todd, peering over his shoulder. "She's a light sleeper."

"So she can check on her widdle baby if he cries?" Brent tucked the bottles under his arm and returned the chair to its place at the table. All the while Todd trailed after him, glancing anxiously toward the ceiling. "Will you relax? Have a drink. That will help."

Todd scowled, but took the bottle of vodka. He retrieved the orange juice from the refrigerator while Brent searched the cupboards for the supersize plastic tumblers their class had sold two years before to raise money for their sophomore trip. They mixed their drinks in silence, listening for footsteps upstairs, then watered down the bottles, wiped them clean, and put them away.

When the harpy didn't come swooping in to bust them, Todd finally relaxed and laughed his way through the Lethal Weapon series like always. They returned to the kitchen off and on, Todd for snacks, Brent to replenish his drink. "We should go get some beer," Brent remarked as they slouched on the sofa watching a half-dozen cars collide and explode. "No one cards during spring break when the students are gone. We can take your mom's car."

"You're not driving, not after that industrial strength rum and Coke you just put away."

It never failed to irk Brent that Todd could drink all he wanted and yet sound as if he were stone-cold sober. "Screw you. I can drive just fine."

"Take your own car, then."

"And wake up my parents getting it out of the garage? Great idea." But Brent stayed put, not really wanting to drive for beer or break his fifty when there were other untouched bottles just a room away.

They were half asleep in front of *Collateral Damage* when the sound of a door opening roused them. "Quick," Todd hissed, bolting to his feet to hide the evidence although their cups had been empty for at least an hour.

They heard footsteps in the kitchen a moment before the light went on. They blinked and looked past the breakfast nook to find Michael setting his backpack on the counter and frowning at them.

"Oh, it's you," breathed Todd, and dropped onto the sofa.

"You better wash out those cups before Mom wakes up," Michael advised, reaching into the cupboard for a glass. "I smelled rum the minute I walked through the door."

"We will," said Todd, and Brent remembered that spill near the sink he had been meaning to clean up.

Michael shook his head and poured himself some milk. "If you make a habit of this, you'll get caught. They'll know if you water down the booze too much."

"Thanks for your moral authority," said Brent.

"In case you haven't noticed, we can't go to the bars and we don't have our own apartment like you," said Todd. "And we aren't doing anything you didn't do."

Michael finished his milk and put the glass in the dishwasher. "I'm just trying to help."

Todd, bleary-eyed from the alcohol and lack of sleep, remained stubbornly belligerent. "If you really wanted to help, you'd invite us to one of your parties instead of making us sneak around."

"One, no one's making you do anything. Two, Mom would kill me if I gave you alcohol. Three, we don't party at our house as much as you think."

"Four, you're an idiot," said Brent.

"I didn't come here to argue with a bunch of drunk high schoolers." Michael took some papers or something from his backpack and stuck them on the kitchen counter by Mrs. Sonnenberg's purse. "If you're stupid enough to get wasted with Mom and Dad right upstairs, that's your problem."

He zipped his backpack closed, hefted it onto his back, and stalked away. A moment later, they heard the front door softly open and close.

Todd slumped against the sofa and groaned. "Man, I can't wait until I go to Princeton."

Brent felt a stab of jealousy. He had tried early admission for

Princeton and had been rejected, though he was still hopeful for Yale. "Does he move back in at the end of the semester? Because if you have to spend the entire summer under the same roof with that loser—"

"He's staying in his apartment." Todd let out an enormous yawn. "And he's not a loser. He's just trying to look out for us."

Brent scowled. "Yeah, I can tell how glad you were to see him."

In response, Todd yawned again. "I'm gonna get ready for bed."

Brent was too irritated to argue. He stalked off to the bathroom, and by the time he returned, Todd had cleaned up the kitchen, turned off the lights, and unrolled both sleeping bags on the air mattresses. He had left the best pillow for Brent. Mollified, Brent climbed into his sleeping bag and said, "Greg and Will are coming over tomorrow. We thought we'd go see a movie and get some beer. Want to come?"

"Where are you going to drink? The arboretum?"

"Where else is there?"

Todd barked out a scornful laugh. "You know, in a year those two are going to be indistinguishable from all the other losers staggering around Fraternity Row every weekend."

"Yeah? How are you going to be any different?"

"I'm going to leave what passes for fun in high school back in high school. I'm not going to be lurking around in the woods chugging beer." Todd thumped his pillow with a fist and rolled over. "And neither are you, once you get out of Waterford. I can't figure out why you like those guys."

One, Brent thought, glowering in the dark, *they don't always have to prove how much better they are than everybody else. Two, they know how to have fun. Three, they understand the importance of friends who stick together no matter what. Four, their mothers didn't treat my mother like something they scraped off the bottom of their shoes.*

Thoughts churning, he lay on his back with his eyes open, but

Todd fell asleep before Brent could think of a retort. With a grunt, Brent crawled out of his sleeping bag and groped his way down the darkened hallway to the bathroom. On his way back, he passed through the breakfast nook and spotted Michael's papers or whatever propped up against Mrs. Sonnenberg's purse. He picked them up and opened the refrigerator door to read them, but it was just the course catalogue from Waterford College with a few passages marked. Brent snorted and stuck the booklet back where he had found it, and as he did, he noticed that Mrs. Sonnenberg had left her purse wide open.

He glanced over at Todd, sound asleep on the family room floor. He reached in for her wallet and leafed through the old photos, choking back laughter at one of the two brothers at about eight and ten years old, their arms over each other's shoulders, beaming with gap-toothed grins. He considered taking money but decided against it, since she was such an airhead she probably wouldn't even notice. But she'd notice missing keys, he thought, lifting the ring carefully to avoid waking Todd. She'd be late for that stupid quilt camp, maybe even get fired. She'd have to walk to that quilt store, too, and maybe get fired there, as well.

Biting his lips together so he wouldn't laugh out loud, Brent stashed the keys in his jacket pocket and climbed into his sleeping bag. A few hours of frustration wouldn't make up for what Mrs. Sonnenberg had done, but it was better than nothing. Too bad he could never tell his mom how he had scored some revenge.

When Brent woke, parched and groggy, the clock on the DVD player read 11:18. He groaned and flopped back against the pillow. He would have tried to fall asleep again if Todd had not sat up and asked if he wanted breakfast. Brent nodded, though he felt too queasy to eat. He padded off to the bathroom and, after splashing some water on his face, he felt a little better.

Mrs. Sonnenberg had left a plate of muffins and a few boxes of cereal on the counter, as if she thought they were too stupid to find the cereal themselves. They fixed themselves some breakfast and carried it back to the family room so they could watch the last of their DVDs while they ate. By that time, Brent had realized to his disappointment that Mrs. Sonnenberg had left in her car, so she must have had a spare set of keys. He hoped he had given her at least a few minutes of frustration, if not the frantic screamfest he had anticipated.

After the movie, they put away their dishes and cleaned up the family room. "Are you sure you don't want to hang with me and Greg and Will today?" asked Brent, giving his friend one last chance.

Todd shook his head. "But call me if you want to do something tomorrow."

Brent didn't bother to try to talk him into it. He packed up the rest of his stuff and left.

He told himself it was Todd's loss, and as it turned out, he was right. The movie was great, and three of the hottest girls in ASB were there—without dates, for a change, so they agreed when Will invited them to The Bistro. They managed to make a plate of nachos and another of mozzarella sticks last two hours, annoying the waitress with frequent requests for the free soft drink refills. When they finally decided to go, it was with enormous pleasure that Brent whipped out his wallet, placed the fifty on the plastic tray with the bill, and announced that he was treating the girls. They squealed with delight and thanked him admiringly in a manner that was more than a little attractive, and Ashley, the prettiest of them with her waist-length blond hair and brown eyes, even hugged him.

They left the restaurant with the girls exclaiming that they'd had a great time and that they should do this again before they all went their separate ways to college. The only disappointment was that the girls turned down their invitation to go drinking in the Waterford College Arboretum, but Brent didn't care because he had managed to get Ashley alone for a minute and she had agreed to be his date for the prom.

He felt invincible as they sneaked back to Will's house and raided his father's well-stocked refrigerator in the garage. Stuffing six-packs beneath their jackets, they hiked along one of the lesser known trails through the arboretum until they came to their favorite drinking establishment, as Will called it, a small clearing where a few fallen trees had created tolerable seats. Night fell before they finished off the last beer, but Brent wasn't worried because his parents knew he and Will were sleeping over at Greg's house, but didn't know that Greg's parents, both sociology professors, were off at some conference in Santa Fe. Brent thought they should have just gone straight to Greg's house with the beer—spring break or not, it was still cold at night—but the arboretum was tradition and Greg worried about his parents finding stray empties.

Hungry and wired, they hiked out of the forest, cracking up as they tripped over roots and fallen branches in the darkness. Main Street was deserted, a rarity for the hour even on a weeknight, with most of the college students long gone and the bars virtually empty.

Will stopped at a legendary dive, the one known for carding even gray-haired alumni and for providing free shot glasses to anyone who could drink twenty-one shots on his twenty-first birthday. He cupped his hands around his eyes and peered inside. "Two, three, four," he counted. "Four customers! They're not making enough to pay for the electricity. Why don't they let us in when the students are gone?"

"Because they don't want to lose their liquor license," drawled Greg, pulling Will away from the window.

They continued down the sidewalk with Will pausing to test every locked door. "All we need is one," he said, yanking on the doorknob of a shoe store. "Locked. And I need some new Nikes."

Brent and Greg guffawed and shoved him along. "Locked," said Greg at a bakery, laughing. "And I need some cookies."

"Locked," said Will. "And I need some—some thread."

Greg laughed so hard he doubled over and nearly fell.

Brent stopped short. "Wait." He dug around in his jacket pocket for Mrs. Sonnenberg's key ring, which he had meant to hide someplace bizarre before he left, like the aquarium or a jar of peanut butter, but he had forgotten. "I think we can get in."

His friends scoffed, and jeered him when the first key didn't work, but their laughter ended when the second turned in the lock. "What are you doing?" demanded Greg, looking frantically over his shoulder.

"Nothing." Brent slipped inside; they followed without prompting. "Let's just look around."

"Don't turn on the lights," hissed Will.

Greg yanked his hand away from the switch as if it burned. "I can't see a thing in here," he complained, stumbling into a display of fabric and knocking it on the floor.

For a long moment they smothered their laughter, shushed each other, and listened with hearts pounding for the police or an alarm. When nothing happened, Brent said, "Be careful, you guys," and shoved over a magazine rack.

Greg laughed and with one sweep of his arm cleared a whole counter of pins and other stuff that went pinging to the floor.

Brent laughed and said, "I hope you have your gloves on."

Greg held up his gloved hands and grinned, but Will said, "Wait. How'd you get that key?"

"Todd Sonnenberg's mom works here."

"Her? Say no more." Will strode over to a bolt of fabric, seized the edge of the cloth in both hands, and flung it so it unrolled in the air. Brent and Greg cheered quietly and grabbed bolts of their own. It became a contest: whose fabric streamer went the highest, the farthest, which cardboard roller knocked over the most stuff when it fell.

Then Greg thought to look for a cash register; they rang up a no sale and cleaned it out without worrying about dividing up the money evenly. "Hey, look at this," exclaimed Will, brandishing a large rotary cutter. "You could do some serious damage with this."

So they each pocketed several and some scissors, since they were on the same rack, then shoved the rack itself until it toppled over.

Brent left the others to ransack the store and wandered into the back office. He gave the ancient computer a shove of disgust and tore the place apart looking for better equipment, but not even the scanner was new enough to be compatible with his system. Annoyed, he flung open file drawers and threw their contents on the floor just for the pleasure of watching the paper fly, but then he spotted a bag with the logo of a bank printed on it, took one look inside, and stuffed it into his shirt. What kind of idiot kept that much cash in an unlocked filing cabinet? Unbelievable.

"Brent, come here," called Greg.

He returned to the main room and found his friends studying something in the dim light. "What?" he asked, picking his way across the littered floor.

"It's a fake ID," gloated Will, "and you'll never guess who's on it."

He held it out of reach and tried to make Brent guess, but Brent wrestled it away from him and gaped at the photo. "Michael Sonnenberg," he read. "Man, this gets better and better."

"Maybe we should think about getting out of here," said Greg uneasily. "The bars are gonna close soon. Someone could walk by."

Brent nodded. "In a minute." He looked around, thinking, until with a sudden flash, he remembered something his mother had said. He stumbled over slippery paperback quilting books on his way to the cutting table, then cleared the shelves until he found the largest carton. One glance inside confirmed it. "Here," he said, shoving the box into Will's arms. "You take this."

arranged so that she would have ample help restoring the quilt shop to order. Bonnie's eyes filled with tears when she saw how many late nights they were willing to endure, at a time of year when their workloads were already daunting enough to weaken the wills of lesser women.

"Do you think Craig could get some of his friends from the physical plant to help?" asked Judy. "It might bend a few department rules, but with more hands and the college's tools, we might be able to finish in time to open next week."

"I don't think Craig's coworkers are necessarily his friends," said Bonnie, nonetheless thanking Judy for the suggestion with a smile. "But I wouldn't ask him anyway."

"Why not?" asked Diane.

Bonnie saw Agnes straighten in her chair, alert and waiting.

"Because Craig and I are getting a divorce."

∞

After the Farewell Breakfast on Saturday, Summer headed straight to Grandma's Attic accompanied by the other Elm Creek Quilters. Only Sylvia and Agnes had remained behind, waiting for the last quilt campers to depart.

All that day they cleaned and repaired and did what they could to raise Bonnie's spirits, but Summer didn't see that they were having much impact. How could they hope to, when Bonnie had lost both her marriage and her life's dream? Channeling her rage into her work, Summer labored in silent fury, repairing shelves, cutting damaged fabric into saleable quantities, and wondering if anyone had thought to question Craig before assuming it was an inside job. The police had questioned Summer thoroughly and with complete skepticism until Jeremy swore she had been with him that night, and she assumed they had given Diane an equally hard time. Had anyone bothered to check Craig's alibi after they grilled Bonnie and her employees? Summer had considered him the most likely sus-

"Why? What is it?" Will peered inside. "It's just some pieces of fabric. Why don't you carry it if you want it so bad?"

Brent had already gone to the far wall, where he scanned the shelves of sewing machines for the one with the most gadgets and highest price. "Because I'm carrying this," he said, hefting a carton.

"Are we done shopping yet?" asked Greg, peeved and anxious.

Brent looked around. They were done. "There might be a back door," he said, as the urgency not to be caught sank in.

They found it and raced outside to the back alley, muffling their laughter as they stumbled into a run, slowed by the weight of their prizes.

CHAPTER NINE

Bonnie resumed her duties at Elm Creek Quilt Camp on the Friday after the break-in. Grandma's Attic was nowhere near ready for business and would not be until she could repair the shelving units, but the broken glass and debris had been cleared away and the salvageable inventory culled from the waste. Once she accepted that she would not be able to reopen right away, her conscience would no longer allow her to ignore her camp duties, no matter how many excuses her friends made on her behalf.

On Friday morning she walked from Agnes's house to the shop just to check on things, too anxious to trust in the lock anymore. After making sure there had not been another burglary, she switched off the lights and left the sign in the window turned to CLOSED.

Then she went around back, climbed into the family car, and drove to Elm Creek Manor.

Her friends greeted her with hugs and words of comfort, taking care, as Bonnie had asked, to keep the news of her misfortune away from the campers. Once she reopened, she would not want them to stay away out of fear that the shop was in a dangerous location or that she was peddling damaged goods.

At lunch, her friends showed her the schedule they had

pect even before learning of the impending divorce, which only strengthened her suspicions.

Summer was teaching a Kaleidoscope-Piecing workshop at Elm Creek Manor when the insurance claims adjuster came to inspect Grandma's Attic the following Monday. After classes, Summer hurried to the shop to help with the ongoing repairs and to find out how the meeting had gone.

Not well, Bonnie's expression told her, although she said it went fine. "I won't know anything for certain until I receive his official statement," she said. "Maybe I should have waited until after his visit to clean up."

Summer glanced around the shop; despite all their work, Grandma's Attic was still a disaster. "They have the pictures we took the next morning, and those from last fall for comparison," she said. "They also have the police report."

Bonnie gritted her teeth as she tightened a bolt on a bookshelf. "The police report is part of the problem. If they decide it was an inside job, the agent says there's a clause in my policy that absolves them from the need to pay."

"They can't do that," said Diane, who had been listening in nearby.

"I'm afraid they can. It's my own fault for signing the policy without considering all the consequences. I never thought it would matter." Bonnie sat back on her heels, bleak. "But what choice do I have?"

Diane looked away, white-faced.

"You can tell them about Craig," said Summer, glancing at Diane and hoping she would second her. But Diane said nothing. "Bonnie, I know you don't want to accuse him—"

"He didn't do it."

"How do you know? Does he have an alibi?"

"Yes." Bonnie set down the wrench and met her gaze evenly. "He was in his office on the computer, logged on to the internet.

Campus mainframe records confirm it. The police informed me yesterday."

"But—" Summer's fury vanished like an extinguished flame. "Then who? If they think it was an inside job, that leaves you, me, and Diane."

"And we all have alibis." Bonnie took up the wrench again and moved to another bolt, tightening it furiously.

"What, then?" Summer looked from Bonnie to Diane and back, perplexed. "Do they think our alibis are fake? Do they think we hired someone to trash the place?"

"I don't know what they think," said Bonnie. "But I want you both to understand that whatever the police believe, I know in my heart that you two had nothing to do with it."

Her vehemence surprised Summer. Until that moment, it had never occurred to her that Bonnie might have even fleetingly considered either of her employees to be suspects.

Summer returned home late that evening, as she had every day since the burglary. Jeremy had kept supper waiting for her. It was supposed to have been her night to cook. She had completely forgotten.

She told him the latest developments as they ate. Loyal customers had stopped by to express their condolences as if they were attending a wake; the best of them brought food and positive attitudes to sustain the Elm Creek Quilters while they worked or, better yet, rolled up their sleeves and asked Bonnie how they could assist. Even with the unexpected generosity, it appeared that they would not be able to reopen the shop until mid-April at the earliest. Fortunately, a second look revealed that the burglars had ignored the storage room, so Bonnie would have something to put on the shelves, though not much.

"I still think Craig is involved somehow," Summer said, brooding. "If I could just figure out how."

"I thought Bonnie said he had an alibi."

"She did, but I'm not convinced it's airtight. Maybe he logged on to the internet before leaving his office, then went back and logged out after trashing Grandma's Attic." She poked at the food on her plate, then set down her fork. She had no appetite but had gone through the motions of the meal for Jeremy's sake. "He's resented Bonnie's success for as long as I can remember. He even seemed to resent her failures, because they at least proved she was willing to take risks he lacked the courage to take."

Jeremy leaned forward and rested his elbows on the table. "You're right to say he lacks courage, so would he really be brave enough to break into the shop just to get some revenge? Wasn't locking her out of their home enough to make that point?"

"You think what he did was an act of courage?"

"That's not what I mean. I was just pointing out that he didn't really need to do it, that he lacks a motive. Whereas this Gregory Krolich guy—"

"Why are you so eager to defend Craig?"

"I'm not," said Jeremy, surprised. "I barely know him. I've only spoken to him once or twice at Elm Creek Quilts functions."

"Bonnie was living out her dream, and Craig couldn't stand it," said Summer vehemently. "It's a typical male response to a woman's success. It's obvious to anyone who doesn't ignore the facts."

Jeremy sat back and studied her. Summer could not meet his gaze. She studied her plate, picked up her fork, and set it down again.

Finally Jeremy asked, "What's this really about?"

"Nothing."

"No, it's something. We should talk about it." His eyes were watchful, his voice steady. "Do you think I don't want you to succeed?"

"I wasn't talking about us."

"I think you were."

"Well . . ." Summer hesitated. "Fine. Let's talk about us. What exactly do you expect to happen when you finish your degree?"

He shrugged. "I'll find a tenure-track assistant position some-where, and a post-doc if none are available. I've already sent out dozens of CVs. You know that. We've talked about this before."

"We've talked about your job, but not about us." Summer took a deep breath. "I am not trying to drag any kind of commitment out of you—"

"Don't worry," he said, frowning. "I know that would be the last thing on your mind."

"What's that supposed to mean?"

"We both know I'm much more committed to this relationship than you are."

"How can you say that? You're the one who's planning to gradu-ate and leave."

"You've known that from our first date."

"When we were just dating it didn't matter."

"I want you to come with me," he said. "That's the truth, and I say it knowing it will scare you off. When I graduate, I want us to leave Waterford together. I want to get married, if your mother hasn't so poisoned you against men that you're afraid to."

Summer pushed back her chair and rose. "How dare you."

"I'm sorry." He followed her into the living room. "That was unfair. I love you, Summer. I want to be with you. But we both know that won't be in Waterford."

"So you do expect me to sacrifice my career to yours," said Sum-mer. He reached for her, but she pulled away. "You're just like Craig."

A muscle in his jaw flexed, but his voice remained steady. "I am nothing like Craig and you know it. I can't believe you're saying these things."

"What's different? You wouldn't destroy a quilt shop, but you would expect me to abandon my dream to yours."

"Is this your dream?" Jeremy countered. "Or is it Bonnie's

dream? Sarah's? You're always saying you want to travel. I've seen the look on your face when you talk about your undergraduate research projects. I've heard you debating theories of historical scholarship with the best students in my department. When I tell you about my research you look—I don't know. Almost envious."

"I'm very happy doing what I'm doing."

"That doesn't mean you want to do it forever."

"I had my chance to go to graduate school. A full ride at Penn. I passed it up for Elm Creek Quilts and Grandma's Attic. I think that shows what my dream is clearly enough."

"Maybe the timing was wrong. Lots of people take time off to work between college and graduate school. You weren't ready then, but maybe you are now."

"Maybe." Then Summer turned and waved him away. "But you're saying I wasted a good portion of my life here. You're just saying this to convince me to leave Waterford."

"I'm not saying that at all, and no one could convince you to do anything you don't want to do." He reached for her again; she stepped back. "You're just afraid to accept what you really want to do because it means admitting your earlier decision might have been motivated by something other than the pursuit of your dream."

"Like what?"

"I don't know. Fear? Uncertainty?"

Summer couldn't bear to hear any more. "I am not afraid to admit my mistakes," she retorted, voice shaking. "And I'll prove it to you."

She stormed off to her room and took down her duffel bag from the top shelf of her closet. She threw it onto her bed and began emptying dresser drawers into it.

"Summer—" Jeremy froze in the doorway. "What are you doing?"

She couldn't look at him. "What does it look like?"

"Summer, don't go." He came to her and put his hands on her shoulders, but she ducked away and continued packing. "This doesn't make any sense. Please don't leave over a stupid argument."

Summer returned to the closet and began taking clothes down from hangers. "What was stupid was moving in here in the first place."

"You don't mean that."

"I do." Summer threw the last of her winter clothes into the bag and zipped it shut. "And don't presume to tell me what my dream is or how to spend my life. Ever."

She tried to avoid his eye as she left, but he blocked the doorway. "Summer." He hesitated, visibly struggling for the right words. "Please don't go."

She could barely breathe as she shoved past him and fled the apartment.

❧❧

The Callahan family sat at the breakfast table, each engrossed in a section of the newspaper. Mary Beth insisted they eat together every morning, but cajoling them into a conversation had proven impossible.

"Here's something you'll enjoy," said Roger, folding his section in half and sliding it across the table.

"What is it?" asked Mary Beth, dubious. She rarely read more of the news pages than the headlines; the national stories were always so depressing and the world news inscrutable. Sometimes she delved into the local news if someone she knew was mentioned, or read the opinion pages if someone had written in about one of her pet causes, but usually she stuck to the features.

In reply, Roger leaned over and tapped a column at the top of the page. Mary Beth frowned and scanned the weekly police report. "What?" Then she saw it: One week ago, Grandma's Attic had been robbed and vandalized.

Why had she not heard this before? Bonnie was no longer a member of the guild, but this was relevant to the Waterford quilting community, and Mary Beth was the center of the Waterford quilting community. She should have been told.

"I heard it was a real mess," Brent offered.

"Well, this is the first I've heard of it." Mary Beth slid the paper back to her husband. "Why on earth would you assume this would make me happy?"

He feigned innocence. "Bonnie Markham's one of those Elm Creek people, right?"

"Yes, but that doesn't mean I'd celebrate her misfortune." She frowned when her husband and son exchanged a look of surprise. Honestly. What kind of person did they think she was?

"You never shop there," said Brent. "You're always talking about how much you hate them."

"And now they'll be too busy to interfere with your quilt guild," added Roger.

"And that quilt for old Mrs. Compson. Now they won't be able to bother you about that stupid quilt anymore."

There was that. Still, Bonnie was the least offensive of the Elm Creekers, and Mary Beth found it unsettling that the criminals had targeted a quilt shop. Why a quilt shop, when robbers usually focused on convenience stores and gas stations? It was unnatural, a strike at the heartland, at home and family and all that quilting represented.

Brent set aside the sports section and rose. On his way to the kitchen with his cereal bowl and juice glass, he said, "I bet Mrs. Sonnenberg is really upset."

Mary Beth considered. "I imagine you're right," she said, and did not try to keep the satisfaction from her voice.

❧❧

A week after the claims adjuster's visit, Bonnie received the written report from the insurance company. Due to the suspicious nature of the crime, they were withholding payment until such time as the authorities could determine an outside party was responsible for the alleged burglary.

Immediately Bonnie phoned the agent who had toured the shop, too shocked for tears. "I don't understand," she told him, although she understood all too well. "Do you mean I won't get anything?"

"I'm truly very sorry," he said. "If it makes any difference, I did recommend you for full coverage, but the board is strongly influenced by police reports."

"But the police didn't conclude it was an inside job," she said. "They said it was inconclusive."

"Unfortunately, that's enough to warrant this decision."

"Then why have I been paying all these premiums all these years?" Bonnie heard the shrillness in her words and gulped air. She must stay calm. "Please. I didn't destroy my own shop. If that were true, why would I want to rebuild so badly? Isn't there anything I can do?"

"You can file an appeal."

She held back a sob. "How?"

She took notes as he described the process, but even before she hung up she realized that even if the board reversed its decision, there was no way, no way she would receive the payment in time to save Grandma's Attic.

◈◈

Gwen was shocked to discover that Summer had moved out of Jeremy's apartment. She was less surprised that her daughter had moved into a suite on the second floor of Elm Creek Manor instead of choosing her old bedroom at home.

"Can we talk about this?" she asked one night after the evening program, when Summer headed for the grand oak staircase in the front foyer instead of the back door to the parking lot.

"There's not much to say." Summer forced a shaky grin. "I thought you'd be happy."

"You don't know much, kiddo," said Gwen, embracing her, "if you don't realize that I'm never happy unless you are."

Bonnie's divorce. Summer's unhappiness, whatever its real cause. Gwen mulled over the events of the past two weeks and decided there had been too much secrecy among the Elm Creek Quilters for far too long.

The next day, she told them about her plans for the new book.

As she should have expected, they praised her idea and exclaimed that someone should have written such a book a long time ago. Summer offered to assist her with her research. Agnes recalled an acquaintance who had also entered the World's Fair quilt competition and who ought still to have the quilt and possibly even some photographs of herself standing beside her entry in the exhibition hall. Each of her friends wanted to help; each assured her that publishers would fight over the right to publish her book and each vowed to buy a copy. When Diane offered to plan her book tour, Gwen laughed and said that academic presses typically did not send their authors around the country, but if Diane wanted to arrange something with the Waterford College bookstore or the independent bookstore downtown, she would have Gwen's blessing.

Her friends' sincere praise rekindled her confidence in the potential of her new project—and gave her the courage to tell Bill about it.

When Gwen asked if Bill was available, his assistant waved her right in, barely looking up from the brochures she was assembling for the Society for the Study of American Culture conference. Usually Martha screened the department chair's unscheduled visitors more carefully, but Bill was a lame duck, and three years' worth of dissatisfaction tended to come out in the last weeks of the term.

Bill was on the phone, so when he gestured to a chair, she sat down and looked at the framed photos on the bookcase, feigning indifference to his conversation, something about next year's hiring budget. Bill's wife and William, Jr. smiled down on her.

Before long Bill hung up. "Gwen," he said. "What can I do for you?"

"I've begun a new research project and wanted to run it by you before I submit a request for travel funds."

"Great." He sat back in his leather chair expectantly. "Let's hear it."

She told him about the quilt contest at the 1933 World's Fair, and how 25,000 quilters—which translated to roughly one of every two thousand American women, given the population at the time—had sought the prize. She explained how a chronicle of the competition would provide an analysis of a folk art, but also fledgling advertising and marketing techniques for a growing industry. She described how a study of the pieces submitted for the exhibition would reveal how "progress" was imagined and defined by a people still recovering from World War I and struggling through the Depression. Her book would capture the mood and values of a nation during one of the most difficult periods of its history.

Bill kept his expression impassive as she spoke. Sometimes his eyebrows rose, occasionally he nodded, but he gave no other sign that he shared her enthusiasm. When she finished, he nodded and mused in silence for a long moment. "Well," he finally said, leaning forward to rest his elbows on his desk. "It sounds like you're on the right track, anyway."

"On the right track?"

"I appreciate how much work you've put into your preliminary exploration, but—"

"But what?"

"Let's face it. This isn't much of a departure from your previous research."

"Ah." She nodded and gave him a tight-lipped smile. "I see."

"Don't get me wrong. It's good that you're focusing on the Depression; you'll find numerous forums for publications, lectures, and so forth. I also see what you're saying about how this contest captured the national mood in a critical era and all that. But couldn't you . . ." He rubbed the back of his neck and looked away before giving her a shrug. "Couldn't you find something else that does that just as well? Something other than quilting?"

"Something like what?" asked Gwen. "Architecture, maybe? Sculpture or painting?"

His face lit up. "Yes. Yes. That's brilliant. I'd go with architecture myself. How did the architecture of the era reflect the values and hopes of the nation? How did the availability of materials or lack thereof determine design? How did the rate of new home building reflect the national economy, and was it comparable to how we use housing starts as an economic indicator today? That would be fascinating research."

"Yes, it would," agreed Gwen. "I'd be interested in reading a paper on that subject. But I would not want to write one."

"What?"

"I've already found the route into the national temper of the Depression I intend to pursue." She stood. "If Depression-era architecture fascinates you so much, then you research it."

"Gwen." He rose quickly and stopped her at the door. "Give it some thought. We're talking about your career here. Do you know what the secretaries around here call you? The Quilt Lady. Is that how you want to be known?"

"Why, Bill," she said. "I had no idea you paid any attention to what your support staff says. I misjudged you."

"You must realize you're sacrificing any remaining chance you had of becoming department chair someday."

"It's a sacrifice I'm willing to make."

She bid him good-bye and shut the door behind her.

She paused for a moment to catch her breath. She had told him, he had balked, as she had suspected he might, but he couldn't stop her from studying what she wanted to study. She had worked too hard to obtain tenure to abandon such a promising idea for the sake of some administrative job she would likely never receive and would probably loathe anyway.

On her way through the outer office, she gave Bill's assistant a cheery smile. "He's all yours," she said.

"Great," said Martha, peering at her over the top of her bifocals. "That makes my day."

Gwen glimpsed a familiar tool in her hand and stopped short. Martha was trimming photographs with a rotary cutter. "You'd better not let Bill see you using that," said Gwen with only a suggestion of the sarcasm Bill had earned. "That's a quilting tool. He might ban it from the campus."

"Is it?" Martha inspected it with interest. "Strange. I don't think he minds it so much. He's the one who gave it to me. And the scissors." She nodded to a gleaming pair of ergonomic shears lying on the desk.

"Really." Gwen picked up the shears and turned them over in her hands. Not a single nick marred the blades. "I thought only quilting shops carried this brand. I suppose Fabric Warehouse might, too."

"Don't ask me. I don't sew. And those aren't leaving my offiice." Martha held out her hand for the shears, and Gwen promptly returned them. "Bill got them from his son. They were left over from some project at the high school. The yearbook committee or some such."

"From William Junior?" That seemed odd. "Since when does a public high school let students walk off with brand-new tools?"

"Don't ask me. I don't have kids."

"Right. Thanks anyway."

"There are worse nicknames than the Quilt Lady," Martha remarked as Gwen left the office. "You should hear what we call Bill."

∞

Bonnie could declare bankruptcy. That option came to her as she sat in the office long after her friends had gone home, pondering her future and struggling not to weep. Until she could reopen, she had no cash with which to pay her bills. Until she could pay her bills, she dared not order new inventory. Until she could order new inventory, she could not afford to reopen. Even if she sold every item on the newly rebuilt shelves, she might not earn enough to pay off her debts after deducting Summer's and Diane's wages from the gross income.

There had to be a way. Bonnie blinked back tears and rested her head on her arms on the desk. She could run the sale herself. The lines would be long—if she were lucky—but maybe the customers would grant her a little extra patience considering the circumstances. She would have to take a week off from camp, at least, which she could not afford to do, but her friends would cover for her without complaint. She could sell the computers, the shelves, the light fixtures, the furniture—students were always looking for cheap items to furnish their campus homes. It would not be easy, but it would be possible.

For a moment she allowed herself a wishful thought: The grand closing sale would be such a resounding success that she would earn enough to pay off her debts, order a truckload of new stock, and reopen better than before. The hope was fleeting. The new rental agreement on the desk beside her provided a sufficient reminder of the new reality she faced.

She had not surrendered yet, but Krolich had won. She wished she could believe him responsible for the burglary, but he had too much at stake to resort to violence, especially since his other tactics were already succeeding.

All she had to do was give the police Michael's name. They would do the rest. Their revised report would exonerate her; the insurance company would meet its obligations. All she had to do was destroy her friend and her friend's son.

She could not. Not even for Grandma's Attic.

He might confess. Michael had made great strides since Sylvia had shown faith in him five years earlier by donating a parcel of land to be developed into a skateboard park. She had led the fundraising effort and had insisted Michael be allowed to advise the designers. That sense of finally belonging to his community, of having a voice that would be heard, had encouraged him to grow from a sullen and troubled adolescent into a young man with a sense of purpose and responsibility. Why had he thrown it away for revenge and a phony driver's license? Didn't he realize she would figure it out as soon as she discovered the confiscated fake ID was missing?

She sat up and wiped her eyes. Of course he had. He had also known that Bonnie would be incapable of hurting Diane by exposing the truth.

Bonnie decided to go home before Agnes phoned, worried about her whereabouts. She gathered her things and locked the door behind her. She headed for Agnes's house, but after a few blocks, she hesitated and returned to the shop to check the door. It was locked, of course, just as it had been the night of the break-in, as she had known it would be.

The next day at Elm Creek Manor, Bonnie took Summer and Diane aside before their afternoon sessions and shared her plan for one last, great sale. "The shelves will be bare when we're through," she said, forcing a laugh. "In fact, if we're really lucky, there won't be any shelves or even lightbulbs to see them by when we're through. But we might just have enough to pay off the last outstanding debts."

"That's a great idea," said Summer, although she looked as if Bonnie had just announced a funeral.

"We'll help any way we can," said Diane. "You know that."

Bonnie nodded. "I know. That's why—" She took a deep breath. "That's the only reason why I can say this. I'm sorry, but I have to ask you to help me as friends. I can't afford to pay you."

Immediately they assured her that was all right, that they had assumed as much, and that they would have shoved their paychecks back into her hands rather than accept them.

"You might as well," said Bonnie, laughing to keep from crying. "They'd bounce."

Diane and Summer laughed and embraced her. She closed her eyes and clung to them.

～

Three days later, Diane had emptied the last of the bran cereal into her bowl and was crumpling up the box to fit it into the trash can when it made a strange clinking noise. She opened the box, removed the bag, and discovered her key ring at the bottom.

She held perfectly still for a moment, then withdrew her keys and threw the rest away. She wiped off the lingering film of cereal dust and returned the keys to her purse, lost in thought.

The morning passed as she pondered what to do. Tim was out of town at a conference or she might have consulted him, but she knew what he would say. She had to talk to Michael.

The afternoon crawled by as she waited for Michael to come home to do his laundry. Finally, two hours after she was supposed to be at Elm Creek Manor helping to register the latest group of quilt campers, Michael entered, a gray laundry sack slung over one shoulder.

He seemed surprised to see her. "Hey, Mom. Why aren't you at camp?"

"I needed to speak with you."

"Yeah?" He grinned and dropped his laundry bag in front of the door to the basement. "So you saw the catalogue? Did you have a chance to talk to Dad?"

Bewildered, she just looked at him until she realized he was talking about the course catalogue and the highlighted passage about Judy's class. "Yes, I saw it. Your father and I haven't discussed it yet."

He frowned briefly. "Oh. Okay. Will you try to soon? Because if I'm going to get a new computer anyway, it would be great to have one before finals."

"Michael . . ." She took a shaky breath. "Please. I need you to tell me what you know about the break-in at Grandma's Attic."

He shrugged. "I don't know much. Just what you've told me. Why?"

She could not speak.

He watched her in silence for a long moment. "You think I had something to do with it."

"Michael . . ." She did not want to admit it; she did not want to believe it. "My keys were missing when I looked for them on the morning before the break-in. I just found them today."

His voice was hard. "Then you obviously just misplaced them."

"I found them at the bottom of a cereal box." For the life of her she could not imagine why he had put them there instead of returning them to her purse. Had someone suddenly walked in on him? Had he hoped to make her think she had absentmindedly put them there herself? "That catalogue you mentioned—I know you came home the night the keys were taken because you left that catalogue right by my purse."

"Yeah? Well, I'm not the only person with access to your purse, you know. It's not like you keep it in a bank vault." He grabbed his laundry bag and glowered at her. "I bet you leave your purse lying around open at quilt camp all the time. I know you think all quilters are wonderful people, but you don't know them. Who more than a quilter would want a key to a quilt shop?"

She had actually considered that, but the campers would not have known that she had a key to Grandma's Attic, and even if one had, a burglar with an interest in quilting would have stolen far more and damaged far less.

"I didn't do it," he said flatly. "I can't believe you think I would." He turned and headed for the door.

"Michael," she called, racing after him and touching his shoulder. "Please. Mrs. Markham will lose everything as long as the police believe it was an inside job."

He jerked away from her. "Yeah? Maybe it was. I don't know and I don't care. All I know is I didn't do it."

He tore open the door and slammed it shut behind him.

Diane reached for the doorknob, hesitated, and released it. She had rarely seen him so angry, but she had too frequently seen him lie with the same persuasive vehemence.

She turned around and leaned against the door.

A sudden movement caught her eye; she glanced up to find Todd standing frozen on the stairs. He had heard everything.

Todd. Michael was not the only one with access to her purse. No, it was incomprehensible.

"Mom," said Todd. "Michael wouldn't do something like that."

Diane pressed her lips together and forced herself to nod.

⟨⟩

Mary Beth sat at the kitchen table going over the social chair's notes for the end-of-the-year picnic. Less than a third of the members had registered, a fraction of the number who had sent in their deposits by this time last year. At the monthly meeting of the guild the previous evening, the social chair had made another beseeching, bewildered plea for people to get their forms in on time, but attendance had been down sharply, so few of the people who needed to get the message were there to hear it. "I don't understand," Dottie whispered, passing Mary Beth on the way back to her seat. "We've never had so many people miss the deadline before."

Mary Beth gave her what she hoped was an encouraging smile, but she doubted two-thirds of the guild had forgotten the date. They simply weren't coming.

"Mom?"

She looked up, startled from her gloomy reverie. Brent was peeking in the doorway, grinning.

"Yes, honey?" she said. "What is it?"

"I know it's early." He emerged from the doorway carrying a large box. "But I know you could use it, so I thought I'd give you your Mother's Day present now."

He set the box on the table, and Mary Beth gasped.

"A Bernina?" She reached out eagerly, then shot him a wry look. "Or it's something else in a Bernina box."

"Open it and find out."

Disbelieving, she unpacked the box to find that it indeed contained a new sewing machine, the sewing machine of her dreams, one with a computer touch screen and more features and attachments than she knew existed. "Brent," she gasped, running her hands over it. "It's wonderful, it's perfect, it's—" She jerked her hands away as if the beautiful sewing machine had scalded her. "How in the world did you afford this? It must have cost you thousands of dollars."

His grin widened. "It's rude to ask the price of a gift."

"Yes, honey, I know, but in this case—" She gazed at the sewing machine longingly. "Is this from you and your brothers? Did your father pitch in?"

"No, it's just from me, and you're still close to the borderline of that rudeness thing."

All at once, she knew. His college fund. "I can't accept this," she said, reluctant. "You can't spend your college fund on gifts for me."

He laughed. "I didn't." He dug in the box for the user's manual and placed it in her hands. "It didn't cost me as much as you think, so just say thank you and read the manual."

"Thank you." Overwhelmed, she hugged him and kissed him on the forehead. "You are such a dear, sweet boy."

He strode from the room, pleased and proud, as she pushed the social chairwoman's notes aside and pulled the shining new sewing machine closer to her place at the table. Then she let out a shriek of delight, tossed the manual aside, and ran upstairs for fabric and thread.

⨳

Two days later, Todd slipped into the desk behind Brent, who turned around and said, "Did you get the answer for the third homework problem? I got 2–i, but that can't be right."

"I have a better question." Todd leaned forward and murmured, "Did you trash the quilt shop by yourself or did Will and Greg help?"

Brent blinked, then assumed a quizzical expression. "What the hell are you talking about?"

"I know you did it, and I know how. What I can't figure out is why. What do you have against Mrs. Markham? Or was it just for the money?"

Brent shook his head, a small, incredulous grin playing on his lips. "What have you been sniffing?"

"My mother isn't stupid. She's going to remember you slept over that night, and she'll figure out you took her keys. And then . . ." Todd sat back and shrugged.

At the front of the room, the Calculus teacher began class. Brent shot Todd a vengeful look over his shoulder as he turned to face front.

For the next fifty minutes, Todd took notes and answered questions and grimly watched his best friend, who did not turn around again.

⨳

Judy met Gwen for lunch on a Wednesday, the one day that week when neither woman taught at Elm Creek Quilt Camp. They had only an hour, so Gwen raced through an update on her research project so they could discuss Summer's abrupt break-up with

Jeremy and Bonnie's plans for a going-out-of-business sale, although neither dared to call it that. Gwen was so forthcoming with her concerns about work and her daughter that Judy was tempted to confide her own secret, but she had not heard anything from Penn since her interview more than three weeks before, so she decided to keep quiet.

When she returned to the office after lunch, her grad students reported that Rick had phoned.

She called him back and left a message on his voicemail, then hung around the lab impatiently waiting for him to return her call. She left to teach her afternoon Introduction to Programming class and raced back to snatch up the ringing phone just before voicemail would have answered.

Mercifully, he delivered the news without a lengthy preamble. "The job's yours if you still want it."

The official offer had gone out in the afternoon mail, he said, but the terms were just as they had discussed during her interview. Rick promised that the letter contained no surprises and that she would not be disappointed.

"Sign the letter of intent and send it back," he urged. "If you know what's good for you. Get out of that hole in the wall and come where the real action is."

"I'll let you know," she told him.

"What? The job of a lifetime gets dumped in your lap and you can't even give me the courtesy of a straight answer?"

"You can wait a few days. You kept me in suspense for three weeks," she reminded him.

"It was a tough decision! Do you think we interviewed just anyone?"

"I know you didn't. Just consider this as a little payback for all the stress you put me through this semester."

She promised to contact him as soon as she had a chance to review the official offer, and then she called Steve.

"Honey," she said as soon as her husband answered, "we have a decision to make."

✥✥

Mary Beth was so shocked to hear Diane's voice on the line that she almost dropped the phone.

"I know I'm the last person you expected," said Diane, and her laugh was, if anything, nervous.

"That's certainly true." Diane had not called the Callahan home in years. Did she intend to apologize? If so, it was a long time coming—one month to the day after she had crashed the quilt guild meeting. Mary Beth waited, wondering why Diane bothered this time when she had never expressed regret for any of her previous insults throughout the years. Because of the severity of her offense? She had certainly jeopardized Mary Beth's standing in the quilt guild, but Diane ought to find that cause for celebration, not remorse.

Then Mary Beth figured it out. Diane wanted the guild's support for that going-out-of-business sale at Grandma's Attic next week. Mary Beth had seen the signs in the store windows, but she remained steadfast in her vow never to cross that threshold again. In a hundred years Diane could not grovel enough to change Mary Beth's mind about that.

After a long pause, Diane said, "I'll get straight to the point, then."

"I do wish you would."

"Have you heard about the burglary at Grandma's Attic?"

"I read the paper."

"Yes, well, I wondered if Brent might know anything about it."

Icily, Mary Beth asked, "What do you mean?"

"I'm not saying he did it, but he might know who did. You see, my key to the shop disappeared after he spent the night here, and the next night the shop was broken into, and there was no sign of forced entry—"

"How dare you?"

"I'm sorry. I know this is a terrible thing to suggest, but—"

"You're darn right it is. I'll have you know that my son was right here at home that entire night. What about your son?"

"Todd was—"

"Not Todd. Michael. He's the troublemaker in this town. Everyone knows his reputation. I bet this wouldn't be the first time he took your keys."

A pause. "You would be right," said Diane, "but he assures me he had nothing to do with it."

"He assures you." Mary Beth snickered. "Oh, that's rich."

"Please, Mary Beth, talk to Brent."

"I'm hanging up now." And she did just that.

She grabbed the back of a kitchen chair for support. That woman, that horrible, cruel, vicious woman. Mary Beth sat down, head spinning. Diane need look no further than her own delinquent son if she was so eager to find someone to blame. Brent was definitely asleep in his own bed that night, not that it mattered because he absolutely could not have been involved, but he was always home on weeknights. Except—Mary Beth tried to remember. The robbery had occurred during spring break. Brent had spent Monday night at Todd's and Tuesday night at Greg's.

She felt a chill but shook it off. She would phone Greg's parents. They would confirm that Brent had spent the entire night beneath their roof.

No one picked up at home, of course. She looked up the Department of Sociology in the phone book and obtained both professors' office numbers from the secretary. Greg's mother did not answer, but his father did.

By that time Mary Beth had worked out her story. She said that Brent had been missing his watch since spring break and they wondered if he had left it at Greg's house when he spent the night.

"I'll ask Greg if he's seen it," he responded, "but Brent should probably check with Will."

"Why?"

"That's where the boys spent the night."

"Are you sure?" Mary Beth's heart thumped. "I was sure Brent said your house."

"No, it definitely wasn't, because Marcella and I were out of town at a conference. We have strict rules against overnight guests while we're away."

Mary Beth murmured an apology, thanked him, and hung up. She did not call Will's parents. She knew they would cheerfully assure her that the boys had indeed been at Greg's house under his parents' supervision the entire night.

Brent had lied to her. Well, she should not be surprised. No teenage boy told his mother the truth all the time. But just because he'd lied about his whereabouts so he and his friends could have some unsupervised fun, maybe even a party or something, that did not mean he had broken into the quilt shop. It hurt his alibi, but nothing suggested he had anything to do with the crime.

Except for the sewing machine, the early Mother's Day present he could not possibly have afforded no matter what he claimed, no matter how much she wanted to believe otherwise.

The realization sank in like a cold stone into a pond. When she could, she rose and climbed the stairs and knocked on her son's door. He was at his desk studying, stacks of books piled around him.

He smiled so affectionately at her that she faltered, but she forced herself to do what she had come to do. "Honey," she said. "I think there's a problem with the sewing machine. I may—I may need to exchange it at the store. Would you mind giving me the receipt?"

His expression did not change. "I think I threw it away."

"Well, do you have the credit card statement? I know you couldn't have paid cash. The store might be willing to accept an exchange with that."

He shook his head. "I did pay cash."

"Oh." Mary Beth looked away, her palm slick with perspiration on the doorknob. "Well, how? If you didn't take the money out of your college account, where—"

"It's not new," he blurted.

"What?"

"It's not new. I bought it at a garage sale. I passed it on my way back from the library and saw some quilting stuff, you know, stacks of fabric and stuff, and then I saw the sewing machine still in the box. They were only asking fifty bucks for it."

"Fifty?"

"I know. I couldn't believe it either. The lady in charge said it was her mother-in-law's. She got it for her birthday but died before she ever had a chance to use it. That's why her kids were having the garage sale, to get rid of a lot of her stuff."

"I thought I knew all the quilters in Waterford," said Mary Beth. "I didn't hear of anyone passing away."

"She wasn't from around here. Just her kids. She lived in a retirement home in Pittsburgh or something." Brent rose, stricken. "I'm sorry, Mom. I know I should have told you the whole truth, but you were so happy. I wanted you to think I had given you something really great."

She touched his shoulder. "You did. It's wonderful."

"Yeah, except it's broken, and now you can't return it."

"I think maybe I can fix it." Mary Beth forced a smile. "I'll check the manual again. You go ahead and get back to your studying. I'm sorry I interrupted."

He hugged her. "I'm sorry I didn't tell you the whole story right away."

"That's all right," she said, patting his back and holding back tears.

The signs in the window called it a Spring Spectacular Sale, but

Summer knew better, and she suspected most of their customers would figure it out when they saw the half-empty shelves and the funereal expressions on Bonnie and her volunteer employees. Bonnie tried to raise their spirits with generous estimates of how much money they might earn over the five days of the sale, but Summer did not need Sarah's accounting degree to know that even if the shelves were bare by Friday afternoon, they would not have earned enough to pay all the bills.

Fifteen minutes before opening on Monday morning, Summer and Diane sat in the back office as Bonnie made coffee and reminded them about a few last-minute price adjustments. "Make sure to tell everyone there will be no refunds," she advised as she filled three mugs with the Daily Grind's house blend.

"What if they ask why?" asked Diane.

Bonnie shrugged and handed around the coffee. "Tell them it's the only way I can afford these low, low prices. Well, here goes." She raised her mug. "Cheers."

"To Grandma's Attic," said Summer.

Diane and Bonnie echoed her, and they clinked their mugs together. They drank, then filed out of the office clutching their coffee mugs as if for warmth.

Through the front window they saw a handful of women already waiting, shopping bags in their arms.

"Summer, would you let them in, please?" asked Bonnie, absently smoothing her red apron.

Summer nodded and hurried to the front door. She welcomed the five waiting women as they entered, but her smile failed her when they halted and eyed the scanty shelves with surprise.

"I know it looks bare," said Summer, "but there are some real bargains here."

"It's a good thing we came early," remarked one of the women. "You're sure to sell out soon."

"Mary Beth wasn't kidding," added the second woman, hefting

her shopping bag, which bulged as if it were already full. "You definitely need this stuff. Where would you like it?"

"Mary Beth?" echoed Summer warily. "What stuff?"

"Donations for the sale," said the first woman. The others nodded and indicated their bags. "What, didn't you know? Mary Beth sent out a letter to everyone in the guild asking us to raid our stashes for fabric and notions for Bonnie to sell."

Bonnie gasped.

"Oh, and blocks for Sylvia's bridal quilt, too." Another woman beamed at Diane and withdrew a plastic sandwich bag from her tote. Summer caught a glimpse of colorful patchwork. "I was surprised she urged us to make them, given her reaction to your announcement at the guild, but she did."

"Her what?" exclaimed Bonnie and Summer in unison, looking to Diane in astonishment. Diane shrugged.

The first woman carried her bag to the cutting table. "May I leave this here while I shop?"

"Of course," said Bonnie, hurrying to assist. The other women followed, and soon a pile of fabric, notions, and pattern books covered a good portion of the table. Bonnie, looking somewhat shocked, waved Summer and Diane over. "Sort all this out, would you?" she murmured, watching the women as they browsed the scanty shelves.

Speechless, Summer nodded. She and Diane quickly got to work while Bonnie attended to the customers. It was obvious that the women had not used this occasion to get rid of their scraps and discards. The minimum fabric cut Summer came across was a fat quarter, the fabric selections included only the same fine-quality cloth Bonnie herself sold, and the pattern books still had their templates.

Summer looked up as the bell over the front door jingled and two more shoppers entered carrying bulging totes. Three more women followed close behind. "Mary Beth is responsible for this?" asked Summer, thrilled but disbelieving.

Diane snorted. "Seems like a guilty conscience at work to me."

Summer shot her a questioning look, but Diane said nothing more, so Summer let it go. Diane would never believe any good could come from her longtime nemesis.

The bell over the door jingled again, and Summer felt a spark of hope kindle. With the donations, and with the support of the guild, they might be able to pull it off.

She longed to tell Jeremy.

Gwen suppressed her guilt as she raced through the last batch of papers, telling herself that at least she was reading and scoring them herself instead of dumping the job on one of her grad students. Between her day job, quilt camp, and volunteering at the whirlwind Grandma's Attic had become, she was stretched to her limit.

A knock sounded on her door. "Not now," she called, glancing at the clock in annoyance. It was time for Jules's weekly conference about his dissertation, but she had warned him to stay away.

"Dr. Sullivan?"

The voice was familiar; she halted in the middle of scrawling a pithy remark about a student's disjointed syllogism and said, "Jeremy?"

"May I speak with you, please?"

She hesitated only a moment before telling him to come in. He entered, unshaven and grim, and took the chair she offered. "Unless you're still looking for the required nondepartmental advisor for your dissertation committee, I assume you want to talk about Summer," she said gently. "I should warn you I'm biased beyond redemption in her favor on every conceivable topic."

"I'd talk to Summer instead, but she won't speak to me."

Me either, Gwen thought, but asked, "Did you have a fight?"

"Yes. Maybe. It's hard to say." He ran a hand through his dark, unruly curls. "We were discussing the break-in when she started tearing into Craig—who deserved every word of it—but then she accused me of being just like him. She said I want to interfere with her career success just as Craig does Bonnie's."

Gwen felt a pang. Jeremy was nothing like Craig, and Summer knew it. "I imagine you didn't take that well."

"That's a safe assumption. I defended myself, which was a mistake. When I tried to find out what was really bothering her, she ran to her room and starting throwing clothes into a duffel bag." His frown deepened. "That's the short version."

Edited, no doubt, for Gwen's ears. "What would you have me do?"

"I'm not asking you to be my advocate. I don't expect you to plead my case. But if you could just get her to talk to me, I would be very grateful. Tell her that I would never ask her to leave Waterford. Tell her that I would never expect her to sacrifice everything she's built with Elm Creek Quilts."

"But Jeremy," Gwen said, "you know very well that one day you're going to leave Waterford."

"Not necessarily."

Gwen frowned and shook her head. "We both know how the system works. If you want a tenure-track position, you have to look elsewhere."

"Then I won't get a tenure-track position. I can still research and write no matter where I live, no matter what my day job is."

"Jeremy—"

"I mean it. This is not the desperate plea of a lovesick kid. We both know there's no one else like Summer in the world, and for some reason she loves me. I am not going to throw that away."

"It's just as unfair for her to ask you to sacrifice your career as it is for you to ask it of her."

"Sometimes life isn't about what's fair. Sometimes it's about what's right. There are an infinite number of jobs in the world, but only one Summer. I'm not going to lose her."

Gwen studied him. She could wait a lifetime and never hear any-one make such an expression of love and commitment to her daughter. Summer at least ought to know that.

"All right," she said. "I'll talk to her."

Judy looked up from her computer at a knock on her office door. "Do you have time for lunch?" asked Gwen, oddly subdued.

Judy quickly switched on her screen saver to conceal her letter of resignation. She was just toying with it; it wasn't as if she had made up her mind. For every advantage to accepting the job she found an equally compelling reason to remain where she was. "I'm afraid not," she said, but Gwen seemed so morose that she added, "I have to finish up some work before heading over to Grandma's Attic, and then I'm teaching at Elm Creek Manor until evening. But I have time for a chat."

Gwen took her usual chair, unzipped the quilted batik jacket she had completed in one of Bonnie's workshops, and frowned at the floor. Suddenly she looked up and said, "Do you think I've held Summer back?"

"Held her back? What do you mean?"

"Do you think I've frightened her away from life? From leaving Waterford, from having an enduring relationship with a man, from, well, everything?"

Carefully, Judy said, "I think Summer has accomplished quite a lot considering she's still in her twenties. And it's not unusual for a child of divorce to be wary of commitment."

"I know that." Gwen shifted in her seat, and for a moment she seemed close to tears. "But sometimes I look at her and I see some-one just going through the motions, someone who's finished what she set out to do and is now just marking time."

"She seems as enthusiastic about Elm Creek Quilts as ever."

"I'm not so sure. She puts her whole heart into her work

because that's her nature. She never does anything indifferently. But sometimes I think her enthusiasm is largely manufactured because she doesn't want to feel like she's letting the rest of us down." Gwen hesitated and said, "Did I ever tell you I persuaded her to go to Waterford College instead of Stanford?"

Speechless, Judy shook her head.

"I did, and you're the only one who knows it but me. And maybe Summer, but I'm not sure. I manipulated her so carefully that even now she might not realize that the decision was more mine than hers." Gwen inhaled deeply. "I felt so horrible afterward, even as I rejoiced in knowing I would have her another four years, that I swore I would make it up to her for graduate school. Then when the time came, she turned down a full ride to Penn."

"That was her choice," said Judy. "She wanted to stay at Elm Creek Quilts and Grandma's Attic."

"But I'll never know if she made that decision because it's what she truly wanted or because I had finally convinced her that she couldn't survive anywhere but here."

Judy shook her head. "Summer seems too confident for those sorts of doubts."

"Maybe." Gwen did not look as if she believed it. "I'd like to think so. But even if remaining in Waterford was the best place for her at the time, that doesn't mean it still is. What troubles me most is that she seems afraid to find out."

"It's never easy to leave the people and places you love," said Judy softly. "Even to pursue a dream. Change can be frightening. Severing ties with friends and family can be worse."

"Summer would never sever her ties with me or with anyone at Elm Creek Manor," said Gwen. "They would stretch, but they would never break, no matter how far away she goes."

"That doesn't make it any easier. What if she takes a risk and realizes it was a terrible mistake? A place that seems so perfect from a distance might be filled with dangers she missed at first

glance. She might find that she's not as capable as she thought, and fail utterly at the job she's longed for."

Gwen barked out a laugh. "I can't imagine Summer failing utterly at anything. She would find a way to succeed even if it didn't come as easily as she had anticipated. All the Elm Creek Quilters are like that. We couldn't have built Elm Creek Quilts otherwise."

"But we had one another."

"Summer will have us in her heart and mind wherever she goes. Besides, if she leaves Waterford, I doubt she'll be going alone." Gwen rose and zipped up her jacket, her familiar grin restored. "And if it doesn't work out, if she does fail utterly, she can always come home. She'll always be an Elm Creek Quilter."

"You're right." Judy returned her smile, tears in her eyes. "It's a lifetime position. We can't quit, or retire, or be disbarred. And thank goodness for that."

"Don't get all misty yet. We're talking about my kid, not yours. You won't have to go through this for years."

Judy laughed. "You never know."

"I don't even know what Summer's going to do," admitted Gwen, "but I want her to follow her heart, even if it leads her away from me. Telling her so will be the least selfish thing I've ever done. I hope I can withstand it."

Judy hugged her and wished her luck, and then Gwen left. Alone again, she sat down at the computer and thought.

Then she touched fingers to keyboard and finished the letter.

Hours after her mother left, Summer sat looking out the window of her guest suite at the moonlit lawn of Elm Creek Manor. She did not like to think of herself as afraid, just as she did not like to accept that her mother had persuaded her to stay in Waterford out of her own fear of loneliness. But as much as she might like to, she could not ignore the plain and heartfelt truth of her mother's words.

There was so much Summer longed to accomplish, s
the world she longed to see. She still loved Elm Creek Q
was proud of all she had done there, but she felt as if she i
ished the task she had set out for herself and was impatient to
on to the next.

She touched her forehead to the glass pane and smiled ruefu.
She loved quilting, she enjoyed teaching, and she had relished the
challenge of nurturing a business from a dream into reality. Why
did she feel something was missing? Why did she keep wondering
what was next and feeling disappointed at the thought of a settled,
pleasant routine? Sure, as long as she stayed at Elm Creek Manor it
would be more of the same, but wasn't that a good thing?

Wasn't she crazy to think of giving this up for something that
might not be as good as what she already had? Even if that meant—
or especially if that meant—leaving Waterford with Jeremy?

Summer sighed and left the window. She pulled a hooded sweatshirt and pair of sweats over the long T-shirt she usually slept in
and padded down the hallway in her stocking feet. Muffled laughter
came from behind closed doors as campers gathered with their
new friends to share quilting secrets and confidences. A light shone
from the crack beneath the library door; inside Sarah was working
on the computer, as Summer had expected. They were all keeping
late hours to compensate for their shifts at Grandma's Attic.

Sarah looked up and smiled sympathetically. "Couldn't sleep?"

"No." Summer curled up on one of the sofas in the center of the
room in front of Sarah's desk.

"Worried about the sale?"

"Not really. We saw more customers today and yesterday than in
the last two months combined, and our inventory is fine. The donations from the quilt guild members have filled half the shelves and
they're still coming in."

"So are the quilt blocks, I hear."

Summer nodded. In a few months, if the Elm Creek Quilters
made several blocks each, they might even be able to make Sylvia

and Andrew a nice lap quilt. The loss of the quilt blocks and their stories from Sylvia's friends and admirers worldwide, though, could not be remedied. No one yet had thought of how to tell the contributors about the theft. It was an unpleasant task they were all willing to postpone. Eventually it would probably fall to Sarah, who was typically the one among them most willing to plunge ahead with necessary work they would rather avoid. Summer wished she possessed a fraction of Sarah's determination.

"Sarah," she asked, "how did you decide to leave your job in State College to follow Matt to Waterford?"

"It wasn't that difficult. I wasn't terribly enamored of my old job."

"You thought enough of it to keep it. You weren't looking for a new job in State College."

"That's true," admitted Sarah. "Well, Matt had been out of work for months and was growing more depressed every day. How could I say no when he finally found something?"

"Because it meant giving up your career without knowing if you'd find anything in Waterford. That's a fairly big chance to take for someone else."

"It wasn't just for him. It was for me, too. I wouldn't have felt happier if I had chosen the certainty of my old job over what Matt needed. Safer, yes, but not happier." Sarah shrugged. "It's just something you do when you're married."

"You mean it's something women do for their husbands when they're married."

"No, not in our case. He would have done the same for me."

"Are you sure?"

Sarah considered. "Yes. I am. That probably made my choice easier. I won't pretend I didn't have misgivings occasionally. There were times I was sure I had made the worst mistake of my life moving to Waterford. I'm sure Matt felt the same way when we first moved into Elm Creek Manor and tried to launch the quilt camp."

Summer thought back on some of the couple's all-too-obvious

arguments during the early years of Elm Creek Quilts and had to agree.

"It was a risk giving up security for the unknown," said Sarah, spreading both arms to indicate the entire manor and everything the Elm Creek Quilters had established there. "But if I hadn't taken that risk, I never would have found my dream. I never would have known how much more I was capable of doing with my life."

"You took a leap of faith right off a cliff," said Summer.

"But I eventually landed on my feet." Sarah smiled. "And you will, too."

On Friday evening, Bonnie waited two hours past the usual closing time for the last customer to leave before locking the door and turning the sign in the window to CLOSED. Judy and Diane, the last volunteer shift of the last day of the sale, had already begun cleaning up, although the store was so bare there was little to do except sweep the floor and carry empty boxes outside to the recycling bins.

Judy and Diane wanted to stay and celebrate the success of the sale. Indeed, thanks to the windfall of donations from the Waterford Quilting Guild, Bonnie estimated that they had earned at least twice the amount of her most optimistic projections—and that was without selling the lightbulbs and bookcases. Until she completed her final calculations, though, she would not know if a celebration was in order.

She sent Judy and Diane home and, from their disappointed expressions, she knew they had hoped to stay and wait for the results of her accounting. She understood, but she guided them to the door and told them she would let them know at the Farewell Breakfast the next morning.

Then she filled her mug with the last of the coffee and set herself to work.

It took hours, but eventually she tallied the entire income from the sale and deducted all her outstanding expenses. She double-checked her calculations to be sure she had arrived at the correct figure.

She was tempted to check them a third time, but it was nearly midnight and her eyes were tearing from lack of sleep and too much time at the computer. Besides, the first two totals matched.

There was no mistaking it: After paying off her last creditor, she would have exactly $56.48 left. She would not have to declare bankruptcy.

But she would have to close Grandma's Attic.

Agnes was the first to know, and Bonnie didn't even have to tell her. All she did was walk in the front door and Agnes understood. Agnes hugged her and offered her a cup of tea, but Bonnie reminded her of their early appointment at Elm Creek Manor the next morning and went off to bed.

She told the others in passing as she saw them at the Farewell Breakfast the next day. Some, like Judy, seemed heartbroken; others, like Sarah, were angry. All asked if she was absolutely sure, if the last option had been exhausted, if there was not some chance, however small, that she could keep the shop open. Her reply was always the same: Unless some miracle struck within the next few hours, Grandma's Attic would not reopen for business.

No miracle came, and it was not until she left Elm Creek Manor in her reclaimed car that she remembered she could still turn in Michael to the police and collect the insurance money. Grandma's Attic would remain closed while she waited for their check to clear, and she would still need to find a way to cover that exorbitant rent, but eventually she would be back in business.

If she could bring herself to do it.

Instead she drove downtown to the University Realty office building. She went inside and asked to speak to Gregory Krolich. Upon learning he was in a meeting, she left a message: Bonnie

Markham will not be renewing her lease. She was halfway down the front stairs when Krolich bounded after her and invited her back inside for coffee and a doughnut while they took care of the paperwork.

The transaction was less painful than she had anticipated. Indeed, she felt numb; she realized that the pain would hit her later, preferably when she was back at Agnes's house, where she could cry and rant and rave, and dear Agnes would sympathize and allow her to drown her sorrows in infinite cups of tea.

Next she drove to her old building—already it seemed a part of her past—and parked in what had once been her usual spot. Craig answered the buzzer so quickly that he must have heard her pull up.

The door buzzed and unlocked; he met her at the top of the stairs, blocking the doorway to the home they had once shared. "So, you brought the car back?" he said, eyeing her warily.

She shook her head. "Not until the lawyers say I have to."

Craig scowled. "What do you want, then? If you're here to divide up the rest of our stuff—"

"I'm here to sign the papers."

At first he just gaped at her. Then a light of immense satisfaction arose in his eyes. "Wait here and I'll get them."

He ducked back inside, and she followed. While he hurried off to the guest room, fairly dancing with glee, she went to the kitchen and rapidly sorted through the stacks of mail. Into her tote bag went a magazine, her alumni newsletter, and two letters from the kids, sent before she had called to explain the situation and give them her temporary address. Listening for Craig, she hurried back to the living room and took several framed photos from the bookshelves. In his triumph, Craig was as unlikely to notice the new bulges in her tote as he was the bare spaces on the shelves.

"Here." Craig returned with a fistful of papers and a pen. He placed them on the coffee table and beamed a triumphant grin at her. "Sign on the dotted line."

Bonnie hesitated. His arrogance was too much to bear, so infuriating and intolerable that she was tempted to walk out. She would still sign—eventually she would have to—but she could drag it out, make him tear his hair out wondering what she intended to do. His grin faltered as she watched him, and she realized she had no desire to put up a fight for something she knew she had already lost, something she no longer wanted anyway.

It was time to move on.

She took the pen and read the agreement slowly, more to make Craig fret than to look for the details her lawyer had warned her about. Then she signed the agreement to sell the condo to University Realty.

Craig snatched the papers away as soon as she added the date. "Nice doing business with you," he said with an insufferable smirk. "If you'd signed this months ago, we could have had the cash right away. Now the lawyers will wrangle over it and take their cut."

"You're lucky I signed it at all, and we both know if I'd signed it earlier I'd never see my half. We also both know we're not as broke as you claim."

He spread his palms and feigned innocence. "You're the one holding going-out-of-business sales. If you can find some cash I've overlooked, naturally I'll split it with you."

Bonnie turned and went to the door without wasting another word on him.

He followed and called to her as she descended the stairs: "By the way, I told the kids you left me. They're furious with you."

She almost laughed. "Whatever you say, Craig."

She waved at him over her shoulder and left.

Two days later, Agnes strode across the Waterford College campus, so determined that towering undergraduates a third of her age jumped out of the way at her approach. Her outrage had not lessened one iota since Bonnie had told her she had signed off on the sale of her home, and Agnes was about to unleash her temper on that despicable man if she had to kick down his office door to do it.

Bonnie had told her not to bother. She was at peace with her decision, and nothing Agnes could say to Craig would change the situation. Maybe not, but Agnes was still determined to show Craig he had made a grave error in judgment when he chose this particular path to divorce. If he thought leaving Bonnie virtually penniless and homeless would make her cower, he was dead wrong. Bonnie was not going to buckle to a bully, not with staunch friends to support her and see her through to the end.

She stormed into the director's office and almost crashed into the same blond assistant she had encountered before. "I'm here to see Craig," she muttered, and tried to duck past her.

"Wait." The woman cut her off. "Do you have an appointment?"

Agnes glowered and nudged her aside; the woman was too startled or too wary about manhandling a senior citizen to interfere. Just before she reached the door, she heard the sharp click of the lock. "Craig Markham," she called out, turning the doorknob in vain. "Get out here and face me like a man, you coward!"

"He's not in," said the blond assistant, alarmed.

"Yes, he is. I see him through the window. Craig!" She rattled the doorknob again. "Don't think you can get away with driving Bonnie from her home. I happen to know she has an excellent lawyer. You'll get what's coming to you!"

"Please, ma'am." The woman moved as if to wrestle Agnes away from the office, but was still reluctant to lay hands on her. "Don't make me call security."

"You go right ahead," said Agnes primly. She had embarrassed Craig and delivered her message. She actually felt much better. "I'll tell anyone who cares to listen the truth about that man."

She turned, and her gaze fell once again upon that distinctive furniture, that unusual combination of Shaker and Arts and Crafts, too worn and mismatched to really suit a professional office. With a frown, she dodged the assistant, set her feet, and gave one of the armchairs a fierce shove.

"Now, really," complained the assistant as the chair toppled over onto its side. Agnes ignored her and got down on hands and knees to examine the bottom of the seat. In addition to a spiderweb and a bright pink piece of chewed gum, she discovered a manufacturer's mark burned into the wood: an intertwined W, K, and M encircled by a wreath of ivy.

Just then the assistant seized her elbow and heaved her to her feet. "Thank you, dear," said Agnes brightly. "I'll show myself out."

She left the office with all haste.

＊＊

"I don't care how," hissed Brent, glancing around. No one could overhear him in the din of the cafeteria, but if his former best friend happened to spot him speaking so urgently to Will and Greg, he would figure out what Brent planned and turn him in before he could act. Brent had no idea why Todd had said nothing so far. It obviously wasn't to save their friendship, which was so far gone it had flatlined.

Will and Greg exchanged a look. "Get rid of everything?" said Greg.

"You heard me. And soon."

"But—" Will gaped at him, stricken. "I gave some scissors and one of those circle cutter things to my dad."

"You moron," Brent seethed. "Get them back. I don't care how. Get them back and then lose them permanently."

He shoved back his chair and stalked away from the table.

Brent didn't bother to stop at his locker before leaving campus. He had just enough time to drive home and take care of the sewing machine before his fifth-period class. His mom had some appointment, a haircut or something, but she would be home after school. He might not get another chance.

He parked in the driveway and ran inside to his mom's sewing room, where he shoved some fabric pieces out of the way, unplugged the sewing machine, and put it on its side. There was no time for elegance. He opened the case and pulled a few wires, then raced to the bathroom for a cup of water, which he poured over the electronic components and the touchscreen. He dried his hands carefully before closing the case and plugging in the cord. There were no sparks, no smoke, when he turned it on, just a blank touchscreen and a sluggish whirring sound when he pressed the foot pedal.

Quickly Brent returned the sewing machine to its place, wiped up the spilled water, and raced back to his car. He had to run a few stop signs and sprint from the parking lot to make it to class, but he slipped into his usual desk a few seconds before the bell. He caught his breath and ignored his ex–best friend's curious stares.

Later that afternoon, he returned from school to find his mother seated in front of the sewing machine, her hands in her lap. She jumped when he greeted her from the doorway. "Hi, sweetheart," she said, her face oddly drawn. "Did you have a good day?"

"Uh-huh." He entered the room and pointed at the machine. "What's wrong? Is it busted again?"

"It appears so." She touched the sewing machine gingerly. "I don't understand. It was working fine this morning."

Brent let out a loud sigh of exasperation. "I knew that deal was too good to be true. I never should have believed that story about some sweet old dead granny who never touched her Christmas present."

"Yes," said his mother. "It does seem rather implausible."

"I'll tell you what." Brent yanked the plug out of the wall and picked up the sewing machine. "I'm going to get my money back. I'll buy you something else for Mother's Day. It won't be as nice as this, but at least it will work."

"I'm sure whatever you give me will be fine."

Brent studied her. "Mom? Is something wrong?"

"No. Of course not, honey. It's just . . ." She looked around her sewing table. "This morning I had some quilt block pieces right here by the sewing machine, but now they're gone."

"Oh." Brent thought hard. He had brushed some fabric out of the way—where? "Here," he said, indicating under her table with a foot. "There's some fabric back there. It must have slipped between the table and the wall."

His mother kneeled down to check, then reached out to gather up the scraps. "Yes. This is what I lost."

Her voice seemed strained. He wished he didn't have to take her sewing machine, but what choice did he have? "I'm really sorry, Mom."

"That's all right." She hesitated. "Brent?"

"What, Mom?"

She sat on the floor looking up at him. "Nothing. Never mind. Don't be gone too long."

"I'll be back before supper," he promised, hurrying out the door, the sewing machine in his arms.

❦

On the last day of March, Gwen turned off her computer, packed her satchel with a heavy heart, and left her office. She had an hour before her first class at Elm Creek Manor. Maybe she would get a cup of coffee and sit at the bus stop across the street from Grandma's Attic and stare at the red-and-gold sign for a while. All too soon some other sign would hang in its place. Bonnie had already promised to save the sign and display it in Elm Creek Manor. No one who saw it, camper or teacher, would ever forget Grandma's Attic.

Just the day before, Gwen had paused on her way home from work to gaze wistfully at the little shop, once such an important gathering place for Waterford's quilters. A woman leaving the shoe store next door saw her and said, "Did you hear it's closing? If I had known they were doing so poorly, I would have shopped there more often instead of driving all the way to the Fabric Warehouse."

Gwen tried unsuccessfully to suppress her anger. "You shouldn't be surprised when the things you fail to support are no longer there when you want them."

She turned and left the woman gaping at her.

Gwen couldn't help her outrage, her disgust. Granted, it was wonderful that Waterford's quilters had rallied to Bonnie's cause at the end, but where had they been in all the months and years before, when the shop balanced on the edge of bankruptcy? Greater support then might have made the difference.

Gwen still couldn't imagine a Main Street without Grandma's Attic.

She sighed and locked the office door behind her, then started as a young man in a Waterford High School varsity jacket hurried by, nearly crashing into her. "Scuse me," he mumbled.

"William?"

The young man halted. "Oh. Hi, Professor."

It was obvious he didn't remember her, but a department chair's son was savvy enough to recognize an occasion warranting good manners. "I haven't seen you since the department picnic last summer," said Gwen. "Are you looking forward to graduation?"

He glanced down the hall toward his father's office. "Um, yeah."

"I can see you're in a hurry, so I won't keep you." She held up a hand as he nodded and prepared to hurry off. "Just one question. Where did you get the shears and the rotary cutter you gave your dad?"

His eyes widened. "Uh, at the store."

"Oh. That's funny, because I heard you got them from school. Which store would that be, then? I'd like to get some myself, but the quilt shop downtown is closing and they don't sell them at Fabric Warehouse. I checked."

"I meant to say I got them at school." Will began to edge away. "*They* got them from a store."

Gwen fixed him with a fierce grin. "Yes, but which one? That's the real mystery, isn't it?"

"I don't know." He backed away. "I'll check and let you know."

He turned and broke into a run.

"Thanks," Gwen called after him. She watched as he disappeared into the department office.

"Professor Sullivan?" someone called out from behind her.

"Yes?" She turned to find one of the custodial staff approaching, a large cardboard carton in her arms.

"I'm so glad I caught you," the dark-haired woman said. "One of our crew just found this a few minutes ago in the boiler room. It was with the trash to be burned, but when some of the stuff fell out, we thought we ought to wait. And since everyone in the building calls you the Quilt Lady . . ." She grinned, and set the carton on the floor. "Well, we thought you could tell us if this is valuable or not."

"What's in the box?"

In reply, the woman opened the lid.

Inside were the missing blocks for Sylvia's bridal quilt.

Chapter Ten

Sylvia

◦≫≪◦

Sylvia sat on the cornerstone patio sipping tea and enjoying the fragrance of lilacs blooming all around her. She looked up from her book to smile fondly at Andrew, who sat beside her tying flies. It was Sunday morning on the first week of Waterford College's summer break, and since the Elm Creek Quilt Camp faculty would be at full strength for the first time all season, that afternoon Sylvia and Andrew planned to embark on an overdue trip to visit Andrew's daughter and son-in-law in Connecticut.

Sylvia was grateful Andrew's children had come much closer to accepting the marriage they had once opposed strongly enough to avoid the wedding. Frequent visits, letters, and phone calls had given Sylvia occasion to show them how much she loved their father, and over the past few months, Amy and Bob seemed to have reconciled themselves to their father's choices. In fact, they had finally realized how fortunate their father was to have found a loving companion. Amy had even confided to Sylvia that she worried less about how her father spent his days so far from his children and grandchildren knowing that Sylvia was there to keep him company.

Andrew looked up and smiled; she reached over and patted his arm. What a comfort he had been throughout the turmoil of the past few months. Sylvia had tried to be that sort of reassuring confidante to her friends, but she wondered how helpful she had truly been. When she had challenged Summer to ask herself why she had not told her friends about her new domestic arrangement, she never imagined Summer would end up moving into Elm Creek Manor. Although she had helped Gwen find a new research topic, Gwen's status in her department and the chair's appreciation of her work seemed unchanged. Her suggestion that Diane tell Bonnie how she felt about her position at Grandma's Attic was moot now that the quilt shop was no more. Sylvia's only consolation was that her meddling had not made matters worse.

Of course, the proposal she intended to make to Bonnie might yet do some good.

"Have you seen Sarah yet this morning?" Sylvia asked Andrew. "I meant to discuss a business idea with her at breakfast, but she didn't come down."

"I saw Matt carrying a tray upstairs to their room."

"Again? That's the third morning in a row."

Andrew grinned. "I guess he's trying to be romantic."

"I suppose." Sylvia pondered this and shrugged. "Well, more power to him. I for one prefer to eat at the table. I don't want to tea-dye my quilts unintentionally."

Andrew chuckled, and both looked up at the sound of the door. "Good morning, all," said Diane, stepping outside onto the patio. "Sarah said you'd be out here."

"Oh? So she's emerged from her boudoir?"

Diane's brow furrowed. "What?"

"Never mind." Sylvia smiled as Agnes exited the manor behind Diane, a battered notebook in her hand. "Oh, hello, dear. So you're here, too?" She glanced at her watch to confirm that she had not lost track of time. "Why so early? We don't have to set up for camper registration for another two hours."

"We'll get to that." Diane rolled her eyes as Agnes returned Sylvia's greeting with an absent nod, seated herself on a wooden bench at the edge of the patio, and slowly paged through the notebook. "Don't expect to get another word out of her. She's had her nose in that old thing since I picked her up."

"Why didn't you wait and come with Bonnie?" asked Andrew.

"At the last minute Bonnie got a phone call from the detective in charge of her case. She's at home waiting for him to come over, but she'll get here as soon as she can."

Sylvia hardly thought that two hours early was at the last minute, but before she could press Diane for details, Andrew said, "The detective needs to see her on a Sunday morning?"

Satisfaction lit up Diane's pretty features. "Apparently there was a development in the case and he needed to speak with her urgently."

"Don't let Diane fool you," said Gwen as she closed the door behind her. "I suspect she had a little something to do with that development."

"So did you," said Diane. "I can't hog all the credit."

Sylvia looked from one to the other in amazement. "What on earth do you mean?"

"My key to Grandma's Attic disappeared right before the burglary," admitted Diane. "I didn't mention it earlier because—well, I had my reasons. One of my son's friends had spent the night, and I thought he might have taken the keys. I had no proof, so I went to his mother."

"Who, ironically enough, happens to be Diane's worst enemy," remarked Gwen.

"Ah," said Sylvia with a knowing smile. "Your notorious next-door neighbor."

Diane nodded emphatically. "Naturally she denied everything and gave Brent an alibi."

"You would have done the same for your sons," said Agnes, without looking up from her notebook.

Diane flushed, and Gwen jumped in. "We all would have. Anyway, while Diane was pondering the mystery of the missing keys, I noticed that my department chair's son had suddenly turned up with a pair of ergonomic shears and a rotary cutter. Since the Fabric Warehouse doesn't sell them, they must have come from Grandma's Attic."

Andrew looked dubious. "He could have ordered them through the mail."

"That's true, dear, but don't you think it's unlikely that a teenage boy would ever peruse a quilt supply catalog?" Sylvia turned to Diane and Gwen and urged, "Go on."

"His story was that he got them from school, which turned out to be an easily disproven lie, but I digress," said Gwen. "So Diane and I independently went to the police with our suspicions."

"Weeks ago," added Diane dryly.

"It wasn't until later that we compared notes. Diane checked with her son, who told us my department chair's son and Mary Beth's son are friends. We passed that along to the police, too, but we haven't heard anything since." Gwen glanced at Diane. "At least I haven't. How about you?"

Diane shook her head.

"Perhaps they needed time to put the pieces together," said Sylvia. She hoped for Bonnie's sake that the detective was not coming over to tell her the case had stalled again.

At that moment, Summer joined them. "Hi, guys." She glanced around the circle quickly. "So we're still waiting on Bonnie?"

As the others nodded, Sylvia impatiently said, "She has another two hours, for goodness' sake. Sarah isn't even here yet."

Summer smiled. "Oh, she'll be along."

Gwen put her arm around her daughter. "How was your date last night?"

Summer's smile deepened so that her dimple showed. "Fine."

"Apparently it was better than fine," said Andrew, a trifle sternly. "She didn't come home until after midnight."

The others laughed as Summer blushed. "We were just talking."

"Uh-huh," said Diane.

"No, really. We have a lot to talk about."

Sylvia was glad that Summer and her young man had reconciled, but she couldn't keep the regret out of her voice when she asked, "Does this mean you'll be leaving us?"

Summer started. "Actually—if you mean am I moving out to move back in with Jeremy, no."

From the corner of her eye, Sylvia saw Agnes heave a sigh of relief, her gaze still fixed on the notebook.

"But—" Summer hesitated, twisting her fingers together. "I think I will be leaving within a year."

"Leaving the manor?" asked Sylvia.

"Yes." Summer glanced at her mother. "And leaving Waterford."

A gasp went up from the gathering of friends. "Why?" asked Diane. It was almost a wail.

"I'd like to go back to school."

Gwen, who knew her best, looked the most shocked. "You're kidding."

"I'm not," said Summer. "I'll hate to leave Elm Creek Quilts, but I really think I need to follow my dream."

"You mean follow your heart," accused Diane. "You're just going to follow that boyfriend of yours."

"That's actually not true," said Summer. "This is something I'm doing for myself. But Jeremy and I are going to make sure we end up in the same city eventually."

Gwen embraced her daughter, tears in her eyes. Sylvia could not make out the words they exchanged, but when they released each other, both were smiling.

"Well." Sylvia cleared her throat. "I'm sure you've given this a lot of thought, and I wish you all the best, but I hope you won't be going soon. We will never be able to replace you."

"I'll finish out the season at least," Summer promised. "After that, it depends on when I can get into grad school."

"I can call my contacts at Penn," offered her mother, but Summer laughed and told her she wanted to do this on her own.

"I guess this is a good a time as any to make my own announcement," said Judy, who had arrived unnoticed in the excitement and lingered near the door looking at least twice as nervous as Summer had.

"Oh, Judy, not you, too," said Diane, dismayed.

Judy nodded, unable to keep the broad smile off her face. "I've accepted a position on the faculty at Penn. I can't imagine what I'll do without my best friends around me every day, but it's an opportunity I can't pass up."

"Yes, you can," said Diane. "You just haven't tried hard enough."

Sylvia's heart sank even as she joined in the laughter. As Judy shared the details of her new job, Sylvia thought ahead to the breaking of the circle of friends. Judy would leave them by autumn, and Summer would part soon after. Elm Creek Quilts would never be the same.

Just then Bonnie arrived, looking dazed. "You aren't going to believe this," she said.

After the bombshells Summer and Judy had dropped, Sylvia would believe just about anything, but she asked, "Do you have news from the police?"

Bonnie nodded and sat down as her friends peppered her with questions. The police had three suspects, she told them, including an additional friend of the two boys Diane and Gwen had named. The parents of all but one of the boys were cooperating with the police.

"Let me guess," said Diane. "Mary Beth."

Bonnie nodded. "Mary Beth still claims her son was home that night, but the police say the other boys refute that." She sighed. "What the police can't tell me is why. It's no secret that Mary Beth and Diane don't get along, but why destroy my store? They're all about to graduate from high school and head off to good colleges in the fall. Why jeopardize their futures for a grudge?"

No one had an answer for her. Sylvia marveled that after all those three boys had done to Bonnie, she still looked as if she felt sorry for them.

"At least now you'll be able to get the insurance settlement, right?" asked Summer.

"I suppose." Bonnie smiled, rueful. "Unfortunately, it's too little, too late."

"Not necessarily," remarked Sylvia. "I have a proposition for you. Why not reopen your quilt shop right here in Elm Creek Manor?"

Bonnie stared at her, and the others gasped in excitement. "That's a fabulous idea," exclaimed Judy. "We have plenty of unused space in the ballroom."

"I was actually thinking of knocking out some walls in the first floor of the west wing, starting with the formal parlor," said Sylvia. "We would have ample space, ideal lighting—"

"And all those captive shoppers when quilt camp is in season," added Diane.

"True enough," said Sylvia as the others laughed, although she hoped to draw most of their business from Waterford. If Waterford's quilters were shown how welcome they were at Elm Creek Manor, perhaps the pointless estrangement between the Elm Creek Quilters and the Waterford Quilting Guild would cease once and for all. "Let's not forget that if local quilters are willing to drive all the way to the Fabric Warehouse, they surely won't object to driving here."

Diane said, "Mary Beth won't like it."

"I think she has enough to worry about, don't you?" said Judy. "Besides, I've heard through the grapevine that she withdrew from the election for guild president. I don't know how much influence she'll have anymore."

"We haven't heard whether Bonnie even likes the idea," said Sylvia, watching her friend. "Perhaps she has other plans."

All eyes went to Bonnie, who shook her head. "This is too much to absorb, too fast," she said. "As much as I'd love to reopen, even in a different location, I have to worry about my basic living expenses first."

"Maybe not," sang out Agnes, holding up her notebook in triumph. "Your ex-husband-to-be isn't as broke as he claims."

She waved them over and held open the notebook so they could all view a curious drawing of an intertwined W, K, and M encircled by a wreath of ivy. "What's that supposed to be?" asked Diane.

"I know I've seen this before, but I can't place it," said Gwen. "It resembles an insignia such as a silversmith's mark, placed on the bottom of a piece to indicate who created it."

"That's very good, Gwen, although this particular craftsman worked in wood and iron and cloth." Agnes's blue eyes were bright with excitement behind her pink-tinted glasses. "You'll recall that a great many years ago I had the unfortunate chore of selling off items from the manor to help support Sylvia's sister, brother-in-law, and myself. I met my husband, Joe, when an antique dealer advised me to consult a history professor from the college about particular pieces." She laughed aloud. "My grandson insisted my notebooks were a valuable record, but I didn't believe him until now."

"What's significant about this insignia?" asked Summer.

"It's the mark of the famous designer Wolfgang Kauffmann Mueller," said Agnes.

"I've heard of him," said Gwen. "He had a unique style drawing from different elements of New England and Pennsylvania history—a little bit of Shaker, some Amish, some German. Scholars often credit him with initiating the Arts and Crafts movement fifty years before it really took off."

Bonnie gasped. "That old furniture in Craig's office."

"Exactly," said Agnes. "His assistant told me he refurbished the offices out of his own pocket, which was my first clue that something wasn't quite right. No offense, Bonnie, dear, but it's no secret Craig is a cheapskate."

Bonnie shrugged. "No offense taken. I've called him far worse."

"So that's where he's been hiding his assets," said Judy.

"Just out of curiosity, Agnes," said Andrew, "how much is this furniture worth?"

"Bonnie's lawyer will have to seek an appraisal, of course," replied Agnes. "But I can tell you I sold a Wolfgang Kauffmann Mueller loveseat for ten thousand dollars, and that was more than fifty years ago."

Gwen's eyebrows shot up. "Considering how much more his work is appreciated now, Bonnie could be looking at hundreds of thousands of dollars."

Bonnie put a hand to her heart and reached behind her for a chair. "He redecorated his office five years ago. That's how long he's been planning this. That . . . that . . ."

"Jerk," finished Agnes.

"That's not the word I had in mind, but it suits him."

The door to the manor swung open and Sarah poked her head outside. "What suits whom?" She scanned the circle of friends without waiting for an answer. "Good. Everyone's here."

Sylvia glanced at her watch. "And none too soon. You're only an hour and forty-five minutes early."

"We have a little business to take care of before the campers arrive." Sarah stepped onto the cornerstone patio carrying a large box that appeared to be wrapped in fabric rather than paper, her husband Matt close behind. "Sylvia and Andrew, this is for you."

Speechless, Sylvia turned to Andrew to see if he knew what on earth was going on, but he looked as surprised as Sylvia felt.

Diane grinned as Andrew accepted the box. "It's a belated wedding gift from the Elm Creek Quilters."

"And one hundred thirty-three of your dearest friends," added Gwen.

"My goodness." Sylvia reached over to help Andrew open it. "And you wrapped it in fabric. Wasn't that clever of you!"

"We thought you could use the fabric later in a quilt," said Summer. "That's much better than tossing more paper into a landfill."

"We should have tied it with fishing line so that Andrew would have a little something extra, too," remarked Judy.

"We'll keep that in mind for their anniversary," said Sarah.

Sylvia eagerly lifted the lid and dug through tissue paper until her hands touched fabric. "Oh, my word, I knew it. You ladies are wonderful."

Diane nudged Gwen. "She hasn't even seen it yet."

"She knows a quilt when she feels one," said Andrew, helping Sylvia unfold it.

Her friends came forward to take the edges of the quilt and hold it open between them. "Oh, my," said Sylvia, and then she could only clasp her hands to her heart in joy.

It was a sampler quilt top in blue, rose, and greens of every hue, all blending and contrasting harmoniously in a frame of split LeMoyne Stars. Sylvia took in the arrangement of rows of blocks and quickly calculated that there were one hundred forty blocks, in every pieced and appliquéd pattern imaginable. Some of her favorites caught her eye: LeMoyne Star, Snow Crystals, Carpenter's Wheel.

"It's very nice," said Andrew, "but you forgot to finish it."

The women burst into laughter.

"We intend for our quilt campers to help us with the quilting," explained Agnes. "We couldn't put it in the quilt frame without you noticing, so we decided to surprise you with the quilt top."

"Don't feel bad, Andrew," said Matt. "I said the same thing the first time I saw it."

"It is exquisite," breathed Sylvia, tracing the appliquéd flower petals in a Bridal Wreath block with a fingertip. "I've never seen anything so lovely. How did you manage to keep this a secret?"

"It wasn't easy," said Sarah, with a sidelong look for her husband. She went on to explain how the quilt had come to be: an invitation sent out to Sylvia's friends and quilting colleagues, the requirement that the blocks represent the maker's relationship to Sylvia, the theft and reappearance of dozens of blocks, and the mad scramble at the end to complete the top.

Sylvia insisted that each of her friends point out her block and explain why she chose it. Sarah eagerly offered to go first, and pointed to an unfamiliar block in the fifth row. "This pattern is called Sarah's Favorite," she said. "And it should be obvious why I chose it, since Sylvia is my favorite person."

As her friends chimed in with their approval, Matt said, "Hey. What about me?"

"Let me amend that," said Sarah, hugging him. "Sylvia is my favorite woman, but you're definitely my favorite husband."

Everyone laughed as Matt shrugged and kissed his wife.

"My turn," said Diane, proudly indicating a block made of triangles, narrow rectangles, and a checkerboard trim along the bottom edge.

"Lincoln's Platform?" asked Sylvia.

Sarah looked perplexed. "Maybe it's one of those patterns that has several names."

"No, just Lincoln's Platform," said Diane, beaming. "I found it in a book. Oh, come on. Don't you get it?"

No one wanted to disappoint her, but one by one they shook their heads.

"Because Sylvia's such a good speaker," said Diane, exasperated. "You know, like Abraham Lincoln. I admire that about Sylvia. Her way of speaking her mind with sensitivity to other people's feelings is an example I try to follow."

"She has a long way to go," remarked Gwen in an aside that was a trifle too loud to be an aside.

"At least no one else chose the same pattern," offered Judy. "It adds variety."

"Thank you, Judy," said Diane. "Someone had to break free of all those Steps to the Altar and Wedding Ring clichés."

"As someone who gave in to cliché and made a Bridal Wreath—" began Agnes.

"I wasn't talking about you," said Diane. "Honestly. I should have just ignored the rules, made a Nine-Patch, and spared myself this interrogation."

Everyone but Diane burst into laughter. "Well, this is my Bridal Wreath block, cliché or not," said Agnes, then she smiled slyly and pointed to a block in the top right corner. "I made this one, too. I imagine Sylvia knows why."

It was a Bachelor's Puzzle block. Shocked, Sylvia shot an accusing look at Sarah, the one person she told about the nickname she and Claudia had secretly given Agnes so long ago. Sarah shook her head, wide-eyed and clearly just as surprised as Sylvia.

"I'm sure I don't know," said Sylvia. "Perhaps because it's a puzzle why Andrew married me?"

"Not to me it isn't," said Andrew, taking her hand.

"That's not it," said Agnes. "Give it some more thought. I'm sure you'll figure it out."

"If not, maybe the answer is in one of Agnes's notebooks," said Diane.

Sylvia ignored the rising heat in her cheeks. Oh, the things Agnes could have written about her back in those days! "If you insist on making me guess, I suppose I'll have to try. Later. How about you, Summer?" she asked, ignoring Agnes's laughter. "What block did you make?"

Summer pointed out a Mariner's Compass block with sixteen points in the center of the quilt. "I thought this pattern suited you best," she said, "because you're beautiful, you're difficult, and you guide us along our way."

A murmur of approval went up from the circle of friends. "Oh, nonsense," Sylvia scoffed. "I'm none of those things, except, perhaps, difficult. On a bad day."

"You can hide behind modesty all you like, but that won't change what you mean to us," said Summer, so affectionately that Sylvia thought she might be forced to return the quilt top to its box rather than endure any more embarrassing praise.

Fortunately, Judy announced that her block was made with Andrew in mind. "Sometimes we focus so exclusively on the bride that the groom feels incidental to everything related to the wedding. I made a Handy Andy block so he would know this quilt is a gift to him, too."

Matt gave Andrew a quizzical look. "'Andy'?"

"Handy Andrew, if you prefer," said Judy with a laugh.

"This one is mine." Gwen pointed out a block near the center of the quilt. Sylvia did not recognize the pattern, which resembled a gold comet streaking across a sunset-violet sky. "I adapted it from a design in a quilt entered in the 1933 World's Fair quilt competition. I chose it because while Sylvia is definitely an original, her art and influences are deeply rooted in quilting's oldest and best traditions. Since I don't know the original name of the block, I call it Sylvia's Shooting Star."

"'Sylvia's Shooting Star.'" Sylvia smiled, amused. "I like it."

"It's high time someone named a block after you," remarked Andrew.

"Thank you all so very much." Sylvia rose and reached out to embrace her friends. "I can't imagine a lovelier wedding gift. The stories of how you chose your blocks make it even more special."

"We're not done," said Sarah, nodding to the box on Andrew's lap. "You missed something."

Andrew dug through the tissue paper and came up with a white binder trimmed in fabrics of the same hues as the quilt. "What's this?"

"Letters from everyone who contributed a block," said Summer. "We asked them to share the stories behind their block choices, too."

Sylvia and Andrew held the binder open between them and paged through the letters, pausing to read some of the names aloud. Sylvia's eyes grew misty as she took in the familiar names of friends and faraway colleagues, quilt camp veterans and students she had met only recently, so many generous friends sending prayers and warm wishes for the happiness of the bride and groom.

"This is truly overwhelming," Sylvia began, then broke off at the sight of a letter from a very dear friend.

March 12, 2002

Dear Sylvia and the Elm Creek Quilters,

My first reaction to your news was to wonder how Sylvia could even think of getting married without me there. I thought we were friends! I would have talked her through those premarital jitters. I would have held her hand or the train of her gown, or both. At the very least I would have brought a nice gift!

Once I got over that initial burst of self-absorption, my thoughts turned to an appropriate block for Sylvia's bridal quilt. I could do nothing less for the woman who restored my art to me.

Our friendship goes back nearly twenty years, founded upon a mutual love of quilts and quilting history. While Sylvia was launching her quilters' retreat, I was working as a quilt artist, lecturer, and museum curator—and struggling with a serious case of "quilter's block" brought on by a recent diagnosis of multiple sclerosis. Although I experienced virtually no symptoms between exacerbations of the disease, I could no longer quilt as I once had. My inability had less to do with my increasing physical limitations, however, than the psychological paralysis of knowing that my life as I had known it was over, and that all the things I loved to do might one day be lost to me.

Sylvia was the friend and mentor who helped me find my way. She encouraged me to create because of my MS, not in spite of it, to use my grief and anger to inspire my art rather than pretend nothing had changed. She taught me to acknowledge that I could no longer do the same work as I had before, but not to accept that I could no longer be an artist.

The work I have created since Sylvia illuminated the possibilities might not be as technically perfect as what had gone before, but it is infused with a passion, a spiritualism, and a deep gratitude and respect for the healing power of the creative process. My art and my faith in God have enabled me to deal with the progression of my disease, which thankfully has been slow, but continuous enough to tax even the strongest will. I almost had to resign my position as museum curator, but thanks to my new medications, I have been able to resume most of my old activities. I almost had to give up my loft, but my daughter and grandson moved in with me instead, so when my symptoms act up, I am not alone. Even on my worst days, I find some way to quilt, whether that means appliquéing quilt blocks or simply examining my fabric stash and imagining new projects. Without Sylvia to encourage me, I would not have even that.

As most of you know, I'm not one to stick to traditional pieced blocks, so I decided to design a new appliqué pattern in the folk art style Sylvia would expect from me. The building in the background is Elm Creek Manor, of course, and the two women joining hands in friendship in the foreground are meant to be me and Sylvia but could be any of the thousands of quilters who have found friendship, solace, and sisterhood at Elm Creek Quilt Camp.

Many, many congratulations, prayers, and good wishes for the happy couple. May their marriage be blessed with love, joy, peace, and the companionship of good friends.

With Love,
Grace Daniels

Sylvia blinked back tears, looked up at her friends, and said, "Thank you."

They smiled, knowing all she meant to convey with those two words.

Her heart ached with joy and with sadness, thinking of the friends who loved her so dearly, of the friends who would leave them too soon, of the inevitable changes that would touch them then and in the years to come. As much as she might wish to capture time and hold it still in that moment, it was a futile wish, and she had lived long enough to know it. Summer and Judy would leave, other friends might follow, and one day, she, too, would part from the home she had loved and abandoned and learned to love again.

But as she gazed upon the block Grace Daniels had given for her quilt, the appliquéd portrait of two women holding hands like steadfast friends, she understood that Elm Creek Quilts was greater than any single woman or even group of women who laughed and cried and quilted within the manor's gray stone walls. Teachers and campers would come and go, and long after the last Bergstrom had passed from the earth, the spirit of Elm Creek Quilts would endure. As long as it stood, Elm Creek Manor would welcome all who gathered there with love and acceptance and the promise of friendships as beautiful and as comforting as the quilts they made.

She gazed upon the smiling faces of her beloved friends and

said, "I know the first order of business after we welcome our new quilt campers."

Sarah, the young woman she loved like a daughter, said, "Layer this top in the frame so we can start quilting it?"

Sylvia laughed. "Yes, of course that must be first. The second order of business, then."

Somewhere, she knew, two quilters who were meant to be among them waited to learn that Elm Creek Quilt Camp sought new teachers.

Odd Fellow's Chain

Bachelor's Puzzle

Sylvia's Shooting Star

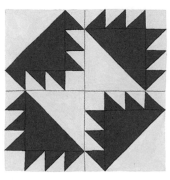

Barrister's Block

Contrary Husband

Lincoln's Platform